James Philip

GEORGE WASHINGTON'S GHOST

The New England Series – Book 5

Copyright © James P. Coldham writing as James Philip 2020.
All rights reserved.

Cover concept by James Philip
Graphic Design by Beastleigh Web Design

THE NEW ENGLAND SERIES

BOOK 1: EMPIRE DAY
BOOK 2: TWO HUNDRED LOST YEARS
BOOK 3: TRAVELS THROUGH THE WIND
BOOK 4: REMEMBER BRAVE ACHILLES
BOOK 5: GEORGE WASHINGTON'S GHOST

COMING LATER IN 2020

BOOK 6: IMPERIAL CRISIS

FUTURE TITLES

BOOK 7: THE LINES OF LAREDO
BOOK 8: THE HALLS OF MONTEZUMA
BOOK 9: ISLANDS IN THE STREAM
BOOK 10: THE GATHERING PLACE

Details of all my books and future release dates will appear first on my web site

www.jamesphilip.co.uk

PROLOGUE

Chapter 1

You and I share a common analysis of the errors our forebears made in earlier wars with the English. Fortunately, His Excellency Il Presidente de Soto, as evinced by the unwavering support he has given the General Staff, understands perfectly the lessons of our ongoing post-conquest struggle with our historic enemies.

A hundred years ago, what are now the South Western territories of the Commonwealth of New England, were provinces of New Spain, administrative entities within the Empire of México. Now our fortresses and mines in Alta California, and guarding the passes of the Sierra Madre are all that remain inviolate north of the Rio Grande. In short, not even the Great Valley of México is safe from the avarice of our enemies, who already covet and send raiding parties to disrupt the gold mines of California which are so critical to our ongoing national development. In every war we lose more ground, or are driven back to our start lines in the mountains or the deserts of our North East; and at home another schism strikes at the heart of our government. And always, those in power – people like you and I, and his Excellency, Il Presidente, whom I believe to be a profoundly good, and wise man – have sheltered behind the myth that we were always doomed to fail.

The enemy is too powerful!

We are too weak!

Frankly, we have never been honest with ourselves. The truth is that in previous wars the English have rarely committed more than a tiny proportion of their Imperial energy to 'swatting away' our piecemeal attempts to reclaim what is rightfully ours.

We, the Mexican people, even today in alliance with our Catholic brothers on Cuba, Hispaniola and Santo Domingo, and in league with our so-called coalition of the willing – which we both accept may not amount to anything meaningful in military terms when the going gets tough – of our Central and Southern American friends, notwithstanding the technical assistance and equipment gifted to us by our German colleagues, cannot hope to prevail if and when even a small part of the nascent military and economic resources of just New England, let alone the rest of the British Empire, are mobilised against us as surely, one day they will be.

Thus, we must accept that in the long-term, we cannot defeat the English on the battlefield.

What we can do, and never have done before with sufficient steadfastness, is to test the moral fibre of our enemies. This time we must fight well-enough and long-enough to discover if New England (particularly the 'Commonwealth' of those pampered East Coast Colonies) has the stomach for the long haul, and more importantly, we must prolong the war for however long it takes to allow the fissures we know to exist between the First Thirteen and the 'Old Country' back in Europe to widen.

In this, I do not think that we can rely on our German friends.

Their interests lie in weakening English power in the Americas and in controlling the oil wells of Gran Colombia, Venezuela and the Southern Caribbean. It remains to be seen how deeply embedded Berlin's Concessions in Sucre, Anzoátegui, and Monagas are in fact, rather than theory. Personally, I doubt if those presences in Caracas, Cumaná and New Barcelona, are worth any more to the Kaiser than that fetid enclave-cum-abomination at San Juan. Nevertheless, if the Germans (while they obsess over oil wells in the Southern Caribbean) are happy to continue to offer our forces ongoing materiel and technical support, and to make available to us intelligence which otherwise would be denied to us, we must 'play along'.

I know that this is as painful to your sense of honour as it is to mine, my friend. Especially, as our Kaiserliche Marine allies treat your people like serfs but we must tolerate it a little longer. If things go according to plan you will soon be rid of them. I think we can take it as read that when the shooting starts Berlin will order its 'advisors in the Indies' to return home for fear of inflaming tensions in Western Europe.

Shortly, all our plans will come to fruition.

For what it is worth I believe that the English will fight this war, at least at the beginning, as they have fought every war with us in the last century. At the outset they will think it is just another 'border war', and that they can deal with us at their leisure.

Little do they suspect that this strategy will not work this time!

Digressing, I think that your perceptive analysis of the lasting effects of the attack by Dominican irregulars on the British Atlantic Fleet in New York Bay two years ago, is spot on. The response of the New England authorities was heavy-handed and chaotic, and alienated large numbers of previously loyal former citizens of New Spain who mistakenly, were under the impression that they were in some way 'safe' in the First Thirteen. You were right to suggest that the attacks tended to dent the Royal Navy's aura of invincibility. The other thing we learned from that episode was that, within the old English colonies the ruling elite were not so much worried about another war with us, as to who exactly they could get to pay for it!

In any event, I reiterate the consensus of the last meeting of the Chiefs of Staff, which has since been formally ratified by the President of the Republic.

We will use all the tools in our arsenal this time.

Moreover, we will demand that the Germans fully participate in the initial stages of the war. We will use all our modern aircraft. We will employ every available submarine against the English...

Extract from a letter dated 3rd February 1978 written by General of the Army of New Spain Felipe de Padua María Severino López de Santa Anna y Pérez de Lebrón, to Vice Admiral Count Carlos Federico Gravina y Vera Cruz, the Chief Minister of Defence and Commander-in-Chief of the Armada de Nuevo Granada.

Chapter 2

A.D. 1978

Saturday 22nd April
El Ojo del Diablo, Provincia Norteña de Sonora

Eyebrows had been raised among his colleagues back at the University of Cuernavaca at El Departamento de Geología de la Academia Nacional de Ciencias Naturales - the Geological Department of the National Academy for the Natural Sciences – when Professor Rodrigo de Monroy y Pizarro Altamirano, despite being six years past the customary 'active service' cut-off point of fifty-five years of age, had volunteered for active military service last year.

He was still the tall, broad-shouldered, rangy man he had been in his prime except, inevitably, not so fleet of foot and he ached in the mornings, and was sometimes, stooped with weariness. His formerly dark head of hair was ever-more streaked with grey, and his face, darkened by the Aztec ancestry that had long been ingrained in all but the most recent generations of migrants from Old Spain, was lined and weathered, set around grey brown eyes which had retained their capacity to unexpectedly twinkle with rueful mischief.

Inevitably, many of his oldest friends, and to a man, the majority of the Fellows in his departmental common room who had arched eyebrows, suspected some unseemly military fervour had gripped their esteemed Dean, whom everybody had assumed had long since bidden farewell to the warrior mantle.

True, Rodrigo was a hero of each of the three most recent wars with the gringo interlopers of New England; last time around, back in the 1960s he had been captured and held by the ungodly, for nearly a year as the bickering about the so-called 'de-militarised zone' dragged on interminably.

It was also true that although he still proudly retained the rank of Teniente Coronel – Lieutenant Colonel – in the Reserve Forces of the Ejército de Nueva España (the Army of New Spain), notwithstanding his long friendship with Army Chief of Staff Felipe Santa Anna – with whom he had fought beside in two of those wars - for several years after the last war had been a prominent, albeit gentlemanly, voice in the Peace Movement, a veritable thorn in the side of successive regimes in México City.

In fact, Rodrigo had been hard-pressed to explain to his wife, Magdalena, why he felt he had to return to the colours. In the end he had had to tell her exactly why he seemed to have 'gone loco'. Only then had she understood; afterwards, she had spoken of it no more.

Other, that was than to observe, tartly: 'If you go and get yourself killed, I will *never* forgive you!'

Which, all things considered, was fair enough.

However, once Rodrigo had learned of the fragmented. frightening stories coming out of the Colorado country, far to the north of the 1964 'border', and beyond the twenty to thirty mile-wide DMZ, in reality a skirmishing zone for raiders and bandits from both sides, he had been inexorably drawn back to the harsh landscapes in which he had made his academic name, prospecting and studying, in his rebellious younger years.

His now famous paper about El Ojo del Diablo – *the Eye of the Devil* – a massive meteoritic impact crater, had eventually established him as Nuevo Granada's, México's, leading geologist. Located at an elevation of over five thousand feet on the great sandstone plateau of the northern Sonora badlands, although eroded by wind and rain for countless millennia and partly filled by drifting sand, El Ojo del Diablo was still three-quarters of a mile across and over five-hundred-feet deep, and its rim still reared, in places some one-hundred-and-fifty feet above the surrounding desert. If ever a man needed to be reminded that his life was but a miniscule mote in the eye of a greater god, he could do no better than stand on the edge of the Eye of the Devil and look down into the void.

Rodrigo had been only twenty-six when he first trekked north into the then 'disputed lands' – turned into 'borderlands' and then 'buffer zones' and finally incorporated into the Commonwealth of New England by the victorious gringos in treaties signed after each successively more humiliating war – in search of adventure, knowledge and yes, if he was being honest about it, fame.

Those were halcyon, free-wheeling days before he had settled down with Magdalena, found academic respectability with his seminal published papers on the stratigraphy of the rocks of the middle and lower grandes acantilados – great cliffs – carved down through over a mile of rock over untold millennia by the Colorado River. As a young man he had been bewitched by the Eye of the Devil, assumed until then by generations of Granadan geologists to be a well-preserved, caldera-like feature associated with ancient volcanism because of its relative proximity to the San Franciscan ridges, themselves thought to be the remnants of ancient volcanoes, some forty miles to the west.

Had he known that day he first looked down into the great impact caldera that the great men in his field would go to almost any lengths to guard their complacent orthodoxy, and that before they finally surrendered would have attempted, in desperation, to have him declared heretic, perhaps, he would have never returned home.

Other than, of course, for Magdalena...

In the end everything had changed, text books had had to be re-written and every aspect of his field rigorously, critically re-evaluated. Eventually, evidence had won the day. The day he found the first fragments of nickel-iron, many of which must have been molten, viscose when they fell to earth, calving from a celestial body probably well over one-hundred-and-fifty feet in diameter with a mass of hundreds of thousands of tons as it plummeted through the Earth's atmosphere at a velocity in excess of thirty thousand miles-an-hour, before exploding on impact with the limestone plateau with a force equivalent to millions of tons of high explosive, had been the moment that Rodrigo's former life had ended.

Another man might have dwelt upon the long years in the wilderness labelled a 'young maverick', when he had been castigated and decried by his elders and every last one of his contemporaries on account of his supposedly 'unscientific ramblings'. Some of the old fogeys, men who claimed to be scientists but invariably trusted the literal letter of Biblical text over 'the scientific method' they claimed to adhere to, had never forgiven him.

Accepting a commission in the Ejército de Nueva España in 1949, had been a blessed relief from the hothouse feuding of Cuernavaca in the old days.

Serendipitously, assigned to an artillery regiment he had persuaded the Army's Office of Ballistics to conduct trials, ostensibly studying the destructive potential of high-powered rounds against sloping cemented plate, and shown the most craven of doubters the conclusive proof of his thesis on the mechanics of crater creation. Those grainy slow-motion sequences of bullets and armour-piercing rounds being fired by experimental high-velocity rifles crashing into sand tray targets had, virtually overnight, made his reputation. Within weeks, he had been the University of Cuernavaca's poster boy.

That was a long time ago, of course.

War and the consequences of the uneasy peace along the Border had denied him access to the high plateau of the Colorado Country for over a quarter-of-a-century. For much of that time only the Navajo and their sometime Apache enemies, and gringo adventurers and bandits had roamed the high plains of the old nineteenth century northern province of Sonora.

Farther back in time these lands had been part of 'the Comancheria' – a huge swath of the South West under the brutal rule of the 'horse people', roving Comanche tribes, the masters of the Southern Plains – not finally vanquished until the 1860s, when Spanish suzerainty had again been bloodily re-established. Mexico, or New Granada as it was in the early years of the nineteenth century, had always claimed Sonora. History, like the desert winds, had slowly eroded its title, long before the 'border wars' with the English had moved the lines on the maps. Even now, hardly anybody lived high on the plateau; and yet so much blood had been spilled over where the lines ought to be drawn on those ancient maps of the 1820s.

It had been so long since Rodrigo's last expedition to *El Ojo del Diablo*, that his old Navajo friends and guides had stopped sending him specimens – rocks and fossils – and he had got on with his career, and with raising his family. And then, a couple of years ago, realising that there was going to be a new war; this time not a series of brave, futile 'demonstrations' but a 'war to the knife' to reclaim all that had been lost since the New Englanders stole the Delta lands, West Texas and the historic, post-conquest borderlands of Nuevo México from the old Empire of New Spain, he had tentatively sought permission to ride deep into the enemy's country, and to return to the Sonoran deserts.

Ostensibly, to all bar a select group of very senior Army officers his mission had been mooted as a long-range reconnaissance, a patrol behind enemy lines but by the time he had crossed in to what had been enemy territory, the gringo lines had splintered so fast, nothing except the harshness of the terrain had slowed his passage north.

It was a surreal contrast to his experiences in the last war. Fifteen years ago, he had been stationed in faraway Alta California, a cavalryman posted to the Modoc Country, a backwater of the war until the English Navy had landed troops to seize the heights guarding San Francisco Bay.

Rodrigo still awakened some nights in a cold sweat, his nightmares turning around the scene that day when those two leviathans – he had since learned they were the battlecruiser Invincible and the battleship Hercules – had duelled with the batteries guarding the Golden Gate while a tide of Marines had swept ashore…

The 'Battle of the Bay' had shaken the Junta in México City, and ended the real fighting inside a month. The politicians had taken fright; terrified that the English would invade the west coast south of Baha California and invade the heartland.

In those days there had been no Triple Alliance, and on land and sea and in the air, his country's armed forces had been technologically backward, outgunned and in the end, effortlessly out-matched by an enemy who had absolute command of the Caribbean and the Gulf of Spain and could roam at will his homeland's Pacific coast, putting ashore raiding parties to terrorise innocent civilians and bombarding ports and cities up to twenty miles inland with impunity.

Those days were gone.

People believed it was because the Germans had given the Triple Alliance new weapons but that was only half the story; the indignity of the unequal armistice of the 1960s had been an iniquity which had galvanised the nation. The old military stranglehold over the government had been discredited: this war was a people's war; a war to restore the pride and sovereignty of the whole Mexican nation over its God-given lands in the north.

Now Rodrigo had finally returned to the deserts of his youth.

He ought to have felt at least a trace of residual guilt at having pulled so many strings to be allowed to lead this expedition.

It was hardly Rodrigo's fault that the Chief of Staff of the Army had once been a subaltern under his command, or that at the end of 1976, his old friend and tutor, Hernando de Soto, had swapped the Presidency of the University of Cuernavaca for the Los Pinos de Oro – the Pines of Gold – Palace, the official residence of the President of the Republic buried deep in the Chapultepec Woods in the heart of the capital, México City.

Il Presidente tried, as a rule, not to interfere with the machinations of the political parties or of the competing military factions but he had never been adverse, behind the scenes, to getting his hands dirty. To most Mexicans he was a gracious, grey-haired figurehead, dignified in his strict impartiality, the grandfather of the nation who had healed the dreadful wounds, still bleeding in the national psyche after the country's humiliation in the last war with the English.

Rodrigo had little doubt that no other man in New Spain could have united the military and the feuding Nationalist, Liberal and Country Parties who together, had formed and unholy alliance with Cuban, Hispaniola and Santo Domingo which in the last few days had carried all before it.

He knew his old friend mistrusted the theocratic fervour of México's allies; but Hernando de Soto was nothing if not a man who understood that sometimes, the enemy of my enemy is my friend. If México was ever to grown into a prosperous modern democracy it needed to throw off the shackles of its imperial past, and stand alone in the arena of the Great Powers. History decreed that it was his country's destiny to demand, by war, to be treated as an equal by the Commonwealth of New England and its English masters.

'The die is cast, my friend,' Hernando had told him. 'We cannot hold back the forces at play in our country. Yes, I am the people's leader; yet no matter my misgivings about the coming war, I must follow the people where they lead. All things being equal, a wiser man than I would agree that we should delay another few months, perhaps a year, while expeditions such as yours unravel the mysteries of the deserts of Northern Sonora, but,' the old man had shrugged, and spread his hands, 'although I give you my blessing to undertake your mission, I cannot forestall the forces already in motion any more than that old rascal Canute, could hold back the tide...'

Several of the Navajo scouts sitting on the ponies around Rodrigo were the sons of men he had known three decades ago; most of the troopers jumping down from their mounts to start setting up camp for the night had never been born the last time he visited this land.

The English had arrived soon after the last war ended in the mid-1960s. They had driven the native peoples off the plateau, beyond the mountains to the west, 'resettling' them in barren mountain passes and valleys bereft of game, and when warriors had attempted to return to their ancestral grounds they had been rounded up, left to rot in prison camps hundreds of miles away, or simply hunted down and killed, their bones left to rot in the desert. Until recently, there had been a great military camp, covering tens of square miles about two days ride north of El Ojo del Diablo.

Rodrigo dismounted stiffly, took off his hat and swished it against his thigh to shake away the dust. A Navajo scout took the reins of his horse.

Some of his troopers – he had told his superiors that he had no need of a 'bodyguard' in the desert, knowing he was safe in the hands of his Navajo 'brothers' – were down on their haunches, scratching curiously at the ground.

"What happened here, sir?" One youngster asked, only a little timidly.

Rodrigo's men knew him to be a fatherly figure who paid little more than lip service to spit and polish, whose real authority had nothing to do with his military rank.

These days, only a dwindling minority of Mexican officers commanded by fear alone; that was another mantra which had fallen into disrepute after the last lost war. The old ways had resulted in defeat after humiliating defeat, a new, model army had had to be created out of the ashes of the old, conscript 'rabble'. All of Rodrigo's men were volunteers. Literacy and a high school education at least up to the age of sixteen was mandatory for all inductees into the Army and its attached Air Force, although not, because Admirals were always the last to adopt modernity over tradition, in the Navy.

That said, even the Navy had begun to adopt the Kaiserliche Marine practice of inducting boy seaman – aged fourteen to sixteen – into what were in effect, military apprenticeships in seamanship, gunnery, engineering, electronics, logistics and all the other specialisations required to keep a modern navy at sea.

Perhaps, the most radical and beneficial of all the changes implemented in the last decade was that the Mexican Army was now built around a relatively small core of professionals, reinforced in time of war by a cadre of fully-trained reservists.

With the abandonment of military rule there had been no need to maintain a large standing army; now three-fourths of the combat strength of the Mexican Army was in its fully-trained, part-time 'Territorial' formations, each at any one time manned and kept 'in being' by a skeleton staff, ready to be fully activated at either one, three, six months' notice, other than when the unit was required to muster for its annual thirty day training camp. In other words, once they had completed their one-hundred-and-twenty-day period of basic training, three-quarters of all trained soldiers spent up to eleven months of each year pursuing their civilian occupations other than when they were undergoing additional specialist education, or weapons or systems familiarisation.

Rodrigo had been surprised, not to say, somewhat taken aback to discover how much things had changed when he re-joined the active list last year. He had re-joined a new, different Army from the one he remembered from the early 1970s. From the modernity of the infantryman's equipment to the flexibility of field tactics, and the remarkable level of personal initiative now demanded of even the most junior private soldier had astonished him; likewise, the professionalism and technical qualifications of the new officer corps had been a real culture shock. It was as if he had left a nineteenth century army and re-enlisted in a late twentieth century one that was, in many respects, indistinguishable from, say...the British Army.

Admittedly, his friend Santa Anna's new model army lacked the bloody-minded esprit de corps of the best British regular units – tradition took scores, hundreds of years to build - but otherwise, the comparison was...unavoidable.

Rodrigo's thoughts wandered a while longer, then slowly began to coalesce as he stared inscrutably at the half-melted stumps of what had, presumably, been at one time a steel tower. Judging by what remained, less than ten feet of twisted, still substantial rusting metal, it might once have been as much as a hundred feet, or more, high. He kicked at the dust and sand underfoot.

Beneath his feet the ground glinted dully.

Like glass...

Only one thing turned sand to glass: intense heat.

He remembered the younger man's question.

"Something burned very hot here, son," Rodrigo said, very nearly lost in rumination.

The native tribes, mainly Navajo but also roaming bands of Apache, had new camp fire legends of lights brighter than the son flashing momentarily in the night, of fireballs rising into the heavens like messengers to the gods of the skies, and of new stars briefly winking in the distance through the mountains.

There was one tale of a village on the ridges overlooking the Verde – Green – River over seventy miles to the south west awakening one morning to discover their tepees caked in the dust of the desert and within days, of men and women and children falling ill with some terrible, killing fever, their bodies wracked with agony as they bled from every orifice.

Rodrigo had consulted the School of Tropical Medicine at Toluca, which had been a magnet for the finest minds in the field of disease control for half-a-century.

The experts he had spoken to had postulated the stories might be explained by an outbreak of a viral haemorrhagic fever of some kind but if that was the case; where had it come from?

What was the infection nexus?

Of course, if one went far enough back into the post-conquest period common European pathogens, viruses and bacterial infections, small pox, measles, diphtheria and all manner of other plagues brought to the New World by the original Conquistadores, and by successive waves of Spanish and Portuguese migration, and then by the unfortunates carried from Africa in slave ships, had run riot among 'American' populations with little or no natural resistance to the new contagions. But that 'infection and transmission' phase had ended in the latter eighteenth and early nineteenth century. Thus, while there were regular outbreaks of haemorrhagic illnesses, like Lassa and Yellow fever, and other local variants in the tropics, indeed, even in the Central Americas, it was unusual to encounter such outbreaks in the north of México, and virtually unknown in the 'contested lands' above the 1964 border.

Perhaps, Rodrigo, had thought initially, the story was just a distorted echo of the post-conquest plague years?

Then, he had spoken to his middle son, Hernan, a newly qualified surgical registrar at the Hospital of the Holy Cross at Churubusco, in the southern suburbs of the capital.

His son was already studying for a degree in molecular biology – he planned to go into research once he had served his 'sentence' at Churubusco – and he had, in a moment, altered Rodrigo's entire mindset.

"I've been thinking about that story you told me about the village where everybody got sick overnight," Hernan had said, on one of his visits to the old family home in Cuernavaca, as he sat down with his father and mother, and two younger sisters. "It put me in mind of the accounts of early investigators looking into the properties of exotic radioactive isotopes. Particularly, the experience of the first researchers began exploring the properties of radium and the possibilities of x-rays. In the beginning they had a poor understanding of the dangers of the radioactive source materials they were routinely handling, and only a very generic feel for the appropriate exposure times of the photographic plates they were using. To cut a long, rather painful story short, as a result, the world found out about the consequences of biological contamination by ionising radiation. Most of the risks seem to centre around long-term cancers but," Hernan had speculated, "if, say, for the sake of argument, a person or an animal was, for whatever reason, to be subjected to a very large, short-term dose of radiation, it might well result in general spontaneous tissue breakdown, in which case bleeding might occur from the eyes, the ears, gums and every other orifice..."

That was when Hernan's mother had peremptorily decided that the subject of people bleeding to death, or logically, drowning in their own blood was not a suitable subject for conversation at the dinner table!

"There are other places like this, Don Rodrigo," one of the Navajo scouts murmured.

Rodrigo stood up.

He had pored over the aerial photographs of those 'other' sites; at least five more of them in a line towards the north east spaced about a mile apart, and to the west, at least two, albeit much smaller craters uncannily similar in configuration to El Ojo del Diablo.

The Navajo had told him about the big camp to the north which, above ground had been systematically dismantled about eighteen months ago. It seemed that the gringos had dug deep 'caves' beneath the desert, and blown these up before they left. However, the broad, arrow-straight concrete roads from the east and the north still criss-crossed the plateau, in the aerial photographs ghostly signposts going nowhere, disappearing into the desert, rapidly being swallowed by the shifting sands.

Rodrigo had never been an overly spiritual man. Notwithstanding, he considered himself to be a good Catholic and had always supported his wife in her determination that their children should be brought up as dutiful adherents to the teachings of the Mother Church.

However, right then he had to fight to suppress the urge to genuflect in front of his men; suddenly, it felt as if ants were crawling over his soul.

His men were gathering around him.

Perhaps, they too sensed the innate evil of this...place.

That the Devil's hand was upon this desolate landscape.

Rodrigo thought he knew what had happened here and it chilled him to his marrow, yet the scientist in him wanted, craved to know more before he took his terrors back to the High Command of the Army of New Spain.

He watched the men of the survey team – all students from the University at Cuernavaca, on what for them was probably going to be the field trip of their lives – going about their business, oblivious to the soldiers and native scouts grouped around the expedition leader.

Every site had to be photographed, measured, samples taken, and in this case, hacked out of the heat-fused earth; tasks that needed to be accomplished in a screaming hurry because, despite the otherwise generally relaxed atmosphere of the incursion into the contested lands thus far, this was still a war zone.

Rodrigo looked to the ridiculously young lieutenant of horse, commanding the fifteen men of the 103rd Republican Reconnaissance Troop, around the circle of dusty soldiers, and at the poker faces of his faithful Navajo scouts.

"Ceterum autem censeo Carthaginem esse delendam," he said, quirking a grimly rueful smile. "So said Cato the Censor over two thousand years ago, to the Senate of the Roman Republic after Rome had been defeated by the Carthaginians in two wars."

"What does it mean, Don Rodrigo?"

Another man, one of the surveyor students stepped into the circle of faces.

"It is Latin," he explained before he reconsidered the wisdom of speaking without his professor's leave.

Rodrigo nodded to him to continue.

"It translates, I think to something like: '*Furthermore, I consider that Carthage must be destroyed.*'"

The older man nodded again.

"I think we have come to a place of death, gentlemen."

Rodrigo let this sink in.

"In the coming days we will survey the rest of the plateau. Then we will return to the south." He straightened to his full height. It would be dusk soon, it had been a long, hard day in the saddle and his people needed to set up camp, heat their rations and sleep if they could in the cold of the desert night. "Let us get about making camp. We will move out one hour before dawn tomorrow morning!"

Rodrigo watched his men going about their work.

Presently, he realised that the student who had spoken lingered at his side.

"Is that what this is, Don Rodrigo?" He asked, grimly. "Our wars with the English, I mean? Some latter-day version of the Punic Wars?"

Rodrigo smiled thinly.

The boy was related to that notorious Imperial playboy, the Duke of Medina Sidonia. His father was that popinjay Pérez de Guzmán's first cousin. Hopefully, if the rumours about some kind of popular rebellion in the old country were true, people like him had been the first up against the wall and shot! Allegedly, young Carlos, a handsome young man, closely resembled the younger 18th Duke at his age.

"I think you know what this is, Carlos," he said lowly, waving a hand at the twisted, heat-deformed stump of the tower less than thirty feet away.

The boy was reading Geology and Roman History, the former an obsession and the latter his 'hobby', he was an exceptionally bright kid, the sort of student who excelled at everything he touched but might as easily, stumble at the first hurdle when he departed the cloistered, insular world of academia. But that was a problem for the future.

"I don't want to believe what I think it is, Master," Carlos de Guzmán confessed, using Rodrigo's formal University title in his anxiety.

His professor shrugged.

"Isn't the lesson of history that great powers, like Rome and the English, one day lose their patience and determine to destroy their enemies? Roman history is your subject, not mine," the older man reminded his protégé, "but didn't Rome get so fed up with Carthage that one day it decided to destroy it so utterly that not one stone remained above another?"

"Yes," Carlos said. He looked to his tutor; his eyes troubled. "But not even the English would destroy whole nations? Would they?"

Rodrigo did not know the answer to that question.

All that he knew was that before him, stretching away to the horizon to the north and the east were the abandoned, secret testing grounds of bombs which might, one day soon, sweep the civilisation of New Spain off the face of the Earth.

Chapter 3

Monday 24th April
Leigh Halt, Kent

His Majesty George the Fifth, by the Grace of God of the United Kingdom of Great Britain and Northern Ireland and of His Other Realms and Territories King, Head of the Commonwealth, and Defender of the Faith, stepped down, shot his cuffs and turned to offer his wife his arm as she joined him on the platform of the railway station.

Normally, the 10:17 from Charing Cross would have swept on past the picturesque rural station at the village of Leigh to Tonbridge, some three miles to its east; but then normally, it only had one, not two First-Class carriages, the second of which, today, had been commandeered by the Royal Party. In the way of these things, the short journey by car to the King and Queen's destination that morning, whether setting out from Leigh or Tonbridge, a little farther away, would have been neither here nor there. However, there would inevitably have been a lot more fuss and bother in Tonbridge, whereas, at a little-used halt in the countryside, the fiction that the 'Royals' were fulfilling a 'private family' engagement was, if not wholly convincing, then at least, plausible.

Predictably, there were a small number of gawping bystanders, eyes agog at the sight of the King and Queen being greeted by the Lord Lieutenant of Kent and the Mayor of Sevenoaks in all their regal and civic finery. Nor had the arrival of a platoon of men in the drab green of the Rifle Brigade, forming an unsmiling, albeit somewhat low-key ring of steel around the halt and hour before the 10:17 from Charing Cross had made its unscheduled stop, gone entirely unnoticed. However, in this part of the Garden of England, none of this really ruffled the tranquility of the locals, let alone impinged upon the customary routines of village life.

For the benefit of the other passengers on the train, the guard had made an announcement respectfully requesting that 'when this service stops at Leigh Halt, would passengers be so good as to remain in their seats and to refrain from leaning out of open windows!'

By and large, most people had respected this request.

This was, after all, England.

The King, dressed in a pin-striped blue lounge suit, his head bare, and his wife, paused and waved, smiling, to the small crowd as their bodyguards guided them unhurriedly to their car and the Rolls-Royce, accompanied by several black Land Rovers drove away to the south on the road for nearby Penshurst.

In the meantime, the train had resumed its journey to Tonbridge and the Channel ports of Ramsgate and Dover.

"Now that we're actually almost there," Queen Eleanor murmured to her husband, for once able to sit in the back of a car without being accompanied by two or three equerries or ladies in waiting, or a government minister or local worthy, and determined to exploit the blissful privacy while she had the chance, "do you really have no idea what the Prime Minister wants to talk to us about, Bertie?"

The King had taken his wife's hand, as he invariably did when they were, however briefly, alone in public.

He sighed.

In point of fact, his ministers had been unusually tetchy about Eleanor's presence at this 'audience'. This was a thing he had found a little odd; it was not as if his views on 'one monarchy, one partnership of King and Queen' were in any way strange. It had, after all, been the implacable mantra of his fifteen-year reign.

His wife, still strictly speaking Her Royal Highness Princess Eleanor, the Duchess of Windsor – because his father had never believed she was of sufficiently 'high birth' to ever be deemed otherwise – had been 'Queen' from the moment of his accession, regardless of whatever all that stupid, arcane protocol mandated. If it was his destiny to have become the accidental King; he was damned if he was going to attempt to bear the burden alone!

His father, the late King had passed away in May 1962 and preparations had been well in hand for the Coronation of his surviving brother Edward; until those blasted Fenians had intervened. He still missed 'Teddy', with whom he had always enjoyed, much to the old King's displeasure, cordial and very amiable brotherly relations: in hindsight, probably because on his part he had never competed with, or been in any sense a threat to his elder sibling.

'You're a lucky beggar, Bertie!' Teddy had said to him wistfully only a fortnight before his death. 'You've got Eleanor, the Navy, and those well-adjusted, sensible boys and girls. All I'm going to end up with is the bloody Crown, which will set off my lumbago every time I put the damned thing on, a wife who can't stand the sight of me and two siblings who can't wait for me to shuffle off this mortal coil!'

The King still missed his life in the Royal Navy.

He had spent twenty-three happy, fulfilling years in the Service. While his three elder brothers had led unfulfilled wastrel lives readying themselves to assume, sooner or later or never at all, the full weight of the crown he, as the youngest, practically forgotten issue – his parents had been in their early forties at the time of his birth – of the house of Hanover-Gotha-Stewart, had, almost anonymously, passed through the Britannia Royal Naval College at Dartmouth in 1941, and subsequently, been regarded with such negligible filial unction that he had been permitted to marry a woman of only middling aristocratic lineage whom he actually loved. The old King had acted as if he and Eleanor no longer existed, which had allowed them to raise their family out of the public eye leaving him free to pursue what in the end, had been a brilliant career sadly cut short by the combined familial predations of age, alcohol, accidents and eventually, the murderous activities of the Irish Republican Army on Empire Day in 1962.

But for the elimination of a substantial part of the Royal bloodline that day he, George would never have been King. His sister, The Princess Royal, Her Royal Highness Princess Sophia, Duchess of Cornwall, and his three brothers: Albert the Duke of Northumberland, and Charles

Duke of York had perished with Teddy, still at that time the titular Prince of Wales and Monarch uncrowned in Dublin sixteen years ago. Since both of Teddy's sons had died in the 1950s without male issue – one in a car crash and the other in mysterious circumstances in Paris, found dead in a high-class prostitute's apartment, at the time a thing hugely obfuscated and publicly announced as a 'tragic death by an unsuspected congenital heart condition' - and Albert and Charles only had the five surviving daughters between them, the 'family firm' had therefore, passed into George's hands.

By then he had attained the rank of Post Captain and was in command of HMS Lion, at the time the Navy's newest, most formidable big-gun capital ship.

Oh, happy days...

He squeezed his wife's hand gently.

"Honestly, I have no idea what this is all about, my dear," he confessed. It bothered him that his ministers saw fit to drag him out into the wilds of Kent when it would have been much more convenient for all concerned to have convened in London, either at Downing Street or St James's Palace, prior to setting out for Berlin for the funeral rites of the old Kaiser.

"It's odd that Sir Hector insisted on Penshurst Place?" Eleanor mused, thinking out aloud.

"Well," her husband shrugged, "on the bright side, I suppose we won't have to get up so damned early tomorrow morning to catch the boat ferry to France!"

Eleanor smiled.

She was the one who had trouble rising at the crack of dawn.

They could have flown to Berlin for the funeral but travelling across France and Germany by train had about it a more dignified, regal ambiance; not to mention being a great deal more comfortable than flying, even if Imperial Airways had suggested transporting the British Party directly to Berlin by seaplane, landing on one of the many lakes and waterways of the German capital.

The Kaiser had finally expired last Wednesday.

Already the German Electors – perhaps the most unholy and mendacious college of 'voters' since the days of the Medici – were gathering in Saxony, presumably sharpening their knives in preparation for the conclave which would crown the next Emperor as soon as possible after the old one was safely in the ground. Or in the case of Kaiser Wilhelm III, concreted into his sarcophagus in the Imperial Mausoleum just off the Unter den Linden.

"Presumably, the whole cast of characters will be at Penshurst?" Eleanor prompted.

"Yes, I should imagine so."

In fact, notwithstanding it had brought the Royal Household's travel arrangements forward a day at literally a couple of hours' notice, it made a lot of sense to get everybody together before setting off for Germany: the Prime Minister, the Foreign and Colonial Secretary, the Chief of the Imperial General Staff, the First Sea Lord and their senior staffers. There had been some discussion about whether the Prince of Wales, William, Duke of Cornwall, the King and Queen's thirty-four-year-old eldest son, should also be in the 'Berlin party' but in the end it had been decided not to call him back from South Africa, where he and his wife, Louisa, Duchess of Fermanagh and Mourne, were in the middle of what was, by all accounts, a marvellously well-received tour. At the last-minute Prince James, Duke of Cumberland and his new wife, the vivacious New-England born Olympian horsewoman, Hannah de Chateau Thierry, now the Duchess of Herefordshire – presently in England before James rejoined his regiment in Australasia - had volunteered to step into the breach to 'beef up the numbers' of the party and to fly to Germany in advance to 'prepare the ground'.

James, the King and Queen's twenty-seven-year-old third son, had always been the apple of his parents' eyes; although not their favourite offspring, that was a thing they had both assiduously avoided even at the peril of being overly hard on the boy in his youth. This was not to say that last year they had not been somewhat taken aback by his request for their blessing to marry Hannah de Chateau Thierry. So 'taken aback' that they had briefly discussed vetoing the match before coming to their senses. James had, morally, if not in strictly contractual terms because there had never been any kind of firm 'understanding' between the families, reneged on his obligations to his childhood sweetheart, Henrietta De L'Isle, to marry the step-daughter of the current Governor-General of Australia.

When their son had broken the news to them neither the King nor the Queen had, literally, known what to say, or which way to look. Philip and Elizabeth De L'Isle were among their oldest, closest friends. It had been awful until first Henrietta, and then Elizabeth, had written to them to put their fears to rest.

Dear Uncle Bertie and Aunt Eleanor, Henrietta had written, *I know you will be angry with Jamie. Please don't be. He and I will always be the best of friends, like always, very much like brother and sister; perhaps, we ought to have said more at the time but we agreed a little while ago that marriage was not for us. Well, not to each other although obviously, I would have been honoured to be connected so intimately to the Royal 'firm'. Jamie was as relieved to be released from our teenage 'arrangement' as I was! I dashed off a letter congratulating Jamie the moment I heard the news. I wish him all the happiness in the world...*

Thinking about Henrietta's letter suddenly dragged the King's thoughts back to the trials and tribulations her father, the Governor of New England, was presently enduring.

The whole Gulf of Spain, the Caribbean and thousands of square miles of the southern and south western Borderlands of New England with New Spain seemed to be on fire. News of one setback – no, call a thing by its real name 'defeat' – after another had rained upon the heads of his Government in London and his Administration in Philadelphia.

The more sensationalist of the newspapers spoke of New Orleans and the Mississippi being threatened; of Royal Naval forces badly mauled and thrown back in disarray; and of open revolt in several of the First

Thirteen colonies, of panic buying emptying the shelves of shops, demonstrations on the streets and of sporadic outbreaks of 'low-intensity' rioting.

Fortunately, the Empire Broadcasting Corporation took a more level-headed, balanced approach to these things mitigating against the need for heavy-handed censorship – a thing the King deplored, mainly because it seemed to him to be nearly always counter-productive - at home, or throughout the Empire. Censorship was, however, a thing under constant review and when the news of the latest 'setback' – well, disaster if one was being frank about it - became widely known, everybody in the Royal Party accepted that the Government might have no alternative but to clamp down hard.

There had been a great battle in the waters south of, and within Mobile Bay, east of the Mississippi Delta, where the damaged battlecruiser HMS Indomitable and several of her escorting destroyers had sought shelter awaiting the arrival of the cruiser Devonshire and her consorts, before making joint passage to the east and hopefully, finding sanctuary in Atlantic waters.

Reports were confused as to specifics; not so unclear about the essentials of the action which had subsequently occurred. A large number of enemy vessels – from the navies of New Spain (Nuevo Granada), Cuba, Hispaniola and Santo Domingo – had gathered in the waters off Mobile Bay, and although gallantly attacked with torpedoes by the Indomitable's destroyers, approached ever closer inshore and engaged the valiant old battlecruiser in a three to four-hour gunnery duel.

Notwithstanding the arrival of the Devonshire's squadron in the middle of the battle, and that the Indomitable's eight 15-inch main battery rifles and modern fire control systems were, it was assumed, greatly superior to the weapons and gun-laying capabilities of her foes, eventually, she had been battered into a burning, sinking hulk as her magazines were emptied, and the Devonshire – badly handled with her own magazines running low - forced to break off the action and withdraw out to sea with three surviving destroyers.

Presently, the wreck of the forty-five thousand-ton battlecruiser Indomitable lay partially capsized in some forty feet of water off Galliard Island. It was feared that at least two-thirds of her fourteen hundred-man crew had perished in the great battle. Of her escorting squadron, only two, badly damaged destroyers survived, having been forced to take shelter beneath the guns of Mobile and Spanish Fort at the head of the Bay.

The Devonshire, meanwhile, with one of her main battery turrets out of action, having sustained as many as a dozen hits and suffered over a hundred casualties had, mercifully, outrun her pursuers as was, for the moment, running for the 'safety' of the Caribbean.

If the loss of Indomitable, four fleet destroyers and some two thousand men dead or missing was a catastrophe; the collapse of imperial naval hegemony in the Gulf of Spain presaged was nothing short of an unmitigated disaster.

The worst of it was that it was a disaster which might not have happened had the Colonial Air Force provided even a few bomber or torpedo aircraft to support the beleaguered Indomitable in her hour of need. Moreover, despite the battlecruiser having been moored in Mobile Bay for well over a week the city's dockyard, beset by alleged 'labour disputes' – shorthand for a mass walk out by the yards' mainly Spanish-speaking and Cuban and Hispanic sympathising work force - had offered her only minimal assistance, and a supposed 'lack of pilotage' had meant the great ship had still been anchored in the lower, outer bay at the time of the attack, seemingly sealing her doom.

That this had been allowed to happen, or rather, circumstances had conspired to create the situation in which the Royal Navy had suffered its greatest defeat – the King was a man who believed a thing should always be called exactly what it was – since the middle years of the Great War over a century ago, was a national disgrace. A disgrace made all the more piquant because it had been well understood *since* the 1860s that a single capital ship, even one as powerful as the Indomitable, was horribly vulnerable to being 'mobbed under' by sheer weight of numbers and firepower of a fleet of individually, much smaller and less powerful warships. There was already angry talk at the Admiralty of traitors 'down in the Alabama River Territory' where the historic European settlement had been as much Spanish and French as British.

However, the recriminations were going to have to wait; for the present, the real significance of the sinking of the Indomitable was that the naval forces of the Triple Alliance now controlled the Gulf of Spain from the Delta to the west coast of Florida, and that there was probably a second, marauding enemy fleet at loose in the Caribbean which might, at any moment, threaten the Lesser Antilles and the whole chain of island colonies all the way down from the Windwards, through the Leeward Islands to Trinidad and Tobago, and the now seemingly precarious enclaves and garrisons, most of them distinctly under-strength and far flung, widely dispersed across tens of thousands of square miles of partially unmapped territory which comprised British Guyana.

Part of modern British Guyana was, technically, still Dutch, and in the west, French remained the first language. Wisely, the government in The Hague had ceded most of its obligations to London back in the 1930s, maintaining trading stations and harbour facilities without the onerous cost of having to defend or administer the colony.

At this distant remove, nobody quite remembered why the French part of Guyana had been quietly gifted to Britain in the small print of the Treaty of Paris. Contemporary thinking assumed that by the time the final text of the great peace settlement was agreed everybody was so cheesed off with the whole business, the one thing that all the parties could, or were will to still agreed about was that whatever typographical errors, cartographic anomalies or outright blunders remained, regardless of how catastrophic they might prove to be for future generations that survived in the two thousand-two hundred and eighty-seven pages of the 'accursed document', they all urgently needed to get out of Paris before another war broke out!

Bordered on the west by the Venezuelan Confederacy, a declared supporter although not full member of the Triple Alliance, and to the east and south by the trackless jungles of Brazil, the giant, chronically impoverished former Portuguese province desperately trying to steer an implausibly neutral course through the chaos enveloping the region, Guyana had long been, in Colonial Office parlance, one of those ancient imperial possessions the Empire would have been much 'better off without'.

Problematically, there were quite a few such 'possessions' like Guyana that the 'progressives' in London might, in a more rational age – if such had ever existed – had they been given a free hand, unashamedly hurried to independence, or partitioned away between its nearest neighbours. But the right moment had never presented itself and besides, not even the Foreign and Colonial Office wanted to start setting 'pragmatic' precedents like that.

Goodness, where would it all end?

India had been stumbling towards dominion status for over fifty years; the last thing anybody in London wanted to do was to start, de facto, selectively calving off bits of the Empire when most of Canada, Australasia, and all bar the Cape Colony in Southern Africa had been successfully hived off into, to all intents, other than in matters of continental defence and foreign policy, self-governing polities. If the Raj could be induced to, more or less peacefully, go down the same route then perhaps the Empire might not actually implode under the weight of its accumulated burdens for another fifty years.

But of course, there was no such thing as 'India', there had not been since the time of the Mughals. The Raj was a collection of religious and ethnic states and principalities – over a hundred of them, although Bengal and the Punjab comprised some thirty percent of the land mass and about one hundred million of the four hundred and eight millions of the population – which, for reasons nobody had ever explained to the King, or anybody else's satisfaction, the 'natives' allowed about twelve thousand Europeans and the eight hundred and twenty-one thousand men of the Indian Army, to *pretend* that they still governed.

It was one thing for Sir George Walpole, possibly the most learned historian ever to occupy the post of Foreign and Colonial Secretary, to aver that 'India does not care who rules it and its peoples will never agree which among them ought to be primus inter pares, *first among equals*,' arguing that ' in a funny way for us to sit in all the big cities and for the Viceroy, whoever he is at the time, poor fellow, to take the blame for everything that goes wrong, suits both the Indian aristocracy, the educated technocracy and the rapidly expanding educated middle classes perfectly. I know there is an apparent ground swell of something ill-informed people in the popular press describe as 'Indian Nationalism' but actually, the present arrangements generally support the aspirations, not to mention, offer a degree of security, to the people who have never really stopped 'running' India. And I don't mean us!"

Of the five main Hindu castes in India – each of which sub-divided into tens, hundreds and possibly thousands of smaller divisions virtually incomprehensible to Europeans – the Brahmins, the priests and teachers, and the Kshatriyas, the rulers and warriors, formed only a tiny proportion of the population but so long as the Raj kept them 'onside', whatever the hundreds of millions of Vaishyas, what in the United Kingdom and elsewhere in the Empire would be regarded, generically, as the middle classes, and the working or lower class, Shudras, effectively the labouring poor, and the Dalits, the 'outcasts', more commonly known as 'untouchables', who did all the most menial work in the society, thought of the British, or the way their great, sprawling country was being run, really did not matter a fig.

While the King was no advocate for this paradigm, which he found deplorable, as more than one of his ministers had said to him down the years: 'We are where we are, sir.'

More to the point, doing the right thing was not, and never had been top of the list of any minister at the Colonial Office where the unofficial motto had always been was: 'Non situ peius!'

Which was colloquially translatable to the majority of the King's subjects without the benefit of a classical education as: *'Don't make the situation worse!'*

Thus, the Guyanese situation had been allowed to fester, its root causes unaddressed and frankly, ignored and even if one accepted that there was never a right time to lance a boil; it was far too late now.

Unfortunately, in the prevailing circumstances risking setting sensible but in terms of imperial realpolitik, positively Quixotic territorial adjustments to the political geography of the broader Empire – like, for example, sorting out the long-standing 'Guyanese Question', an FCO headache for well over half-a-century – always ran into the sand.

Quick sand, that was, meaning that in the circumstances of the present war the Empire was left holding a huge, indefensible acreage of land far from home which nobody, literally nobody in the British Isles except a few Colonial Office stalwarts, knew anything about, or cared a damn!

War, as any historian will tell one, has a nasty habit of pressing the fast forward button of human affairs, invariably with the predictability of a chess board kicked over in the middle of a long game. While it might be possible to remember where the pieces had been before the great upset, predicting where they actually landed was another matter entirely!

And now it was far too late to mitigate the consequences of decades of Imperial inertia. The unthinkable had happened.

The war was barely a month old and already it seemed if not yet certain, then at least possible that centuries-old British suzerainty over its island empire in the West Indies was collapsing, like dominoes...

The car ground to a halt.

The King snapped out of his introspection.

Guessing as much, his wife half-smiled.

"I think we've arrived, Bertie," the Queen murmured.

Chapter 4

Monday 24th April
William Penn House, Philadelphia

It was election time in the late spring in the Crown Colony of Virginia but not in Pennsylvania. Throughout the First Thirteen and their laggardly Johnny-com-lately, and depending on how one counted these things also Vermont and Maine fellow 'founding' colonies of North America - there was constant argument about who was first and last and suchlike in olden times – making up the 'historic' East Coast-New England Commonwealth, there was absolutely no consensus as to which was the best time of year for elections, or for that matter, much else. Which was probably why each individual colony so resented it when London, or its representative, the Governor of New England, in Philadelphia, sought to inflict unifying political and administrative protocols and standards.

Granted, these days, more or less everybody grudgingly agreed that whether they liked it or not, there were certain advantages to having a uniform Commonwealth railway gauge, Brunel's so-called 'standard-medium-permanent way', uniform systems of measurement, the 'Imperial' system of feet, inches and yards, etcetera, weights and underlying commonalities in jurisprudence, and so forth.

Unfortunately, where there had always been violently articulated divergence, was on the subject of rates and the appropriateness of local and commonwealth-wide taxation. This was hardly odd because although each colony claimed to have its own 'take' on the subject – none of them liked paying it (tax, that was), with some claiming Biblical justifications – in general, and as it was key to the whole topic, upon how exactly war should be waged on the shores, and upon the seas around, New England in particular.

Which, counter-intuitively, was why the Chairman of the Virginia Colonial Legislative Council, Roger Emerson Lee III, presently the Director of the Organisation of the Chairmen – there were no women, nor had there ever been – of the sovereign Colonial Legislative Councils of the First Thirteen, plus Maine and Vermont, had come to Philadelphia, in Pennsylvania, to make the opening set-piece speech of his campaign to be re-elected to the VCLC back in Richmond approximately six weeks hence. Just turned fifty-seven years old, handsome in that traditional fleshy Virginian planter fashion, and scion of one of the five wealthiest 'old' dynasties in New England, he was vain, thin-skinned and unfussy about detail, or for that matter about letting the truth get in the way of a handy epithet, and operated as a rule, as if he had a God-given entitlement to do...well, pretty much whatever he wanted to do, whenever he wanted to do it.

Again, counter-intuitively, in recent years people tended to remark that his was never a thing which had served him as favourably as by rights it ought, with the vapid society women who tended to flutter around the sons of old money in in either Virginia, or the seat of imperial power in Philadelphia, for although he had had many mistresses, nowadays they circled, ever-ready to hand a juicy new barb to journalists and *the great man's* political opponents.

Lately, those numerous opponents had observed, perceptively, that the key thing which best characterised the inner man was that with the coming of the war, Roger Lee saw only opportunity. Opportunities to smite his enemies, to aggrandise himself with fat new military contracts and to paint himself as the great national leader he but hardly anybody else, had always believed himself to be. Now, as the recently anointed Director of the Organisation of Chairmen of the Colonial Legislatures of the Fifteen - which had never been a constitutionally recognised position – which made him the spokesman for his fellow Chairman of the Chairman bar one – Florida – of the Crown Colonies that actually mattered, he was convinced he was finally making progress!

That day, his audience was a select one.

By invitation his Whig allies, and a sprinkling of his newly acquired, unlikely philosophical bedfellows, racist Christian fundamentalists who demanded 'separate development', or *Getrennte Entwicklung*, as the more extreme Lutheran sects insisted on calling the policy, filled the old hall that day, sat in cliques amongst the great and the good of the nexus of the banking, industrial and commercial affairs of New England. In fact, Roger Lee's supporters were hugely outnumbered by the real movers and shakers of the Commonwealth, the men who controlled the steel mills and factories, the banks, the railways, who oversaw the giant construction combines carving the permanent way and two and four-lane tarmac roads into the wilderness of the West, and increasingly, the men who would build the war planes and land cruisers, the ships and the bombs which would win this latest contretemps with the 'damned Spaniards'.

Gadfly opportunists like Roger Lee, had never been a man to contemplate long-term consequences when he saw personal profit, or a chance to stab an enemy in the back. His detractors, of whom there were countless, jested sourly that Lee was the sort of man who would have given Judas Iscariot a free pass for his share of the thirty pieces of silver.

Here, in the midst of the seat of Colonial power in New England, every seat in the relatively small, historic hall where once, two centuries ago the traitors of 1776 had plotted their failed rebellion, was taken and newspaper and TV people stood at the back, waiting for the fireworks to begin.

Nowadays, from the outside the old building looked like one of the white-washed non-conformist Wesleyan chapels which dotted the counties around the city. Set in leafy grounds in the heart of the great, booming metropolis of imperial Philadelphia, the city fathers had long ago, ripped out the old fittings, and turned it in a community theatre and function room for the local Parish Council. Normally, casual visitors were discouraged; its doors were locked and the gates to the plot of land upon which it sat, barred. Unlike in Boston where public references to 'the tea Party' or to the so-called 'Boston Massacre' had always been banned outright, either in tourist literature, directional or location signage, in Philadelphia, the building was still actually called 'Liberty Hall' on street maps of the city's financial district.

However, while outside there was a rusting commemorative plaque on the north wall of the building facing Chestnut Street bearing the names of the signatories to that wicked 'Declaration of Independence' who had been executed for their treason back in 1776; it was very much in the shadow of the twelve-feet high bronze statue of General William Howe – mounted triumphantly on a rearing thoroughbred - the victor of the Battle of Long Island, and the scourge of the Hudson Valley campaign which had sundered the defeated First Thirteen and brutally crushed the rebellion even before the winter of that fateful year, 1776, had clamped down across the land.

In their mercy 'the English' had only executed twenty-four of the fifty-six signatories, and many of those spared had subsequently pledged renewed allegiance to King George III, and quietly been compensated for the land and miscellaneous property sequestered by the Crown in the autumn of 1776. However, for John Hancock, President of the traitorous Second Continental Congress, there had never been any question of clemency although once he was safely buried the witch hunts had ceased, and there had been no more hangings.

Even two centuries ago the then, nascent Empire, understood that the business of 'the Empire' was business itself, and pogroms and blood-letting – while they had their place – were generally, bad for business.

Since the modern-day traitor Isaac Fielding had re-labelled William Penn House as 'Liberty Hall' in that scurrilous diatribe 'Two Hundred Lost Years', there had been a movement to have the 'execution plaque' taken down, or perhaps, removed to the Colonial Museum down on the west bank of the Delaware River.

In any event, it was a strange place to launch *a Virginian* election campaign; even given that Roger E. Lee was the sort of politician who only really ever went out of his way to talk to the converted.

One of Lee's distant ancestors, Henry 'Light Horse' Lee, an obscure minor figure in the revolt of 1776, whom, in their wisdom the English had 'graciously rehabilitated', supposedly to found the most 'loyal' of 'loyal families'.

History knew 'Light Horse' as the man responsible for so badly fortifying Manhattan and Long Island that George Washington and the Continental Army, had they escaped the clutches of the Howe – 'Black Jack' the Admiral and William the ruthless soldier - brothers at the Battle of Long Island, in August 1776, would have had no choice but to have fled up the Hudson Valley in disarray. Later, the British had installed 'Light Horse' as Governor of Virginia, demonstrating a Georgian sense of humour few had, until that time, suspected in the Americas, the first of several members of the Lee family to occupy the position, in which post he had, probably to nobody's surprise, proven to be as inept as a colonial governor as he had as a general in the Revolutionary Army!

Funnily enough, although Roger Lee frequently cited 'Light Horse', he hardly ever mentioned *Robert E. Lee*, the solitary 'great' man of the clan; the man who might have won the Great War a year early but for a sniper's bullet cruelly finding its mark in the forests of the Argonne in 1865. Perhaps, his reticence was because even Roger, in some crevice of his consciousness knew, just knew, that he must only pale into insignificance in the presence of such unparalleled greatness…

"My friends," he began, with his arms apart, hands raised like a whiskey preacher, "thank you for coming here today at this momentous time in our history. Once again, we find ourselves confronted by a terrible war that was none of our own doing; into which we, the peoples of New England have been dragged by the incompetence and inattention by a foreign regime which knows little of us, nor cares…"

Lee was genuinely surprised when this opening verbal salvo did not strike a stronger resonance in the hall, or rather, hardly any response at all bar a few desultory mutters of concurrence, and one or two half-hearted claps.

Otherwise his audience simply stared at him.

War was far from, per se, bad, for the great men of New England.

In fact, all the evidence was that it was good for business.

"Many times," Lee went on, clearly disappointed, "I took my fears, my forebodings to the Governor's office. But was I listened to? NO! Now look where we are today!"

Problematically, any seasoned watcher of politics will confirm that even a man so full of his own importance that it never occurs to him that even his political allies regard him as a self-serving buffoon, can perchance stumble upon a magic, opinion-changing formula. Usually, by accident. In Roger E. Lee's case, it helped his cause that he was a man compulsively addicted to the sound of his own voice and that he had the moral compass of an alley cat, because sometimes it took a lifetime to trip over, unwittingly, a cause which perfectly matched one's meagre gifts.

"Now we are about to reap the whirlwind, my friends!"

Still, no reaction other than a few noncommittal shrugs.

Roger Lee bored on.

"The *English*," he complained angrily.

Here and there people were shifting uncomfortably in their chairs.

Most New Englanders considered themselves to be English, or of Irish, or Scottish, or Welsh stock, or just plain British; it was only when you went further out West that people started calling themselves Louisianans, or Missourians, or Kentuckians, or Dakotans or Columbians, or by nicknames and abbreviations derived from the ancestral names of native tribes or lands upon which they lived, like Iowans or Lakotans, or Arizonians, or Mesans. Whereas, here in the East, everybody knew they were 'of their colony' yet also New Englanders, intrinsically in some way British unless they had had the sad misfortune to have come from some other European land.

"The *English* have already lost Jamaica and one of their battleships. At this very moment one of their monstrously expensive new aircraft carriers is sitting in Hampton Roads like a burned-out wreck. Look what has happened to stock prices in the last week! And that was before the disastrous news from the South West started coming in. Is it any wonder that the *English* tried to keep all that from us?"

A disinterested observer – not that there were any of those in the room – would have been hard-pressed to tell whether the souring mood of the audience was affirmative, or negative towards Roger Lee.

"Balderdash!" A man at the back yelled.

Chairs scraped as other men rose to their feet.

"Is it? Is it?" Roger Lee bellowed. "Who do you think the English will force to pay to replace the ships they are frittering away, or for the lost revenues from Jamaica, or for the armies and the aircraft they will need to keep the Spanish from fording the Mississippi in a couple of months?"

"Go back to Virginia!"

But of course, Roger Lee had a microphone and his detractors, did not and he had never been very good at listening to whatever anybody else had to say to him.

"Here, in this city, reside the criminals who have led us to this sad pass; the men in Government House who will surely tax us to kingdom come to pay for their blunders!"

Pennsylvanians tended to be a lot harder-headed about most things than their southern brothers and sisters. For example, nobody in the colony fondly cast their minds back to the slave-owning past, and modern industry, shipping and commerce had long ago made the colony prosperous. There were none of the ghettos and poverty-stricken backwaters one found in most Virginian cities, and in the north the old plantations had been replaced by modern arable and cattle farms. In the south, Virginian agriculture still depended on cotton and tobacco, on vast estates dependent on a large number of low-paid workers, many first or second generation Hispanics from Cuba and Santo Domingo, or the descendants of African slaves, most of whom were trapped in the southern colonies by penal indentures, or for the want of education and the skills necessary to find employment in the factories and offices of the middle and upper colonies of the East Coast, most of whom denied welfare and Poor Law support to 'outsiders'.

The Royal Navy had long been the biggest single employer in Virginia and the Carolinas, coincidentally, those same colonies the least taxed, per head of their populations, of any of the First 'Fifteen' for much of the twentieth century. In Philadelphia, the man or the woman on the street, insofar as they thought about it at all, was not preoccupied with how much tax they paid but by how little some of the other colonies, like Virginia, for all its complacent superiority and sneering condescension of its neighbours, paid!

Roger Lee may, or may not have been aware of this. He was not a man who read widely, if at all, or who was not known for his capacity for original thought. Like many career politicians he was always too preoccupied looking for the next wagon to hitch his horse to. Politics was the game he played to give his life meaning, because nothing else ever had.

He talked a lot about his family but his wife, Emily Beauregard Lee, was a semi-recluse hardly ever leaving the family's vast Arlington Estates – which straddled the Potomac for several miles north and south of Arlington itself – and his five surviving children; idle, spoiled brats aged between twenty-one and thirty-four, of whom the eldest, Jackson, now an independently wealthy sometime merchant banker, was the only one who had threatened to make anything of himself, and tellingly, had estranged himself from the clan in recent years.

Roger had been perfectly happy to escort potential New Granadan, Mexicans as they called themselves, and Cuban tobacco-men clients around his plantations before the Empire Day atrocities, and afterwards. In fact, the man had been positively pro-Spanish – even to the degree of learning a smattering of conversational Spanish - until that was, he discovered that his spinster sister, Amelia had supposedly had a 'dalliance' with the then Spanish Ambassador in Philadelphia, the Duke of Medina Sidonia, whom he had publicly challenged to a duel.

That affair had laid him low for a while.

Not least because, much to Roger Lee's surprise, the Spaniard had responded by offering to give him 'satisfaction' either with the sword or the pistol 'on the field of honour'.

Suddenly, Roger had dropped out of sight, re-emerging eventually after his attorneys had allegedly advised him that 'reluctantly, I must decline Medina-Sidonia's challenge on legal grounds'.

Amelia, a bookish, plain woman in her forties who had been completely under her brother's thumb, having lived in his house all her adult life, had since struck out on her own, in the last year publishing a book of short stories for children, and two slim volumes of what her agent called 'English-style country verses'. There were even rumours of further 'dalliances', titillatingly for the tabloid press, almost exclusively with younger men. It had also transpired that under the terms of her and Roger's father's will; forty-nine percent of the family's estates had been left to her and her descendants, in perpetuity, a thing which had never been a problem while she was unmarried, and a near-recluse companion for Emily Beauregard Lee.

All in all, the 'Spanish affair', now some thirty months ago, still had a lot of people smirking behind their hands whenever Roger E. Lee's name was mentioned.

A more empathetic, less thick-skinned man would have found it intolerable but Roger, once he had dodged – quite literally – the bullet in declining to meet the Duke of Medina Sidonia on the field of honour, had carried on as before.

Which only went to show that if he had ever been a man motivated by idealism, patriotism or fellow feeling; these days he was just in it for himself. He had no scruples about lighting a fire under the respectable, oh-so-superior burgers of Philadelphia.

"WHO DO YOU THINK IS GOING TO PAY FOR THIS WAR THE ENGLISH HAVE GOT US INTO?"

The great and the good of the city were heading for the exits.

"WHEN THE SPANISH COME MARCHING UP BROAD STREET AND TAKE A LEFT DOWN CHESTNUT STREET: WHO IS GOING TO STOP

THEM?"

Only the converted were still sitting, uneasily in their seats.

Roger Lee did not care; at the back the reporters were scribbling like Empire Day had come early and their lives depended on submitting their copy first!

None of this would go down well north of the Potomac but Roger Lee did not care a fig about that. He knew that back in Richmond and across the Carolinas and in deepest Georgia this would make a positively seismic impact. Perhaps, his Planters' Group on the Virginia Colonial Legislative Council would finally, after a gap of nearly a dozen years, regain its majority?

War was not just good for business.

It was good for politics, too!

Chapter 5

Monday 24th April
Rancho Mendoza, Unincorporated District of Northern Texas

The horsemen looked down into the jagged shadows filling the arroyo which carved across the rocky desert. Last week's rains had transformed the now, mostly dry, channel into a raging torrent for a couple of days. Judging by the dark clouds gathering in the west and north, in a day or so all the gullies and dried up streams feeding the stream would flood again. Every time it rained up country, the waters slashed the ranch in half and there were always cattle who were in the wrong place at the wrong time; as every cattleman knew, there was nothing quite so dumb as a steer sheltering from the wind in an arroyo in a rain storm.

A rancher working this country found out about the vicissitudes of the life soon enough. In the olden days – fifty years ago in the time of Don Carlos Mendoza, whose family had run herds on this land since the early nineteenth century – there had been sporadic troubles with the Comanches and the Wichitas, and now and then very occasionally, with the Tawakoni. Nowadays, a wise rancher co-existed with the native peoples, took care to cultivate good relations with tribal elders, turned a blind eye to hot-headed young bloods cutting out the odd steer, especially when winter was biting hard.

These days the Buffalo hardly ever came this far south, not for twenty years now. People said the rate of settlement on the Great Plains east of the Mississippi had thinned the herds that the first western explorers had claimed stretched from horizon to horizon. Some scientists said the herds of Bison had only grown so big because the diseases the Spanish had brought to the South West in the sixteenth century, had 'winnowed' out the heart of many of the tribes, and that it was only recently, as the natives gained some natural immunity from those pestilences that their populations were gradually on the rise again, albeit from a level that was a pitiful fraction of what it had been two or three hundred years ago.

Not that many Texan ranchers gave a damn about that; it was hard enough running herds in this country without wasting time pondering the consequences of ancient history.

Several neighbouring ranchers had started to fence off their ranges, not so the owner of Rancho Mendoza. Nothing so antagonised the tribal elders as white men stringing mile upon mile of barbed wire across their stolen ancestral lands.

The tall man sitting on his loyal chestnut mare, at ease in the saddle as if he had been born with the reins loosely held in his right hand as he rested his left on the worn, leather pommel as he studied the country around him with hooded eyes beneath the broad rim of his canvas hat, had been brought up to respect the ground, and to live in harmony with nature. To work with it, not to fight it. And besides, when it came to barbed wire, he had already seen way too much of the filthy stuff in his life.

There were four horsemen resting their mounts on the bluff above the arroyo, three men and a young woman whose straw blond hair tangled and whipped in the gusting breeze. They all felt the strange, desert moisture in the air and knew it threatened another storm overnight.

"Junior reckons there are five hundred head over there, Pa," the young woman said, waving into the distance across the other side of the deep gully.

The arroyos cutting across the ranch filled with wind-blown sand most of the year; presently, they were 'clean', their sides sharply delineated by the recent rains which, in places, had drained into them so hard it had over-topped their sides.

"Nothing for it, Connie," the tall man told his daughter.

Christened Constance Dandridge, the latter, middle name in the now out of fashion southern tradition of preserving a girl child's maternal family name, his youngest issue had been 'Connie' from the day she came squalling, lustily, into the world.

Rancho Mendoza had an outstation – a couple of well-made cabins and some holding pens – located about six miles north west, where a couple of hands, and sometimes their families, wintered, keeping an eye on the northern extremities of the range. They might be cut off up there for a couple more weeks at this rate, especially if the coming rains were as bad as they had been in the last few days.

"I guess so," Connie conceded.

The other two men exchanged looks and shook their heads. They were a father and son whose family had been in the service of Rancho Mendoza forever. Like many so-called Texans, their tanned faces and lean, whiplash frames were the result of generations of inter-mingling tribal, Spanish and New England-settler bloodlines. In these parts, few people were readily identifiable as 'English' or 'European', like the father and daughter. However, whereas other 'old world' ranching dynasties in this part of Texas tended to import East Coast wives for their sons, the sons of the man everybody in this part of the territory called 'El Jefe' – *the Chief* – or just, respectfully Don Jorge, had married local girls. George junior, whom all his contemporaries just called 'Jorge', the Hispanic version of his given name, had married a Creole girl with Mexican blood, and Jedidiah had got hitched, only last year, to the youngest daughter of a Tawakoni elder.

"The rains will come again, Don Jorge," the older of the two Spaniards – Texas had been a mixing pot of the empires of New England and New Spain for centuries and hereabouts, allegiances were familial, political, emotional rather than an inheritance from the place one's ancestors had been born – observed, with a sigh and a shrug which in another context might have seemed positively Gallic. "That landing field down at Trinity Crossing will be flooded again, I shouldn't wonder."

The tall man on the Chestnut mare nodded.

He was a man of few words who was content with in his thoughts. Many assumed he was aloof but actually, his distance and his quietness, was an innate shyness he had never really thrown off other than in the company of his family and closest friends.

Trinity Crossing was the nearest real town – no kind of city, just a community straggling along the Trinity River either side of a seasonal ford – some thirty miles to the south. In the last few months the Army had started setting up re-supply depots on the east bank of the river, work had started on a spur off the railway line down to San Antonio to connect Trinity Crossing to the West Mississippi network, and the small, dirt strip aerodrome outside the town had been taken over by the Colonial Air Force. From what they had heard out in the country the military had not been in any kind of a hurry; and the thirty or so troops billeted in the town had, or were in the process of pulling out. Supposedly, the airstrip was still not 'operational', whatever that meant.

From what people up country could see the Army and the Air Force had been even less well prepared for this war than they had been for the last two or three!

The tall man grunted, turning to the older of the two men in the party.

"I've been thinking, Pablo," he confided, as the sound of an aircraft, its engine buzzing like an angry bee, fell down to earth from the south, "about what happens if the Mexicans come north."

The two men had known each other all their lives.

Although one was master and the other faithful retainer, no man or woman listening to their discourse would think they were anything other than very old friends.

Which, in fact, they were.

"We could drive the herd to the east?" The other man murmured, without enthusiasm.

"I know, but that's back country. The spring is late this year…"

"The Army might requisition the herd?"

The tall man nodded and the two men lapsed into silence.

Pablo's son, Julio, and Connie had let their mounts track backwards a few paces; they grinned, one to the other. They were of an age, not quite twenty and nobody could figure out why they were not sweethearts.

Well, not in public, at least.

Out here on the range with only their fathers for company, chaperones far too preoccupied with 'big matters' to watch over them, they were safe to 'carry on' as they pleased.

They had been sweet on each other since they were children; yet as ranch siblings they were also inbred with a pragmatism that had long ago made them older and wiser than their years. Connie was going to a college in the East that summer; she might not be back for two years. By then she and Julio would both be twenty-one, and that would be the right time to decide what to do next.

Connie took off her hat, sat forward on her mount, a handsome black gelding her father had given her for her eighteenth birthday. They had all been in the saddle for several hours and her face was a little grimy as she turned to look up as an antique biplane wobbled towards them, and then turned over the arroyo to head almost due south.

"A Fleabag," she declared. "Those things look so frail you half-expect them to fall out of the sky at any time!"

Connie spoke Spanish in an oddly French-accented way. Spanish and English, and for reasons nobody had ever explained to her, one of the dialects of the Wichita, had always been spoken, virtually interchangeably on the Rancho Mendoza since time immemorial. From habit, she and Pablo tended to converse in Spanish; particularly when they were in the company of 'Easterners', most of whom only spoke English. In any event, given that their respective fathers were talking in the first language of the Commonwealth today, they were being awkward, sticking to Spanish.

That again, was another of their 'little ways', foibles remarked upon all the time by their mothers but unremarked by their respective fathers.

Connie and Pablo turned their horses to watch the Fleabag crab across the sky as it slowly followed the line of the arroyo down to where it met the fork of the Trinity River. Lately, they had seen higher-flying, much more modern silvery-winged warplanes and transport aircraft flying to the south west.

They assumed the aircraft must have navigated from Caddoport on the Red River, tracking along the railways lines to the west before using the upper reaches of the Trinity River as way points signalling the way down to the transit aerodromes around San Antonio some two hundred and fifty miles to the south-south-west. Those aircraft probably used Waco and Round Rock, there were supposed to be navigation beacons at both, as further way markers on their flights to the south.

"Pa says the Mexicans won't come this far north," Connie said quietly.

Pablo shrugged.

A hundred years ago, Trinity Crossing had been the site of a border fort of the Empire of New Spain, and the whole South West had been half-a-dozen provinces of the great sprawling dominion ruled from México City all the way from the Pacific to the Red River.

In school all Texan children were taught that once upon a time that 'dreadful empire' had stretched from the northern shores of the Latin Americas to the Texas Territory and the banks of the great Mississippi. In both Pablo's and Connie's great-grandfathers' lives the Inquisition had ruled the ground upon which they now stood. And now, it was said, that the Catholic Triple Alliance had embarked upon a new crusade to reclaim the lost lands from the heretic usurpers of New England...

"What are you two plotting?" Connie's father called, fondly gruff.

It was Julio who replied, turning in the saddle.

"Do you think the Mexicans will come this far north, Don Jorge?" He asked, suddenly serious.

"Maybe," the older man said. "But swallowing San Antonio will choke them awhile first. That's what towns and cities do to invading armies. They suck in troops and when they fall it is hard to get an army moving again afterwards."

Connie's gelding stamped his hooves as she guided its proud head around.

"What do we do if that happens, Pa? I mean, if they come this way>"

Her father pondered this a moment.

"I've been thinking a lot about that a lot," he confessed.

"The Army will probably requisition the whole herd, anyway," Julio's father said disgustedly. "Like they did in Don Jorge's father's time."

That was before Connie and Julio had been born. It was an era lost in family history, folklore and legend. Even at the time of the last war the young people had barely been toddlers, recollected little and knew only what their elder siblings had told them; snatches of more myths, fragmented gossip. The old folk never talked about their time away at the wars.

Connie knew her father had been some kind of hero in that last war. Girlishly, she had always assumed he must have been a hero each time he had gone away; how could he be anything else. As a child she had wondered why so many visitors to the ranch called him 'Colonel', and the way everybody in Trinity Crossing very nearly bowed and scraped when he came into a room; but in the way of such childhood things, not really thought much of it.

Julio's father had gone off to war with him, too.

They said he had been wounded, very nearly died in one battle and lately, after a day in the saddle he was noticeably stiff, and often had to be helped down to the ground, a thing he clearly hated. Other, that was, when the helping hand was that of Connie's father. For they were old soldiers both.

"Will you go away again, Pa?" She asked.

Her father shook his head, quirked a rueful half-smile.

There was something faraway in his grey eyes for a moment as he glanced to Pablo and his old friend grimaced as they shared an old, unspoken joke.

"No," Connie's father sighed, "I hope not, sweetheart."

Chapter 6

Monday 24th April
Penshurst Place, Kent

The Royal couple had been welcomed to the old house by the Governor of the Commonwealth of New England's thirty-five-year-old eldest son, Viscount Frederick Philip Anscombe De L'Isle and his vivacious Indian wife Usha, known within the family as 'Pippa'. 'Freddie' De L'Isle had followed his father into the Guards and was presently attached to the Household Cavalry, a duty he had temporarily been relieved from to perform the honours at Penshurst Place.

"Freddie you look marvellously recovered from that fall you had at Windsor last autumn!" Queen Eleanor beamed the moment the bowing, scraping and curtsying was over and done with.

The dashing cavalry officer's wife was heavily pregnant with their third child and Eleanor began, gently, to berate her husband, whom, like all the De L'Isle offspring had grown up regarding the 'accidental' King and Queen as forbearing and attentive godparents and as quasi Uncles and Aunts.

That was the thing the King and his consort missed the most; the easy informality of those days when they were both 'minor' royals; as ordinary a family as it was possible to be.

"Oh, Pippa," Eleanor scolded fondly.

Usha's father had been the Minister for Bengal in London for many years, a wise, professorial, witty man who had brought up his four daughters in the 'English way', ignoring criticism from nationalist quarters – principally, gangs of religious zealots, Hindus and Islamists - back home in Calcutta. "I feel terrible that we've forced you to stand outside in the cold!"

"The rest of the party is gathered in the old Banqueting Hall, sir," the younger De L'Isle respectfully informed the King as the two couples went inside. For the time of year there was a persistent, bitter wind gusting across the Kentish Weald, a thing the King and Queen tried not to interpret as an ill omen for their coming journey to Germany.

Normally, there would have been a full reception line in the drive and on the steps to the mansion; however, that had been deemed 'too public' and the King had not troubled to delve deeper into the matter. His father would have demanded a band, fanfares and that every notable from twenty or thirty miles around attended him on his arrival 'in the county'; but that was not the sort of monarchy that the firm of Bertie and Ellie ran!

The King and Queen had visited Penshurst Place many times over the years. Situated just thirty or so miles from the sprawl of London, it offered a welcome haven of tranquility. Their own children had played and occasionally, fought with Philip and Elizabeth De Lisle's large brood and it had been fascinating to observe the often, parallel development of the De L'Isle youngsters and their own 'brats'. Of the De L'Isle brood, Freddie, the oldest and Henrietta, the youngest, had always been the real stars. Freddie had assiduously cultivated the persona of the devil may care, polo-playing horseman soldier: and it was only a matter of time before he abandoned his military career and followed his father into the Diplomatic Corps. And as for Henrietta, after her recent adventures in Spain, she probably had the world at her feet!

At one time there had been a suggestion that Henrietta might join the Royal Household; but she would have hated being a Lady in Waiting, she was far too free a spirit.

"I received a letter from Hen yesterday," the Queen confided to her hosts, passing inside out of the chilling breeze.

"Good old Hen," Freddie De L'Isle guffawed. "You just can't keep her down, what!"

Although it had not come into the hands of the Sidney family until around 1552, when the child-king Edward VI had awarded it to Sir William Sidney for the services he had rendered his late father, Henry VIII, of 'six wives' fame, there had been a manor house at Penshurst Place since the fourteenth century. Back in the sixteenth century, the estate's previous 'holder' had been Sir Ralph Fane, whom Edward VI had had executed for treason. Every courtier walked a very narrow line in those days!

Sir William Sidney's son, Henry, had married into the Dudley family, themselves murkily entwined in the affair of Lady Jane Grey but survived with his head, and later established one of the most famous gardens in England in the grounds of the old house.

Subsequently, Henry's son, Sir Philip Sidney, the warrior, poet and Elizabethan courtier who died aged thirty-two of wounds received at the Battle of Zutphen had been but the first of a small regiment of heroic De L'Isles. Notably, the 2nd Baron De L'Isle and Dudley had won membership of the Order of the Garter for leading the charge that broke the French Royal Guard at Vers-sur-Selles and completed the encirclement of the great fortress of Amiens in 1860, early in the Great War, long before the influx of troops from the Empire eventually turned the course of the conflict in France.

That was rather uncomfortable history for any monarch; given that the fall off Amiens had sparked a bloody revolution in France which had, within eighteen months seen the citizen armies of the 1st Republic fighting on the side of the British invaders against Austro-Prussian aggressors on the Rhine. In the resulting chaos the whole of France had been ravaged, Paris fought over twice and then thrice...before the final armistice.

So much for ancient history...

The leading members of the rest of the 'Berlin Party' had been circled in conversation as they awaited the arrival of the Royal Party, now they shook themselves out into a dutiful reception line to greet their Sovereign.

Heading the line was the Prime Minister, Sir Hector Hamilton, for once unaccompanied by his wife: Sir George Walpole, the Foreign and Colonial Secretary was next in line in the dark, wood-panelled drawing room; to his right hand was the Chief of the Imperial General Staff

(CIGS), the white-haired and moustachioed Field Marshall Lord Francis de Selincourt Tremayne of Kandahar, and to complete the quartet, the sparse, dapper figure of the First Sea Lord, Admiral of the Fleet, 7th Viscount Julian Wemyss Troubridge, the man responsible, in league with the now C-in-C Atlantic Fleet, Cuthbert Collingwood, for the abandonment of the big gun in favour of naval aviation in the last decade.

Eleanor always found herself thinking about the remarkable resemblance between the Royal Navy's two greatest 'living' men, and their – in portraiture - Georgian predecessors: Collingwood was a big, bluff, red-faced man who spoke his mind without fear or favour, albeit one with a remarkable knack of working behind the scenes to get his way; while Troubridge was the spitting image of that first Admiral Collingwood's friend and heroically fated, comrade at the Battle of the Channel at the beginning of the nineteenth century, Horatio Nelson, that most tantalisingly enigmatic of naval icons.

"My, my," the King declared, "I know we're off to a funeral in Germany tomorrow but you fellows all look like you've got guilty consciences!"

Said by her husband in jest to break the ice because they were, after all, among friends, coincidentally, that was exactly the impression Eleanor had formed the moment she laid eyes on the quartet.

Sir Hector Hamilton grimaced.

He glanced around, uncharacteristically, clearly unhappy to be in the presence of so many staffers and courtiers.

Freddie De L'Isle lightened the mood: 'Perhaps, if we moved into the Banqueting Hall, sir," he suggested to the King. "Light refreshments have been laid on."

Both the King and the Queen exchanged raised eyebrows when the doors to the great room, with which they were so familiar, were shut behind them, excluding all bar their hosts and the four great men who had travelled separately to Kent for this rendezvous.

Freddie De L'Isle bowed his head.

"Forgive me, sir. Pippa and I were asked to accommodate the subterfuge necessary to facilitate this meeting, I hope you will not feel I have gone behind your back. Sir Hector emphasised the gravity of the situation and I felt it was my duty to, er, facilitate matters in my father's absence abroad. With your permission, sir," he requested, a little uncomfortably, "Pippa and I shall leave you to your deliberations."

The King met the younger man's troubled gaze.

He patted the younger De L'Isle's arm.

"Think nothing of it, Freddie," he assured him, "think nothing of it."

Eleanor and Usha De L'Isle exchanged pecking kisses and then the younger people were gone, and the big, oaken doors clunked shut at their backs.

The King's stomach was rumbling, and he was glad to survey a silver tea service, and several plates of savouries laid out on a table under the windows. Now that he was looking around the room, he noted that there was a film screen set up at one end and a semi-circle of comfortable chairs arranged, ready and waiting.

Poor Freddie and Pippa, they must have felt absolutely dreadful having to play their part organising this charade.

Whatever it was that was actually going on!

"What is this, Hector?" He inquired of his Prime Minister, his tone momentarily that of a captain of a ship awakened in the middle of the night by a routine report which could have waited until the morning. "What the Devil is going on?"

The King had been looking around for a movie projector, his scrutiny seeking something large, clumsy and metallic; now his eye settled on a small, dull, scarcely larger than a child's hand device, roughly aligned with the big screen at the southern end of the room in front of the waiting chairs.

Eleanor decided that her husband's most senior advisors were ill-at-ease, unusually awkward in the Royal presence. That would never do!

Touching her husband's, elbow she moved to the table.

"Shall I be mother?" She offered brightly.

This seemed to break the ice.

Julian Troubridge stepped forward.

"There is a film concerning an extremely confidential matter, sir," he explained. "We are agreed that, as they say, a single picture may convey more than a thousand words. Respectfully, if Your Majesties would indulge us a few minutes? You will have many questions and the answers will, well, make more sense once you have seen the, er, movie, that we have had prepared…"

A frown began to harden on the King's face. Soon after he had taken command of HMS Lion – the best part of twenty years ago, now – he had had a dream, a nightmare one night. He was on the bridge of the leviathan, roaring along at nearly thirty knots and suddenly a lookout reported a rock, directly in front of the ship. Instantly, he had ordered the wheel to be put over and…nothing, nothing whatsoever had happened except that the battleship had ploughed ahead even faster…

He studied the faces of the other men.

While both of the politicians were looking a little sheepish; and the CIGS was avoiding his eye, the First Sea Lord, on the other hand, seemed quite cheerful, almost relieved. It was as if the four men were about to confess their sins…

Tea cups clinked in saucers.

Soon, Eleanor had organised the men around her. Bringing up a brood of clever, competitive and frequently quarrelsome children was marvellous preparation for marshalling a group of men of a certain age, notwithstanding that the men in question were among the great men of the Empire.

Everybody took their seats; the King and Queen in the centre flanked by Sir Hector Hamilton and Sir George Walpole to their left, and the two military men to their right.

Troubridge had a small, grey remote-control unit in his hand.

"If I may, sir?" He inquired tersely.

"Carry on."

The screen flickered to life as the lights in the room dimmed.

There was no commentary on the movie itself.

Instead, the First Sea Lord spoke.

"The first pictures you will see are of a secret base in Newfoundland at the head of Placentia Bay, Your Majesties," he explained.

On screen there was an aerial view of a port, dockyards and what appeared to be a tanker farm built to the model of such Royal Navy oiling facilities all around the globe.

The aircraft taking the pictures – which were amazingly, pin-point clear and of astonishingly high definition – circled lower, and lower until it became obvious that the 'tanker farm' was built on high ground overlooking the empty anchorage.

"The tanker farm hides and underground complex approximately the size of nine or ten football fields," Lord Troubridge declared.

The camera shot altered, now it was on the deck of a ship offshore, focusing on the hillside next to the small port. In the distance a section of shoreline began to change colour, darkening. It was some moments before the King or the Queen recognised what they were looking at; a huge blast door slowly revolving forward, and sinking beneath the cold, northern waters.

"There are six 'pens', each of which can serve as either a maintenance or a construction dock. The steel doors protecting the individual pens are four feet thick and each bunker has twenty-three feet of reinforced concrete above it, and at each longitudinal side, in addition to some thirty feet of earth and rubble on top of them."

"Most impressive," the King murmured.

"The complex was designed to be resistant to a conventional armour piercing bomb twice the size of the largest munition of that type ever dropped from an aircraft, and," the First Sea Lord hesitated, "a ground blast hit within one hundred feet of any part of the facility by an atomic bomb with an explosive yield in the range of mid-tens of kilotons of munitions-grade high explosives..."

The construction of such weapons, and of such bunkers – categorised as 'defensive infrastructure under the protocols of the Submarine Treaty of 1966 - were explicitly forbidden.

"First Sea Lord," the King growled, warningly. He would have continued, voicing his growing concerns had not he been suddenly transfixed – there was no other word for it – by the long, low, black shape which had begun to emerge from the shadows of the concealed dock.

There was a moment of shocked silence.

"Is that a," the King gasped, flabbergasted.

"Yes, sir," Lord Trowbridge said quietly. "That is HMS Splendid, the first of her class, going to sea after her acceptance trials refit in October 1973."

No, none of that sunk in for several more seconds.

"Bertie," Eleanor murmured, touching her husband's arm, "your mouth is hanging open, darling. If you're not careful, you'll swallow a fly."

The King shut his mouth, knowing that he was not going to be capable of coherent speech for several seconds to come. Leastways, not until his roiling thoughts began to calm a little.

What he was looking at was not one of those ugly, iron, bodged together, two or three hundred-ton coastal submersibles that the Germans had experimented with in the early 1960s, or that the Cubans were supposed to have constructed in more recent times. What he was looking at was a big, very long – possibly over four hundred or more feet - vessel with a bridge, conning-tower, whatever it was called, structure streamlined like a giant whale's fin, that soared perhaps thirty feet above the near wave-swept rounded pressure casing. Which itself did not look remotely metallic, rather it seemed rubbery, and somehow, granular.

"The vessel's pressure hull is covered in acoustic tiling, sir," his First Sea Lord informed him. "The material is rubbery to the touch; additionally, that shielding – essential to isolate the operating noise of the boat's machinery from the outside world – is covered in a synthetic material which mimics the effect of a shark's skin, reducing the hull's resistance to the water as it moves through the depths."

"How big is that ship?" The King asked, momentarily too awed to be angry or actually, to be thinking at all about the earth-shaking implications of what he was looking at.

"She's over six thousand tons surfaced, nearer seven thousand-three hundred submerged, sir. She has six twenty-one-inch torpedo tubes forward and storage capacity for twenty-seven fish."

"Torpedoes?" The Queen asked, by then in 'polite inconsequential conversation' mode, as she too began to assimilate the momentousness of the mind-boggling secret that she and her husband had just been let in on.

"Torpedoes, yes, Ma'am. They come in several variants. The standard Tigershark Mark III with a contact detonator or magnetic initiator, the Searcher Mark VII, that's a fire and forget wholly electrical – very quiet and doesn't leave a wake – fish that locks onto its target and homes in on it," Lord Troubridge paused, picked his next words with infinite care, "and, of course, the Mark XX, that's a *special* munition."

"Special?" The King snapped, breaking from his reverie.

"The Mark XX is an ultra-long-range weapon – twenty-five plus miles - which can be configured to carry a *special* physics package, sir."

"A nuclear bomb, you mean?"

"Yes, sir."

The movie was carrying on in the background showing HMS Splendid blowing her ballast tanks and dipping beneath the surface. There was a sequence shot in the submarine's gleaming, antiseptically clean and air-conditioned control room; it was like something out of a science fiction movie about space travel!

"Well over a decade ago, *My Government*," the King said with barely contained icy cold rage, "solemnly signed an undertaking with the German Empire to desist from all warlike underwater research and development, to scrap all our existing operational submersibles of one hundred and fifty tons or more, and to absolutely curtail for a period of not less than twenty-five years, the development of nuclear power for military purposes."

"Yes, sir," the First Sea Lord agreed, blandly, as if he really did not see what the problem was.

The King glared at his Prime Minister and his Foreign and Colonial Secretary. The latter had actually, briefly, been Prime Minister around the time of his untimely accession to the throne, and the former 'first among equals' for most of the last decade.

It was the Queen who asked the really obvious question.

"How on earth did you keep the building of *that* ship secret, gentlemen?"

Sir Hector Hamilton looked to the floor while he gathered his courage.

The First Sea Lord, obviously deciding it was best to make a clean breast of matters as soon as possible, stepped into the breech with an alacrity typical of what the Senior Service still termed 'the Nelsonian spirit'.

"HMS Splendid is one of eight vessels either already in service or expected to join the Fleet in the next year or so. Prior to the launching of the first of the 'S' class boats, three experimental vessels were commissioned, two of which are presently on active service."

The King was suddenly on his feet.

"Stop that bloody film!"

Everybody else rose to their feet, except Eleanor, who decided that if the men in the room were temporarily incapable of keeping a level head, then she must.

"Bertie," she suggested quietly, "I am sure that our *friends* had a very good reason for keeping this from us?"

She understood that this was one of those rare moments when her dear, profoundly decent husband needed to be reminded that the men who had just sprung the shock of the century on him, were still their 'friends'.

"They've got a damned odd way of showing it!" The King retorted, grimly.

The Foreign Secretary cleared his throat.

"Forgive me, sir," Sir George Walpole prefaced, not really very apologetically. "I suspect, that at present the matter of how we kept this secret for so long is not as big a problem as the fact that, contrary to all expectations, we have actually kept it secret for so long. Personally, I cannot imagine the German Empire would have acted so recklessly in the West Indies and in fomenting Mexican aggression in the New England South West, had it been aware that the new aircraft carriers were but the visible hilt of the shining new sword that we now have in our hands."

The King stared at his old friend.

Speechless...

"I fear," his minister sighed, "that the secret, such as it is, has been kept too long and that now, the problem is that we must reveal it to the world before," he shrugged, tight-lipped, "the German Empire steps even closer to the edge of the abyss."

Chapter 7

Wednesday 26th April
Imperial Airways Pier No 2, Gowanus Bay, Long Island

Maud Daventry-Jones had decided it was all very well for her best friend in the world, Leonora Fielding nee Coolidge, to tell her to 'play it cool' but that the advice completely ignored the present state of her hormones. Similarly, the proud attendance of her parents, dressed in all their Sunday finery, a large part – it seemed - of the population of New York, and judging by the unruly, jostling throng gathered behind the barriers, the entire press corps of the Commonwealth of New England, was not about to inhibit her one little bit.

Appearances be damned!

The man she had fallen in love with, who had recklessly gone off to war and, despite his own admirably self-effacing account of events, gallantly assisted in saving two damsels in distress – to wit, the Governor of New England's daughter and a well-known, adopted daughter of the twin-colony, Melody Danson – not to mention an innocent four year-old-child from the wicked clutches of the Spanish Inquisition, in a purely *Boy's Own* story of derring-do, was about to step back onto New England soil!

So, how on earth was she supposed to 'play it cool?'

Maud was fidgeting like she had an itch she could not scratch.

"Well, for goodness sake," Leonora sighed. "Try not to hug the poor man to death," she advised. "There will be plenty of time for that later," she added, teasingly.

Maud had no idea how her friend, so soon after giving birth to her first baby, had so swiftly recovered, apparently in every way, from the messy, traumatic experience. Leonora was her old, willowy, stylish, self-assured self and without her the last few days would have been even more intolerable than they had been!

Nevertheless, in her state of heightened existential angst, right then, Maud would have been okay with her returning hero ravishing her on the boardwalk in front of...everybody.

Not that she imagined, for a moment, that Albert Stanton, reporter extraordinaire of the *Manhattan Globe*, and as soon as his book about Kate and Abe Lincoln came out later that year, a sure-fire runaway best-selling author, was the sort of man who would take advantage of a girl in public.

Maud had been in a turmoil – a complete mess, really - ever since *that* first telegram came through from the British Embassy in Lisbon, Portugal.

IT IS WITH GREAT PLEASURE THAT I AM ABLE TO INFORM YOU STOP AT MISTER STANTONS PARTICULAR REQUEST STOP THAT HE IS ALIVE AND WELL STOP HE SENDS YOU HIS MOST HEARTFELT FELICITATIONS AND HOPES TO BE REUNITED WITH YOU SOONEST MESSAGE ENDS.

The Ambassador would never make a half-way competent romantic novelist but Maud had got the gist of things. Her beau was alive and well and the first thing he had thought about was getting back to her!

Or rather, after he had filed his copy with *The London Times* and the *Manhattan Globe*, wholly proper and professional conduct which she was not about to take umbrage over because, after all, he was heart and soul a newspaper man.

She could no longer deny or resent that, than Leonora could rail against the man she had fallen in love with and married, Alex Fielding, being a daredevil aeronaut!

Then Albert's letter had reached her.

I was an idiot to go to Spain...
There were so many things I never had a chance to say to you...
Will you ever forgive me?
I will be counting down the hours to when I hold you in my arms...

'Men!' Leonora had groaned, finally getting her hands on that first missive from Portugal. 'Can't kill them; you've got to love them!'

Which was a bit rich coming from the woman who had fallen for Major, now Acting Commander Alexander Fielding of the Royal Naval Air Service, a man who wore his fighter pilot's soul on his sleeve and to whom, she was utterly devoted.

Whatever she said!

Maud had understood that her friend's crankiness was solely on account of her own hero's absence, probably, knowing Alex, single-handedly fighting the whole Army, Navy and Air Force of the Triple Alliance with one hand tied behind his back...just to make it a fair fight!

The great silvery hull of the CEREBUS, one of the older of Imperial Airlines fleet of 'C' class trans-oceanic flying boats, drifted closer, its flank almost imperceptibly bumping up against the padded bulwarks protecting her plates and the ribs of the old pier. All four of the aircraft's three-bladed propellers were stilled, each stopped at a different angle, although her engines creaked and hissed as they cooled down.

A steward opened the cabin door and dogged it back.

And then *he* stepped out and stood, for a moment, blinking myopically into the bright light of the morning. It would have been dark when he boarded the aircraft at Southampton, and for most of the flight across the Atlantic.

Maud was running before she realised it.

Somebody was screeching with delight and for several steps she did not realise it was her.

Albert Stanton saw her coming towards him – at what seemed like a hundred miles an hour - and braced himself to catch her as best he could. A lean, spare man still not really physically recovered from the hard knocks and the privations of his time on the run in Spain, he was a little afraid he was about to be bowled over or worse, tackled directly into the cold waters lapping beneath the pier.

He need not have panicked.

Maud decelerated at the last moment and then the lovers were locked in a blissful embrace, perfectly oblivious to the frantic clicking and clattering of camera shutters. It was a clinch broken, very reluctantly, only when the participants began to turn blue from lack of oxygen.

"I missed you," the man gasped.

"I missed you even more!" Maud claimed breathlessly.

Albert Stanton slowly become aware of the huge welcoming committee for the first time, and the deafening storm of...applause. Although sorely tempted to kiss Maud anew he determined to be strong, mostly on the grounds that a pleasure delayed was likely to be a pleasure multiplied later, and tried to stand tall for the cameras.

He clutched Maud's left hand in his larger, right mit.

She was quivering with excitement.

"This is what it must be like to be movie stars," he whispered, looking to her.

Maud giggled.

The *Manhattan Globe* man had been introduced to Maud's parents last year, when he was covering Maud and Leonora's running battle with the Colonial authorities over the wrongful imprisonment of members of the Fielding-Lincoln family. However, this was a little different, very much an encounter with the mother and father of the bride to be.

Dazedly, he shook Maud's father's hand.

Maud claimed that despite the impression the old man made on strangers that her father was a 'good sport' underneath; Albert Stanton asked himself how far down one had to drill to get to the 'good stuff'. Her mother was a rotund, cheerful lady with her daughter's mischievous, twinkling eyes. She kissed her daughter's beau on the cheek with no little enthusiasm.

Albert Stanton ignored the clamour all around.

"Sir," he said in an approximation of what he hoped was his most serious, decisive tone, "forgive my temerity but I won't beat about the bush; I would like to ask you for your daughter's hand in marriage." He weakened. "if that's all right with you, sir?"

Had the man not retained a firm grip on Maud's hand she would have been jumping up and down and clapping her hands together in a jig of joy.

Leonora Fielding rolled her eyes.

Men!

If that's all right with you...

Leonora had no idea what exactly her own husband had said to her father, who, by any standards was a much scarier and harder case than Maud's sweet, somewhat fuddy-duddy old man.

Alex had probably said something along the lines of: 'Look, I've already knocked up the girl; so, you had jolly well better let me take her off your hands before people start to notice the bump, what, old man!'

"I've already volunteered to be maid of honour!" She announced loudly.

"Well," the father of the would-be bride decided, ruefully, "that settles it. Don't you think, Mother?" This latter, he inquired looking to his wife who was already moving to hug her daughter.

Albert Stanton had tried to sleep on the flight from England.

Failed, dismally.

In the event, leaving Melody and Henrietta, and little Pedro, had been a much bigger wrench than he had expected. This was hardly surprising, thinking about it, they had gone through a lot together. Both women had hugged him very nearly to death.

Albert Stanton still had no idea what to make of the arrival in Viano do Castelo, in Northern Portugal of Alonso Pérez de Guzmán, 18th Duke of Medina Sidonia, the handsome castellan of the Comarca de Las Vegas, sometime diplomat and cavalryman, now seemingly an agent of the Spanish Government in Exile in Lisbon, headed by the estranged wife of the King Emperor Ferdinand, Queen Sophia, by reputation a woman capable of extraordinary mendacity. Even more baffling, were the man's relations with the two women who had shared his roller-coaster life and death flight across the wilds of a country disintegrating into civil war.

Melody Danson was clearly the Spaniard's mistress, and not remotely coy about it; and as for Henrietta, goodness, well, she was scarcely less *familiar* with de Guzmán, whom, incidentally, seemed to be a decent enough fellow, than her friend. Disconcertingly, the two women had never, at any time, bothered to hide their own, presumably, *intimate relations*, leastways, not in front of him or from what he had seen, from the disinherited, apparently, now Catholically ex-communicated nobleman.

Albert Stanton had always thought he was a broad-minded sort of man. He had heard the rumours about Melody Danson, not given them a second thought; the woman was clearly at ease with herself without ever going out of her way to flaunt her predilections. In Spain, far away from the stupid, old-fashioned orthodoxy of the religiously inclined in the First Thirteen, both Melody and Henrietta had made no secret of their mutual affection, one for the other.

Unfortunately, sooner or later that was going to be a problem for her father, the Governor of New England...

"You went all dreamy back there in the car?" Maud asked him as they spilled out onto the forecourt of the hotel in the Hamptons, where her parents had organised a modest – by the standards of well to do Long Island families – homecoming ceremony.

"Sorry, I was back in Spain," he grinned uncomfortably, "and Portugal. I'm afraid I'll probably have moments, now and then, when some of those things come back to me, for a while yet."

Maud clamped herself on his left arm.

"I shall distract you!" She promised. "Daddy will want a long engagement, by the way. But that simply won't do! We need the bands to be read toot sweet so we can get down the aisle as soon as possible."

"That sounds like just the ticket," he agreed.

Leonora Coolidge button-holed the hero a little while later.

"I've been out of it for most of the last forty-eight hours," he confessed. "What's the latest news about Alex?"

"His ship is at Norfolk. The Perseus 'tore up a turbine' or something in the battle to save the Ulysses. So, Perseus was in dry dock for a few days; she may already be mended by now. Alex is hoping to fly up here for a day or two, maybe at the weekend. I'm not holding my breath."

"I heard he was in the thick of things?"

Leonora pulled a face and shook her head.

"The stupid man," she said with a severity mocked by the fond pride in her eyes, "spent so much time flying around making sure all the pilots coming back to the Ulysses, which was on fire from one end to the other by then, flew on to try to land on the Perseus that he ran out of fuel. He was in the water nearly a day before he was picked up!"

That was more or less what Albert Stanton had heard; it was always good to get corroborative information, especially when the man concerned was a friend.

"No news about Abe, I suppose."

Leonora shook her head.

"Poor Kate..." The man made an effort to put on a brave face. "I'm sorry, I didn't mean to be a wet blanket."

Leonora laughed, patted his chest playfully.

"My best friend just got her knight in shining armour back. That's good enough to be going on with for the moment!"

It had come on to rain which meant everybody had come inside, where it was stuffy and noisy in the ground floor rooms Maud's father had rented for the occasion.

"Oh, I wish we could just be alone," Maud complained.

This was the way the man felt about it too.

"We'll say good bye to your people and go back to Manhattan," Albert Stanton said with rare impetuosity, his courage rapidly diminishing.

"Yes!"

While Maud's parents had obviously planned to bask in the reflected glory of the new hero in the family a while longer, they had the good sense to know that the young people badly needed a little time together.

Leonora had already departed.

"I have a baby to feed and your mother and father's friends are incredibly boring," she had said on the way out, pausing to briefly drape herself around Albert and to hug Maud in a long sisterly embrace.

Most of the press corps had taken Leonora's exit as their cue to race back to their offices on the other side of the East River, to file their copy and get their photographs developed.

The lovers had got a taxi to the nearest rail station, Bridgehampton, waited over an hour for the stopping service to go on down the line to the last halt, Amagansett, and then return west along the single-track. The line only became two-way at Good Ground, which serviced the Hampton Bays area. There was a lot of talk about the line being closed to the east, the days when two daily trains carried fresh fish to the markets of Brooklyn and Manhattan were long gone since Colonial Highway 107 had been extended all the way to Montauk. Notwithstanding, there was always such a hullabaloo from the wealthy locals on this part of Long Island that the New York Railway Company had, to date, carried on running the whole line at a small, albeit worsening loss for most of the last twenty years. Elsewhere along the East Coast commuter services had been electrified in the fifties and sixties; all except the 'marginal lines' which one day would inevitably, be abandoned.

Maud cuddled up against Albert Stanton, he contentedly put his arm around her shoulders as the train, just a two-carriage service pulled by an old diesel locomotive clattered and jolted back towards the city they both called home.

Knowing that it would be chaos at the landing pier, Albert had taken the precaution of asking Imperial Airways to deliver his luggage – only a couple of small cases, mostly filled with clothes and shoes purchased in London, a dozen second hand books discovered trawling the capital's second hand and antiquarian bookshops, and a few miscellaneous toiletries - to his East Side apartment.

The carriage had filled by the time the train rattled over the King Edward VI Manhattan Bridge and squealed to a stop at the Broad Street elevated terminus.

"Where shall we go?" Maud asked shyly. A little of the euphoria of earlier in the day had evaporated, otherwise, her yearnings were unabated.

"I think," Albert Stanton grinned, "the returning hero deserves dinner with his lady fair?"

"Yes," Maud nodded enthusiastically. "And then I'd like very much to be seduced, please!"

Chapter 8

Wednesday 26th April
Edificio del Ministerio de Defensa, Churubusco, Mexico City

General of the Army of New Spain Felipe de Padua María Severino López de Santa Anna y Pérez de Lebrón rose to his feet to shake the hand of the German Ambassador, Walther von Hagen, and his Military Adjutant, the monocled Colonel Dieter von Seydlitz-Hesse.

Both of Santa Anna's visitors towered over him, the Ambassador a broad, hearty Bavarian from an old Wilhelmstrasse dynasty, Seydlitz-Hesse a sixty-three-year-old, angular, hawk-browed Prussian career soldier and one-time mentor of the Kaiser presumptive, Kronprinz Wilhelm.

The Mexican Defence Minister and Chief of Staff of the Army was a man of approximately average height, physically unprepossessing, almost anonymous until one met his gaze and then the quiet, dazzling clarity in his grey brown eyes seized an interlocutor's whole attention. And when he spoke it was always with soft, reasonable authority which left nobody in the room in any doubt that he, and he alone knew the way forward.

He waved his guests towards comfortable chairs in his sparsely furnished, very nearly bare-walled office overlooking the sprawl of the modern city. Like other newly-built military installations in the capital the Defence Ministry Building was brutally functional, totally lacking in ornamentation; gone were the days when precious treasure was wasted on pandering to the egos of the men in uniform who had ruled Mexico, as if it was their personal fiefdom, for much of the last century.

Santa Anna studied the two Germans.

The great men of the Wilhelmstrasse in faraway Berlin had not imagined, for a minute, that Mexico would actually – true to its sacred national promise to its allies – actually invade the New England South West. This war, the men around Count Lothar von Bismarck, the Foreign Minister of the Reich had reasoned, would be like all those of the last fifty years; border skirmishes, small land grabs to deter the English from interfering with the mines of Alta California and Sonora, designed to make it impossible for the British Empire to exploit the oil reserves known to lie beneath Texas and the continental shelf in the northern reaches of the Gulf of Spain.

The 'long peace', and the coming of democracy to the Mexican Republic a dozen years ago, had redirected the wealth of the country's mines into the public purse. Previously, the war lords and their minions had siphoned off the fruits of the land; now there were modern hospitals in all the big cities, public servants got paid regularly, the sick no longer starved on the streets, new roads and railways were under construction and industry, previously hamstrung by corruption and the country's medieval, chronically under-invested infrastructure, had leapt ahead. The economy had grown at over ten percent for each of the last eight years, and fuelled by the runaway growth of the mining sector, foreign currency had poured into the country.

"I think you know why we are here today, Minister," Walther von Hagen suggested.

Santa Anna nodded.

The German Empire had been perfectly happy to collude in the Triple Alliance's re-armament programs, and by implication, connive in its preparations for war. What the wise men of the Wilhelmstrasse had not banked on, was the war breaking out this year, nor next year and consequently, no steps had been taken to stockpile essential raw materials sourced from the region by the Reich. And now it was too late to do anything about it.

Problematically, while the islands of the greater Antilles – Cuba, Hispaniola and Santo Domingo – only exported cotton, tobacco, sugar, exotic fruits, spices, hard woods and trinkets to the Fatherland, Mexico had, in recent years become a key supplier of key strategic minerals and this trade had, thanks to the British blockage of the Caribbean and the Gulf of Spain, and anticipation sooner or later, of the long Pacific west coast of Mexico, cased overnight.

"It is my government's view that things," Von Hagen hesitated, "need to be placed back on a more even playing field." He was one of those profoundly undiplomatic diplomats the Wilhelmstrasse often despatched to friendly, and client states. Always something of a bull in a china shop, many of Santa Anna's colleagues in the Cabinet of Il Presidente Hernando de Soto, regarded the German Ambassador as an uncultured oaf, frequently joking among themselves at the expense of the man's often pigeon-Spanish. "There is a feeling in Berlin that things have rather got out of hand..."

Santa Anna smiled a saturnine smile.

"To the contrary, *things* are going very much to plan, Herr Ambassador."

"Dammit, Felipe," the German protested, "we're bloody lucky Gravina's adventures haven't landed us all in a general war with the British!"

Santa Anna raised an eyebrow.

The President of the Republic, family members and a small number of old friends might casually employ his Christian name but he had always resented it when a man used it without his leave.

He carried on smiling, as if in sympathy.

Simply stated, because the Germans had not expected war *this year*; neither had the English.

The British Lion had been caught half-asleep and as yet, he had not fully awakened. Axiomatically, had the Wilhelmstrasse known that war was imminent it would have instructed all its citizens to return home, including the technicians who kept the Californian gold mines open and elsewhere, who had overseen a doubling in the production of silver in the last five years. Such an exodus would have shouted 'war' to the whole world; as it was there were still at least a hundred thousand German nationals 'trapped' in the 'war zone', and the great traffic in copper (of which, globally, Mexico was the third largest producer), and in sodium-sulphide, fluorite, celestite, and calcium inosilicate (of which it annually supplied upwards of one-third of all European demand) had come to a grinding halt. At the same time, the flow of oil from Curacao and the refineries at Aruba, and from the newly opened fields in the Venezuelan jungle territories had dried up.

While it was unfortunate that the German Empire was going to be the first to feel the pinch – the British could easily substitute supplies from elsewhere in their dominions – that had always been inevitable and there was very little, if anything, that Santa Anna could do to soften the blow.

Or, that he would have done to soften the blow, had it been within his power and he was a little irritated that the Germans, who were, after all the unwitting architects of the situation they now found themselves in, had not worked that out for themselves by now!

Dieter von Seydlitz-Hesse grunted like a boar with a huntsman's dog clinging onto his hind leg, and scowled so hard Santa Anna was a little afraid his monocle was going to shatter. The German was an old soldier invalided out of the Army in his forties by a near fatal brush with fever in Africa.

"While there are bulk materials which cannot for the moment, be shipped to the Reich," he sniffed, looking down his nose in the way that only Prussian aristocrats and British Guard's officers could, "minerals such as graphite and strontium might be smuggled past the blockade with relative ease."

The German Ambassador leaned forward in his chair.

"It has also been suggested to my principals in Berlin that ways might be found to enable gold and silver to find their ways onto the international exchanges?"

Since the Battle of the Windward Passage the price of gold and silver had begun to steadily inflate, and in the last week, race ahead. Needless to say, the German Empire had belatedly woken up to the fact that the British, having grimly clung to the so-called 'Gold Standard' ever since the Great War of the last century, now sat on a mountain of the stuff, and the Kaiserliche Schatzkammer – the Imperial Treasury – in Berlin, did not. Apparently, the German Reichsmark had already lost over twenty-five percent of its convertible value against the pound sterling. German pensioners living in England or anywhere else in the British Empire were facing penury, and there were suggestions that several of the larger German banks might shortly be confronted by unprecedented margin calls.

Santa Anna doubted either of his guests understood, or cared about such ephemeral details; leastways, not until their own bankers went to the wall and they were faced by the prospect of having to sell family heirlooms to make ends meet.

"That will not be possible," he explained urbanely. "Much consideration has been given to how to finance the war to liberate the lost lands of old Mexico."

Santa Anna was tempted to suck his teeth, and gloat a while. He resisted the temptation; these men were his guests and it was a poor host who mocked his visitors.

Von Hagen and con Seydlitz-Hesse were prisoners of their prejudices and lack of imagination. Neither they, nor their masters in Berlin had ever really troubled to understand Mexico, its people or its national aspirations, other than in where they exactly corresponded with some bizarre Germanic world view in which Mexicans, Cubans, Hispanics and Latins in general, were no more than intellectually and culturally challenged tools to be wielded for the greater good of the Grosse Reich.

At first Berlin had handed out penny parcels of military and economic assistance; then, when the Germans realised that the Mexicans were anything but paupers, they had greedily exchanged aircraft, ships, guns, and exchanged technology in return for gold and silver and discounted copper ore. It was as if the Germans had hardly noticed that all the while new factories were sprouting along the Caribbean coast, and dotting the Great Valley of Mexico; or that Mexican arms, airframe and engine plants were turning out improved versions of the originally supplied land cruisers, vehicles, infantry weaponry, aircraft and power plants, and that shipyards on the east coast were building new, sleek frigates and destroyers that outgunned the latest hulls on the slipways at Hamburg and Kiel.

Meanwhile, the first generation of Mexican students who had passed out of the German Technische Schulen – Technical Schools – in the late 1960s, were now driving the second Mexican industrial revolution. Twenty years ago, the country had still been an agricultural backwater littered with the ruins of nineteenth century factories, abandoned irretrievably flooded mines, a land still mainly lit by fire. Nowadays, in many cities at least, visitors from Old Spain marvelled at the modernity of the architecture, the new hospitals, and the pylons of the electricity grid remorselessly marching out into even the remotest corners of Mexico.

But the Germans had seen none of this; or if they had, they had not recognised if for what it was, Mexico belatedly stepping into the twentieth century and determined to assert its rightful place in the pantheon of great nations.

One day, perhaps, the German Empire would open its eyes and, as fashionable New Englanders were known to remark: 'smell the coffee'. However, that was beyond the comprehension of Santa Anna's visitors.

"The matter of the gold," von Hagen groaned, "is most pressing, Felipe."

"Yes, I agree," Santa Anna concurred politely. "However, possibly it is a thing better discussed with my colleagues at the Finance Ministry, Walther."

"Dammit," Dieter von Seydlitz-Hesse complained, as if he did not see what the problem was, "you're the only man who can make things happen in this country!"

Santa Anna did not rise to this.

He folded his hands in his lap.

Undeniably, his word carried disproportionate weight in the high councils of President Hernando de Soto's Grand Council of State – the equivalent of the British Cabinet – yet to say that other voices were unimportant was a misnomer. True, he could, occasionally dominate discussions in Cabinet; but at the end of the day if he was out-voted, then, that was that. He always went along with the expressed view of the majority. That was what the word 'democracy' meant!

"Can we not come to a private arrangement with you, Felipe?" The German Ambassador proposed. "I know you have to pay lip-service to all that nonsense the civilians spout…"

Santa Anna slowly got to his feet.

The Germans, looking askance one to the other, did likewise.

"Gentlemen," the Minister of Defence declared, "thank you for your time. Our meeting is at an end."

Chapter 9

Thursday 27th April
Imperial Concession, Guaynabo, San Juan, Santo Domingo

Baron Hans Dieter von Schaffhausen was well aware that he would never have ended up in a place he personally considered to be the rectum of the German Empire, if he had not slept with the wrong woman. Namely, the witty, marvellously sensible, unutterably lovely woman whom, thirty-two years ago, Captain Lothar von Bismarck – then, like von Schaffhausen, just completing his military service – but now and for many years, Foreign Minister of the Reich, had been scheduled to marry in the High Cathedral of Saint Peter in Trier.

Thereafter, Lothar had become one of the great men of world affairs, and von Schaffhausen had eventually, after a middlingly unremarkable career in the Diplomatic Service, ended up as German Minister for the Guaynabo Free Trade Zone, on the easternmost large island of the archipelago of the Greater Antilles.

That said, the German Minister at Guaynabo had no doubt whatsoever that he was the luckier of the two men. Poor old Lothar had spent the last quarter-of-a-century married to a woman he plainly did not care for – and the feeling had been mutual if the gossip was to be believed – wrestling with the impossible problems of the old Kaiser's infantile grasp of the realities of foreign relations. Whereas, he, the man who had cuckolded the 'golden boy' of their generation, had perambulated around the globe with the love of his life and their ever-expanding clutch of offspring.

Even the posting to Santo Domingo had been, until lately, mostly a blissful idyll.

Von Schaffhausen's fiefdom amounted to Guaynabo, itself a part of the Pueblo Viejo barrio – a term used hereabouts on Santo Domingo to signify a township, a farming community or simply a patch of untamed jungle, of which there was still a lot on Santo Domingo – and the barrios directly to its south, Frailes, Santa Rosa, Guaraguao, Mamey, Rio, Camarones, and Hato Nuevo and Sonadora, straggling eight or nine kilometres into the interior. In all, von Schaffhausen's little kingdom encompassed some sixty to seventy square kilometres of real estate in which some thirty thousand people, the overwhelming majority Dominicans, lived and worked.

The climate was hot, humid and the capital city of Santo Domingo, San Juan, which abutted on the eastern boundaries of the Concession, and watched over it from the opposite side of Bahia de San Juan, was a dirty, disease-ridden and home to the inevitable collection of religious nut cases one tended to encounter in these parts. The Spanish had never made anything out of Santo Domingo, originally 'Puerto Rico', the *rich port* of the first waves of European interlopers. Subsequently, the Mother Church had achieved nothing but to inculcate an extreme, violent strain of messianic evangelistic Catholicism in the general population.

The revolutionary liberators of the island, and their descendants, had been too busy squabbling amongst themselves for the last hundred years, to do anything about the periodic famines – how bizarre was that on a tropical island that ought to have been a paradise on earth? – or the obscenely high rates of child mortality among their people, let alone done anything to build up their *Holy Republic's* economy. Of course, the great men of 'the revolution' had always managed to find money for their fine haciendas in the hills, guns for their army and police forces, and even to maintain a rag-tag navy.

Had he been a man so disposed, Hans von Schaffhausen might have long ago despaired and retreated, like so many men in the foreign service of the Empire, into an anaesthetised alcoholic or drug-induced stupor as he saw out the final years of his career. However, he had never dwelt overlong on his misfortunes; whatever people in Berlin thought, he had had a long and fulfilling career and even here, in Guaynabo these last few years, and mostly, he had had a lot of fun.

Angela loved the heat, the year-round blaze of colour of the vegetation and the company of their three youngest children – their eldest, Hans junior, commanded a destroyer in the Baltic Fleet, and Gretchen, had married an English archaeologist, and was in Oxford completing her post-doctoral studies in Latin American history – Wilhelm, Karl and Amelia, all now in their teens, all talked of one day using their Foreign Ministry bursaries to go to university in New England and return, if it was possible, to live and work in the Americas.

When the call from his wife was put through to his second-floor office overlooking San Juan Bay, von Schaffhausen had picked up the handset, and trailing the connecting wire, wandered out onto the balcony to enjoy the breeze that sometimes fluttered off the water in the mornings.

The battered, fire-scorched hulk of the SMS Weser, one of the merchant motor vessels secretly taken in hand by the Kaiserliche Marine under the 1971 Naval Estimates, to be converted for commerce raiding in the event of war, was alongside the so-called 'Liner' quay about a hundred metres away. The ship was in a sorry state, still leaking diesel from ruptured plates, listing two or three degrees to starboard as her combined Kaiserliche Marine and Royal Navy crew – leastways, the survivors – did what they could to keep the ship afloat and to make emergency repairs.

Further out, anchored in the middle of the bay, the antique Dominican armoured cruiser San Miguel trained her two 190-millimetre, and her casemate-mounted 127-millimetre guns on the still, near-sinking commerce raider.

"How are things this morning, meine Liebe?" The German Minister's wife inquired with her customary brightness.

Von Schaffhausen guffawed.

"Tolerably dire, mein Liebling."

"Oh, dear, as bad as that?"

Actually, as was invariably the way of things, now that he heard his wife's voice on the other end of the typically crackly Dominican line – one of his pet projects had been to bury the current, tangled over-ground telephone network within the Concession underground but there had never been the necessary funds to start the project – things did not seem anywhere near as 'dire' as they had a few minutes ago.

Angela had always had that effect on him. Perhaps, for the good of the Fatherland he ought to have let her go, unsullied to the altar at Trier with Lothar?

No, she would have been wasted on his old friend...

Everywhere they had gone on their travels Angela had been a marvel. Here, her personal project had been to open up and develop the formerly tented 'fever ward' extensions to the small German Hospital at La Puntilla, organising the other ex-patriot women, trawling the small, German community for anybody with nursing experience. Inevitably, the Dominicans had refused to help; and even if von Schaffhausen's requests for medical and humanitarian assistance from German ships in the region, or over-optimistically, from home had ever been answered before, it was unlikely that the blockade of the Concession by sea and land would be lifted to allow such aid in now.

Less than six weeks ago, two great cruise ships of the Hamburg-Atlantic Line had been moored in San Juan Bay, their wealthy passengers filling the grubby, down-at-heel hotels of the Dominican capital, their Imperial Reichsmarks and British Pounds Sterling fuelling the sclerotic wheels of the island's failing economy. When there was a liner in port the Concession came alive, like that mythical Scottish village, a 'Brigadoon' in the tropics. The harbour front bars and restaurants came alive, people from the surrounding villages poured in to sell their wares, not to mention their daughters and sometimes, their sons, to the oh-so-respectable burgers from the German heartland who came to San Juan to party, and to taste forbidden fruits in the knowledge that practically everything was for sale. It was like a never-ending carnival and von Schaffhausen's job had been to make sure the party never stopped. Mostly, he and Angela picked up the pieces, overseeing the administration and the welfare of the German families living in the Concession.

They had known that Guaynabo was just one of several colonial 'pressure release valves' of the Empire; a place where Germans could come and behave in ways they would never get away with back home. There were other enclaves and concessions which served similar roles as tax-free free ports where none of the normal social mores applied. There were limits, of course. Hardly anybody ever got away with actual murder, for example; nevertheless, it was hardly any great recommendation for Germanic culture, or the virtues supposedly held so dear back in the Fatherland. People said the British had their own 'Guaynabos, Mediterranean fleshpots and Asiatic opium dens' but for the British those places were incidental, lost in the vastness of the Empire and economically insignificant; for Germany, such blots on the face of the globe were the Wilhelmstrasse's only viable, self-supporting overseas domains. Even oil-rich Aruba and Curacao – ceded to Berlin in an annexe to the Submarine Treaty - on the southern shores of the

Caribbean, which ought to have become the oil well of the German Empire was still little more than a seedy tropical Babylon, like Guaynabo.

Von Schaffhausen groaned just to think about that.

Instead of letting the Kaiserliche Marine, or one of the great Ruhr industrial combines take over and develop the oil fields and build new refineries, fearful of allowing the Navy, or any of those lower-middle class upstarts in Essen *usurp* the prerogatives of the Wilhemstrasse, Lothar von Bismarck, that peerless arbiter of geopolitical affairs who knew absolutely nothing about industry or commerce, had entrusted Aruba to a gang of merchant adventurers sponsored by his aristocratic friends at Court!

But then that was how the German Reich worked.

The British Empire had achieved practically everything it had achieved by allowing any Tom, Dick or Harry to 'have a go'; a thing no Teutonic mind could ever permit. Now, those geniuses at the Wilhelmstrasse had blundered into a regional war so stupid and ill-conceived that it boggled the German Minister's credulity.

The scene visible from his office balcony was just the thin end of a rapidly worsening wedge. The Liner wharves were unoccupied – apart from the Weser – the bars in the town were mostly shut, the two brand-new modern hotels built to welcome the Hamburg-America trade and to put up visiting businessmen and diplomats were deserted, and even within the boundaries of the Concession, Dominican men, women and children were begging on the streets.

Fortunately, his beloved wife was used to him drifting off into his thoughts.

"Hans, have you been listening to a single word I've just said?"

"Forgive me, mein Liebling," the German Minister apologised, realising he had been brooding.

"Never mind," his wife said with her customary happy forbearance.

"I am a bad husband," von Schaffhausen chuckled. "I do not deserve you…"

"No, you don't," Angela agreed, happily. She sighed, sobering by degrees. "I just got back from the hospital," she explained. "We didn't lose anybody last night. That's two nights in a row. I think the crisis may have passed."

"That is good…"

Kapitan zur See Albrecht Weitzman, of the Weser, had succumbed to his wounds – for the want of antibiotics, most likely – on Tuesday afternoon, the twelfth wounded man brought ashore to die. That brave officer had been cut down early in the action with the two Dominican torpedo-boat destroyers Inquisitors in the San Juan regime had sent out to illegally arrest his ship.

"I must get on with things," his wife declared. "Chin up, meine Liebe."

Von Schaffhausen remained on the balcony, surveying the aquamarine waters of the bay now smeared with the diesel still seeping from the Weser, for some minutes after his wife hung up. Presently, he was disturbed by a polite cough.

It was Paul Meissner, his Private Secretary. Twenty-three years-old and less than six months into his first overseas posting since joining the Foreign Service of the Wilhemstrasse, the young man was a graduate of the University of Göttingen. Unlike many of the young tyros Berlin had sent von Schaffhausen down the years, Paul was a fluent Spanish-speaker, and more than competent in translating Portuguese. Like all University entrants to the Foreign Service it went without saying that he spoke English 'like an Empire Broadcasting Corporation newsreader'.

"Leutnant zur see Kemper and Korvettenkapitän Cowdrey-Singh are here to see you, Minister," the young man reported dutifully.

Von Schaffhausen blinked out of his thoughts. Suddenly, he was all business, jovially urgent. He switched to English.

"Wheel them in! Wheel them in! Try and get one of the girls in the office to bring us some decent coffee, please!"

Paul Meissner nodded his head in acknowledgement.

The young man was still getting used to the bear-like, seemingly irrepressible energy of the man who had been exiled to Santo Domingo eight years ago, and it seemed, forgotten thereafter by the Wilhelmstrasse. Normally, overseas postings were for three, and very occasionally, five years. The length of von Schaffhausen's 'sentence' at Guaynabo was unprecedented; back in Berlin it was whispered that it was all to do with some ancient feud between Count Bismarck and the House of Schaffhausen but it was all so long ago, that nobody knew for sure.

Back at the Wilhelmstrasse, Paul had been warned that 'your Minister has gone native'. In one way, von Schaffhausen had – he actually liked Santo Domingo and most of its people, just not its leaders or priests – but in another way, he was every inch a German patriot, organised, and a stickler for propriety.

That had surprised Paul Meissner, given that his chief presided over a veritable den of iniquity. He had been even more surprised to discover that away from the relatively small, 'party area' of the Concession mainly situated around San Juan Bay, the Concession was run very much like a little piece of Germany transplanted to the tropics. It had its own small garrison of Kaiserliche Marines, a German police force, a small modern hospital staffed by mainly volunteer ex-patriot women, and a couple of shops well off the well-beaten tourist path selling beers and delicacies from home. Further, although the port and dockyards were run mainly by local workers and stevedores, it was invariably managed with very nearly Teutonic efficiency.

Of course, everything had gone to Hell, as the English might say, 'in a handcart' in the last fortnight.

Nobody had the faintest idea what had got into the Dominicans' heads thinking that they could arrest a German ship in international waters!

That was insane!

Clearly, somebody in the Palace of the People on the hill on the opposite side of San Juan Bay must have had some kind of psychotic episode...

Anyway, that was what the Minister's wife, a most formidable and outspoken lady had said when the news broke. Unexpectedly, right from his first day on Santo Domingo, Frau von Schaffhausen had extended an open invitation to her husband's new Private Secretary to dine with the family at the weekends, and indeed, for his first weeks on the island he had been a guest at the Minister's Official Residence, very much under that formidable lady's mother hen wing. Suitable accommodation for young men fresh from Germany was hard to come by in the Concession; and the Minister's wife always took a very personal interest in making sure newcomers were 'safely' inducted into the ways of the community, and 'properly' settled.

Acting Leutnant Klaus Kemper, the twenty-one-year-old Captain of the Seiner Majestät Schiff Weser, and Commander Peter Cowdrey-Singh, RN, formerly the Executive Officer of the sunken HMS Achilles, were unlikely comrades in arms. The Indian-born Englishman was tanned, bearded, his facial scars still pinkly angry and his bearing stiff, as if he was in constant, niggling discomfort from his unseen wounds. Kemper looked like a schoolboy; lanky, pale-skinned with a crop of ginger to blond hair with uncertain, greenish eyes that spoke, eloquently, to the nightmare through which he had been navigating in recent days.

Kemper saluted the Minister, Peter Cowdrey-Singh simply shook von Schaffhausen's hand. The German Minister waved his guests to take seats in the shaded, cool area of his office where occasionally, the breeze circulated.

The wind had shifted in the last few minutes.

Distantly, the sound of the Weser's labouring pumps carried into the room. It was a faraway roaring, thumping like persistent gunfire just over the horizon.

"Paul, stay please," von Schaffhausen decided. He had never got to the bottom of why, exactly, Peter Cowdrey-Singh had been on the bridge of the Weser, nor when, within minutes of the opening of the battle poor Albrecht Weitzman was cut down, the Anglo-Indian had assumed command, ordering his own men – effectively up until then passengers, quasi-prisoners – to fight beside their German comrades, and fought the ship.

Had he not stepped in the Weser would probably have been sunk, or possibly captured by her assailants. It was a moot point which of the two eventualities could have had a more malign impact on Dominican-German relations.

Inevitably, the Dominicans wanted the heads of both young Kemper and of Peter Cowdrey-Singh and the other thirty-three surviving members of the crew of HMS Achilles.

"How go the repairs to the Weser?" Von Schaffhausen inquired of Leutnant Kemper.

"Slowly, Herr Minister," the young man apologised, as if it was his fault those Dominican destroyers had raked his ship with cannon-fire and achieved half-a-dozen hits with larger shells, killing and wounding over a hundred men. Kemper glanced to his companion.

"If the pumps stop, she'll sink onto the bottom, sir," Peter Cowdrey-Singh grunted, resignedly. He leaned towards von Schaffhausen. "I must ask you again, sir," he apologised tersely, "what communications you have received from *your side* as to the arrangements for the repatriation of my men?"

Von Schaffhausen grimaced.

"I have received no reply to my request for matters to be clarified, Commander."

The other man thought about this. Slowly, he rose to his feet.

"In that case, I am serving no useful purpose here, sir. I will return to the Weser…"

"Commander, I was hoping we might have a more constructive conversation…"

"About what, sir?" The Royal Navy man retorted, quietly indignant. "About how the Kaiserliche Marine attacked Achilles and murdered hundreds of my men? Or about how it was left to Captain Weitzman, on his own initiative, to attempt to do the decent thing for the small number of survivors of that war crime? Or about how the *great* German Empire is powerless to do anything to clean up the mess your lords and masters at the Wilhemstrasse have made of things?"

The others had risen to their feet, also.

Von Schaffhausen groaned.

"Things are more complicated than you realise, Commander Cowdrey-Singh. There have been further battles at sea. The Indomitable has been sunk and one of your new aircraft carriers has been badly damaged. Your Navy has withdrawn from the Gulf of Spain and the Caribbean; on land the army of New Spain has routed Colonial forces in the mountains and deserts of the South West. Consequently, the governments of the Triple Alliance are in a triumphal, unreasoning mood." He hesitated. "Moreover, the sad death of the Kaiser has left," he hesitated again, "a vacuum of power in Berlin. Nobody is making any decisions until the new Emperor is elected. Until then, please, I ask you to be patient. I have given you my word of honour that I and the forces under my command will defend the German Concession, and *all* those under its protection."

"Herr Minister," Peter Cowdrey-Singh replied, brusquely. "You have sixty Marines and an ad hoc German civilian militia of seventy or eighty men and boys to defend a community of what, three hundred expatriates and civil servants. If those maniacs across the bay cut up rough there is absolutely nothing you, or anybody else can do about it!"

The trouble was, von Schaffhausen knew, was that the battered and rightly, embittered Royal Navy man, was right.

At the moment the only thing that was stopping the Inquisitors dragging his English 'guests' and the Weser's German 'criminals' to the Inquisition's torture cells, was a lingering – possibly fast-evaporating - fear of the wrath of the German Empire.

Sooner or later somebody in the Dominican regime was going to realise, that with the demise of the old Kaiser the German Empire was temporarily, in a state of near paralysis.

Chapter 10

Thursday 27th April
Big Springs, Unincorporated Crown Territory of West Texas

William Lincoln 'Bill' Fielding had not known what to do with himself when he got out of prison last year. By then he was pretty much alienated from his brothers, and his old Getrennte Entwicklung Congregation had cast him out – in retrospect, not such a big problem because he had lost his faith – and he was broke. Worse, there were still people out there looking to recoup the gambling debts he owed them.

Playing cards and betting on horse and dog-racing were other things he had got out of the habit of, or simply dumped, like his belief in a merciful God, while he was in prison in Albany. Finally getting to confront his Pa had been a cathartic, transforming moment. It was weird the way he still felt guilty sometimes about punching out his Pa that way; even though he knew he would likely have killed the old fool if his brothers had not grabbed him.

Initially, he had not thought it was a very good idea talking to Albert Stanton; but the others, Abe and Alex, had pretty much opened their hearts to him and he had turned out to be a reasonably straight arrow kind of guy. For a newspaper man, leastways.

'You're a qualified mechanical engineer, right?' Stanton had said to him afterwards. The Manhattan Globe man had picked him up at the hostel in Brooklyn Heights where he was dossing down most nights, taken him down to Brighton Beach for a beer and fish and chips.

Despite Bill's suspicion the two men had got on okay.

'Yeah,' he had conceded.

'With a lot of hours tuning and repairing high-performance speed boat engines?'

This too, was true, Bill could hardly deny it. It had been his work, for, among others the Long Island Speedboat Company at Gowanus Cove – on several of the boats which were driven at high speed into the sides of the battleships in the Upper Bay - which had originally got him into so much trouble after the Empire Day atrocities.

'Yeah,' he had agreed, again.

'Alex tells me the CAF are crying out for guys like you. Three square meals a day, a roof over your head, work clothes provided and, according to your big brother, the Service pays top rate for qualified men.'

Bill reckoned that Alex had put the newspaper man up to it.

At the time he could not afford to be prideful; truly, pride had gone before his fall from grace and now, somehow, he had to atone. If not to God, then to himself and his kith and kin, whether they still cared for him or not.

Citing his elder brother as a reference, he had breezed through the CAF's candidate technician selection process. Notwithstanding, he had still had to do the normal ninety-day induction 'square bashing', to endure the interminable kit inspections, the calisthenics and the route marches carrying a combat pack, personal weapons – a rifle, a pistol and a bayonet – and pass a final selection panel to get into the Colonial Air Force Reserve. Most new recruits then got hived off to a training establishment to prepare them for their chosen branch of the service, or in quieter times, discharged straight back into civilian life on a small annual retainer or one-third pay; however, Bill had been posted directly to the newly re-activated Patuxent River Naval Air Station in the Colony of Maryland, located, blissfully in the middle of nowhere, far, far away from his creditors.

At first the CAF had had him working on re-conditioning old engines; mainly antique junkyard power plants like the ones which powered all those Bristol Vs, VIs and VIIs used by weekend pilots and amateur enthusiasts but within a couple of weeks he was transferred onto a crew servicing Goshawk scouts and Sea Eagle torpedo bombers; completely different beasts.

He had not looked back since. A month ago, they had put a third stripe on his sleeve, promoted him Flight Sergeant (Technician) signifying that henceforth he was responsible for his own crew and on Squadron service, for the 'safe and appropriate maintenance' of his allocated aircraft.

Assigned to the 4th Colony of Maryland Squadron, flying Goshawk Mk III scouts, he had boarded a rickety transport for the long, bumpy flight down to West Texas in February. In retrospect, he ought to have known that the storm was about to burst. They all ought to have known. On the other hand, the 4th Maryland was very newly formed, in the process of receiving its Goshawks literally as they came off the production lines back East, as soon as they could be ferried to Big Springs.

If the isthmus upon which the Patuxent River Naval Air Station had seemed to be in the middle of nowhere; Big Springs actually was. It was so named because several 'big springs' came to the surface within several miles of each other in the middle of what was, and to most intents, remained, extremely sparsely populated former Comanche tribal lands. In the last decade local cattle barons had attempted to fence off huge tracts of grazing land for their cattle; one enterprising rancher had even tried to stake a claim to the de-activated – to all intents, abandoned - airfield some miles north west of the town!

Bill and his crew joked that ranchers like that were the first ones to complain when the CAF did not defend them against the Dagoes!

Life at Big Springs, a 'forward base', was very basic.

Everything was under tents and if you walked anywhere at night you had to put your boots on and carry a flashlight. There had been a lot of rattlers slithering about the last few days, little ones, probably just hours old; but it was the scorpions that you really had to look out for. By day the dusty prairie seemed lifeless, at night every kind of malignant biting, poisonous beastie imaginable seemed to come out to play. Coyotes howled through the darkness, insects, and huge, bird-like moths formed in clouds around any source of light. Worst of all, even for men like Bill born and bred on the upper East Coast it was cold, really cold at night; all the more of a shock to the system when as the summer approached during the day a man needed to be a 'real Englishman' to be dumb enough to voluntarily go out in the noon day sun.

During the last Border War there had been a few solid, four-square permanent buildings: a boxy control tower, half-a-dozen small hangars – no use whatsoever for the Squadron's big modern gull-wing Goshawks – and half-civilized barrack and messing accommodation, at Big Springs Air Station. No more. Either the locals had robbed out the wood or it had rotted away. There were still old-fashioned buried fuel tanks in the sand; they too had been abandoned after the last war, and never properly drained so when the ranchers had siphoned off the last of the good stuff, they had left the tanks open to the elements. All the piping was gone, presumably now plumbing the haciendas out in the wilderness.

It went without saying that the top brass back East were complacently under the impression that CAF Big Springs was still a potentially fully-functioning aerodrome in well-preserved state of 'mothballing', rather than just a patch of West Texan desert.

Nobody ought to have been surprised.

Alex had always told him the 'big men' in charge during the last war had been 'clowns'.

In any event, it had fallen to Bill and the rest of the Squadron's advance guard to create a functioning military airfield from scratch. Everything had had to be flown, or more prosaically, trucked in from hundreds of miles away. The 'heightened tensions' on the Border and elsewhere had all seemed a long, long way away when Bill had finally jumped down from the back of the five-ton Bedford CAF lorry, he had hitched a lift on for the final leg of the trip to his new duty station from San Antonio.

There had been no airfield waiting for them.

Bill probably had not been alone in wondering if he and his new mates had not been dropped off at the wrong place. Understandably, there had been a few grouches, from rookies and old-timers alike; but on the reverse side of the coin there was real satisfaction in turning a patch of desert into a working CAF aerodrome ahead of the arrival of the first Goshawks.

The Goshawks had been a long time coming, arriving in ones and twos from mid-March onwards. The spares, high octane fuel and lubrication oils, and the ammunition to get them into the air and to enable them to fight had not begun to arrive in serious quantities until the beginning of April. That was when everybody knew, for certain, that the people back East thought that there really was going to be a war. Before then the CO, a veteran of the last 'unpleasantness' who had been running his family's plantations near Atlanta prior to his untimely recall, had talked about 'deterrence' and 'showing the Spanish that we're serious'; suddenly, he was talking about making sure all his pilots got as much time in the air as possible before the 'curtain went up!'

Ahead of the delivery of the first aircraft nobody on the Squadron had been warned that 4th Maryland was to be equipped with 'modified' Mark III Goshawks, officially designated Mark III-Gs. Effectively, the standard scout design had been 'stripped down' and fitted with underwing hard points to enable the carrying of 'external munitions'; bombs or rockets. The most striking 'mod' was that the armour-plating behind the pilot's seat had been removed, the pilot's oxygen bottles reduced in size and capacity and re-positioned beneath his legs, and the rear cockpit bulkhead, essentially, the top element of the main wing spar had been moved rearwards by about fifteen inches to ensure that the aircraft's centre of gravity remained consistent with the reduced weight, and altered structural loading of the airframe.

The priority for the CAF was to be, henceforth, the support of the troops on the ground. The hard points under the gull wings of the Goshawk looked ugly and the pilots swore they cost them ten to fifteen miles an hour of straight-line airspeed at most heights; not that they were going to spend a lot of time above thirteen or fourteen thousand feet with only twenty minutes – rather than the original sixty-five minutes – oxygen supplies!

There was, however, a single upside to the clumsily implemented modifications to the Squadron's Goshawks. Bill Fielding had not been the first man to recognise that there was scope – assuming one could inveigle or persuade an amenable pilot to co-operate – for a man to 'joy-ride' in the space behind the pilot's seat; especially, in that honeymoon period before the old man got wise to the practice and banned it.

Personally, Bill had just got in under the wire the day before the new Squadron Standing Orders were posted. However, pilots tended to be a cussed, awkward lot and now and then one or other of the 'scout jockeys' cheerfully cocked a snook at the CO to take one of his ground crew men up for 'a spin'.

Bill's own pilot, Flying Officer Gregory Torrance, a Canuck with a more than usually casual attitude to authority even for a scout pilot – he would have got on well with Alex! – had surreptitiously taken a tart he had met in Big Springs up to 'loop the loop'. It seemed she had objected to being 'stuffed behind the seat' and ridden on his lap. That had not worked out so well, the poor woman had puked up her breakfast all over the inside of the cockpit. Typically, 'Greg', like most men from north of the New England border he was a real gentleman, privately apologising 'for the mess' to Bill and ensuring that a couple of crates of beer had turned up to thank the rest of the crew for cleaning up 'the mess', and neglecting – at Bill's behest - to record the incident, or the extra work it had occasioned, in the aircraft's maintenance log.

The war had come to Big Springs without warning.

The morning the shit had hit the fan, Greg Torrance and two other *unarmed* 'B' Flight Goshawks had been conducting a navigation exercise some miles to the north of the field, when about a dozen enemy aircraft, which looked suspiciously like German BMK-57F radial-engined scouts in the red and yellow livery of the Air Force of New Spain, had attacked the aerodrome.

There had been no warning that day three weeks ago.

Those aircraft had approached at better than three hundred miles-an-hour at zero feet, their propellers and slipstream kicking up rooster tails of desert dust, with their machine guns blazing; zoomed into steep

65 | Page

climbing turns and dived back down, guns hammering, releasing a blizzard of twenty-five-kilogram blast bombs. Inside less than two minutes the whole aerodrome was wrecked and all bar one Goshawk – miraculously untouched in its newly completed blast berm - wrecked. Four of the forty-one dead and thirty-eight men seriously wounded that day had been pilots, killed when a bomb went off in the slit trench adjacent to the Officers Mess tent, where they had dived as the first wave of Mexican attackers had roared overhead.

Nobody, other than a couple of officers who had blazed away with their service revolvers, or a warrant officer who had launched several flares into the path of strafing scouts – to no effect - had fired a shot in return.

The attack, executed with clinical precision and brutal determination, had lasted less than a minute.

Greg Torrance's three-Goshawk flight, short on fuel had been forced to try to land between the craters. One aircraft had put a wheel into a bomb hole, ground-looped and been written off.

Remarkably, by the next morning they had got the field back into use, repaired the dirt landing strip, dispersed and camouflaged the three remaining serviceable kites, and settled down to wait for reinforcements and replacement aircraft from the East which never came. Instead, Big Springs soon became a collection point for the lost sheep from the other, shattered squadrons nearer the front, and within days the airfield had turned into a scaled down version of a chaotic flying circus, with three-hundred-and-fifty-mile-an-hour plus Goshawks flying alongside Bristol biplanes capable of only a third of that speed, and a handful of Navy Sea Eagle bombers, putting up token combat air patrols, and mounting two or three plane ground attacks, usually at dusk because wherever the 4th Maryland's planes flew to the south and west they were always outnumbered five or ten, and sometimes twenty-to-one.

A week or so ago, they had learned from a shot down 'Mexican' pilot that what they had mistaken for BMK-57Fs were called F-2 Estrellas Fugaces - *Shooting Stars* - by the enemy, whom, it seemed, assembled the airframes in factories in the southern, Vera Cruz Province.

Apparently, 'most of the' engines still came from Germany...

The 'Shooting Stars' were not the only nasty surprise. The Mexican version of the Sea Eagle was a single-engined low-wing monoplane dive bomber, the B-3, that plummeted down upon its targets in a near vertical swoop with air-sirens mounted under its wings blaring an unearthly, terrifying banshee wail that only changed its note when the aircraft had dropped its bomb and had begun to pull out of its dive.

This latter machine looked like a monoplane version of an experimental Deutsche Luftstreitkräfte three-seater which was widely demonstrated at international shows in the mid-1960s, the SWF-44, one of a series of 'trial designs' developed to the pre-production stage by the Stettin Wasserflugzeug Funktioniert (Stettin Seaplane Works), which at the time hosted the Prussian Aerospace Development Design Bureau.

To the Mexicans, this aircraft was the *El Vengador.*

The Avenger...

Mercifully, these two aircraft, both seemingly in plentiful supply, were the only real surprises of the war in the air to date. Unfortunately, this was only a small mercy. Likewise, the fact that the abject defeat of the CAF in the air had been put into the shade by the humiliating rout of Colonial forces on the ground.

Before the war the pundits had focused on the superiority of Empire-made land cruisers to their Spanish counterparts, which they massively outgunned, and much had been made of the thickness of the angled armour protecting those leviathans.

Huge play of the railheads close to the front guaranteeing the flow of fuel, munitions, food and all the other things a modern army needed. Moreover, it had been claimed that each new settlement in the disputed Borderlands would be a strongpoint 'choking' off the enemy advance, while at sea, it had been taken for granted that the Royal Navy would blockade the Gulf of Spain; making impossible any 'flanking landings' behind the Colonial front lines.

All of which had turned out to be total horse manure!

It did not matter if 'our' land cruisers were better than 'theirs'; *they* had hundreds of the bloody things and *we* had a couple of dozen. *They* had a dozen infantry divisions – albeit advancing at the speed of a mule or a horse – and *we* had more or less, three understrength brigades, say the equivalent of about ten or eleven under-strength battalions of riflemen, watching over a thousand miles of desert and mountainous border.

Tellingly, in the air, nobody had planned for an attack by hundreds of modern aircraft flown by men who obviously knew exactly what they were doing!

And as for the Navy...

At sea, well...where the fuck had the Navy been when Mexican and Cuban Marines, and several brigades of blood-sucking Dominican Inquisitor-warriors had come ashore at Corpus Christie and Lavaca Bay and once they had over run the ineffectual militia garrisons, systematically slaughtered *all* the men and boys, and raped *all* the women and girls?

Bill Fielding flinched involuntarily as the next Mexican ranging shot whistled overhead and detonated somewhere in the vicinity of the old 1960s tanker farm.

Everything had gone to Hell in a handcart.

There was nothing he could do about that.

Right now, the bastards were still firing ranging shots from their positions in the burning town of Big Springs, targeting – thus far without success - the runway from which what was left of the CAF in the South West had been fighting, unavailingly, to stem the inexorable advance of the invaders.

About twenty aircraft had managed to get away in the last couple of days. They said San Antonio was not yet encircled, although that was probably just a matter of time. Beyond San Antonio only the desert and the prairie, was going to slow the enemy down...

Bill Fielding wiped the sweat and grime off his face with a filthy rag.

He slammed shut the cowling above his head.

He held up his right hand, making an 'O' with his thumb and forefinger.

Simultaneously, the man behind him on the battery cart flicked the switch and put a jolt of current into the alternator of the starter motor of Acting Flight Lieutenant Greg Torrance's Goshawk's 1,260 horsepower Gloucester-Royce radial engine. There was a bang, then another and suddenly the four-and-a-half-ton aircraft was vibrating like it was in a storm.

Bill stepped back, staggering away from the blurred circle of the scout's propeller. The man at the battery cart had not waited for orders and sprinted for the safety of the nearest slit trench.

Bill had sent the rest of his crew away in the last lorry, the other man was one of the farmer militiamen who had turned up at the field, initially demanding to be flown out, and then just to be fed. He had given Bill a black look when he ordered him to sit at the cart but hit the switch when the time came.

Weekend soldiers cost the exchequer a pittance; the trouble was, they could not fight their way out of a paper bag in a war like this. Bill would have felt sorry for the man had he not already seen too many better men die.

The pilot was hanging half out of the cockpit.

He was yelling at Bill.

"Kick the fucking chocks away and get up here pronto, man!"

Bill Fielding blinked, uncomprehendingly.

"Quick, get in behind me before those bastards find the range with those big guns in the town!"

The scout was rumbling, rolling in a cloud of dust towards the runway as the first full salvo of four 75-millimetre rounds screamed overhead and fell among the blast berms where the planes that could not be saved were already burning. Everything which could not be moved had been heaped onto those flames in the last few hours, and a pall of acrid black smoke hung over the ruined airfield.

Bill Fielding swung his leg over the cockpit combing as the Goshawk bumped savagely over the edge of an old half-repaired bomb crater, which even though he was half-in, half-out almost launched him into thin air. A moment later he grabbed the back of the pilot's seat and poured his lean, hungry frame into the narrow space.

"Hang on, old man!" Greg Torrance bawled before his voice was drowned out. He kicked the brakes, lined up the scout with the end of the runway and pushed the throttle up to and through the gate.

The pilot made no attempt to pull back the cockpit hood.

Bill was deafened, aware only of the thunder of the engine and the hurricane backwash of the Goshawk's giant three-bladed propeller.

The scout was picking up speed, bounding down the mile-long dirt strip.

Geysers of smoke and dirt erupted in the near distance. Bill shut his eyes. The aircraft shuddered; seemed to stop for a split second.

Then flipped jarringly to the left.

This is it!

Bill had contemplated getting back on better terms with his maker in recent days; but he had been too busy, not yet got around to it. Possibly, he suspected, he ought to have made time to atone. Now, well, it was too late...

He waited for one of the wing tips to dig into the West Texan dirt, and for the Goshawk to cartwheel to its fiery death.

But when he opened his eyes the aircraft was thrumming healthily, climbing hard, he could feel as much in his bones and around him the sky was clean, cold, and for the first time in weeks he started to cough the dust of the desert out of his throat.

Life goes on...

Perhaps, there was a God after?

A merciful God who actually, contrary to the evidence of his previous life, gave a damn about whether Bill Fielding lived or died...

Chapter 11

Friday 28th April
Ducal Palace of Vila Viçosa, the Alenteo, Portugal

Now that the time of the audience was nearing, Melody Danson was starting to get nervous, positively anxious. Contrarily, mainly about things she hardly ever usually got het up about; but then she was about to be introduced to the Queen in Exile of the Empire of Spain, Sophie Catherine Magdalena, Princess of Aragon and Navarre.

'It will be sufficient to address the Queen as *Your Majesty*, and thereafter, as in the English tradition, *Ma'am*," Alonso had explained. 'Her Majesty speaks English excellently but she will probably take it as a compliment and an earnest of good faith if you initially converse in Castilian.'

Alonso Pérez de Guzmán, 18th Duke of Medina Sidonia, formerly the castellan of the Comarca de Las Vegas, not to mention several other large estates in Castile and Leon, and Melody had recently learned, still the owner of numerous other estates in Portugal, including commercial properties in Lisbon and land in the Algarve, was a mine of useful information.

If only he stopped trying to fill her head with facts and insights when they were in bed together – and the balance of her mind was somewhat skewed - she would probably learn a great deal from him!

Granted, they had to do something to fill in the gaps between the long, delicious spasms of ecstatic coupling and it seemed such a pity to waste any of the time they were naked together just sleeping; even so, she tended to be distracted in the darkness, flesh against flesh and she usually had to check everything he had told her later when she was in that particular state of...grace.

"Oh, God!" She muttered, looking at herself in her compact, a pretty silvery thing Alonso had bought her in the capital - for the umpteenth time.

She had had her wonderful mane of angry red hair shorn right down to her scalp escaping the Inquisition in the Mountains of Madrid. Time, the intervention of four weeks or so, had repaired her near 'bald bits' and a couple of sessions with a stylist who knew exactly what she was doing had made her look half-way human again but even so, she still missed her lost hair...

I look positively boyish, androgynous...

Whereas, Henrietta, even with her hair cut like a boy's, still looked achingly...womanly.

Sometimes, life was just not fair!

With her flaming hair and pale complexion Melody had tended to avoid the sun as a child. Even though it was still spring, spending so many days outside, trekking across the countryside had left her with an unfamiliar tan, and unlike Henrietta, she had burned a little so now she was constantly dabbing her face and forearms with moisturising cream.

I must look like something the cat dragged backwards through a hedge!

She had no idea what Alonso saw in her.

"I look a mess!"

Alonso had taken her shopping, again, in Lisbon yesterday; that must have been an excruciating experience for the poor man. She kept asking him what this, or that dress looked like and he always just looked at her as if she was a movie star.

"The lipstick is too much..."

It was hard to believe it was a fortnight since she and Henrietta, and Albert Stanton carrying little Pedro, had splashed across that treacherous ford on the River Douro, pursued by bullets kicking up the water, and finally set foot on the soil of Portugal. The two weeks they had been on the run, hunted, harried and forever in mortal fear for their lives already seemed like some kind of strange, formative dream.

It had been a wrench saying goodbye to Albert Stanton a week ago. They had understood he wanted to get back to New England for all sorts of pressing reasons, not least to get re-acquainted with certain Miss Maud Daventry-Jones and the crying need to sell his story, *their* story to the highest bidder. That was business he would have concluded with one of the big London publishing houses, before he boarded a plane to return to New England.

Henrietta had spoken to her parents several times over the transatlantic telephone link, and Melody, for the first time in twenty years had felt the need to hear her own mother's and father's voice. They had been oddly...tearful; it was as if it was the first time, she had really registered how much they still cared about her. She had thought they were distant, somewhat indifferent to her life and career and now, belatedly, she had discovered that she had been wrong, all along.

It was a funny old world...

She and Henrietta had talked about going home, and Pedro. Neither of them could make up their minds if the fact that he was Alonso's – love-child, bastard – son, these things still mattered in the Iberian Peninsula and certainly would in some quarters in New England, changed anything. It certainly changed nothing about the way they both felt about him – Pedro, that was, because Melody was still struggling to get to the bottom of Henrietta's feelings vis-à-vis Alonso. The only thing she knew for a certainty, was that her friend-lover-partner's emotions about the Duke of Medina-Sidonia were, well, complicated and foremost in their decision to remain, pretty much indefinitely, in Portugal was to give the boy a chance to get used to his new surroundings, and to them. Pedro already treated them like his mothers, Henrietta more so, unsurprisingly, since Melody was never going to be any kind of maternal exemplar. The boy still slept with them, or Henrietta when Melody was 'being wicked' with Alonso, which was whenever she got the opportunity.

I have been completely wanton with Alonso...

I ought to be ashamed of myself...

But I am not.

I wonder what that means?

Melody decided not to re-do her lipstick.

The mood she was in she was likely to paint her whole face!

"Oh, God," she groaned anew.

She fixed her lover in her almond-eyed gaze.

"This isn't real, Alonso. No matter how I, you, either of us would like to go on like this forever, we can't. It just won't work."

The man smiled a rueful smile and leaned over to kiss her forehead and rest, for a moment, his right hand on her nether regions.

God in Heaven, I love it when he does that!

"Oh, fuck... What if I inadvertently swear or blaspheme in front of the Queen?"

"You won't."

"But I might!"

It was too ridiculous: this whole 'audience thing' was freaking her out in the way that being on the run for her life from the Inquisition and being shot at, had not!

Perhaps, she rationalised, it was just getting out of the car after the ninety-mile drive from Lisbon to be confronted by the magnificence of the Ducal Palace of Vila Viçosa?

"Why is the Queen of Spain living so close to the border, Alonso?" The question popped up in her head, like interrogatives often used to in her previous life as a detective.

"Two reasons," the man shrugged. "To be close to the children she has lost, and," a sad pursing of the lips, "to send a message to her enemies in Madrid that she has no fear of them."

Melody knew very little of the real story of Queen Sophie's escape from the mob besieging Aranjuez Palace outside Madrid, as it happened, on the same night that she and Henrietta had been spirited out of Chinchón, minutes ahead of the Inquisition.

Alonso had confided to her that Don Rafael, the faithful family arms man who had saved the women's lives that night, had been killed in the course of a second, failed attempt to rescue other members of the Queen's court from Toledo, where they had sought sanctuary and been, in the way of things in a civil war, betrayed by countrymen they had mistaken for friends.

Melody had known Alonso must have wept many, many tears for his father's old retainer, and down the years, his own good and true friend and mentor. It was but one more cruel cut to bear. One way and another they had all passed through a dreadful vale of tears in recent weeks...

Melody had expected a regiment of footmen in full ceremonial livery, terrifyingly elegant, and a gaggle of intimidating ladies in waiting.

Instead, a small middle-aged woman with bird-like eyes and pecking mannerisms as she spoke, materialised before the couple and addressed Alonso as if Melody was not there.

"You may present your lady to Her Majesty, Don Alonso." The trio walked several steps, their feet ringing dully on the marble floor. "You will be received in the Orangery."

Much to Melody's surprise the woman she had come to see rose to her feet and smoothed down her stylish, grey calf-length dress as her visitors entered her presence in what seemed like a very plush greenhouse attached to the side of the palace.

Queen Sophie was about Melody's own height, and age. Her hair was raven black to her shoulders, she was slim, poised and her blue-grey eyes seemed oddly, amused.

She was not alone.

Both the royal princesses were present.

The nine-year-old Infanta Katherine, and her younger sister, seven-year-old Infanta Margarete gazed curiously at the newcomers with their wide, Hapsburg-Bourbon eyes. Both princesses were dressed as any proud, upper-class middle class mother in New England might dress their daughters, in a style Melody would have called, if pressed, expensively but not in a fussy way which was liable to stop an adventurous young girl climbing a tree or wanting to engage in the normal rough and tumble.

Melody felt a twinge of pain to think that both the royal princes, Alphonse and Charles, aged respectively sixteen and twelve, were with their father, presumably locked away in the Escorial Palace thirty miles from Madrid, where, it was said, the streets were still littered with decomposing bodies.

Just to send a message to any surviving rebels.

Alonso had said it would be alright to bow; Melody was terrified that if she attempted to curtsy, she might, in her agony of nervousness, fall flat on her face.

'Prostration is not necessary in this enlightened age,' he had reassured her, smiling wryly.

So, she bowed. And was astonished when the Queen of Spain held out her hand to be, very timidly, shaken by her visitor.

Melody tried hard not to grin like a gargoyle.

"Perhaps," the Queen suggested to Alonso, in English. "If you might give me a few minutes alone with Miss Danson, Your Grace?"

"Of course, Your Majesty," Melody's escort assented, with a naturalness which suggested to her that this request had been anticipated in advance.

Melody's confusion, now peaking, turned her introduction to the two princesses into a blur.

In a moment the youngsters were dismissed.

"Remember not to stray from the gardens!" Their mother called after them in Castilian.

Melody was starting to calm down, and to take in her surroundings. There was a small circular, probably wrought iron, table nearby, with several wicker chairs. A bottle of Champagne and half-a-dozen glasses were neatly arranged.

"My daughters had hoped they would be allowed to sip wine every day now that we are no longer in Spain," the Queen observed ruefully.

Melody's heart rate had slowed to a regular, pedestrian pace.

She and the Queen were wearing dresses of a similar style, although Melody's was a peach-tinted red contrasting with her host's grey.

"I first tasted wine when I lived in Spain with my parents, Your Majesty," Melody volunteered in Castilian, rather blurting the words because she was still nowhere near as in control of herself as she thought she was.

The Queen of Spain in Exile smiled, seemingly touched that her guest would volunteer to speak in her native language, as if it was a courtesy she had not expected and was therefore, doubly appreciated for the respect the gesture implied.

"Yes, Alonso reminded me that your parents are Thomas Ransom and Violetta Daingnton; I recollect being fortunate enough to have been present at several of their virtuoso house concerts as a girl." Queen Sophie made no move to return to her seat.

Melody tried not to flinch under the other woman's intently sympathetic scrutiny.

"It must have been quite a challenge growing up with two such perfectionists as parents?"

"Yes and no," Melody shrugged, unsure how to respond. Honesty was probably best: "They taught me the importance of intellectual rigour without ever," she paused, "holding it against me that I did not want to live the lives that they had lived." She smiled, tight-lipped. "Well, that they still live, actually. They have a big house, miles from anywhere in the wilds of Vermont..."

"Do they still play?"

"Yes. Every evening."

"And have they ever forgiven you for not filling their big house in the country with children?"

Again, Melody shrugged.

This was *not* the conversation she had expected to have with the Queen Empress of Spain in Exile; sometimes, life was full of surprises. So, she went with the flow.

"No," she shook her head, "I think they got used to that around the same time that I did."

Queen Sophie gestured for her to walk with her.

Together the two women emerged into the afternoon sunshine. Nearby, there was a sisterly squabble in progress between the two royal princesses.

The Queen looked to her companion.

"You are not at all like me," she said, sighing a little laugh.

"Oh, I don't..."

"Forgive me. It is just that I was afraid that you would be exactly like me. But I am glad that you are not."

Melody halted, unable to do anything about the spontaneous frown forming on her lips or the questions in her eyes.

"You're the Queen of Spain and I'm a lawyer turned detective turned spook who just wants a quiet life," she said, despite her best intentions, a little peevishly.

Queen Sophie nodded, seemed to inadvertently chew her bottom lip for a moment.

"You must understand that Alonso and I grew up together, or rather, when we were teenagers, we moved about within the same fringes of the same court society. In another age we would have married and lived happily ever after but," a waving away motion of her right hand, "it was not and could never be. It would have been, literally, the death of us both. But I still remember the way I felt about him; and I am confident that his recently expressed, foolishly suicidal loyalty to my person, reflects that he too shares that memory. But..."

"But," Melody echoed, utterly confused.

Am I really having this conversation?

She was tempted to pinch herself.

The other woman took pity on her.

In fact, Melody got the distinct impression, that she was a little guilty to be unburdening herself to a stranger.

"I will never again be the Queen of Spain," the other woman said, "and while I live, there will be no government in exile, or pretender to the Catholic Throne of Madrid. *Not in my name.* In time, I will negotiate a truce, and accept whatever penance must be served to guarantee the safety of my daughters. Alonso must accept that. I will have no more bloodshed in my name to recover a throne which almost certainly cannot survive another generation. To be frank, I tried my best to nudge and to tempt my country into the modern world, and I failed. I must live with that. Even if it breaks my dear Alonso's brave heart."

The women began to walk, very slowly down aisles bordered with freshly planted shrubs and colourful borders. They were in a walled garden with lemon and lime trees interspersed around the walls, and the spring air hummed with the buzzing of bees.

"This palace was the seat of the House of Braganza. The last King of the Portuguese of that house, gifted it to the nation when he went into exile in London. His grandson practices law, at the Lower Bar of Lincoln's Inn, I believe. Perhaps, one day my family will find something useful to do with themselves. Presently, I am an embarrassment to the government in Lisbon, reliant wholly on the charity and forbearance of the present Royal House of Portugal."

They reached a corner and began to walk back towards the Orangery.

"A Papal Bull has been promulgated excommunicating my person, and that of Alonso, and his heirs, in perpetuity from the Grace of God and the communion of the Mother Church. The King, my husband, has already seized the estates of the Medina Sidonia family, and taken Alonso's *former* wife, the Duchess Amelia, under the protection of the Crown."

Melody tried to work out what all that meant in practice; coming to the general conclusion that things had worked out as badly for Alonso as she thought they had.

Queen Sophie sighed.

"Alonso is no longer married to his wife. Ironically, he only married her because my husband, Ferdinand, willed it. I think that at the time, he was terrified that I would elope with him. Amelia is pious to a fault, a beauty of the cold, dreary sort and she and Alonso's two daughters have maintained a separate house for the last ten years. My husband, the King is also a similarly pious, not very clever man and I would not be surprised if he does not, at some stage, seek to set Amelia up as some kind of platonic mistress cum confessor."

Melody was starting to think she had had a reality bypass.

"In any event, in the sight of God, and the Spanish state, Alonso is no longer married to Amelia. He is a free man. Free to re-marry. His old career is over. His new life is before him and now that he has been reunited with his son, I can have no further claim on him. At least not as his Queen, if not his friend for that I can never cease to be."

Queen Sophie, realising Melody was a little bit shell-shocked by all of this, took sympathy on her.

"So, for his sake and for Pedro's sake, Alonso must marry a strong woman to keep him on the straight and narrow. Plainly, it seems to me that this is a thing much complicated, and obliquely, much simplified by the self-evident fact that he is clearly bewitched by two such women!"

Melody was blinking uncontrollably.

The exiled Queen Empress smiled, halting at the door to the Orangery, her gaze following the progress of her daughters, the two Infantas, as yet just children unaware of the maelstrom they had escaped, gleefully chasing each other around the garden.

"You will need to discuss this with Lord De L'Isle's daughter, obviously," the other woman said, taking Melody's right hand in her own and fixing her with a stare that was nothing if not regal, "but please, do not delay overlong. People will begin to talk and that would cause us *all* much pain which frankly, is best avoided at this time."

Melody did not remember walking back into the Orangery, or sitting down, or a footman materialising to pop the Champagne cork, or to half-fill the fluted glasses with the bubbling, fizzing issue from the chilled bottle.

The Infantas had run in, breathless.

They had been allowed a sip of Champagne each and dismissed, indulgently, so that they could continue their chasing game outside.

"To what are we drinking?" Alonso, who had drifted into the Orangery, materialising by Melody's side, asked of his Queen.

"Miss Danson and I have had a very interesting conversation," he was informed in a gently teasing voice.

"I am intrigued."

"I am sure that *Melody* will tell you all about it, in due course. In the meantime, I want to hear all about her adventures in the Mountains of Madrid with the Lady De L'Isle!"

Chapter 12

Friday 28th April
Charlottenburg Palace, Berlin

Eleanor, Queen Consort and Duchess of Windsor, never really felt relaxed in Berlin. Partly, this was because her command of the German language was 'schoolgirlish', and unlike her husband, she was not actually closely related to anybody of any importance in the city. There was also the fact that in Berlin most German men of a certain class – the ruling class – treated women with barely veiled condescension or as ignorant, pretty faces to be 'talked at'. Whereas at home, or practically anywhere in the Empire no invitation to her husband would have specifically excluded her; here in Germany, other than in respect of wholly social events, or designated political ceremonies, she was automatically excluded, ignored as if she did not exist.

Bertie simply would not put up with it anywhere else.

Even here, he still got a lot hotter under the collar than she did, bless him.

"None of the bloody Electors trust any of the others!" The King seethed, coming into the drawing room where Eleanor was writing a letter to Elizabeth De L'Isle, in response to her old friend's latest fascinating missive on the subject of her daughter's adventures, and miraculous escape from Spain.

Eleanor looked up.

"Apparently," she reported brightly, "Henrietta and her companion, Ms Danson, rescued a young boy, just four years old, during their adventures," she explained brightly. "An orphan, by all accounts. It seems their escape was masterminded by several of the Duke of Medina Sidonia's arms men. I can't wait to sit Hen down and hear all about it from her own lips!"

This completely took the wind out of her husband's sails.

As she had known it would.

"If you were the Prince of Bavaria or the Princess of Lower Thuringia," she posed, smiling, "or the Bishop Protector of the Palatinate," she went on, "would *you* trust *any* of the other Electors, Bertie?"

"No, I suppose not," the King agreed with a sulky ill-grace that he regretted a moment later. "I'm sorry, my dear. It's just that here we are three-quarters of the way through the twentieth century kicking our heels in a country with a governmental system stuck in the bloody middle ages!"

"What do Sir Hector and Sir George think of all this?" Eleanor inquired.

The Prime Minister and the Foreign Secretary were as frustrated as their monarch; except, because they were intrinsically political animals, they were more adroit at concealing their angst. Had it not been for the war in the Americas and the dreadful catalogue of secrets the royal couple had carried with them to Berlin; the last few days might have been a prime jamboree of diplomacy, a melting pot of the nations. As it was, the paralysis at the heart of the German Empire suddenly seemed horribly dangerous, and the electoral system first designed to settle the question of the succession upon the death of a Holy Roman Emperor in times immemorial, had endless potential to be a disastrous global banana skin!

The twenty-four Electors: princes, a couple of princesses, one Duchess and various 'Protectors', could vote for whomsoever they pleased at the forthcoming 'Imperial Conclave', due to commence early next week. Although, from the outside it seemed odds-on that the Kronprinz, presently the uncrowned Kaiser Wilhelm VI of Prussia, the mercurial forty-four-year-old son of the old Emperor, ought to be a shoe-in at the Sanssouci Palace – Germany's rival to the magnificence which had been Versailles before it was destroyed in the Great War – the traditional seat of the Kings of Prussia and in more recent times, of the German Emperor. However, nothing was quite so disruptive or corrosive as an Imperial election; and as was traditional, the most bizarre rumours were freely circulating in the city. Laughable as it might seem, many in the Crown Prince's retinue constantly obsessed about suspicions that several of the more Catholic Electors favoured a Hapsburg, or even a revanchist Bourbon candidate. Of course, this was patently absurd because *not even* an Elector could seriously expect the people of the Grosse Reich to stomach a dispossessed French princeling on the throne, and the only available substantive Hapsburg contender would be the embattled King of Spain or one of his teenage sons, all of whom in terms of bloodlines were more Bourbon-Medici-Aragonese than Hapsburg other than in name. Nonetheless, that such improbable possibilities could be discussed at all, was illustrative of the unusually febrile atmosphere in the capital and the reason why so many of the great men of affairs presently resident in the city, literally, dared not go home until a generally acceptable new Emperor was actually crowned.

Infuriatingly, in accordance with twentieth century tradition – supposedly to avoid intimidation or bribery – Kronprinz Wilhelm was effectively, in purdah, inaccessible to the Electors and they to him, for the duration, other than in the course of holy worship, or in the joint fulfilment of ceremonial state obligations. Practically, and ludicrously, this meant that several of the Electors, members of the old Kaiser's inner circle were not allowed to talk to other members of the interim Reich Administration.

The right and the left hand of the government literally did not know, and where not permitted to communicate, what was going on with each other.

And people honestly believed that the Germans were the most rational, organised nation on the planet!

"Hector and George dined with cousin Albert last night," the King sighed. His distant relative, the Duke of Saxe-Gotha, was one of the two Thuringian Electors, very much a man staunchly in the Crown Prince's camp.

Eleanor knew that cousin Albert – goodness knows how many times removed – had the rare knack of making her husband dyspeptic. It was ever thus if families. She had always found Albert harmless enough, albeit a little over-bearing, and a little too fond of the sound of his own voice. Not to mention, for a man with such a colourful past – in rotund middle age he remained an incurable philanderer – rather too self-righteous. He was also an inveterate schemer. Wealthy, having never had to seek, let alone pursued a profession other than opinionated lordliness, Albert had made a career of scheming for no better reason than, he could. At times such as these when it seemed to many that 'everything was up for grabs,' the only certainty in an uncertain world was that *cousin Albert* was probably having the time of his life.

Meanwhile, the over-large gang of visiting monarchs, politicians and diplomats in Berlin to attend the funeral of the old Kaiser and the anointment of his successor, had been farmed out around the numerous summer and winter palaces of the capital and its surrounding royal estates; the Charlottenburg had been reserved for the British and, as they dribbled in from all over the world, the representatives of the Dominions. By tradition only the Dominions, not colonies, not even the larger ones sent representatives to the great set-piece pageants of foreign states. Therefore, while Chief Ministers and Governor-Generals from Dominions, such as South Africa, Australia, New Zealand, the nefarious Maharajas of a clutch of self-governing states within the Indian Raj, and representatives of the largely self-governing sparsely populated Canadian dominions planned to attend the State Funeral of the old Kaiser, the King alone represented New England, Labrador and Newfoundland and the majority of all those other places stubbornly painted imperial pink on maps of the globe.

Dominion status had been mooted for the First Fifteen New England colonies as long ago as the 1880s, mainly in recognition of the role New Englanders had played in the victory of 1866. Had there been more enthusiasm – in the event there had been virtually no interest in the idea whatsoever then, or since baring that from a few eccentrics, like Isaac Fielding and his republican-leaning adherents - on the other side of the Atlantic, it might have happened without a great deal of fuss and bother, and more or less passed on the nod.

The trouble was the world, and New England had changed out of all recognition in the last hundred years. The process of settlement had exploded west from the historic colonies in parallel with the westward march of northern, Canadian expansion until now, the imperial writ ran from coast to coast, the bothersome South Western corner excepted. And with that unfettered expansion had come unstoppable economic growth that was now the well-spring of the whole Empire. The 'final canalisation' of the St Lawrence and the linking of the Great Lakes, completed only in 1955, financed almost wholly from grain and ore revenues mainly from Canada, to whom Dominion status had been granted as long ago as 1951, had literally, opened up the New England west to industry and agriculture, promoting a boom that had run out of control for the last twenty years.

Now, grain from the prairies west of the Mississippi had rendered the famines of Bengal, Rajasthan and the Punjab things of a past, dark era. And huge, sprawling frontier cities had sprung up along the shores of the Great Lakes, their never-ending hunger for labour drawing people from every corner of the Empire. It was hardly surprising that Philip De L'Isle sometimes grew so exasperated with the insularity and the westward 'blindness' of the 'great men' of the East Coast who were still so wedded to the old country, that they refused to glance over their shoulders at the 'new' New England conquering the fastnesses of their unimaginably bountiful continent...

"Um," Eleanor declared philosophically, giving her husband a wry gaze, "you've got that faraway look in your eye, again, mein Liebe."

The King grimaced sheepishly.

"Forgive me, my love, I was thinking about everything we saw when we were in New England a couple of years ago," he confessed. "I don't mean our time in the East. I was thinking more about those great factories, the steel mills, the row upon row of huge grain silos at Buffalo, and all those big ships plying their trade on the Great Lakes. And," he shrugged, "travelling on that train across the prairies, sometimes rattling through endless fields of ripening wheat and corn from morning to dusk. And thinking, as inevitably one must, how little the people at home, or in the wider Empire, or in the First Thirteen, truth be known, and certainly not here, in the heart of Europe, understand that in New England there lies a sleeping giant..."

"I've invited Ranji to join us for luncheon," Eleanor said, changing the subject in an attempt to raise her husband's spirits. "Hopefully, you two can cheer each other up talking about cricket!"

The news instantly broke her husband's preoccupation.

Major General His Highness Jam Saheb Ranjitsinhji Vibhaji III Jadeja of Nawanagar, was the flamboyant, raconteur grandson of the most remarkable cricketer ever to come out of the sub-continent.

'Ranji', like her husband – strangely, given that he had been a gunnery specialist, a thing requiring the finest imaginable exactitude – notwithstanding his unquenchable love of the summer game was a man almost completely lacking in hand-eye co-ordination when it came to holding a cricket bat or attempting to take a catch in the field.

Nevertheless, the Chairman of the All India Cricket Board of Control and the Honorary Life President of the Marylebone Cricket and Lawn Tennis Club, the arbiter of the laws and standards of both sports at Thomas Lord's Field next to Regent's Park, and the King were old friends from their school days at Harrow. Regardless of whatever else was happening in the Empire, they always fell straight into an animated debate about the state of their national summer games (Cricket and Tennis) and the perennial problem of what on earth their respective Cricketing elevens were going to do about the blasted all-conquering Philadelphians!

On that particularly sore topic, while now and then the Australians or the South Africans put up a gallant but doomed fight against the terrifying New Englanders – whose bowlers bowled like the wind and whose batsmen seemed to be wielding mighty tree trunks, not the matchstick forty to forty-five ounce bats of their foes – who time and again mercilessly reduced their foes to dispirited, often gibbering shells of the men they had once been...

Eleanor giggled.

Her husband had already brightened, shaken off his broodiness.

"And after luncheon I plan to take a stroll in the grounds..." Her voice trailed off because she very nearly had to bite her tongue to stop herself saying: "Because we probably won't be welcomed back again when we make our shameful confession about the Submarine Treaty to whoever turns out to be the new German Emperor!"

She was relieved her husband was not reading her mind, or if he was, he hid it well.

"Yes, Ranji and I do tend to jabber on a bit about bat and ball, and the politics of the International Cricket Council," the King conceded apologetically.

Cricket and Association Football – respectively the national summer and winter national games - were alike to Eleanor; once, early in her marriage she had suggested, in all earnestness, to Bertie that both games would be much improved as a spectacle if each side had their own balls...

Their marriage had, fortuitously, survived that first crisis and flourished; which only went to show what could be achieved if there was a little bit of good will and plenty of give and take on both sides.

When they were first married, they had holidayed and travelled in the German Empire, a thing impossible since the late 1950s although visitors from Germany often quietly called on the family in London or at one or other of its country retreats. But discreetly, for discretion had been the key word in all 'higher-level' Anglo-German contacts in recent times.

However, the next visitor to the royal couple's rooms was not the cheery Jam Saheb of Nawanagar, it was a very grim-faced Sir Hector Hamilton, who thus far in Berlin had cut a sorry, somewhat diminished figure. He had kept the 'great secret' from his King for what he had determined were the best possible of reasons, his motives had been good, patriotic but he had wilted under the white heat of his monarch's anger, and hardened political operator that he was, he was not about to recover his equilibrium any time soon.

"Hector, what is it?" Eleanor asked anxiously. "You look as white as a sheet?"

The Prime Minister bowed.

"George Walpole stayed behind at the Embassy," the newcomer explained. "Telegrams are coming in all the time. We have received reports that the redoubt defence lines around San Antonio in Texas have been breached, and that our reserve forces of last resort, are in full retreat."

The King's face darkened, his scowl deepened.

"I regret that I must report that there are no substantial forces between the invaders and the Mississippi River, sir," Sir Hector Hamilton went on. "But," he added, holding up a hand. "That is not the worst of it, forces of the Triple Alliance supported by many warships are reported to have seized the port of Pensacola. If this is true, then it is likely that the Delta and the city of New Orleans may soon be cut off and in due course, besieged; or worse, the enemy may strike east and isolate Florida from the rest of New England."

The King compelled himself to take several long breaths.

It did not help.

"And?" He asked tersely, knowing that there must be more very bad news.

"*And* an enemy squadron is reported to be bombarding English Harbour on Antigua, our main garrison in the Leeward Islands…"

Eleanor was bewildered.

She looked to her husband.

"I don't understand," she confessed. "What on earth is the Navy doing about all this, Bertie?"

Chapter 13

Friday 28th April
HMS Surprise, 35 nautical miles SW of Bermuda

Surgeon Lieutenant Abraham Lincoln, RNAS, had adjusted to the sameness and clockwork routine of life on board HMS Surprise faster and with a lot less angst, than his friend. Ted Forest, notwithstanding he was still recovering, rather than rehabilitating from what had been life-threatening wounds, freely confessed he was getting 'cabin fever', shut up in their claustrophobic new world.

'I joined the Air Service because I hate confined spaces and I actually like the wind in my face!'

For Abe, this surreal entrapment below the waves, was a priceless opportunity to regain his mental and physical equilibrium, and to allow his battered body and perturbed psyche to heal itself. Of course, he worried about Kate, and what she must be going through, probably thinking in her heart that he was dead but there was nothing he could do about that and, hopefully, all his wife's grief and hurt would, in time, be repairable, if and when he eventually got home. If he had died on the Achilles, or on Little Inagua, Kate would never have known where his bones lay. As it was, although his and Ted's sojourn on the Surprise seemed interminable – this was actually only their fifteenth day aboard – it would surely end one day. In the meantime, he had been devouring the submarine's medical library like a starving man suddenly presented with a banquet fit for a king!

And the quietness was pure bliss...

However, he was not quite so sure about the tiny electric shock; well, more of a persistent tingling of the band around his left wrist which warned him that there was about to be a boat-wide announcement which he was required to listen to, over the ether via the earpiece permanently in his right ear.

Apparently, unlike on surface ships, blaring alarms and exhortations over the boat's speaker system were an 'absolute no-no' when the Surprise was creeping around several hundred feet beneath the surface trying very hard to be as stealthy as possible.

The wrist band also served the purpose of allowing the Officer of the Watch to establish exactly where every man was at a given moment. It was a court martial offence to remove the band while on board; likewise, woe betide a man who took out his earpiece, or mislaid it, or placed it more than the specified two-and-a-half seconds out of his immediate reach.

"This is the Captain!"

Abe put down his book. Today, he was 'slumming it' in the Petty Officer's Mess, like every other compartment on the vessel far too small to swing a cat in – leastways, not enthusiastically – in his constant quest to not get under anybody's feet. He was a lot better at that than Ted Forest, who, now that he was up and about – limping and on crutches - was a bundle of nervous energy keen to learn everything that was to be learned about the great mechanical whale, which had swallowed them off Little Inagua a fortnight ago. Abe would have been more curious but then that would have spoiled his friend's fun; Ted clearly enjoyed explaining everything he had discovered to him of an evening, or morning, or whatever, one soon lost track of time, day, night and all that nonsense, on board a nuclear-powered submarine.

"You will all have been asking yourselves what we have been doing twiddling our thumbs the last couple of weeks," the Captain prefaced, speaking quietly, as if each and every man on the boat was standing directly in front of him, "while our chums up top have been getting it in the neck. Other than ferrying our gang of half-tame Royal Marines ruffians to their next rendezvous with unpleasantness, that is!"

That 'gang' of ruffians were the only reason Abe and Ted were still alive. Ted would almost certainly have died of his wounds, infection for want of antibiotics back on Little Inagua, and Abe had not exactly been in tip top form by the time the Marines jumped on him.

The 'ruffians' had gone on another 'excursion' about a week ago; reporting back with no little satisfaction, or irony, that *this time* 'the Royal Naval Air Service had been so good as to leave them some Cubans and Dominicans to kill.'

There had been much jocular banter in the Wardroom about how it hard been for the Marines to move around Little Inagua, 'what with continually falling over all the dead bodies lying about everywhere!'

The Captain went on: "You may be aware that until now our rules of engagement have been to avoid detection and to not initiate contact with the enemy. At zero-one-zero-zero hours this morning GMT, we received new orders authorising us to attack and sink the Cuban submersible we have been tracking the last three days, and any other enemy submarine we encounter within a fifty-mile radius of *any* our surface units or bases ashore."

The Captain paused, as if he was checking the deckhead chronometer in the Control Room.

"In approximately seven minutes the boat will come to Attack Stations. For your information all six bow tubes are loaded, with tubes One and Three already flooded down."

Abe thought there was going to be more.

"That will be all."

Submariners, Abe had learned, did not tend to make much of a fuss about anything in particular.

"Ah," Ted Forest announced cheerfully, hobbling clumsily into the compartment, "there you are!"

Considering that he had a broken leg in a cast – and that he had had two, by no means minor, 'tidying up' surgeries on his abdominal bullet wound in the first forty-eight hours he had been aboard the Surprise - the boat's surgeon had been frankly astonished that Ted was: one, so 'chipper'; and two, up and about and obviously already so well 'mended'.

Abe had told his medical colleague that you could not keep a good man down, and resisted all blandishment to try to persuade his friend to 'take it easy'.

His own shoulder wound had healed nicely and like his still pink facial wounds, presently rather obvious given his sunburnt countenance and torso, would in time, fade.

'No lasting damage,' Surprise's surgeon had concluded.

Abe put down his book and looked up.

"Well," he frowned, "I could hardly get out and go for a walk outside, old man!"

Ted Forest maneuvered his 'gammy' leg under the Mess table and sat down beside Abe.

"This is true," he agreed, chuckling. "*Torps*." He explained confidentially, "says we'll probably just creep up behind the other fellow and launch a homing fish at him from about a mile away."

'Torps' was the Torpedo Officer, a fresh-faced boy who looked far too young to be out of school, let alone in charge of two dozen of the most advanced naval weapons on the planet. Actually, the fellow was in his mid-twenties, a graduate in marine mechanical engineering of the Southampton Institute of Technology who had been head-hunted for Project Poseidon in his last year at college over four years ago.

Most of the men on board the Surprise were unmarried, some many years younger than men holding similar ranks and discharging comparable burdens of responsibility in the rest of the fleet, like 'Torps' recruited directly into their specialisations, who had not been back to the British Isles or New England since signing on for Project Poseidon.

Both Abe and Ted had been briefed, in a cursory fashion about what it was to be '*a Poseidon*', a club of which they were honorary members for the duration of 'this patrol'. They had been cautioned in no uncertain terms, at no little length, exactly what the uniformly dire consequences of divulging anything – anything whatsoever – they had seen while aboard HMS Surprise to an unauthorised person (which was practically anybody in the world including the majority of the members of the current Government), would be for them.

Further, they had been warned that it was unlikely they would be 'released back into general service as soon as the boat returns to base' because 'a suitable, credible cover story will have to be manufactured to explain how you survived the loss of the Achilles in the Battle of the Windward Passage and escaped back into Colonial hands.'

"It is the middle of the night topsides," Ted explained, "and the other chap is probably on the surface re-charging his batteries. We've been tagging along several hundred feet down listening to his propellers to keep in touch. Apparently, the other boat, they think it's a Cuban-built variant of the original three hundred-ton German Mark II coastal model, has got a noisy bearing on its starboard prop."

"How on earth can they tell that?" Abe asked, regretting it immediately. "No, no, don't tell me!"

His head was already so full of secrets already he hardly needed to know any more!

Abe's wristband tingled.

"Here this! Here this! Attack Stations! Attack Stations!"

Nothing much seemed to happen except a few men tip-toed past the open bulkhead door.

Some twenty minutes later there was another electric tingling.

"Attacking! Attacking!"

It was all very unreal.

When Abe had dive bombed the former Kaiserliche Marine light cruiser Karlsruhe there had been fire, smoke, chaos. His Sea Fox had pulled up and flown through the fumes spewing from the warship's funnel; he had seen the Achilles's other two aircraft shot to pieces, and the wreckage of one of them crash into the side of the Karlsruhe.

But the Surprise was fighting a distant, remote, antiseptic war that felt almost like cold-blooded murder; and it offended Abe's hunter's soul not to be literally, or even metaphorically, looking one's foe in the eyes.

His wrist tingled.

"REMEMBER BRAVE ACHILLES!"

There was a short pause.

"FLUSH TUBE ONE!"

Neither man definitively recognised the moment the Mark XX semi-passive homing torpedo left its tube over two hundred feet away. That there was a very subtle tremor throughout the submarine was hydrodynamically undeniable; however, the injection of a small quantity of compressed air, instantly trapped by baffles at the mouth of the torpedo tube as the munition was launched, was to all intents, undetectable other than by a seismograph aft of the torpedo room bulkhead.

"This is really cold, Ted," Abe said quietly.

Less than three weeks ago, the two men had gone to war in an obsolete biplane launched off an old ship, the last of her class, on her last commission. Achilles had been beaten into submission by two newer, bigger cruisers, and he and Ted had been shot down by modern high-performance aircraft; and that they had survived had been nothing short of a miracle.

But those men on that small, diesel-electric submarine in the Surprise's sights were helpless, dead men walking.

The intercom circuit was live.

"FISH ZERO-ONE HAS ACQUIRED BANDIT ONE. TARGET LOCK CONFIRMED. BANDIT ONE CONSTANT BEARING. REPEAT CONSTANT BEARING."

The deck beneath their feet inclined as the submarine turned to port, her bow dipping downward.

"TARGETTING TELEMETRY...NOMINAL. TIME TO IMPACT..."

"TEN SECONDS..."

"FIVE SECONDS...FOUR...THREE...TWO...ONE..."

"BINGO! CONFIRM BINGO!"

Abe and Ted Forest looked at each other.

Waiting.

The faraway rumbling was barely audible, unfelt.

And that was it.

"PLEASE BE AWARE. THE BOAT WILL RUN DEEP. THE BOAT

WILL RUN DEEP. STAND DOWN FROM ATTACK STATIONS. ALL PERSONNEL TO CRUISING STATIONS. REPEAT. ALL PERSONNEL REPORT TO CRUISING STATIONS!"

"How many guys are there on a Type II boat?" Abe asked, dully.

"Twenty, maybe twenty-five."

Ted punched his friend's arm playfully, knowing Abe had killed many, many more Dominican sailors and marines on Little Inagua with a long rifle, and when he had run out of ammunition, with a bayonet, or the hatchet he had retrieved from the wreck of the Sea Fox.

"It's a damned good thing the Spanish haven't got boats like this one," Ted Forest observed, trying to sound cheerful.

Abe shook his head.

"Until a couple of weeks' ago, I had no idea *we* were capable of building a thing like this!" He retorted, waving his arms about him.

Ted Forest shifted a little uncomfortably.

Abe frowned concern.

"My bloody leg is itching," his friend complained. "Can't bloody scratch it with the bally cast on it!"

In a way this was an apt metaphor for their present situation: they were aboard a top secret vessel that was not supposed to exist, would both much rather have been ashore and yet their lives, and their careers were on hold until...well, they did not know that either, and there was nothing they could do about it. It had also occurred to each man, separately, that given the Surprise and the project which had created her was so secret, and that – like it or not - they both now knew so much about it that, whatever their heroics and adventures, that *they* might actually be something of an embarrassment to the Empire.

In fact, it might be more convenient for everybody if they simply disappeared, either temporarily, or...for good.

How hard would that be to arrange?

After all, everybody back home already thought that they were dead...

Abe shook his head.

The Empire did not do that sort of thing!

"I think that knock on the head I took back on Little Inagua is still playing tricks with my thinking," he admitted, sheepishly.

"Yes, well, I definitely need my head examining if I ever go flying with you again!" Ted Forest chided him.

"Oh, yeah of so little faith. Let me tell you that that last landing turned out a lot better than I thought it was going to five seconds before we hit the ground!"

Ted was encouraged by the fact his friend had not completely lost his sense of humour. He well understood that Abe must be going through a mental wringer knowing that Kate had to think he was dead. It was bad enough for Ted himself; he might not be married but he had made a goodly number of friends since he arrived in New England, and they would, presumably, been a lot cheerier had they discovered that news of his death was premature. What made it worse, and guiltily nagged at their souls, was that nobody would tell them how many of their crew mates had gone down with the Achilles, or what else was going on in the world. Not that the average crew member on board was any better informed.

The Spanish have torpedoed a couple of our ships. There are half-a-dozen enemy submersibles at large in the Gulf of Spain and the Atlantic...

But which ships had been torpedoed?

Like the majority of the Surprise's crew the two fliers had no idea where the ship was, or had been, at any time after she submerged off the north coast of Little Inagua.

Abe and Ted were prisoners, albeit captives in a gilded technological cage which in other circumstances would have been like an Aladdin's Cave.

Abe went back to his reading.

Ted Forest tried to make himself more comfortable and to have a nap.

A few minutes later their wristbands tingled.

"Mister Lincoln and Mister Forest report to the Captain's cabin at your earliest convenience!"

Chapter 14

Saturday 29th April
Imperial Concession, Guaynabo, San Juan, Santo Domingo

Hans von Schaffhausen stepped onto the deck of the SMS Weser and clambered up to the bridge. The wreckage had been cleared away, and the blood hosed off the planking since his first visit to the ship but the constant clanking of the pumps told their own, sad story.

Commander Peter Cowdrey-Singh, RN, had greeted the German Minister informally at the head of the gangway; Leutnant zur see Kemper, the boyish captain of the crippled merchant raider crisply saluted von Schaffhausen.

The three men stepped to the bridge wing to view the big cruiser cautiously edging into the poorly marked deep-water channel of San Juan Bay, fighting the tide to turn to starboard, so as to safely pass inshore of the San Miguel, the ancient Dominican ironclad still pointing her guns at the Weser.

Peter Cowdrey-Singh raised binoculars to his eyes and studied the SMS Emden, the second ship of the Mainz class 5.9-inch-gunned light cruisers. He noted the static Mark II air search ELDAR aerials at the ship's fighting top above her conning tower, the main battery gun-director ELDAR mounts, small half-dishes which scanned through thirty degrees either side of the target bearing, the two port and two starboard directors, fore and aft, each triangulating and continually correcting for error. He took it all in with cool, professional detachment. The Royal Navy had adopted a completely different ELDAR fire control solution making it possible, in some circumstances to slave a whole squadron's main batteries to that of the flagship.

He could see that the German cruiser – which, along with the Breslau – had been involved in the bombardment of Kingston, Jamaica and in supporting the subsequent invasion of the Crown Colony, was in need a little time in dockyard hands. She was heavily rusted in places; crude patches had been welded over a couple of holes in her hull amidships and her seaplane crane was missing.

The Emden's crew was lining the rail, and she was flying her Imperial Ensign. Clearly, her captain was in no mood to allow standards to drop while he still commanded. That said, this must be a very sad day for the Germans still on board the ship.

The quayside north of the Weser was being made ready to receive the cruiser, and within hours she would be handed over to the Dominicans, with every last good German coming ashore.

"I bet they'll need a couple of tugs to get her *out* of the bay," Peter Cowdrey-Singh remarked idly, looking from bow to stern of the handsome ship as her captain handled her with marvellous adroitness in the confined, relatively shallow waters. It took a rare seaman to so confidently handle his ship in a strange harbour, especially when he was about to surrender his command to a bunch of religious maniacs…

"Kapitan-sur-See Wallendorf was a champion yachtsman in his

youth," von Schaffhausen re-joined sombrely. "He will be sad to learn that his old friend, Weitzman, now lies in the German cemetery."

The Englishman saw the muddy water churning under the stern of the cruiser, the head of the ship swinging towards him. Slowly, slowly, the Emden crept closer to the Liner wharf.

Captain Wallendorf was indeed a master ship-handler, that much was readily apparent even to the uninformed. He judged it to a nicety, slow astern on one propeller, slow ahead on the other. Riding the incoming tide, the cruiser drifted, almost imperceptibly broadside on to the dock, the distance narrowing, narrowing...

Lines were hurled.

The Emden kissed the fenders.

There was less than twenty feet of clearance between the warship's raked, clipper stem and the stern of the half-wrecked commerce raider.

"I shall speak with Kapitan Wallendorf," von Schaffhausen told the two officers, "I am sure he will be amenable to taking you and your men under his protection, Commander Cowdrey-Singh."

Von Schaffhausen had been given to understand that a Hamburg-Atlantic line ship had been despatched to collect the crews of the ships of Rear Admiral Erwin von Reuter's former Vera Cruz Squadron, some two thousand six hundred men in all, and to transport them home to Germany. The dwindling band of survivors from HMS Achilles ought, it was thought, be safe in the company of the four-hundred-and-fifty remaining Kaiserliche Marine men shortly to disembark from the Emden. Moreover, the attitude of the Santo Domingo regime to its German guests within the Concession should, by rights, be immeasurably improved by the handover of the modern cruiser, some months in advance of the originally agreed date.

Peter Cowdrey-Singh had no say in the matter either way; the decision had been taken to try to get his people off the island with the German navy-men. His people were already preparing to go ashore from the Weser under the protection of the Emden's disembarked Marine detachment. Wisely, von Schaffhausen did not want to use his own troops unless he absolutely had to; he, after all, was still going to be living here when hopefully, his 'English guests' were long gone.

There were already over three hundred Dominican officers and men aboard the Emden, shadowing their German mentors or actually filling posts on the ship's duty roster, supposedly ready to take over at a moment's notice.

The former Executive Officer of the Achilles seriously doubted 'the natives' were remotely ready to take over, let alone to fight the Emden. He remembered coming on board the Achilles to re-commission her. It had taken at least a couple of months to master the old ship's ways and to build the proficiency necessary to operate her efficiently. Building up her fighting power had taken much longer. By the time she was engaging those cruisers in the Windward Passage the old girl had been in mid-commission, at a peak of battle worthiness. However, from what he had seen of the locals thus far, and the slovenly habits of the men manning the San Miguel the locals literally did not have a clue!

Giving them big modern ships like the Emden 'to play with' was an accident waiting to happen.

Good riddance was all he had to say about it!

Down on the dock many of the Concession's wives had come down to greet the Emden's arrival, children had been allowed out of their Saturday morning classes – the Concession was a little piece of Germany transplanted to the tropics with the same rigid school week and hours, five-and-a-half days as per the standard model of the German Empire - and there was an almost festive atmosphere. The Concession's military band was blasting out tunes from home while saluting guns had swapped whiplash reports with each other on shore and on the cruiser.

It was all a hollow pretence, an act to show the Dominicans that it took more than the guns of a museum ship anchored in the bay to intimidate them!

Von Schaffhausen was hoping that Captain Wallendorf would have up to date news about the other ships of the Vera Cruz Squadron, and the latest fighting in the region. He no longer trusted anything he received from the Wilhelmstrasse, and the Dominicans jammed the British Empire Broadcasting Corporation's wavelengths. According to the regime on Santo Domingo the Royal Navy had been annihilated by the hand of God, and the true warriors of the Cross were rampant in the southern territories and colonies of New England. Elsewhere, the Windward and Leeward Islands would soon fall like 'rotten fruit' into the hands of the one true faith. Invariably, all this tended to be happening in a 'sea of blood'; which was a little too crass to be taken seriously by von Schaffhausen, or by any of the other sensible Germans of his acquaintance.

The only thing which had really surprised him since the Battle of the Windward Passage – a shameful affair that offended practically everything von Schaffhausen believed in – was that San Juan had not been bombed by a swarm of British aircraft, or bombarded into smithereens by naval artillery. In fact, but for the hyperbole and hysteria of the Dominican governing regime, the Weser episode and that old ironclad moored opposite the waterfront below his office window, he would not have known that this island was at war with the most powerful, and ruthless, empire that the world had ever known.

Peter Cowdrey-Singh watched the Emden tying up, and gangplanks being secured. The German Minister, who seemed a decent type, had confided that the two heavy cruisers, Breitenfeld and Lutzen, and the still dry-docked Karlsruhe – which Achilles's Sea Foxes had handled so badly – were to be, or had already been, handed over to wholly Mexican or Cuban crews, and the other 'light cruiser', a sister ship of the Emden, the Breslau was to be crewed wholly by 'Hispanics' from Santo Domingo's western neighbour, Hispaniola. All the surviving German destroyers had been taken over by the 'Mexicans', the erstwhile New Granadans, who seemed to be the brains behind everything that the Triple Alliance did.

Having imagined he understood a little bit about the tortured religious and political realities of this part of the world; he had discovered, to his cost, that he had got a lot of things wrong. For example, while the Mother Church seemed to be an integral part of the governance of the Greater Antilles – Cuba, Hispaniola and Santo Domingo – New Granada, or *México*, as seemed to be the modern customary usage in this part of the world, was a kind of quasi-democracy in which church and state were constitutionally separate, albeit co-operative entities. Further, 'New Spain', a generic term he had employed for as long as he could recollect to describe, in vague terms, the Central Americas from the southern shores of the Caribbean to the line of the Rio Grande river in the south western borderlands of New England, including the vast gold and timber-rich Alta California territory which stretched half-way up the Pacific coast to Canada and included much of the Oregon Country, was actually the term the Catholic Church and the countries under its umbrella called *all* of the lands surrounding the Gulf of Spain. Therefore, to be a Mexican or a Cuban, Hispanic or Dominican, or to Colombian or a Venezuelan or even to a Guyana, or a Portuguese Brazilian, practically everything south and west of the Crown Colony of Georgia and the Carolinas was, in the eyes of the Mother Church, to be a citizen of 'New Spain'. Moreover, nobody within the 'Triple Alliance' – another misnomer because it had more than three members – regarded the 'Border Lands of Sonora, or Texas, let alone the Louisiana country – any of it - as 'English"; furthermore, Florida was no more or less than a 'stolen colony', and Jamaica was now a freed 'slave state'.

Peter Cowdrey-Singh had decided that he could never be a diplomat. Diplomats had to put aside their anger and their grudges, prejudices and scruples. He doubted he would ever trust a German again, and as for the bloody Spanish, well, the sooner the Atlantic Fleet got its act together and sorted this mess out the better!

He had no idea whatsoever what he was supposed to make of von Schaffhausen's assertion, that had 'the British Government extended an olive leaf to the Mexicans after they overthrew the idiots who caused the last Border War,' there would have been no opportunity for Germany to step into the regional vacuum of power. The German Minister had concluded that, as unlikely as it seemed now, there had been a genuine window of opportunity for a lasting peace, back in the mid-1960s at around the time the British and German empires were squaring up to each other in Africa and the Mediterranean; a simmering quarrel only ever thinly papered over by the Submarine Treaty.

The Emden sounded her fog horn.

One last blast of defiance.

Chapter 15

Saturday 29th April
Trinity Crossing, Unincorporated District of Northern Texas

The swirling wind had been gusting up to fifty miles-an-hour when Acting Flight Lieutenant Greg Torrance had decided, having circled for nearly twenty minutes, that he was going to have to risk attempting to land on the already muddy, well-puddled strip about a mile north east of Trinity Crossing. As it was, he had very nearly cut it too fine, with the Goshawk III's engine misfiring as he gunned the throttle and the turned for what would be, one way or another, his final approach.

Clinging on, buffeted in the narrow space behind the pilot's seat and the cockpit bulkhead, Flight Sergeant Bill Fielding, had heard the misfiring engine's note alter, steadying as his pilot thinned the mixture as lean as he dared without risking seizing the fuel-starved Gloucester-Royce radial.

'THIS IS GOING TO BE BUMPY!' Greg Torrance had yelled.

Needless to say, Bill Fielding had already worked that out for himself!

The Goshawk had previously made several low-level passes over the field and been waved off each time, presumably because the dirt strip had been reduced to a quagmire by the cloud-burst they had passed through south of Trinity Crossing. The problem was, that there was no other strip within fifty or sixty miles, and crash-landing in the deserts flanking the Trinity River and its nearby forks, held little attraction as the darkness closed in. At least if they crashed here there was an outside chance somebody would pull them from the wreckage.

Bill Fielding felt the undercarriage lock down.

There was loose talk about the new generation of 'jet' aircraft being configured with nose wheels so they could land 'fully upright'. That made sense because with the 'jet' installed – as was suggested - in the back of the aircraft there would be plenty of space for landing gear, guns and all sorts of other equipment to be installed in the front end of the machine...

However, the Goshawk was a conventional tail-dragger with a small fixed wheel just under the tail. Which was going to be really bad news if the mud was more than a couple of inches deep. If the mud was any deeper the scout was liable to dig in, pivot on its undercarriage and pitch forward onto its nose, where, its prop, still spinning at an ungodly speed would come to a grinding halt as it tore itself, and the engine – right in front of Greg Torrance and his passenger – to pieces. Thereafter, it was fifty-fifty that whatever fuel, and more dangerously, petrol vapour remaining in the main fuel tank, exploded.

In fact, one unsettlingly plausible scenario was that the Goshawk would get stuck in the mud on landing, still travelling at around a hundred miles-an-hour, pitch forward and land upside down, trapping the two men...

Bill Fielding shut his eyes and prayed.

Sometimes, no matter what crisis had afflicted one's faith there was simply nothing else to do.

In the event, the scout had skidded, aquaplaned in a flurry of red mud and water for about a quarter of a mile - at one time sideways - before it came to a steaming, creaking halt in the scrub about thirty yards from the rain-swollen lake at the western end of the field.

Much to Bill's surprise...*upright.*

Bill and his pilot had trudged out to inspect the mud-spattered Goshawk the next morning as the rain – apparently the leading edge of a tropical rainstorm which was sweeping west across the Texan hinterland – periodically a Biblical deluge, lashed down.

Nobody was going to be moving the scout until the ground around it, rapidly turning into a quagmire in which a man sank up to his lower calves with every step, eased and the southern sun had burned down for several days. The two men, and a couple of bedraggled fitters dragooned to accompany them, just took one look at the aircraft and turned away. They had discussed camouflaging the scout but even that was pointless, the Goshawk had already collected so much muck and mire as it skidded to a halt that from the sky it would almost certainly be indistinguishable from the desert and the scrub around it.

It had transpired that Greg Torrance was the senior pilot at Trinity Crossing. Before the war the country aerodrome, as neglected since the last Border War as their previous home – no more than a dirt strip and a few shacks, had been home to a pair of old Bristol Vs the locals used for finding lost cattle and keeping an eye on raiding Indian parties. In the last month the Army had half-heartedly taken over, basing a flight of four R-2 Fleabags, small, slow, unarmed canvas and dope single-seaters which had first taken to the skies nearly forty years ago, and only been retained in service as artillery spotters for no better reason than that the Army could not afford to replace them.

A couple of the Fleabags were still airworthy, as apparently were three of the other nine aircraft which had landed, or crash-landed at the field. It seemed that in recent days at least one Goshawk and one Sea Eagle, had over-flown the strip and decided they would take their chances elsewhere, or in the desert. So, apart from Greg Torrance's, probably written off Goshawk, what remained of the CAF in the West seemed to be the two Fleabags, and two twin-engine Gamecocks, sturdily built metal skinned biplane scouts of a type which both the newcomers had thought to have been phased out of squadron service over a decade ago.

Returning from inspecting his Goshawk, Greg Torrance had summoned everybody at the field to a meeting in the one, leaking shack large enough to accommodate the thirty-three CAF men, and twenty or so local militiamen at the field. By then he and Bill Fielding were starting to get a better feel for their new home.

The township of Trinity Crossing was about three miles to the south west, straggling along the banks of the Trinity River just above its eastern and western forks. The population of the surrounding country had been, perhaps, around two to three thousand but a lot of people had fled east or into the desert, mostly heading north and east. It seemed that a company of mounted men, supported by a mortar platoon which had been in transit west before the storm, now guarded the presently flooded ford across the Trinity River which had given the local township its name. These men were, it seemed, under the command of a local 'old-timer', a veteran of the last 'couple of wars', whom Greg Torrance had determined to set out and find that afternoon once they had 'got a grip of things at the field'.

The land west of the river tended to flood most springs, although this year the rains had come early. Apparently, every two or three years a tropical rain storm swept the country hereabouts, usually the leading or trailing edge of a dying hurricane which had battered the Gulf coast. Once the storm had passed the desert would bake dry, stone-hard again within days.

Trinity Crossing had long been a nominated 'redoubt position of last resort' in Colonial military training exercises. Not that anybody had ever imagined any invading force could threaten a position this far north of west, which was probably why nobody had ever thought about lengthening the runway at its only air strip. This was hardly surprising since it was obvious – searingly so – to Bill Fielding, who hardly considered himself to be any kind of strategist, that the Colonial military had given precious little thought to anything in particular about what happened next if their 'tripwire' front line was breached in one, let alone all along the line. 'Tripwire' was one of those weasel military words, inferring that if the enemy 'tripped' the 'wire' and thereby, announced his coming, then forces, pre-positioned and equipped reserves, behind 'the front' would – as if by magic – miraculously respond and repulse them. However, when push came to shove there had been no reserves, no pre-positioned forces, significant or otherwise, capable of halting, or even threatening to inconvenience the invaders. In the air and on the land, and from what he could guess, at sea, the Spanish had pretty much swept all before them!

There was an old – two or three decades at least – faded map on the end wall of what had been the 'club house', mess room and bar of the ramshackle pre-war aerodrome. Rumour had it that the nearby town was 'dry', run by a gang of neo-puritan settlers – the country wing, or to be more charitable, country cousins of the East Coast 'separate development', or *Getrennte Entwicklung*, societies of the more extreme wing of the Lutheran Church, of which Bill had been a practicing member most of his adult life until Empire Day, two years ago. Bill had stared at that map; any fool could tell, even from that old, probably not very well-drawn map, that Trinity Crossing, the arroyos and valleys of its western and eastern forks to the north, in no small measure because of the flooding that was likely to inundate the countryside to its south, was potentially excellent ground upon which to consolidate and build-up forces for a counter-attack, perhaps, sometime in the early summer.

The land around Trinity Crossing was generally flat, good land cruiser and artillery country apart from where the rivers cut through the terrain. A great limestone chalk ridge – the White Rock Escarpment -

rose over two hundred feet north to south and effectively, cut off any line of march on the key 'crossing' of the Trinity River – the only one for tens of miles north or south – from an enemy coming from the south west. A few mortars, a couple of anti-tank guns and a company of rifleman could hold off an Army for days, possibly for weeks from those heights.

Always assuming, that was, that there had been any reserves in the first place.

Which there had not been, nor would there be in the foreseeable future because clearly, what was patently obvious to a relatively newly-minted non-commissioned officer in the CAF, had not been in any way as obvious to the all-powerful imperial masterminds who were actually responsible for the defence of the Commonwealth of New England.

The rain hammered down, and water from the leaks in the roof trickled and dripped into ever-widening puddles on the dirt floor.

"Okay, chaps!" Greg Torrance called out. "Listen up, please!"

Gradually, the crowd fell quiet.

Bill Fielding's pilot looked around.

Torrance was a tall man, supposedly a big advantage for a Goshawk jockey because it meant he had long levers to stand on the rudder pedals and haul back on the stick, not to mention it meant he sat higher in the cockpit and was better able to see trouble coming from farther away than a shorter man. He had been fleshier when he and Bill first encountered each other but then, so had Bill; they had been down to hard tack and brackish water by the time they had made their escape.

Having discovered last night that there were no working radio sets at the field, Bill had already surveyed the other aircraft, and all the wrecks, with a view to salvaging the components required to put at least the communications deficiency right.

"Bill's in the process of cobbling together a radio set," Greg Torrance announced, "so, we should soon be back in contact with civilisation. In the meantime, we need to get weaving."

There were murmurs of dissent.

"I'm in charge, now," the pilot went on, an edge in his voice. "You chaps are in uniform, and I'm the ranking officer. I don't care what has happened down on the Border. You and I are subject to military discipline and you will obey my orders…"

It was uncanny that this was the very moment that the door at the far end of the shack creaked open and a tall, distinguished-looking man accompanied by three equally soaking wet companions, one of whom was a blond-haired woman, stamped into the building, shaking the rain off their broad-rim hats.

"Or what, sonny?" The tall man, of indeterminate latter middle age with a deep, gravitas-rich voice and a manner to match belying his militia battledress bearing two thin chevrons on his biceps, said. The man's face was lined by a life lived in the open air, chicken pox-pocked, and although weathered, handsome still. There was no real challenge in the question. The man was simply curious and gently, sceptical.

Greg Torrance was immediately struck by the man's presence: one of those rare men whose entrance really does change the atmosphere of any gathering, and to whom everybody instinctively looks to for guidance. The crowd between him and the two CAF men parted, and as the newcomer and his companions approached, they were greeted with respectful nods of acknowledgement.

The young pilot swallowed hard, and tried to retain his composure.

"That depends, Corporal. I'm not about to give you chaps a pep talk. The mere fact that most of you are here means that you didn't just roll over and surrender as soon as the first Mexican rifleman walked towards you." He glanced to Bill Fielding for moral support. "Flight Sergeant Fielding and I were the last chaps out. Bill managed to get our kite fixed while the Spanish were shelling our old field at Big Springs. It strikes me that we're all in pretty much the same boat. We keep waiting for the top brass to organise a defensive line but it hasn't happened yet. Well, I'm fed up with taking a beating and watching our chaps running away."

Practically everybody was looking at the tall man in the corporal's uniform.

Greg Torrance pointed at the map on the wall.

"This is as good a place as any in this sector. If our side hangs on to this bit of the northern Texas Territory then the Spanish will leave a massive open left flank if they carry on driving towards the Mississippi..."

The tall man was standing very nearly in front of the much younger aviator.

"The Spaniards will have to get across the Red River if they plan to invade the Louisiana Country between there and the Big Muddy, son," the other man observed, merely stating the obvious and clearly at pains not to pick a fight with, or in any way do down the CAF man. "In the meantime, we've only got a hundred or so effectives here, and down at Trinity Crossing."

This rather took the wind out of the sails of the younger man.

The one hundred-and-eighty miles of desert and prairie west of the Red River – to all intents, as formidable a barrier as the great Mississippi itself – was an entirely different proposition to the forests, swamps and bayous blocking the one hundred-and-seventy tortuous miles beyond the Red River to the Mississippi, and much of the ground to the south was impassable to wheeled, or even tracked vehicles.

Talk of Santa Anna driving all the way to New Orleans was, perhaps, a little premature; a litmus test of the panic in the air.

"At the moment, yes," Greg Torrance agreed, nodding. "I would just remind you that there were only three hundred Spartans at that pass at Thermopylae, they held back a hundred thousand Persians. And besides, they didn't even have an airfield."

The Corporal sighed.

He glanced over his shoulder to the men cramming the room and to his companions, whom Torrance could now identify as a Hispanic-looking man in his fifties, a younger man who could have been his son, and a blue-eyed young woman – booted and dressed in riding gear like the others – and then back to Greg Torrance.

"We've got families hereabouts," he explained. "Most of us have got

Mexican kith and kin, and proud of it. We hear what those boys back East say about the Mexicans; but take it from me, they know squat. A lot of people in these parts don't believe they'd be any worse off living under Il Presidente de Soto, they say old Hernando ain't so bad..." He shrugged. "I met General Santa Anna a couple of times back in the day. He's a man like you and I, son. He's got a wife and kids, and he wants the best for them. Just like I do for my family. A hundred years ago this country was a part of the Empire of New Spain, all of us around here grow up speaking Spanish."

The younger man felt his face burning.

For all that there was a strange absence of malice in the other man's voice, almost sympathy, in fact, the scout pilot began to bristle with anger.

Bill Fielding watched, figuring that the older man was trying to rile Greg Torrance; not really questioning his military but his moral authority to claim leadership. He was mightily relieved when his friend refused to rise to the bait.

"You may be right," Greg Torrance shrugged. "I've never lived under a Catholic theocracy. What's your name, friend?"

The Corporal straightened.

He was six feet tall if he was an inch, his shoulders stooped unless he was making an effort to stand with his head held high. Stepping forward, he had the gait of a man who has spent his life on horseback, a stiff erectness of posture that oddly defined him in this rag-tag collection of fleeing CAF personnel and local militiamen.

"Washington," the older man said gruffly. "George Nathaniel. I was Mayor of this County a few years back. I have a ranch up river. I was Colonel of the North Texas Brigade in the last war; I thought I was done with soldiering after that."

Greg Torrance frowned.

"Aren't you in the wrong uniform, sir?"

"I resigned my commission in sixty-seven," George Nathaniel Washington cast his eyes down onto his battledress. "This was the only tunic in the4 stores in town that fitted me."

George Washington...

Bill Fielding stared at the man.

That name had caused him and his family untold grief.

"Well, Colonel," Greg Torrance sighed. "I was about to try to talk everybody into extending the runway, digging slit trenches and defending this field as something of a forward reconnaissance, patrol and sally point," he explained, feeling a little foolish. "But that was when I was still under the mistaken impression that I was the senior officer present. Patently, that is not case."

Torrance and beside him, Bill Fielding came to attention and saluted the other man.

Around the room, unbidden, almost in groaning existential relief that at last somebody had stepped forward, others began to do likewise.

George Washington stood like an island in the stream, oddly apart and for a moment, an onlooker might have suspected he was seriously contemplating refusing the command which was being thrust upon his shoulders.

In saying that he had 'resigned' his commission he had stretched the truth somewhat. In fact, he had requested to be assigned to the Reserve on the grounds that he could not afford to devote more than a month a year to military duties; after all, he had a family that depended on him and a ranch to run. Similarly, when he said he had been Mayor of Trinity Crossing a 'few years back', actually he had been Lieutenant Sheriff of the District of Northern Texas until a little less than a year ago, to all intents, the King's representative for most of the several thousands of square miles of the Unincorporated Territory between the Trinity and the Red Rivers.

In both war and peace, duty and service had always weighed heavily on his now stooped shoulders.

George Washington had no fond memories of war, or of leading men in combat. He had been happy, content, in his element ranching the country of his youth before his head had been turned by the bright lights of the East, first at William Penn College in Philadelphia, then as a 'Sword Student' in England at Sandhurst, through baptisms of fire in India and Egypt, where his regiment had guarded the army of men digging that great ditch across the desert to link the Mediterranean to the Red Sea, before returning a decade later to the land of his birth where brutal attrition and defeat had elevated him from brevet battalion command to acting Brigadier, 1st Texas Mechanised Infantry in the last Border War. Afterwards, they had made him substantive Colonel, stuck a Military Cross on his chest and offered him a garrison post down on the Border.

Nobody had tried to stop him returning home, by then his twenty-two-year contract with the British Army was at an end, and he had earned the right to give his young family an idyllic home overlooking the valley of the west fork of the Trinity River. It had seemed like a good place to bring up his boys and he and his wife, Mary Dandridge, the Punjab-born daughter of an Indian Army officer, had been happy enough, even when the droughts of the last few years bit hard.

He had known that this new war had been coming a long time; only the fools in Philadelphia had not noticed the writing on the wall, turned a blind eye to the emissaries of the Mexican Republic who had travelled these lands with impunity, salting the battlefield and seducing the unwary and the Catholic-minded to defect, or leastways, to stand aside when the armies of New Spain came north to reclaim what, to a man, its fighting men believed was their birth right.

There had been many times over the years when he had asked himself if he ought to try to do something about the malaise but he had fallen out of contact with old friends from his Army days; and wanted only to build a new, second life in this country; God's own land.

George Washington met the eye of the dapper, dark-eyed man beside the young pilot. Unlike Torrance, who seemed relieved to be able to pass on the burden of command; Sergeant Fielding was giving him a very odd look.

As if he had seen a ghost...
The older man returned the salutes.
Oh, well!
What will be; will be.

He looked around the room, made eye contacts with two men who had until then, been anonymous in the crowd.

"William, Israel," he said, in that moment taking command. "Take a couple of men with you down to Trinity Crossing. Requisition that bulldozer they've been using to lay out the new town square and any tractors you can lay your hands on. While you're at it, shake out anybody who hasn't reported for militia duty as yet, and summon the townsfolk to a public meeting in the Chapel for six o'clock this evening. I will address the County at that hour. Any questions?"

There were no questions.

George Washington turned to Greg Torrance.

"You will command all pilots and air crew. Please report to me later this day how many aircraft are airworthy. You spoke of building a radio?" This was posed rhetorically. "Good. We'll need more than one. Once you have got us back in contact with headquarters, send technicians to the local farmsteads and haciendas; most of the estates and ranches have their own radio sets. Borrow them if possible, otherwise, requisition them."

"Yes, sir," the two CAF men chorused.

"That is all. Please carry on."

Chapter 16

Monday 1st May
Portsmouth Admiralty Dockyards, Norfolk, Virginia

Commander Alexander Lincoln Fielding, sporting the ribbon of his newly acquired Navy Cross on the left breast of his uniform jacket beneath his wings, wandered with the other officers from the Perseus, back down the length of the huge, drained graving dock. No 4 Dock was one of three at Portsmouth which had been extended by some one hundred and fifty feet to accommodate the Navy's big carriers. The dimensions of the dock and the ship in it boggled the human imagination. Leastways, it boggled Alex Fielding's credulity, and as anybody who had ever met him could attest, he was not a man easily impressed!

The great, looming hulk of the wounded, thousand-feet-long, forty-four thousand ton – that was just empty! – HMS Ulysses blotted out the sky above his head as it rested on a thousand, precisely placed wooden blocks positioned so as to evenly spread the weight of the leviathan. Everything about the mighty, beached whale of a ship was stupendous, from her keel to the top of her island bridge she was higher than most skyscrapers, her four enormous three-bladed screws could drive her through the water at over thirty-three knots – that was thirty-seven-and-a-half miles-an-hour on land – and she needed a crew of over three thousand men to steam, fight and to launch and recover her design complement of eighty-two fighting aircraft.

Two things had saved the leviathan when that torpedo had ruptured and ignited – by one of those cruel twists of fate that war manifests struck her Achilles heel – the aft high octane fuel main and sparking a fire, initially on the rearward hangar deck which, fanned by the movement of the ship, had roared unstoppably up onto the flight deck where the last of the carrier's Sea Eagles, fuelled and bombed up had been neatly lined up for take-off.

Much of what followed had already been intensely analysed; inevitably, and fundamental questions had been asked about the design of the Royal Navy's huge new fleet carriers.

What had been learned – nothing quite so accelerated 'learning' as actual battle experience – was both troubling and oddly, reassuring.

It had been a pure fluke that the torpedo had hit where it had and caused a theoretically improbable rupture in a heavily armoured high-octane conduit. However, despite this the Ulysses had survived.

Lessons...

Firstly, the fire had broken out, and the seat of that fire had remained, contained within the armoured box of her hangar deck, which ran over two-thirds of the length of the vessel, and despite the main fire main also having been cracked by the torpedo hit which was the cause of all the problems in the first place, the hangar deck's integral fire suppression system had, on its first test in earnest, almost certainly saved the day.

Secondly, although the fire had spread – via the after aircraft elevator

– to the flight deck where several aircraft, their fuel and bomb loads had been consumed in the blaze; fortunately, the majority of the Ulysses's aircraft had already taken off, and the deck crew had managed to push five of the ten aircraft still on deck over the side before the fire engulfed them and their munitions had started 'cooking off'.

Several bombs – including three five-hundred pounders - had exploded on the flight deck and the fires, up top, had raged for well over an hour-and-a-half most of the damage had turned out to be relatively superficial. The design concept of making the flight deck an integral 'strength deck' had been wholly vindicated. Likewise, the associated concept of building the hangar deck as, in effect, a giant armoured box, had ensured structural integrity was never threatened and that once the wreckage of the four planes undergoing servicing near the seat of the fire had been cleared away, and the stern elevator repaired – probably the most challenging element of the repair program – the ship would swiftly be back in business.

As to the flight deck, the dockyard was already peeling and cutting away the distorted, splintered plating directly above the still intact armoured roof - up to three inches thick - of the hangar deck, preparatory to 'resurfacing' the rear four hundred and forty-seven feet of decking.

Obviously, nothing was as simple in practice as it was in theory; the landing systems had been destroyed, as had the hydraulic mechanisms tensioning the 'traps', the steel hawsers, wires that 'caught' a plane when it landed, and light anti-aircraft weaponry and other equipment had been wrecked but essentially, the ship was sound and it was confidently predicted, that in between six and eight weeks she would be ready to rejoin the Fleet.

As yet, the dockyard had done nothing about the fifteen feet wide by seventeen feet high hole caused by the explosion of the submarine-launched single torpedo – one of at least four launched at the carrier, apparently – which had struck the ship's port side approximately sixteen feet below the waterline between frame fifty-six and fifty-seven, some two hundred-and-thirty-five feet forward of the stern.

The ship's plates were twisted inward as if Ulysses had been hit by a giant sledgehammer.

The fish had exploded on contact with the outer plating and its warhead, its effect multiplied by hydrostatic forces, had punched through the carrier's double hull like a fist through paper. The Navy's boffins had studied the hole and determined that it had been caused by the detonation of approximately seven hundred-and-fifty pounds of, probably, 'enhanced high-explosive'.

'Bloody hell,' Alex Fielding thought to himself, 'no wonder the powers that be decided they wanted to ban submarines back in the mid-1960s!' And, 'no wonder the top brass is absolutely livid that two of their biggest ships – the battlecruiser Indomitable, and now the Ulysses - had, thus far, been so badly damaged by internationally *outlawed weapons*.'

Worse, the very existence of the Spanish submarines had forced the Fleet to fight at long-range and compelled a hurried, somewhat ad hoc re-writing of the rulebook of naval warfare.

It was hardly any surprise that people in New England, and presumably, back in the Old Country, were presently asking themselves what the Navy was doing?

The answer, of course, was that the Navy was licking its wounds prior to getting stuck in again with a vengeance. However, with the sinking of the Indomitable in Mobile Bay, the crippling of the Ulysses and the loss of so many of her aircraft – although most of her birds had landed on the Perseus there had been no room for all those kites on her flight deck so they had had to go over the side – and the threat of the submarine menace ever-present, there was an awful lot of head-scratching going on at Norfolk trying to work out how exactly, the Royal Navy was going to reassert its supremacy over the waters of the Gulf of Spain and the Caribbean when clearly, not even Atlantic waters were safe!

Alex had been staring into the dark depths of the great gash in the carrier's flank for some moments, unaware of anything going on around him.

"It's Fielding, isn't it?"

For once in his life Alex had been, quite literally, lost in his thoughts.

He had steered clear of the gaggle of senior officers down at the other end of the dry dock when he had descended into its depths. He was killing time before he boarded his flight to Bronxwood Aerodrome that afternoon; by tonight he hoped to be holding his nineteen-day-old son, Alex junior, in his arms for the first time.

Leonora's parents said the baby had his nose. He could not see it himself, or at least, not in the photograph Leonora had sent him of his then, day-old first born. Every baby he had ever laid eyes on looked exactly the same to him but he knew it would be different once he got to hold the little sprog in his own arms.

He would never have visited the dockyard had he not been in such a state of high anxiety about his forthcoming, seventy-two hour-long furlough on Long Island. Which was crazy, not like him at all. Leonora had obviously spun some web of bewitchment about him. That said, now that he was down here, he was fascinated, especially looking into that dark chasm in the great ship's flank.

The new carriers were of all-welded construction; a technique that saved weight – on a ship the size of the Ulysses, up to five or six thousand tons – and, Alex had been assured more than once, made any ship, especially a really big one, a significantly tougher 'nut to crack'. Apparently, rivetted ships of yore had 'worked', much as old-time wooden sailing ships had; and absorbed a little of the motion of the seas. Modern ships were 'stiff', unbending and more easily repaired. Farther aft the sparks of several oxy-acetylene torches showered down the side of the carrier.

The torpedo had stove in the longitudinal, strengthened 'mine bulkhead' – in future they would call that a 'torpedo bulkhead' – seven or eight feet inboard of the outer hull. The impact point had been below the ship's tapering armoured belt, three-and-a-half inches thick in places, and flooded one of the Ulysses's three port fire rooms. Despite the ship being at Battle Stations with all watertight doors dogged shut, each of the three port-side fire rooms had flooded to varying degrees although all the initial fatalities – some twenty-three men – had occurred in the compartment directly breached by the hit.

In all, one hundred and forty-seven men had lost their lives and another two hundred and four had required hospital treatment, of whom nearly fifty had suffered disabling burns.

The man who had called out was approaching.

Alex half-turned, still a little distracted.

Suddenly, he straightened, and put his shoulders back.

It turned out he had been ignoring Admiral Lord Collingwood, C-in-C Atlantic Fleet and the second most senior officer on the latest Navy List.

In desperation he threw a belated salute.

The great man, accompanied by a bevy of staffers and civilian dockyard officials, seemed to tower over Alex. He had only met the C-in-C once, last week when he had pinned that damned medal on his chest. He still thought *that* was a nonsense. If his instruments had been working properly, he would never have had to ditch in the sea, and as for all that tosh about being the 'Pied Piper' of the Atlantic Fleet leading all of Ulysses's returning strike aircraft back to the Perseus, well, that really was gilding the lily!

All he had done was stooge around the Ulysses making sure that the returnees knew which vector to fly to find the Perseus, at the time about eighty miles away and closing the distance with a mighty bone in her teeth.

True, the chill of the sea as he floated around in his little inflatable 'bath' waiting to be picked up, or to drown – he had expected there to be sharks and been disappointed – for the best part of two days had not been a lot of fun. Still, it was good to have had a chance to have a nice long think about things and the feeling in his hands and feet was coming back nicely...

"I was informed you were supposed to be taking a few days well-earned leave, Commander Fielding?"

"Yes, sir. I'm just killing time before I fly out..."

"Jolly good!"

Alex realised that Lord Collingwood, a large, ruddy-face man with eyes that missed absolutely nothing, had gently waved away the rest of his entourage.

The two men stood a few feet apart from the others.

"When I joined the Navy," Collingwood remarked cheerfully, "a hit like that would have sprung every rivet for ten, fifteen feet or more either side of that hole. Ulysses would have been out of action for six months!"

Alex had no idea what he was supposed to say; so, for once in his life he held his piece.

The C-in-C peered into the chasm above them.

"You and I both know that no plan survives first contact with the enemy. We knew the Spaniards, the Triple Alliance were preparing for war and had been for some years," he confessed, without deprecation, simply stating a fact. "But German re-armament in Europe meant that the priority was home defence, the security of Europe, not that of New England which, when all is said and done, is just one among several imperial imponderables. India is another, obviously, and of course, Africa baffles us all." He gestured at the great hole in the ship. "We even anticipated *that*, or something like it. Crying wolf, however, was never an option for reasons which will become clear to you in the days, or at most, the weeks to come."

Alex opened his mouth to speak, bewildered.

"I planned to have this little chat with you when you returned from Long Island, Commander," Collingwood confided. "So, this encounter is serendipitous. I want you to accept a permanent commission in the Royal Naval Air Service. It goes without saying that your present rank would be made substantive. I have plenty of sea-going captains with the aggressive, never-say-die spirit we are going to need in the coming months, and possibly years. However, the RNAS is still young, and its esprit de corps a fragile thing threatened by its rapid expansion. I badly need chaps exactly like you to command *my* carrier-borne air wings."

"Er, I don't know what to say, sir," the younger man admitted.

"When you get back from leave you will be returning to Perseus; but only briefly. Report to me when you get back from leave and I'll brief you fully on what I have in mind for your future employment."

Now Alex was blinking like an idiot.

"Our enemies have not rushed into war, Commander," the older man continued, with the unstoppable certainty of a battleship driving through an Atlantic blow. "It was naïve for anybody to think that once the fighting started, it can be switched off, as if by magic. Personally, I did not think things would go so badly for us so quickly; but I knew we would suffer reverses and that, as now, we would be on the defensive and may well be for some time to come. Contrary to public perceptions, our Government in England, and at the highest levels here in New England, understood well enough the storm that was coming. Unfortunately, the peoples of the Empire are not ready, or receptive to the truths of the modern world. Presently, our foes are sowing the whirlwind that one day, they will come to rue. In the meantime, we must stand firm."

Alex had taken it as read that as soon as Perseus had re-victualled and re-armed, and that new aircraft were delivered to bring her air group up to full strength, the Atlantic Fleet would put to sea to smite the Triple Alliance a great, war-winning blow.

Lord Collingwood patted his shoulder.

"Go on leave. Get to know your new son, Fielding. The war will still be here, waiting for you when you get back."

Chapter 17

Monday 1st May
Ducal Palace of Vila Viçosa, the Alenteo, Portugal

The first time Melody had met Queen Sophie and the two Infantas, she had had no idea that the small family only occupied a handful of rooms in the western end of the great palace, or that most of the security – troops and armoured vehicles, and the police manning roadblocks on many of the routes into and through the town of Vila Viçosa – were stationed there solely because the King of Portugal, Carlos III of the House of Orléans-Bourbon, was in residence.

Bizarrely, after a revolution which had exiled the House of Braganza at the beginning of the century, twenty years later the Portuguese parliament had gone, cap in hand to little known side-line of two otherwise extinct Franco-Spanish dynasties in a bid to quell sectarian and ideological schisms and restore what had been, for over half-a-century an obedient, compliant and largely unifying monarchy. That this arrangement had 'worked' for the Portuguese, halting a slide towards civil war and possibly, strengthened democracy over the years was a thing which had had academic historians performing any number of intellectual and perceptual somersaults ever since.

Queen Sophie, Queen in Exile, made no secret of her admiration for the role her Portuguese counterparts had played in the 'quiet revolution' which had seen Portugal transitioning from a failing, bankrupt mother of a sprawling, disintegrating empire forty years ago, to embrace modernity, the arts, and a land whose universities, particularly those of Coimbra and Lisbon, were every bit the equal of their Parisian and British counterparts.

She had nothing but praise for King Carlos II, a quietly-spoken, man who had always led a blameless, fairly anonymous life before he came to the throne; an impeccably constitutional monarch and a rigorously non-partisan head of state, the Portuguese having adopted the 'British model' of kingship back in the 1920s. Carlos, a bookish, scholarly man, kept his head down, only appearing to his people, usually accompanied by his wife, the Queen Consort, Elisabetta, a marvellously comforting, matronly woman, in times of state ceremonial, crisis or tragedy and then, discreetly, returning to his 'quiet' life in a corner of one or other of the Royal Palaces his unwanted regal role compelled him to inhabit.

The most conspicuous member of the Portuguese Royal Family was Carlos's eldest son, the Prince Royal, now in his mid-thirties who often stood in for his father on overseas forays, and actually, seemed to enjoy the public notoriety he enthusiastically cultivated as 'the People's Prince', attending sporting events and generally living the celebrity lifestyle the King, plainly, despised. It was said that the Prince Royal's French wife, Princess Antoinette Johanna, a willowy blond Austrian-born apparition, who might have stepped straight off a Parisian catwalk, had a knack of invoking mild apoplexy in her regal in-laws; in any event, the couple never stayed at Vila Viçosa.

Melody had imagined her first audience with Queen Sophie would be her last one. Which only went to show that she had been wrong about a lot of things lately.

On her second visit to the Palace, Queen Sophie had introduced Melody to sixty-three year-old Queen Elisabetta, who turned out to be as bubbly and energetic as her public persona, and to Melody's discomfort had instantly started asking her astonishingly perceptive and well-informed questions about the cases she had solved working as a detective in the Crown Colony of New York!

It transpired that the Queen Consort of the Portuguese, an avid reader of detective non-fiction, and fiction and, a fluent English-speaker, liked nothing better than to sit down in front of the television set and watch taped recordings of British and new England crime dramas and whodunnits!

It was all a little bit overwhelming...

Yesterday, Melody had marshalled the courage to press Queen Sophie further about what she had said to her during their first bewildering encounter. In retrospect, everything had seemed unreal that day, and Melody badly needed a little clarity.

Today, Alonso had had to go to Lisbon.

Apparently, the Spanish Government – if such a thing meaningfully existed at present, which was a moot point – had started legal proceedings to sequester the Medina Sidonia estates in Portugal. Or rather the authorities in Madrid had commenced actions to pass the administration of those estates to the Mother Church in Portugal, disregarding the fact that under Portuguese Law a Papal Bill of Anathema – ex-communication and disinheritance, etcetera – had no foundation in Civil Law within the borders of Portugal or its overseas dominions, territories and protectorates.

Nevertheless, the futile cases still had to be disputed in the courts.

Thus, Alonso had had to stop pleasuring her at the crack of dawn that morning, to set off for the capital, over ninety miles away, a think Melody resented more than somewhat.

"I'm not ordering you," the exiled monarch laughed, "to marry Alonso. Either you, or your friend, Lady de L'Isle. I'm just saying that it would be the best outcome for Alonso, and whomsoever took him on in matrimony."

Recently, there had been times when Melody suspected her life was turning into a series of scenes from a Restoration comedy of errors.

"Look," she tried to explain, "I'm Alonso's mistress. We're fairly discreet about it but it is not exactly a state secret," she had reminded the Queen, whom, even though she was never anything less than regal, had demonstrated a wickedly dry sense of humour and self-evidently, intuitively seemed to treat Melody like a kindred spirit. "So, obviously, I'm middlingly stupid about him. But Henrietta…"

"Ah," the other woman sighed. She thought for a few seconds, and seemed to come to a decision. "Throughout our lives, and especially when Alonso was on his travels in the Philippine lands and in New England, he wrote to me, and I to him. The farther away he was the more often he wrote. Almost daily, these last few years, after he was banished to New England..."

"Banished?" Melody interjected.

"Oh, yes."

"Because of Pedro?"

The Queen was thoughtful.

"Let us just say that when the circumstances of the child's birth were brought to the attention of the King's ministers," she shrugged, smiling tight-lipped, "there were consequences. Poor Alonso became, unofficially, you understand, persona non grata at the Escorial. What with one thing and another his posting to the Philippines and later to Philadelphia was for the best."

Alonso had never said anything to Melody about writing letters to his Queen but then she had always allowed the men in her life their little secrets; that was the deal, she had her secrets, they had theirs.

Queen Sophie continued, a wryness in her eyes if not her voice: "You must understand that in Spain there were always several competing *courts*. The King's, the Mother Church's, the Navy's, and the Army's, and mine, and imperial diplomats abroad would traditionally communicate, as they saw fit, with each, or all according to the trust invested in them by whichever faction they imagined to be in the ascendant in Madrid; often, although not invariably, a thing determined by the attitudes and vested interests of the aristocratic and military classes. Oddly, and certainly counter-intuitively, it was much easier to sustain a confidential correspondence with Alonso when he was in the Philippines or in Philadelphia, than it was when he was in Spain. But that is by the by, as they say."

Alonso had warned Melody that the Queen turned away most prospective visitors: although few foreign officials wanted to complicate their government's affairs by treating with an exile, there was a plethora of private citizens either seeking her support for treason, or to beg for this or that indulgence, few if any of which she was in any position to entertain, and numerous agent provocateurs scheming to implicate her in spurious intrigues against the factions vying for power in Madrid.

So, a purely social visitor, like Melody, was a breath of fresh air.

"I learned many things about New England from Alonso's letters," the Queen explained. "For example, he was fascinated when the Governor, Lady De L'Isle's father, a man for whom he has the most profound respect, brought you in to 'ventilate' the Empire Day farrago. Henrietta had mentioned your name to him several times before then but he had taken what he had heard with a pinch of salt. And besides, the only woman in New England who had remotely interested him until you accepted the poison chalice, had always been Henrietta." The Queen smiled, a little sadly, Melody thought, albeit for a fleeting moment and thereafter she almost suspected she had imagined it. "Whom," the other woman went on, "he clearly adored, then as now."

Melody said nothing.

"Poor Alonso, it is just like him to fall for the one woman in New England who was, literally, untouchable."

They had spoken of other things, both a little distractedly.

Alonso was ex-communicated, his Catholic marriage automatically annulled; and he was, therefore, now free to marry whomsoever he pleased.

"May I write to you, Your Majesty?" Melody inquired when the women were parting.

The Infantas had been summoned and Queen Sophie had walked her visitor to the inner gates of Palace. The two women were simpatico, felt comfortable in each other's company and had, possibly, already formed the basis of an enduring friendship.

"I would be deeply offending if you did not, Melody," the other woman replied. "If, and when, we meet again, in private, I would much prefer you to simply refer to me as 'Sophie'." This was accompanied by an uncharacteristically nervy, short laugh. "I think in years to come I will be in need of 'real' friends."

Nevertheless, Melody had bowed her head.

"You and me both," she speculated ruefully.

Afterwards, returning to her hotel room she had laid down on the bed and, exhausted, fallen into a deep dreamless sleep. Everything was clear, her mind was strangely uncluttered. It was dark when the knock at her door awakened her. Groping for the bedside light switch she had stumbled to the door.

Alonso had smiled.

Melody stifled a yawn.

Oh, God! I must look a mess...

The man stepped into the room and reached for her.

She stepped away. "No, no," she muttered, shaking her head.

"What is it?"

If Melody had been more awake, her head less befuddled she might have not blurted her reply so gauchely, as if she was in some way an injured party.

"Why didn't you tell me you loved Henrietta all along?"

If Melody had ever suspected – and she had not – that her lover was a natural-born dissembler, she would have been comprehensively disabused of the notion a moment later.

The man hesitated, sighed.

"Because... In Philadelphia... Even had Henrietta done me the honour of reciprocating my affection she would have been in an impossible situation; especially, after the Empire Day atrocities. And yes, before you ask me," he went on, "I do feel guilty taking you from her, even though I know that sounds ridiculous!"

Melody was not angry.

This was more about resolving her own emotions.

She turned away but did not resist when the man came up behind her and gently wrapping his arms about her, drew her against him, his lips nuzzling her left ear.

That was cheating!

Men!

Chapter 18

Tuesday 2nd May
Charlottenburg Palace, Berlin

"You're joking!" The King spluttered in disbelief.

Five minutes ago, he had been enjoying a convivial luncheon with his wife and a couple of old Kaiserliche Marine friends and their spouses, confidently expecting to enjoy a few days sightseeing and catching up with a clutch of his godchildren. Everybody had expected the Court of Electors – the twenty-two kings, princes and counts, and two princesses of the German Empire – to sit in deliberation for most of the rest of the week. After the endless, wearying, dispiriting funerary ceremonial of the last three days, it had seemed reasonable to expect the Electors to take their time; not to sit down, shut the doors, cursorily chat amongst themselves for a couple of hours and then come out with a verdict before the crowned heads of Europe, and the world leaders still hanging around in the German capital, had had time to digest their luncheons!

Moreover, despite the nervousness of his advisors, practically everybody had taken it as read, that the Crown Prince, forty-four year-old Wilhelm, the old Kaiser's eldest surviving son, was the only serious candidate and although the Court of Electors might haggle and privately seek certain assurances – mainly about the status and privileges of individual Electors – that in the end they would surely row in behind him.

This was in no way an unreasonable expectation.

History bore exemplary witness to the fact that the one thing it was safe to take for granted, was that whatever their faults and foibles, the members of the Court of Electors, tended to be a notoriously unimaginative, and very cautious bunch when they sat down to appoint a candidate to safeguard a tradition dating back to the time of Charlemagne the Great..

Which made the transparent eccentricity of what the King had just been told all the more…*extraordinary.*

Sir George Horace Walpole, the King's Foreign and Colonial Secretary, was as surprised as anybody. In fact, he was struggling to keep a straight face, undecided whether the whole thing was some huge practical joke or simply, a very, very bad dream.

The sort one might expect to experience after recklessly experimenting with hallucinogenic drugs…

It happened that the King of Bavaria, Ludwig Maximillian VI, was a mild-mannered, God-fearing man in his late fifties who had never really taken much interest in getting involved with his kingdom's internecine political machinations. By all accounts he was a decent, somewhat indecisive man, rather hen-pecked by his wife, Alexandra, a waspish woman younger by some fifteen years who had thus far born him two teenage daughters, and latterly, begun to meddle around the edges of the turbulent Munich political hothouse.

"They've named poor old Ludwig Emperor?" The King demanded,

only partially ventilating a positively volcanic excess of sudden existential angst. He turned to his wife, who had followed her husband out of the dining room and heard the raised voices. "They've only gone and passed over Willie for that chap down in Munich!"

"Ludwig?" Eleanor murmured, dazed. "Surely not?"

George Walpole coughed respectfully.

"I fear there is no doubt, Ma'am. The Proclamation of Succession has already been promulgated. The Imperial Government has resigned pending the pleasure of the Emperor designate."

"Marvellous!" The King muttered in exasperation. "What the Devil is going on, Walpole?" He put, testily, to his Foreign and Colonial Secretary.

"If I was to speculate, sir," his old friend offered, "I'd say that the Electors have had their fill of strong leadership."

The Queen shared her husband's anxiety.

"Willie won't take this very well, Bertie," she said, voicing what they were all thinking.

The Kronprinz – or rather, the former Kronprinz – was not a man known for his patience, of for his propensity to take a slight, less still a punch to the solar plexus like this, with a smile. Moreover, given that Wilhelm was now King of Prussia, by far the most powerful economically and militarily, and in terms of population and geographic weight three times the size of the next three largest 'electorates', the decision of King Wilhelm VI of Prussia's fellow Electors was nothing short of...dangerously *eccentric.*

"The Government has resigned, you say?" The King queried.

"Yes," his Foreign Secretary nodded, "although in theory the ministers will stay in post in the interregnum before the new Kaiser makes his own appointments, sir."

"Have you spoken to Lothar?"

"Count Bismarck is currently incommunicado," Walpole explained, trying to conceal how worried he was by his counterpart's unwillingness to either take his call, or for his staff to agree a time or a venue for a meeting. No matter how fraught things had been in the past the two men had always been able to thrash things out, face to face. "I suspect, Lothar is fully occupied attempting to ascertain from the new Kaiser's advisors their attitude to the pressing matters of the day."

The King remembered his luncheon guests; it was inexcusable ignoring them this way!

"I'll rely on you to keep us abreast of developments, George," he declared and ushered Eleanor back into the dining room.

That there were no riots on the streets of Berlin that afternoon was probably a good sign; however, neither the King or the Queen, or their senior ministers took much comfort from this. They had come to the German capital with a secret to manage, and to divulge to, they assumed, the Crown Prince, upon his accession to the Imperial Throne. Now they had no way of knowing if 'coming clean' would be for the good, or ill. Or even if Wilhelm, bless him, given that he had been the candidate of both the Army and the Navy, would meekly accept the decision of the other twenty-three Electors.

Concern deepened on this score as the minutes ticked by without anybody being able to contact the disposed Crown Prince. If he chose to seize the throne denied him by the princelings of the other half – well, slightly less than half by population, wealth and acreage of land – it was well within Wilhelm's ability to mount a coup; Berlin was, after all, the capital of his kingdom, Prussia.

As time went by the phone lines to London began to burn.

And then, at around seven that evening, as the light faded and dark, rain-bearing clouds began to collect over Saxony, a cortege of half-a-dozen big black limousines pulled into the square in front of the Charlottenburg Palace, the red and blue lights of several motorbike outriders sparkling brightly through the light rain and the thickening darkness.

"King Wilhelm of Prussia requests an audience, sir," the King's Secretary reported. "He apologises for quote: 'suddenly turning up like this"

"Summon the Foreign Secretary please."

The King was already on his feet.

Six black-garbed troopers of the Prussian Royal Guard had preceded their monarch into the building and taken up protective positions, and postures, the muzzles of their automatic rifles pointed to the floor, their eyes searching, searching as if they fully anticipated a battalion of assassins to spring, as if by some dark magic, from the doors, or even from the very walls themselves of the high-ceilinged reception room. Fortunately, the men and women of the British Royal Protection Squad were not entirely unaccustomed to the uncompromising methods of their Germanic counterparts, and contented themselves with merely fingering their mostly, concealed and rather more discreetly carried firearms. The principle which applied was: *when in Rome behave as one has observed the Romans behaving.*

Wilhelm Frederick von Hohenzollern, Wilhelm IV of Prussia and until a few hours ago, Crown Prince and in effect, de facto Regent, of the German Empire, strode into the Charlottenburg Palace in the uniform of a Colonel of the 1st Mounted Regiment of the *Deutsches Heer,* the Imperial German Army, his ceremonial sword jangling at his side.

He wore the tabs of the *Grosser Generalstab* – the Great General Staff – on his lapels. The King tried hard not to frown: he had never known his cousin to sport *those* tabs in all the years of their acquaintance and had a horrible premonition that everything could suddenly fly out of hand at any moment.

The forty-four year-old son of the former Kaiser was hot, flushed, and angrily impatient until he realised that Eleanor and one of her ladies in waiting were present. Instantly, he mellowed, bowed gallantly and miraculously, with a supreme effort of will, sobered.

"I', sorry about this," he growled. "Turning up like this without a by your leave, and all that! I must speak to you alone," he continued, looking directly at the King.

The monarch raised an eyebrow.

"And with Sir George and Ellie, obviously," their visitor agreed tersely.

Eleanor stepped forward and assured him that they were delighted to see him. Because it was her, Wilhelm almost believed it. Soon his seconds and the crowd of courtiers had been invited to leave the day room into which Wilhelm, the Royal couple and the Foreign and Commonwealth Secretary had gravitated.

Nobody sat down and briefly the only sound was of the rain beginning to batter at the tall windows overlooking the landscaped grounds of the Palace.

"The bastards didn't tell me until the old fool was dead," Wilhelm complained, starting to pace. By way of a preamble it failed to communicate anything other than his seething inner outrage. "And none of those bloody 'Electors' have a clue! Not one of them! And as for that dummkopf Ludwig..."

The King and Queen exchanged looks.

It was Sir George Walpole who asked pertinent question.

"Forgive me, Your Majesty," he bowed imperceptibly. "Might one presume to inquire what exactly 'they' did not tell you?"

The King of Prussia scowled, shook his head like a Rottweiler just out of the rain.

"The dummkopfs didn't tell me that *we*, the Reich, started, systematically – they were very proud of that - breaking the bloody Submarine Treaty practically the day my dear, lamented, demented if you ask me, father signed it!"

If Wilhelm noticed the way his interlocutors' jaws must have dropped, momentarily, very nearly to the marbled floor at their feet, he was far too wrapped up in his own roiling internal angst to remark upon it. His tone was one of a man betrayed and yet, grudgingly proud; for he was a man clearly caught betwixt and between any number of violently conflicting emotions.

"Dammit, Bertie," he complained. "If I'd known what was going on, I..." He threw his arms about theatrically. "No, that's not true! Actually, I don't know what I'd have done about it! Those 'people' the old man collected around him never trusted me. Now I think about it I wouldn't put it past them to have nobbled half the Court of Electors. Thirteen of the two-faced traitors voted against me," he snarled, "for that nutzloser Haufen Scheiße, Ludwig!"

Useless pile of shit...

Immediately, he apologised for his intemperate language.

He looked to Eleanor.

"Forgive me, please. I am not quite myself today, Ellie."

"That's quite understandable, Willie," she cooed comfortably.

"Anyway, I had to tell you about the Submarine Treaty nonsense," Wilhelm continued, no less agitated. "My father has done enough damage already with us going to war, or some such, over a stupid misunderstanding over the folly and duplicity of a stupid old man, what!"

The King viewed his cousin.

Beside him his Foreign Secretary was wearing a gravely troubled countenance, and he knew that his wife was looking to him for a lead; and yet, he was torn, desperately hoping his own shame was not as transparent as it felt to him, as he met Wilhelm's imploring gaze.

"Yes," he murmured, "now, about the Submarine Treaty..."

Impulsively, the younger man, having paused pacing, resumed his movements as if unwilling or unable to meet the King of England's eye.

King George opened his mouth to speak but was pre-empted, beaten to the punch by Wilhelm.

"It's incredible! Unbelievable! *They've* been building a couple of experimental nuclear-powered ships, and what *they* call a 'test bed' submarine 'hull' in the Baltic. Apparently, *they* hollowed out a whole damned island up there so they could carry on without being seen."

"Ships?"

"Yes, *they* towed a couple of uncompleted heavy cruiser hulls from the yards at Stettin. I know virtually nothing about the submarine, other than the fact it is still about a year away from launching. *They* seemed to have been concentrating on *their* bloody bomb project. There's a facility down in South West Africa, near Walvis Bay. *They've* already tested a couple of small devices down in the Southern Ocean somewhere..."

By this time the King and his wife were silently distraught; and had the former Crown Prince been able to step beyond his own agonising shame he would have realised that he was not alone in his guilt.

So, when Sir George Walpole made as if to question Wilhelm further, his own monarch cut him short.

"Dammit, George," the King muttered. "Enough of this double dealing!"

When the King of England employed his 'captain on the bridge' tone, everybody in any room in Christendom stopped what they were doing, thinking, or planning and looked to him.

Wilhelm was only human.

He halted mid-stride and looked to his fellow monarch.

The older man was grim-faced.

"I regret to have to confess to you that you are not the only one whose government has been keeping you, or I, in the dark, Willie. Before the Queen and I left England, we too, were briefed about matters of which, until a few days ago, I assure you on my word as an officer and a gentleman, that we had absolutely no inkling."

Eleanor moaned a soft sigh.

"Bertie and I were livid when we discovered what had been done in our name."

"I don't..."

The King raised a hand, unwilling to allow his cousin to voice additional hostages to fortune.

"We too, the British Empire, have been systematically flouting the spirit, and the letter of the Submarine Treaty, Willie. My ministers asked me to broach this matter with the new Kaiser, whom, we all confidently expected to be *you* at the earliest possible time."

Wilhelm was too stunned to say anything for some seconds.

Then: "You've got the bomb?"

The older man nodded.

"We have had it for several years, actually."

"And ships?"

"Submarines, yes."

"And you never knew?"

Both the King and the Queen shook their heads, emphatically.

Presently, Sir George Walpole became aware that he was the sole object of attention in the room. He had always intended to come clean at some stage, one day but his good intentions had been thwarted, first by his losing office and then when he was back in government, by the diktat of successive Prime Ministers, Chiefs of the Imperial General Staff, and to a man, the last three First Sea Lords.

"I was Prime Minister at the time Project Poseidon was initiated, Your Majesty," he confessed to the King of Prussia. "That was prior to the signing of the Submarine Treaty but I acquiesced, when the decision was taken to redouble the Empire's efforts to build a viable atomic weapon and to harness the power of the atom for future civil, and as a priority, military uses. We suspected, and later became aware – in general terms – that the nuclear planning and design bureaus active in the German Empire prior to the Treaty, had not been disbanded post-signature and ratification. Likewise, we were cognisant of the German Empire's experimental establishments on Rugen Island and upon the Peenemunde Isthmus. As for the Walvis Bay facility, we have been monitoring that for some years, at first because we assumed it was a base from which agents of the German Empire and their Boer collaborators, were attempting to foment an uprising against our interests in the Cape. Later, we detected traces of radioactive contamination some miles offshore, and in the northern Cape, and drew the obvious conclusions that relatively small Uranium bombs must have been tested somewhere in the Kalahari Desert. That would have been about three years ago."

Wilhelm's mouth opened and shut.

Words would not come as the revelations assailed him, pummelling him from every direction as if he was a defeated pugilist being driven across the ring in the last seconds of an already lost prize fight.

A dreadful rage began to play, like fire, in his dark eyes.

He had come to humbly abase himself before *friends*; and they had treated him like a dummkopf...

His honour meant nothing to these people!

"What you mean is that *you* meant to come to Berlin and present me, as the new Kaiser, with a fait accompli!"

"No, that was not our intention, Willie!" The King remonstrated irritably.

The King of Prussian glared at him.

"It might not have been *your* plan, Bertie. But what of your government?" Wilhelm waved derisively at George Walpole. "You bring with you the man who sees himself as the puppet master of the civilised world! The man who would keep the German beast in its cage! The man who wrote the Submarine Treaty to ensure that the German Empire could never achieve the living space it needs, or to obtain the oil it must have if it is to ever rival the industrial might of New England!"

Lebensraum...

Oil...

"Unbelievable!" Wilhelm cried out. It was like a roar of pain; signifying the final betrayal. "I come here to try to make things right with people I once thought were my family, my friends and what do I get? Stabbed in the back! That's what I get for trying to do the right thing! I seek peace and what I discover is that you 'people' have been laughing behind my back, behind my father's back, behind the back of the whole German people!"

If the King, Queen or the immediate object of Wilhelm's ire had been so naïve as to take comfort from the fact that they were being berated by the King of Prussia, not the Kaiser, they were soon to be disabused of the last scintilla of their complacency.

"Damn you, Bertie! Damn you! I thought you at least were a man I could do business with!"

"Willie, I *am* a man you can do business with!" The King barked angrily, which was probably the worst thing he could have done.

"Seriously?" The King of Prussia bellowed. "I came here to make things right. To start my reign with a gesture of good will. I was going to offer to scrap Projektende der Tage..."

Project End of days...

"I'd have sent half the bloody Kaiserliche Marine to the breakers if that was the price for a treaty that gave the Empire lebensraum and access to the oil fields that we need to fulfil our rightful racial destiny!"

Nobody tried to gainsay him.

"Why on earth would I make a deal with the bloody Russians if we could sort everything out with our Aryan brothers in England and its White Dominions? But, oh no! You have to trip us up at every bloody turn! I don't know how *you* did it," Wilhelm shouted at Sir George Walpole, "but if you think persuading those dummkopfs to Elect that prissy old fart Ludwig is going to stop me," his face was red, he was sweating and when he spoke spittle flecked the air, "you've got another bloody thing coming!"

With which, he turned on his heel and stormed out of the Charlottenburg Palace.

Chapter 19

Tuesday 2nd May
Gravesend, Long Island

Alex Fielding had been a little – just a little because the events of the last year or so had confirmed him in the opinion that faint hearts never won a damned thing in this world – *thoughtful* about bringing his wife and baby son back to what had been the Fielding family home of his youth.

On the face of it the Jamaica Bay Road district was not exactly Leonora's *style* but he suspected that these days neither the high life, or living in a Shinnecock Hills mansion was her *thing*, either.

He had taken his gurgling, barely three-week old son Alexander Lincoln Fielding from his wife's arms to allow her to get out of the car – an old sportster he had borrowed from an old CAF friend for the duration of his brief leave – and was loathe to hand him back.

"I always knew you were just an old softie!" Leonora declared triumphantly.

"Guilty as charged!"

Leonora viewed the old house, boarded up since the time of the Empire Day atrocities, the garden in front of it overgrown, something of an eyesore.

"Weird," she sighed. "That I've never been here until now."

"It's the first time I've seen the old place in years," Alex admitted. In other circumstances it might have been a good place to bring up a family." He hesitated. "This is the sort of size of place the Navy provides for Commanders and their families..."

"Are you trying to say that you want me to move down to Norfolk?"

"No," Alex chuckled, flashing a smile, rocking his baby son in his arms.

"Oh," Leonora was stupid about her husband but she was not, per se, dumb about anything in particular and guessed that he had brought her out here because he had something on his mind. "Come on! Out with it, Mister!"

"I will be going back to Norfolk, *this* time. But in a couple of months, maybe sooner, I'm likely to be headed for the West Coast. Vancouver probably. Then, probably to the Sandwich Islands. The Navy is building a base the size of Norfolk out there." It all came out with a guilty rush. "The war with the Spanish isn't going to be over any time soon, or maybe not this year or next. We weren't ready and it will take a while to get up to speed, re-arm and all that stuff. Besides, looking ahead, it seems that the Government back in England is as worried about the Japanese, and the Russians, I suppose, in the Far East almost as much as they are about the Spaniards right now. Anyway, to cut a long story short, I've been asked to work up a new air group on the West Coast."

"And you said 'yes'," Leonora decided, not really needing him to spell out any of the reasons why. She had had her eyes wide open marrying Alex Lincoln Fielding. "What about me and your son?"

Alex was feeling anxious; an odd sensation.

"I rather hoped you'd come with me, actually."

Leonora nodded noncommittally and wandered up the path to the porch of the house, the knee and waist high vegetation brushing her skirt.

"Who owns this place nowadays?" She asked.

Her husband followed in her footsteps.

"My Pa never made a will. I'm the oldest, I guess I own it."

Ever practical, Leonora asked: "Why haven't you sold it?"

"Never got around to it. Or even really thought about it..."

"What are the Sandwich Islands like?" Leonora thought they were talking about tropical islands in the middle of the Pacific Ocean but it paid to check.

"Paradise."

"There's no such thing."

"I reckon I'm in paradise every time I'm with you, my love," Leonora's husband declaimed gallantly.

She scoffed at this: "Men!"

Until then she had been thinking more about moving into an apartment in Manhattan, on the West Side within walking distance of Maud's place. Of course, at the moment Maud was a little preoccupied with her own, personal hero. She guessed her friend would dive head first into domestic bliss, a thing Leonora had never seriously contemplated for herself. And yet now she was being asked to be a 'proper' Navy wife.

It was a funny old world.

"Vancouver? You said Vancouver? That's cold and rainy and winter goes on half the year up there?"

"Well, the base is actually some way to the south. A place called Tacoma, in the northern Oregon Territory." Alex hoped he was not sounding too vague or evasive, knowing that his wife was not the sort of girl to allow him to get away with fobbing her off with a lot of 'need to know' excuses.

With this to the forefront of his mind, even though Admiral Lord Collingwood had, strictly speaking, dismissed him by that stage of their conversation in the huge graving dock at Portsmouth; Alex had stood his ground, taken his courage in his hands and respectfully asked the great man what exactly he had in mind for him.

The C-in-C Atlantic Fleet had thought about it, probably contemplated keeping him on tenterhooks but then, with a mildly amused, harrumphing sigh, gestured for him to walk with him as he continued his inspection of the wounded Ulysses.

'Yes,' Admiral Collingwood had grimaced. 'Fair enough...'

The second most senior flag officer on the Navy List had confided to Alex how he meant to give the Spanish a 'really sharp kick in the backside at the earliest opportunity' within the month. Longer-term, with ships drawn from the Pacific Fleet and the Squadron already based at Vancouver, he planned to definitively tip the strategic balance before the end of the year.

'In the last war we put troops ashore at San Francisco, scared the life out of the enemy. They sued for peace after that. This time around they are stronger, they have better aircraft, and an army that doesn't turn tail and run at the first sign of trouble. Moreover, they've made their plans for the long run; we haven't, so we too, must now play the long game. Back home they will allow themselves to get distracted by the inhabitants of the Greater Antilles but the Cubans, Hispanics and Dominicans are nothing without the wealth, industry, oil of the southern Caribbean and the ideological, not theocratic motivation of the Mexicans. The Mexicans are the real enemy in this war and we must never take our eye off the ball!"

Unfortunately, that was not the way the East Coast New England media was reporting the war. The popular call was to invade Hispaniola or Cuba and supposedly 'cut the Triple Alliance in half!' As for the collapse of the whole eastern flank – effectively, the line of the Rio Grande – it was a case of lions being led by mules! Everybody from the Governor in Philadelphia to the Prime Minister in London was being blamed for the 'woeful state of colonial defences in New England', the 'obsolescence of the Royal Navy's big ships and the inept, brainless tactics of the admirals.'

Remember Brave Achilles was the mantra of the Colonial Legislatures of the First Thirteen; if only the 'great men' in Government House and at Fleet Headquarters in Norfolk had a tiny fraction of the pluck and never-say-die spirit of the men of the Achilles, all would be well in the blink of an eye!

And as for the Navy's hugely expensive new fleet aircraft carriers; the first time they had seen action their squadrons had been decimated and one of them had very nearly been destroyed by 'a single mine'.

A mine...

Nobody was brave enough to say the 'S' word.

The battlecruiser Indomitable had been torpedoed by enemy destroyers, it seemed; not the submersible that one of her escorts had rammed!

In retrospect, Alex now realised he had just been a kid in the last war, wet behind the ears and lucky to live through it. In the process he had learned to fly – really fly – and developed a psychological carapace it was likely he was going to need in the coming months, and if things went badly, years.

Up here on Long Island the war was an awfully long way away. Legislators were still discussing the proposed colony by colony reintroduction of the draft. Wisely, the Governor was giving the First Thirteen the opportunity to exert their 'colonial responsibilities' as well as their 'colonial rights' before he mandated conscription across the board. Presently, the unemployed, and in the view of the armed services, far too many 'unemployable' men were only trickling through recruitment centres, their numbers padded out by returning veterans and the odd patriot. It was not good enough. Volunteers from the sparsely-populated Canadian dominions were not going to fill the gaps in the line, nor, in the short-term were troops from the Old Country, or India, Africa or Australasia. Worse, the rout in the South West had finally proven that the poorly trained local militias and the understrength, ill-equipped and poorly-trained formations parsimoniously supplied by the East Coast colonies were no substitute for professionals such as the regular troops of the Indian and British Armies.

The catastrophe of Mobile Bay was no kind of rallying cry.

Likewise, the saving of the Ulysses.

The Navy had thus far managed to keep secret the flight of its last major warship in the Gulf of México, the cruiser Devonshire, which after disengaging from the action off Mobile Bay had had to flee from yet another rag-tag fleet of old ironclads and smaller, relatively modern frigates and destroyers, finally escaping into the, where it was dodging Triple Alliance hunting groups somewhere southeast of Jamaica as, with her magazines nearly empty and her bunkers running low, she crept eastward to rendezvous with friendly forces.

When Alex had left Norfolk the two cruisers and five destroyers had been departing harbour to reinforce the Fifth Cruiser Squadron already on station waiting to meet, or in extremis, to enter the Caribbean to aid the Devonshire.

Leonora sat on the step and took her son back, rearranging his shawl. Alex settled beside her and together they stared at the car parked beyond the bushes, which were swaying gently in the breeze.

"I think about what happened to Abe," she confessed suddenly. "I don't know what I'd do if the same thing happened to you."

Alex tried not to think overlong about his youngest brother's fate. Missing meant dead most times; and Abe had been missing a long time now. He thought about that day he had visited Kate in Norfolk. She had been in denial. Perhaps, that was the best way to be?

"I'm indestructible."

"No, that's the trouble. You're a tough guy but you're not indestructible."

"They're making me a CAW," he said defensively. "Commander Air Wing, that mean's I don't get to fly regular missions. Or, necessarily, to fly at all!"

"No," his wife smiled ruefully, "you won't let that happen."

They had known this moment would come, sooner or later.

Leonora made a confession.

"I knew what I was getting into the first time I saw you, Alex," she sighed. "Remember, that was the time you tried to get me killed?"

The man guffawed.

"That was a heck of a day, wasn't it?"

Leonora gave him an unconvincing long-suffering look.

Her husband chuckled roguishly.

"Honestly, tell me that wasn't the most fun you'd ever had in your life?" Alex pressed, a mischievous twinkle in his gaze. "Well, until you sprung me from jail. After that, we really, really had some fun!"

She leaned against him.

"Yeah," she admitted reluctantly. "And yes, again."

Feeling a little left out young Alex began to cry.

"I think he's hungry," the sleep-deprived mother groaned, irritated that every eye in the houses nearby was most likely staring at them through lace curtains. She stood up, turned around and with her back to the street put her son to her left teat, quieting him instantly.

Alex got up, a little unsure what he was supposed to do.

"As soon as he's had his fill he'll piss or poop his pants," Leonora declared, mildly accusatively, "just like a man!"

Alex put his arm around her and kissed her hair.

"I'm sorry. I shouldn't just dump all this on you out of the blue..."

"Don't start apologising for everything, sweetheart."

"Sorry," he retorted.

Leonora giggled.

"Don't be. Until I met you, I was going to be rich and idle all my life. I guess I'm still rich, I am an heiress, after all. But the idle bit had already got old by the time you tried to get us both killed on Empire Day. I didn't think I'd ever be a Navy wife but I suppose that's better than being a rich bitch wife of a banker or a lawyer, or a politician, so, I'm okay with that. Maybe, following you around the Empire was the way it was always supposed to be. Anyway, what's the choice? Staying here on Long Island making another baby with you every time you come home every two or three years? Or actually being your wife?"

Alex shifted on his feet, suddenly foolish.

"You've got all this worked out, haven't you?" He concluded ruefully.

"I was rich and idle, spoilt too, when I met you. I wasn't ever dumb. I wouldn't have married you if I wasn't prepared to follow you wherever. To the ends of the earth, and all that stuff."

She turned her face to him; they kissed unhurriedly.

And then, right on cue, as predicted junior pissed and pooped his pants.

Chapter 20

Wednesday 3rd May
Trinity Crossing, Unincorporated District of Northern Texas

The storm had passed over, the last of the rain having fallen some forty-eight hours ago but the chalky ford across the river was going to be impassable for days, or more likely, weeks. Presently, the Trinity River was in spate and low-lying parts of the sprawling town along its banks were several feet deep in muddy water.

Fifty-seven-year-old George Nathaniel Washington had ridden to the airfield that morning with two of his gauchos, kids he had known most of their lives whom he regarded as kith and kin, from Rancho Mendoza on the grounds north of the east fork of the Trinity River. He did not think he needed bodyguards – his second-in-command, Flight Lieutenant Torrance seemed to have an irrational fear of 'bad Indians' and 'Dominican assassins' – because he knew this country like the back of his hand, this was his home and he was too old to start living in fear at his age.

Nevertheless, riding with young Tom and Henry, he could briefly, forget that he was a soldier again. Presciently, Mary, his wife, had warned him that if he 'got involved' this time around 'they will only make you a general'; and, it was already looking like she was right. Bless her, Mary was usually right. He had known that sooner or later his friends in the Red River highlands would turn to him; it was simply that the arrival of that young tyro, Torrance had hastened the process.

He had left Rancho Mendoza in his old friend Pablo's capable hands. For the while, Pablo's boy, Julio, and his daughter Connie could make themselves useful at Trinity Crossing. Mary had told him not to worry about whatever the youngster got up to 'now that nobody is watching them all the time'. She had always been more laissez faire about 'what the kids got up to' than he had. Not because she had been brought up in India where the 'goings on' within the expatriate community, not to mention its 'dalliances and interactions' with members of the local native gentry, were intrinsically scandalous, which they were in some places; but simply because Mary always chose to see the best in people.

That was a rare gift.

From what he could gather from the High Command in the Delta, everybody assumed that the Mexicans would move north *and* west from San Antonio, and in that event Trinity Crossing was the place to make a stand. He thought that was unlikely, not least because he doubted the Mexicans had the fighting manpower, or the logistics train to sustain two separate lines of advance.

And besides, the Mexicans were not the incompetent idiots those fools in the East painted them!

His old sparring partner General Felipe de Padua María Severino López de Santa Anna y Pérez de Lebrón, the Chief of Staff of the Mexican Armed Forces, was not going to send his troops this far north. That would be too much of a gamble and Santa Anna was just not that kind of general.

It had astonished Washington that hardly anybody in New England remembered Santa Anna from the last war, or had troubled watch his inexorable rise to power in México with anything other than idle, passing interest. But then people on the East Coast had been sleep walking most of the last decade when it came to Nuevo Granada and the rapid modernisation of its political and military infrastructure.

Personally, Washington had guessed the Mexicans would wait a while longer; return to the negotiating table with its new army, its modern air force and a navy that was beginning to warrant the name, a democracy demanding its place in the world and a settlement of its centuries' old territorial claims to land taken from it by force majeure by the British. But in a few years New England would have an air force of jets, the Empire could out-build any two or three other navies on the planet and sooner or later, the oil of Texas and offshore in the Gulf of Spain would persuade the government in London to properly fortify the border, and then, because the men in charge in México City were – contrary to the badinage filling the East Coast press -profoundly rational, they would know that their ever-shortening window of opportunity had closed.

So, Santa Anna had – probably with immense reluctance – concluded that a new war, right now, was the only way to guarantee a front row seat at the peace table, next year or the year after. The trouble was that the people in Philadelphia and London did not get it. They still believed they were dealing with a tin pot, banana republic run by a gang of fanatics. Nothing could be further from the truth. From the aftermath of a relatively bloodless revolution in the wake of the defeat in the last Border War, México had democratised, more or less in the same Parliamentary fashion as the Home Islands. Neither President Hernando de Soto nor Santa Anna were dictators or military strong men, and the current war was not some impulsive aberration, it was an expression of Mexican nationhood, the one thing that united most of the great, sprawling nation...

This war had been coming for years

This war had been wholly avoidable.

De Soto and Santa Anna were men London could have done business with had it not been for those idiots in the First Thirteen...

George Washington had to bite down on his anger.

He needed to think clearly.

Best case, worst case scenarios.

If the enemy came this far north *and* got across the river – both unlikely, in his humble opinion - then there was precious little to stop them marching a few miles to the north and following the railway all the way east to Caddoport on the Red River.

But George Washington did not think Santa Anna was that greedy. In his old foe's place, he would be still be coming to terms with the outrageous success and lightning speed of advance of his forces. Those Mexicans fighting in the suburbs of San Antonio must have outrun their supply train, be living of the land and any loot they chanced upon. They would be exhausted, formations would have lost combat coherence, and sixty or seventy percent of their vehicles would have broken down by now. Their pack animals would be literally dying on the hoof. The safe, rational thing to do was to consolidate San Antonio as a logistical and transportation hub, fortify the town and then, when the troops were well rested, press on to the east, threatening the Red River line while amphibious operations were prepared to blockade the Delta. Another man might have allowed himself to get carried away with his good luck; but not Santa Anna...

No, the safe thing to do would be to consolidate San Antonio as a logistical and transportation hub, fortify the town and then, when his troops were well rested, press on to the east, threatening the Mississippi line and the Delta.

In the meantime, it did no harm to operate on the presumption that Trinity Crossing might one day soon be New England's last redoubt in northern Texas, or perhaps, one day, become the logical staging point for a counter-offensive to retake San Antonio. If nothing else, it sharpened his men's minds, kept them honest in the conduct of their duties.

From what George Washington had learned from Greg Torrance and his chief mechanic, Bill Fielding, the Spanish had bombed all the railheads to the south, and the retreating army had torn up the rails of all of those expensively built lines to nowhere in the south west as they retreated. Washington had watched those tracks being laid all over southern and western Texas, extended into the Sonoran deserts, and people said, blasted through the mountains. Those tracks were supposed to guarantee that reinforcements and supplies could be swiftly, efficiently delivered to the fighting men at the front in the event of war but there had never been enough rolling stock, or men guarding the borderlands; the reliance upon 'bastion' settlements and militiamen had been, to his mind, just plain dumb. Frankly, little better than an abdication of responsibility and now they were all paying the price for their neglect and negligence.

Every single one of those carefully, expensively built-up depots north of the demilitarized zone were now in Spanish hands, and the surviving colonial troops running ahead of the invaders, were heading due east.

The three riders had halted on a rise north of the town.

"The Spanish can read maps just like we can, boys," George Washington observed wryly, gazing out across the partially flooded landscape of forest and grassland framed by the scrub and rock of the desert beyond the floodplains of the shallow valley bending away to the south for as far as the eye could behold.

God's own country...

"They came at us all along the border," he went on, the two youngsters, neither eighteen yet, listened respectfully. "They'll halt a while, maybe around, or a little way beyond San Antonio and down on the coast. Maybe they'll wait to link up with the force coming up from the south. If they do, they'll meet up a long way south of here. Sometimes, armies get as disorganised advancing fast as an army in full retreat. They outrun their supplies, run out of ammunition. Sure, they captured our depots but we use different calibre rifle ammo, .303 against 7.92-millimetre metric, and artillery 3-inch imperial as opposed to 75-millimetre metric. Their land cruisers probably don't use the same lubricants as ours. So, they'll halt, reconsolidate, regroup awhile before they come on again. If we're lucky we'll get a couple of weeks, more likely a month or two, to get our act together."

As of yesterday evening, courtesy of Flight Sergeant Bill Fielding and a couple of self-confessed 'radio hacks' the latter had identified, several wireless sets were now in full working order, enabling him to make contact with Western Command in New Orleans.

Those idiots had no idea what was going on.

Not that this surprised him; given that the man who had presided over the preparation for and the actual, wholly predictable shambles west of the Red River in the last few weeks, was 'Chinese' Forsyth, who, in the way of these things was at the tail end of a highly self-publicised but otherwise average career, being rotated, in unhurried stages back to the Old Country before he was finally put out to pasture.

By repute, it was said Lieutenant General Sir Roger Forsyth was - despite having earned the sobriquet 'Chinese' ruthlessly putting down rebellions around the British Concession of Shanghai in the 1950s - a gentle, bookish soul who had spent most of his twenty years or so in Asia learning occidental languages and patronising archaeological, anthropological and botanical expeditions, several of which he had led, apparently with no little distinction.

Well, he had plenty of new ruins to peruse now!

Washington had gleaned precious little satisfaction from his thirty-minute conversation over a swooping, noisy scrambler link to Forsyth's headquarters in the Delta.

The man had talked airily about trading territory for time.

He had also ordered that all livestock was to be destroyed ahead of the approaching Spanish 'horde'.

Scorched earth...

Blowing up oil well heads...denying the enemy the fuel to continue the war!

Washington had no intention of participating in that kind of crime. He had, as tactfully as possible, attempted to put Forsyth right.

This was *his* country the other man was glibly talking about laying waste; and potentially, *his* cattle and other Texan and border-landers' livelihoods. Forsyth needed the support of every Texan and ordering them to wreck their country was not going to cut the mustard.

Worryingly, the C-in-C was perfectly happy, 'reconciled' was his exact word, to allow the Spanish 'in their own good time' to close up to the margins of the Delta and 'if they want, up to the western bank of the Mississippi', which was just plain crazy.

It also illustrated how poorly the C-in-C understood the ground for which he was responsible. It angered – but did not surprise – Washington that a man so ignorant was calling the tune. It riled him even more that he was having to argue with the idiot within his, uninformed terms of reference.

'You can't do that, sir,' George Washington had said in exasperation. 'If they take New Orleans the river will become a highway into the interior...'

'Don't talk rot, man!'

Washington had tried to point out to the idiot that unless Santa Anna was advancing with an 'engineering cohort' equipped to ford a major continental river system, there was precisely no prospect of the Mexicans crossing the Red River; so, how on earth the invaders were going to 'close up to the Mississippi' was a mystery to him.

However, this line of reasoning also fell on deaf ears.

It seemed that Forsyth was about to fly into the San Antonio 'enclave'. He felt a flying visit would stiffen the resolve of the garrison; something of an oxymoron if Greg Torrance was to be believed. San Antonio was where everybody, soldier or civilian was fleeing towards now that the Spanish had landed on the coast at Galveston Island.

The chaos of the sprawling conurbation – before the war a boom town city of well over a hundred thousand souls, oil men, ranchers, chancers and shysters of every description - which was surrounded by industrial sites and small hamlets on the prairie, now choked with survivors, retreating troops and refugees would, inevitably, suck in Mexican troops and block the advance of the invaders for several days, possibly weeks regardless of whether the defenders put up a fight.

Unfortunately, Forsyth was obviously one of those senior officers honestly believed that men like him who had survived the trial by fire of a public school-education in the Old Country, could achieve anything they set their minds to!

Washington's attempts to discover if there was anybody co-ordinating the operations of the Army south and west of San Antonio, or even if it still existed, the CAF and the Royal Navy in the Gulf of Spain, had also drawn scorn.

That 'was not the concern of a middle-ranking field officer', he was informed.

Washington had tried to be diplomatic.

'I propose to send out mounted scouts to establish the lines of advance of enemy forces in my sector, sir,' Washington had reported, realising that it was pointless having an argument with a man who had no idea whatsoever what was really going on anywhere between San Antonio and Alta California. 'I urgently need aviation spirit for the aircraft under my command...'

That apparently, was a matter he needed to take up with the Quartermaster of the Colonial Air Force.

Whereupon, Forsyth had delivered a pep talk and hung up with the thought that, apparently, all would be well because 'the ground is in our favour!'

Which was nonsense because all the things which had gone wrong before, during and after the last Border War were repeating, except on an exponentially more disastrous scale. And this time there was an idiot in command who seemed to think ceding hundreds of miles of territory east of the Delta and allowing the enemy to over-extend his lines of communication was the answer to everything!

In the last war New Englanders had been able to count on at least the tacit support of the native peoples of the region; in the last few years the 'free land' settlement policy planting alien communities, many of which had virtually popped up overnight, in the middle of the ancestral lands of the ancient tribal populations, had meant that this time around if the tribes co-operated with anybody, it was going to be with the Spanish.

Washington had left Greg Torrance trying to contact somebody, somewhere capable of trucking him enough high-octane petrol to get his airworthy aircraft into the air. His Goshawk was going to need a 'little tender loving care' before it flew again but he was optimistic that the pair of intact Fleabags would come in useful for 'field observation' if only he could get hold of some petrol!

The call had gone out around Trinity County for all able-bodied men to report to the airfield, with, if they had them, long rifles and spy glasses. Washington had requisitioned all the stores in the town, including the communal grain reserve. The town's elders had been unenthusiastic, complaining that the war was still a long way away. Luckily, for all that Washington's local knowledge and exploits in the last conflict with the Spanish counted for nothing with Chinese Forsyth; his own people had, reluctantly, seen the light and fallen in behind him.

George Washington went on staring at the floods.

No, he decided, the Spanish were not coming his way any time soon.

San Antonio was the best part of two hundred-and-fifty miles to the south-south-west. Strategically, New Orleans or one of the port towns on the Mississippi, possibly Natchez, about one-hundred-and-fifty miles up-river from the Delta might actually be a long-term objective of the next stage of the Mexican offensive. The Delta lands and the lower reaches of the great river constituted legitimate contested ground, whereas historically, the Spaniards' claims on anywhere north and east of Trinity Crossing were purely hypothetical since those territories had never been administratively incorporated into the old Empire.

However, he did not believe it; Santa Anna had to know that a march to the Mississippi or the Delta was the equivalent to the German march on Moscow in the Great War. Pure folly, destined to end in untold grief and Washington was pretty damned sure that the Mexicans had already committed their best troops.

The other thing they forgot too easily back East was that history mattered; war was not just about what was possible or practical, it was also about folk memory and national identity.

Once the Spanish moved a few days march east of San Antonio, they were going to start trespassing upon what had been French Louisiana at the time of the failed East Coast rebellion in the 1770s, lands subsequently ceded to Great Britain as part of the settlement of the Anglo-French wars of the late eighteenth and early nineteenth centuries. It was one thing for foreign troops to trample on 'Unincorporated' Colonial territories which had been legitimately, formerly part of the

Empire of New Spain but the Louisiana Lands, stretching from and including the whole Delta and hundreds of miles either side of it, all the way up the Mississippi very nearly to the border with the Canadian Dominions of Manitoba and Ontario, remained, inviolably, British sovereign soil. Logically, in defiling that 'soil' an invader would be crossing a very significant Rubicon because from that moment onwards, the war ceased, *de jure*, to be 'colonial' and became 'imperial'.

George Washington was confident that Santa Anna and Il Presidente de Soto, would be mindful of that distinction because in the event *that* line was crossed, the British Parliament would be bound to – if it had not already been promulgated - to invoke the so-called Sykes-Temple Rule, which specified that the violation of the territorial integrity of one Colony, Dominion or other land deemed to be equivalent to that of the United Kingdom, shall result in an imperial declaration of war against that 'violator'.

Granted, such a declaration of war had already been made but thus far only in respect of an entity named 'the Triple Alliance', in response to the attack on HMS Achilles and the invasion of Jamaica.

It seemed to George Washington that the British Government had been vacillating over declaring war against a named country, possibly because it was playing some kind of secret diplomatic game with the German Empire. It was odd how legal niceties clouded the conversations Government House in Philadelphia must be having with those self-seeking planters, bankers and merchants in the *founding colonies.*

Oh, how those fine gentlemen must be twisting and turning, arguing that it was the Empire's responsibility to fund a 'colonial war', and resisting any blandishment to modify their entrenched resistance to the imposition of 'war taxes' in their individual Crown Colony fiefdoms. It was all semantics; somebody had to pay whatever price it eventually took to clean up this mess. Inevitably, the First Thirteen did not want to pay their share of the bill; they never had before. Even more inevitably, no East Coast colonial legislator wanted to have to take responsibility for taxing their voters; much better if all the blame was heaped on the Governor of the Commonwealth of New England when he stepped in to lance the boil. That way the Governor and the English back in the Old Country would take all the blame for heaping the cost of the war onto New Englanders.

Those East Coast scoundrels had got away with it in the last war when the full cost had been borne by the British Exchequer. The bankers of New England had made huge fortunes on the loans they had made to the Government in London, and generations of mill and factory owners had grown even fatter on bountiful military contracts. Contracts upon which the 'English' taxpayer was still paying interest because of the 'war loans' taken out in the early 1960s to save the miserable skin of those same patriotic colonists!

In the meantime, the defence of the borderlands had been denuded of real soldiers, the ranks filled with amateurs, colonial militiamen who had by and large, turned tail and run away when the first shot was fired.

"This is going to be a long war, boys," he frowned, carefully nudging his mount's flanks, leading the other two riders down the gentle slope towards the dry end of Trinity Crossing.

"Are we going to go down south and sort out them Dagoes, Colonel?" Henry Sullivan asked.

"Not any time soon, son," the old soldier chuckled. "For the time being we'll collect any strays that come our way, and wait on reinforcements. Hopefully, we'll get some of our aircraft back in the air soon. In the meantime, we'll carry on fortifying the town. It'll give everybody something to do. At times like this people always feel better when they're doing something."

Chapter 21

Wednesday 3rd May
HMS Surprise, North East Providence Channel, The Bahamas

Abe and Ted Forest were escorted forward. After about a quarter-of-an-hour there was a quiet hissing of air and the vessel ascended. Both men had surrendered their alarm wristbands and signed over their earpieces and were thus, out of the 'quiet command loop'.

A bearded petty officer nodded and acknowledged a communication. He turned to the two aviators.

"The Pirates are just breaking out their boats, gentlemen." He beckoned to Ted Forest; whose leg was still splinted. "We'll send you up first, Mister Forest."

The two aviators had done an impromptu tour of the submarine earlier that day. Simply to say 'thank you' to the men of HMS Surprise, and the 'Pirates' – the boat's Special Forces Unit – for well, saving their lives, basically.

Surprise's Captain had come forward to say his farewells and to ensure that they were fully prepared for their send off.

'There will be a couple of fellows on the aircraft which collects you, they will brief you on the officially concocted story detailing how exactly you were rescued from Little Inagua, and where you have been in the intervening period. I imagine that the truth will probably come out sooner rather than later," the older man had grinned ruefully.

HMS Surprise had stalked and killed a second enemy submersible two days ago, this time as the target was alongside a supposedly neutral – Norwegian registered – merchantman, which the submarine had also torpedoed and sunk without warning.

Without warning, and without ever – attack periscope apart – breaking the surface of the ocean. It seemed the Spanish submarine, a larger, five or six hundred ton version of the first one they had destroyed south of Bermuda, had been refuelling and taking on board perishable foodstuffs at the time she was chopped in half by the half-ton warhead of the Tiger Shark Mark XI torpedo which hit it a few feet abaft of its conning tower.

Like the first 'kill', this one was conducted with quiet, deadly precision. The merchant ship had broken up as she sank, the rending of hull plates and the crash of machinery breaking loose had followed her down into the depths as the Surprise had silently slipped away from the scene of the crime.

'Do you think there were any survivors?' Ted Forest had inquired of the submarine's Executive Officer.

'Probably,' the other man had shrugged. 'Not our problem, I'm afraid. Our rules of engagement forbid us to assist or to take on board survivors – be they enemy combatants or neutrals - other than for purposes of interrogation.'

Ted had later confided that he thought this was unnecessarily harsh, and speculated it was probably contrary to the international treaties concerning the treatment of combatants, or for that matter, non-combatants who were injured or who wanted to surrender.

Abe had thought about it.

He was still a little awed by the effortless efficiency of the submarine as a killing machine. It was like watching an execution, not a hunt.

'Remember brave Achilles," he had retorted grimly.

'It just seems, well, unfair,' Ted had countered, a little wary of his friend's mood and perhaps, remembering – as if he was ever going to forget it – Abe's murderous rampage on Little Inagua.

'Not cricket?'

'No.'

Abe had smiled sadly.

'It is just war, Ted. Us or them. I'm sorry if that sounds cold but that's as complicated as it is, no more or less. Kill or be killed and I, for one, vote for going on living every time.'

Ted had let it go.

Now they waited, on tenterhooks for the hatches to be sprung and to again draw cool, unfiltered sea air into their lungs. For the first time they became aware of a sense of motion under their feet. Several crewmen had warned them that the 'boat rolls like a garbage scow' in any sort of sea when she was on the surface. Luckily, it transpired that it was calm up above.

Ted clambered up the ladder awkwardly, one run at a time. When he reached the level of the casing strong arms lifted him through the hatch.

Abe followed, clambering out onto the hull, wondering at the discernible yielding 'give' underfoot as the submarine's rubbery acoustic skin yielded to his weight.

The men of the deck party pulled the inflation lanyards of their life jackets; had they been activated inside the boat they would never have got through the pressure hatches.

It was pitch dark but a couple of members of the deck gang wore odd-looking headsets, with peaks that appeared to come down over their eyes. It was a few moments before Abe realised that they must be wearing some kind of infra-red night vision equipment. Two Royal Marines, faces blacked and garbed in black fatigues guided Ted into a rigid inflatable like the one which had lifted them off the north beach of Little Inagua. It was eased off the casing into the water. The boats engine purred and it circled, returning, pushing its rounded snout up against the Surprise.

'Jump in, sir," Abe was invited jocularly.

Actually, he fell into it.

Seconds later the boat was forging away from its mother ship to where, darkly emerging from the night a twin-engined Mallard seaplane bobbed silently on the extraordinarily flat, glassy seas. Abe imagined he could make out the dark hump of land to his right, and assumed these waters were sheltered by it. Nevertheless, for any part of the Atlantic Ocean to be as smooth as a millpond was positively bizarre.

The Mallard was rocking from side to side, its wing-tip floats slapping the surface of the sea. Again, Abe discovered that the best way to transfer from the ceaselessly moving inflatable was to fall into the rescue aircraft.   Several strong arms grabbed, guided and generally arrested Ted Forest's otherwise precarious entry into the passenger cabin.

The hatch shut, and was promptly dogged.

The port engine coughed into life.

Then the starboard.

The pilot ran up both motors, throttled back briefly.

By then Abe and Ted had been strapped in.

The Mallard started moving, turning, searching for the slightest of breezes to take off into, or failing that a current to kick up a wave to help bounce the machine into the air. Picking up speed the seaplane started to judder through the top of the water, her engines straining.

On and on, until suddenly the shaking stopped.

"We're taking you two to St Augustine. We plan to present you to selected press, radio and TV reporters around noon tomorrow, after which you'll be flown up to Norfolk. Lieutenant Lincoln, your wife will be informed of your safe return to New England shortly after we put you ashore in Florida."

The man saying – or rather, shouting above the roar of the engines – was about Abe and Ted's age, around his mid- to latter-twenties. In the very dim, red light of the cabin he was hanging on for dear life as the aircraft climbed, bucking and slipping through the turbulence as it tried to climb through the clouds.

Immediately, Abe was struck by the contrast between the antiseptic, futuristic modernity of HMS Surprise and the clattering, rattling old seaplane. It was as if he had stepped back into a thirty or forty-year-old technology, gone backwards in time. It also prompted another thought: If we have so effortlessly mastered the depths of the oceans; might we not have also, and as secretly, conquered the skies too?

"We're going to need you chaps to memorise your scripts before we present you to the New England people. There will probably be stuff in there that you don't like; that's too bad. You follow the script. That order comes straight from Lord Collingwood."

"You said my wife will be told I'm alive when we reach St Augustine?" Abe checked, in that moment not giving a damn what nonsense the Navy wanted him to spout tomorrow.

"Yes, the senior Naval Liaison officer supporting the relatives of the crew members of the Achilles, will be in his office overnight waiting for my call. He asked me to ascertain if he should wait until the morning to give your wife the good news. People knocking on one's door in the middle of the night can be very worrying..."

"Kate will want to know as soon as possible," Abe said, his voice thickening with long pent-up angsts.

"You're sure?"

"Yes."

Abe was exhausted, utterly spent which was strange because he had been physically inactive for most of the last few weeks, and ought to have been brimming with youthful energy. He sensed it was the same for Ted Forest.

"We believe that there were a number of other survivors from the Achilles, including Commander Cowdrey-Singh," the two aviators were being told. "The Germans published a list of some fifty or so survivors. Your names weren't on that list. One report is that the other survivors may be held captive on Santo Domingo under the protection of the German Minister at Guaynabo, San Juan. Frankly, we don't know what to make of it. So, you two will be the first of the Achilles's *heroes* to come home."

In the darkness the other man could not see the anger in Abe's and Ted's eyes.

"We're not bloody heroes," Abe grated.

"Of course, you are!"

"We just did our duty, that's all," Ted Forest insisted.

"Like it or not you chaps are bally *heroes*!"

Chapter 22

Wednesday 3rd May
Berlin-Spandau Railway Terminus

The King and Queen, their ministers and the rest of the original party, accompanied by the one hundred and seven accredited diplomats – including the Ambassador, Sir Evelyn Baring – all peremptorily expelled by personal order of the King of Prussia, Wilhelm VII, had been driven across the city as darkness fell.

Nevertheless, they had seen the bodies lying on the street and buildings burning in the near distance, heard the regular thump and crump of artillery pieces. A pall of smoke hung over the Reich capital as the blood-letting went on unabated.

It seemed that the Deutsches Heer – the Imperial German Army - had acclaimed Wilhelm Emperor, the High Command of the Kaiserliche Marine had swiftly fallen into step with the generals, with only the Air Force, the one service not dominated by Prussian officers, dithering before eventually, splitting down the middle with individuals and squadrons taking different sides.

Wilhelm's men had mounted a dawn *coup d'état*, arresting all thirteen of the Electors who had voted in favour of Ludwig of Bavarian's accession to the Imperial throne. Ludwig himself, and his wife were presently being held at the notorious Moabit Prison, located inside the massive DG - Deutscher Geheimdienst – *German Secret Service* Complex in the Mitte District of the city.

The old Kaiser's security service, officially the German Secret Police Service, had acquired a dreadful reputation in the early years of his reign but had been, albeit only somewhat, rehabilitated in the public eye in recent times. However, this was unlikely to be much comfort to those who fell into the DG's hands at a time such as this.

It seemed that the King and Queen had witnessed only the beginnings of Wilhelm's rage at the Charlottenburg Palace. Without risk of over-egging the case, it was obvious that he must, thereafter, have suffered some kind of psychotic episode. The great imperial city had shuddered with explosions and gunfire, the banshee wail of sirens had been continuous, countless aircraft had flown low over the rooftops while the German State Broadcasting Network had played martial music interspersed with orders – not requests – for calm, notifications of a twenty-four hour curfew, warnings that rioters would be shot on sight and that, contrary to the evidence, everything was, quote: 'Under control and there was no need for the citizenry to worry...'

Stray and spent bullets had hit the Charlottenburg, one had cracked a window within feet of where Queen Eleanor had been sitting that morning. After that the Commanding Officer of the Royal Protection Detail had virtually frog-marched the King and Queen down to the basement, where, shortly afterwards they were joined by the Prime Minister, Sir Hector Hamilton and Foreign and Commonwealth Secretary, Sir George Walpole.

Count Lothar von Bismarck of Hesse-Kassel, Foreign Minister in the old Kaiser's government had found the British party sheltering below ground. He was grey with weariness and mental fatigue. Although he was one of the Electors – despite his 'electorate' being essentially honorific – he was not one of the Electors who had allowed whimsy or, in the circumstances, more likely narcotics abuse or congenital imbecility to sway him towards the person of the Kaiser elect, Ludwig. Not actually a great admirer of Wilhelm, he had nevertheless, always done his best to excuse and explain his cousin's quirks and excesses down the years. It was, the British party assumed, only a combination of his past forbearance and unimpeachable public loyalty, and the fact that he had actually cast his vote for the King of Prussia, which meant he was still at liberty and acting, insofar as it was practical in the present extraordinary circumstances, as an agent of the self-appointed new Kaiser.

Looking every minute of every hour of his near sixty years, the newcomer bowed to the King and Queen and began to apologise profusely for the indignities 'the situation must inevitably impose upon your most honoured persons...'

His voice had trailed away into the musty, dank air of the crowded basement as he met the gaze of his oldest remaining friend in Christendom.

Ignoring the ire of his monarch and the even colder rage of his Prime Minister, George Walpole had put a fraternal arm of friendship around the German minister's shoulders.

The two men had sparred, in academia in their younger days and latterly, in the less brotherly sphere of realpolitik for the last, ever-more troubling decade. Whereas, on Walpole's part, their diplomatic encounters had been interrupted now and then by the vagaries of the workings of democracy in the United Kingdom, this was not a cross that Lothar von Bismarck, whose family had been to all intents, under the Germanic Imperial system, the hereditary masters of the Wilhelmstrasse for the last century ever had to bear.

'How have we come to this?' Bismarck sighed, shaking his head.

Eleanor, seeing a good man distraught with shame for acts over which he had no control but nevertheless, still felt palpably responsible, stepped forward and gave him a hug. This was not a thing she had often had occasion to do, notwithstanding Lothar, two years her senior, was actually her nephew.

In that moment there was a horrible sense of familial, royal and patriotic duties getting irretrievably tangled, torn, warped and the Queen knew as well as anyone in the room that there were things were going on around them – unforgivable things – which would taint Anglo-German relations for generations to come. The scale of the disaster was as incalculable as it was intangible, such was the surreal atmosphere of that dreadful day.

It was obvious that no man felt the dire consequences of the catastrophe unravelling about him more keenly that Lothar von Bismarck.

In preparation for his life-long career; first as a junior secretary in the Kaiser's Colonial Office followed by a succession of increasingly senior posts until eventually, he succeeded his father at the Wilhelmstrasse, the German Foreign Office on the Unter den Linden in Berlin, Lothar had spent two years at Harrow, and subsequently studied Classics and Medieval History at Balliol College, Oxford, where he had first met with many of the men with whom, it was anticipated, he would work with, and more often against, in pursuance of his Kaiser's policies in later life.

In comparison with the giant, somewhat fiercely over-bearing persona of his illustrious forebear depicted in nineteenth century portraits and monochrome photographs – the acknowledged guiding hand behind the Treaty of Paris, the man every German child was taught was the 'saviour of the First Reich' – Lothar was a man constructed on slighter, more dapper lines belying the fact he was the 'Iron Man's' great-great grandson.

Born into an age when in polite German society to be an Anglophile was a thing to be greatly admired and respected, a mark of distinction; and in England to be regarded as a Teutophile or Germanophile, was viewed as thoroughly 'good form' and demonstrative of a man or woman having a healthy surfeit of 'the right stuff', Lothar had always taken unquenchable pride in his familial connections to the Royal Family. His mother was Eleanor's eldest sister, a thing that was until he was in his twenties just an incidental matter but then the atrocity of Empire Day 1961 had occurred, and suddenly, his aunt had become, overnight, the Queen Consort of the King of England, and his old friend 'Bertie', George V, and thus, by an accident of history Lothar von Bismarck presently found himself nineteenth in line of succession to the English throne.

Bizarrely, at one stage back in the 1950s he had actually been seventh in line to the British throne but – much to his relief - the present King of England's offspring had, of late loyally, dutifully and with no little gusto been producing new royal princes and princesses at a rate which far outstripped the demise of their seniors in the Royal blood line. Inevitably, in the last few years as tensions bubbled just beneath the surface, in Germany the Press took a malicious pleasure in teasing Lothar about his 'British antecedents'. For example, cartoons of him hob-knobbing with the Royal Family, referring to the King as 'Bertie' and the Queen calling him 'Bissi', appeared in the papers every time he was accused of being 'soft on the Brits'.

To his immense mortification he had been sent to the Charlottenburg to deliver a personal message from the Kaiser by acclamation.

Kaiser durch Akklamation.

Lothar von Bismarck had choked on the words.

He could hardly look King George in the eye.

'It is my Kaiser's command that I inform you, Your Majesty,' he intoned, grieving for times now forever past, 'that you should remove your Royal person from the lands of the German Empire this day. My Kaiser states that he no longer considers himself to be related to the

Windsor branch of the Anglo-Germanic blood line. He declares that you and all members of your court and of your government, including the diplomatic service, are hereby deemed persona non grata in the Empire. All diplomatic and governmental relations with the British Empire are henceforth severed. Further, all British Empire assets on German soil are hereby forfeit.'

The German Foreign Minister shook his head.

Despairing now...

'Further, it is decreed that the airspace above the German Empire is closed to British Empire aircraft. Likewise, German waters are closed to all British vessels upon the seas. Ships of the merchant marine of the German Navy will no longer salute, give respect or right of way to any British or British Empire registered merchant vessel or Royal Navy ship...'

By then George Walpole was staring at his friend, aghast.

It had taken some minutes for the German Foreign Minister to read the full text of the hurriedly prepared Königliches Kommando – Royal Command – and when he finished, shamefaced, for his listeners to take in its dreadful ramifications.

It had been the King who summed up the mood in the basement, while outside, the capital of the Reich was burning.

'Presumably,' he had inquired, stiffly, 'somebody will have the courtesy to let my ministers have this in writing at some stage before we depart Berlin, Count Bismarck?'

Everybody was carefully keeping their distance from the King and Queen as the train began to drag slowly out of the Berlin-Spandau terminus.

The windows of the carriage rattled with the concussion of a series of heavy explosions, mercifully at least a mile from the line.

The King looked to his wife.

"Gott im Himmel," he murmured distractedly. "I never thought I'd think it, let alone say it," he remarked, 'but thank God for Project Poseidon!"

Chapter 23

Thursday 4th May
El Palacio de Los Pinos de Oro, México City

In the weeks since Rodrigo de Monroy y Pizarro Altamirano's last visit to the Presidential Residence, set among the pines of the Chapultepec Woods which was once the site of a pre-Columbian Aztec Palace, the Army of the Republic had placed a ring of steel about it.

Armoured personnel carriers blocked both the roads into the forest surrounding the palace and combat troopers of the elite Assault Corps patrolled the grounds. Every visitor's pass was checked at the outer and inner gates, and even senior politicians and uniformed officers were required to submit to body searches before they were permitted to proceed further into the compound. Moreover, nobody was admitted at all unless their visit had been pre-authorised by the Office of Presidential Security.

Fortunately, a female member of President Hernando de Soto's secretariat was waiting at the door of the Residence to usher Rodrigo and his University of Cuernavaca faculty colleague, Arturo Gutiérrez Ortiz Mena, past the final security checks.

"Hello, Don Rodrigo," the girl, she was barely twenty and the spitting image of her mother at her age, smiled shyly.

Margarita Medina-Mora Icaza, President de Soto's niece, had been permitted to take a sabbatical half-way through her second year at Cuernavaca, where she had been studying Modern Languages – English and German – to serve as an intern on the Presidential Staff for the duration of the current emergency. The majority of such student applications were rejected, nothing was so important to the Republic than the education of its children and young people but Hernando de Soto had made an exception for his niece, albeit on the solemn condition that the moment the emergency was passed, she would resume her studies.

The young woman's long jet black hair was restrained in a very sensible pigtail, she wore no make-up, foregoing the bright nail paints most young women of her class carried like badges of honour, and she was respectably dressed like a matron twice her age, covered up from neck to wrists, all the way down to her mid-calves.

She and Rodrigo hugged briefly, very correctly, much as he and his own offspring did in public.

Margarita's mother had died in childbirth when she was only seven years old and her father, a diplomat presently in Manilla in the Philippines, not really knowing what to do with her and her two elder brothers, had never re-married. The two boys had been packed off to military colleges, Margarita had been handed from family to family until, just after her tenth birthday she had been all but been adopted by the de Soto's, who had treated her as the daughter they had never had. In no time at all she and Rodrigo's twins, Rudolfo and Marija, who were her juniors by only a month or so, had become, and still were, inseparable.

Unfortunately, Rudolfo was still not talking to his father at the moment on account of Rodrigo's implacable refusal to allow him to volunteer for militia service. The boy still had over a year of his degree course at Cuernavaca to complete and until he was twenty-one, he needed *his* permission to make a mess of his life!

Needless to say, Margarita's 'escape' to *Palacio de Los Pinos de Oro* – the Palace of the Gold Pines – had rubbed still more salt into Rodrigo's son's wounded pride.

"Marija says that Rudi," Margarita said hesitantly, speaking lowly as she led her charges deeper into the Residence, "isn't quite as angry, anymore, Uncle."

"Ah... That's good to know, my dear."

Margarita took the two men into an ante-chamber occupied by an older woman, the President's Appointment Secretary, a formidable lady whom he had brought with him from the University two years ago.

"Why, Professor Altamirano!" This woman smiled, rising from her chair and coming around her desk to shake Rodrigo's hand. She turned to the other, younger man and extending her hand again said: "Professor Icaza, it is a great honour to meet you at last."

This rather disconcerted Arturo Gutiérrez Ortiz Mena, a rather junior member of the faculty of the University of Cuernavaca. He was a stocky, and even today, a little unkempt, seemingly distracted man in his late thirties who rarely socialised, or played 'the political game' within the tight-knit academic community. To everybody's surprise he had married a former student some ten years his junior eighteen months ago, who had already presented him with a baby daughter. His wife, a plump, bubbly presence had not made any attempt to 'tidy up' her new husband; presumably, on the grounds that she liked him just the way he was. He had turned up for his meeting with the President of the Republic in a jacket with leather patches over both the elbows.

The President was not alone when, a few minutes later the two academics entered his office, a cool, sparsely decorated large room with tall windows along its southern and western aspects.

General of the Army of New Spain, Felipe de Padua María Severino López de Santa Anna y Pérez de Lebrón, rose from an armchair as the two University of Cuernavaca men came in.

Santa Anna, the man who had used his position as Chief of Staff of the Mexican Armed Forces – the 'Army of New Spain' title was a meaningless honorific these days and had been for a century – to cement the hold of the National Democrats on power in the pre-de Soto era, was wearing a plain Army dress uniform with no badges of rank other than, on his left breast pocket a small tab which read: *Gen. Santa Anna.*

It was a standing joke that all of Santa Anna's predecessors had eventually expired of exhaustion under the weight of the multiplicity of the medals they wore, 'all the time!' But then, of course, unlike most of his predecessors, Santa Anna did not pretend to, or for a moment plan to be, the dictator of México.

He was a man of average height, fifty-six now, still trim with a relatively full head of hair, a man to whom a uniform seemed like a second skin. Only a lieutenant colonel at the time of the last war with the English, he had been the man whose troops had stemmed the rout and later, as revolution threatened, ordered the troops under his command to interpose themselves between the rioters in México City and the trigger-happy para-militaries of the old, sham-government coalition which had sent so many of the nation's sons to their death untrained, under-armed and disgracefully badly led in the borderlands with New England.

Back in those days the country had been teetering on the verge of civil war and *he*, Santa Anna, had stepped briefly onto the political stage and given the old regime a chance to peacefully step aside, to avoid a bloodbath. After that, his promotion to the top job had been axiomatic, and for the last nine years he had worked tirelessly to re-build and to re-equip, and to instil a wholly new esprit de corps in the Mexican Army, Air Force and to his enduring chagrin, only to a lesser extent, in the Navy, whose officer corps still doggedly fought to remain the preserve of the old, conquistador aristocracy. That said, he and Vice Admiral Count Carlos Federico Gravina y Vera Cruz, the Chief Minister and Commander-in-Chief of the Armada de Nuevo Granada, and he, generally 'knocked along' well enough, and Santa Anna was only too well aware that at sea, he was, well, *all at sea...*

Besides, all revolutions had their price.

That México's most recent revolution had been largely peaceful, and that the country had reaped the rewards of that these last ten years as never before, was a price worth paying if its only cost, albeit a substantial one, was that the Navy had retained much of its former independence. Moreover, while Gravina rightly basked in the glory of being the High Admiral of the Fleets of the Triple Alliance, he – and more importantly, his quarrelsome admirals and captains - were going to be far too busy to meddle in the affairs of the state at home, or attempt to interfere with the able men entrusted with prosecuting the war in New England.

Arturo Ortiz Mena was staring wide-eyed at Santa Anna.

"We meet at last, Professor," the soldier half-smiled, shaking the academic's hand and making eye contact. He turned to the dishevelled younger man's companion. "We meet again, old friend," he said wryly, his grip dry, hard.

"The honour is all mine, General," Rodrigo re-joined.

"Don Rodrigo commanded the rear guard in the retreat from the Rio Grande Country," Santa Anna informed Ortiz Mena, "he and his men fought like lions. They saved what was left of the Army. But for Don Rodrigo there would have been no Army left to stop the Republic descending into another civil war."

It took Arturo Gutiérrez Ortiz Mena some minutes to get over what was probably a partial anxiety attack and to find a voice that was not a half-choked, gasping whisper.

Hernando de Soto, in academic life as in the Presidency of the Republic, had always made allowances for nervous students, or for visitors initially being more than somewhat over-awed in his presence. Strong coffee was brought in by Margarita, who swiftly scurried out again, leaving the great men to their deliberations.

The four men were sitting, informally in arm chairs around a low wooden table, very much as if they had been invited to Hernando de Soto's tutorial room at Cuernavaca, or to his hacienda in the hills overlooking the campus.

"General Santa Anna and I have read your reports, gentlemen," the President prefaced, his expression contemplative as if he was parsing some arcane philosophical proposition.

Rodrigo had only got back from northern Sonora six days ago, having despatched a provisional field survey report marked MOST CONFIDENTIAL AND SECRET – PRESIDENTIAL EYES ONLY under seal, by air as soon as his expedition passed through the lines.

He had been unwilling to trust the hundreds of soil, rock, vegetation and water samples he had collected to a small courier aircraft, and needed to warn Arturo Gutiérrez Ortiz Mena, to prepare his laboratory in advance.

Those samples had been delivered to Cuernavaca by a Carlos Pérez de Guzmán escorted by a small guard detachment, while he had taken a train to the capital to brief Hernando de Soto and Santa Anna five days ago.

"Er," the younger academic murmured, "my report was hurried, very provisional, lacking in the rigor normally expected by the University…"

The President of México smiled indulgently.

"You will have plenty of time to apply your customary rigor to subsequent papers, Professor," he assured him, every inch the nation's favourite grandfather. "It may be that you have already done your country a great service."

Santa Anna nodded.

"Don Rodrigo will have briefed you on the findings of his field survey in the Colorado Country and the deserts of Sonora, Professor?" He checked, not a man to take anything for granted.

"Yes, General."

"Forgive me, my University background was in mechanical engineering and ballistics," Santa Anna continued, self-effacingly – a frequently demonstrated character trait that people who did not know him very well invariably found disconcerting in such a 'great man' – "and security considerations have prevented me from sharing the contents of your paper with specialists on my Staff who are better informed than I on these matters. Might I ask you, and Don Rodrigo to brief me anew on your findings." He spread his hands. "In layman's terms, perhaps?"

Understanding that his University colleague was still a bag of nerves, Rodrigo took the lead, giving Ortiz Mena a little more time to collect his thoughts. He began to recount his expedition's trek north, climbing onto the great plateau bisected by the Colorado River and its tributaries, and what they had discovered beyond *El Ojo del Diablo*.

"We surveyed eleven separate sites where devices of varying explosive potential, and possibly, different types and configurations had probably been tested above and below ground. Common to each of the above ground sites were the remnants of a what may have been very tall towers or scaffolds of extremely robust steel construction. We also came upon several 'crater sites', the largest of which was six-hundred-and-twenty feet across and some sixty feet deep, with a rim of about fifteen feet in height above the surrounding desert. In two places we came across depressions of similar proportions, except, obviously, absent the elevated rims of the other craters. These, we assumed must have been the result of tests conducted underground..."

Arturo Gutiérrez Ortiz Mena had been fidgeting.

Suddenly, he interjected: "At some stage the idiots must have finally realised that the ground burst tests threw countless thousands of tons of heavily contaminated sand into the lower atmosphere likely to pollute the land downwind for many tens of miles!"

The other three men looked to him.

"Sorry," he mumbled. "This is all very... *disturbing*," he apologised.

This, coming from the lips of the only man in the country who might, one day, qualify as one of the globe's leading experimental physicists and was already, one of the brilliant minds beginning to explore the implications of the theoretical constructs of the latest quantum 'Uncertainty Theories' merging from British, German and French universities, was even more chilling than the stark descriptions in Rodrigo's survey report.

Tellingly, anywhere else in the Catholic Americas, and assuredly in Cuba, Hispaniola or Santo Domingo, the Head of the University of Cuernavaca's relatively new, still embryo Department of Nuclear Physics would have been arrested, imprisoned and almost certainly tortured by the Inquisition until he recanted his heretical notions. In México, while the more evangelistic and traditional adherents of the teachings of the Mother Church still frowned upon the black magic involved in the unravelling of the building blocks of God's Divine Creation, nobody seriously demanded to have theoretical physicists burned at the stake.

Well, not for the last twenty years or so, leastways.

"My provisional analyses of a representative samples of the soil, rock and sand-fused-glass sent to my laboratory by Don Rodrigo is," the physicist went on urgently, his brow deeply furrowed, "still very provisional, I must emphasise, very rushed work, most unsatisfactory... However, the initial results are most troubling..."

Chapter 24

Thursday 4th May
Royal Naval Air Station, Virginia Beach, New England

The call had come through to Albert Stanton's Manhattan flat at a little after two o'clock that morning. As it happened, had the telephone not rung, very nearly off the hook, at a moment when he and Maud Daventry-Jones were in between coupling – in itself a very rare thing in recent days – the call would have gone unanswered.

He had listened, sweaty and breathless with Maud's fingers tracing tingling lines across his back and walked tantalisingly down towards his groin as he propped himself on an elbow in the darkness, at first not really appreciating what was going on.

'Abe's alive?' He muttered and then was suddenly awakened by a surge of undiluted, briefly intoxicating relief. 'And...'

He had got up to speed after that, albeit a little distracted by his partner's toying with his now again enthusiastically tumescent member.

'That's a tight timescale?' He had queried when informed that Surgeon Lieutenant Lincoln and his fellow flier, Sub-Lieutenant Ted Forest would be landing back in Norfolk that afternoon.

'Just get down to the Imperial Airways pier at Brooklyn by four o'clock and we'll fly you straight down to Virginia...'

'Okay... Okay... Look, I'll be bringing a colleague.'

'That's fine. Just be there by four!'

He had collapsed onto his back, and started chuckling.

'Abe and his friend, Ted Forest are alive. There's going to be a big welcoming home ceremony. It sounds like the Navy is making a real party of it.'

Maud had swum on top of him, straddling his ever-hardening erection before gently raising herself to peer at him in the gloom, supported by her forearms resting on his chest. The press of her upon him, the sensation of her flesh touching his at every possible point was...sublime. His hands began to roam over her hips and buttocks., easing her down onto him.

He slid deep inside her in a moment.

'Come with me to Norfolk,' he had decided.

Maud had moaned dreamily; which he took for an affirmative.

They had made love again and consequently, very nearly missed the chartered Imperial Airways seaplane, the Centaur II, which had been about to cast off when they ran down the pier.

The boarding officer had raised an eyebrow when Albert introduced his fiancée as 'my assistant' but fortunately, Albert Stanton was such a well-known face in New York, not to mention much of New England that he and Maud were swiftly waved aboard without the normal document or accreditation checks, to join the unlikely crowd of dignitaries, journalists and 'snappers'.

Seats had been reserved for the couple near the back of the passenger cabin.

Maud was hugely impressed by the way her lover seemed to know everybody, and they him; and soon, she realised, they would recognise her also. After her campaigning with Leonora last year she had happily backed out of the limelight; it was one thing to be photographed in handcuffs, or covered in the paint or dye one had tried to throw at a policeman or a member of the judiciary, another entirely to be recognised everywhere one went thereafter. Although, that said, she had no problem at all being photographed on Mister Albert Stanton's arm!

Maud had clung to Albert's hand all the way down to Norfolk, a flight of a little over two hours, touching down in Hampton Roads as dawn was breaking on a clear late spring morning. She had gazed in fascination at the great grey warships which seemed to fill the anchorage as the big seaplane's course prescribed long, sweeping turns before with a final roar, swinging into the sheltered waters of Willoughby Bay.

Breakfast had been laid on for the 'visitors' flying in from all quarters in one of the hangars at the Royal Naval Air Station at Virginia Beach, about half-an-hour's drive on Navy buses from the landing stage.

Maud felt like she was a girl again, sitting in the back of her parents' car setting off on a summer holiday, or for a spring or autumn weekend in the country. Granted, today she was not bickering with her brother or pestering her poor mother and father for ice cream or chocolates. Today, she was far too preoccupied with the last few days...making up for lost time with her very own hero!

And, my oh my, how they had *made up* for that lost time!

Several times every night and at least once every daytime, too.

Maud had decided that she was going to be very happily married to Mister Albert Stanton!

The Royal Navy had thought of practically everything; apart, that was, for washrooms for the relatively small female contingent in the welcoming party. If ever a woman needed to be reminded that it was a man's world; the provision of 'public bathroom facilities' for the female half of the population, *always* confirmed it. Nevertheless, she had quiescently queued with the others, sanguine for once because nothing was going to rain on her parade.

The day Albert had got back to Long Island they had headed straight for her plush West Side Apartment and fallen, literally, straight into bed. The next few days she had visited his flat, a much better potential love nest, collected some 'things' from her place and pretty much, moved in with her beau and quickly, lost track of time. Albert was already working on a book about his adventures in Spain, and being keenly courted by likely publishers.

Coincidentally, he had only spoken to Kate Lincoln yesterday. Maud had listened from the bedroom, realised that her husband-to-be was conversing not with a woman in the news, or a 'contact' but with a friend who had, incongruously, possibly been as worried as she had been when he was reported lost in Spain. Albert had proudly told Kate that he and Maud were to be married 'as soon as possible.'

It was only a few days ago, that Kate's husband had been officially posted missing presumed dead, one of the hundreds of casualties of the first barbaric act of the war in the south and west.

"What do you think about the stories coming out of Germany, Albert?" One older, trench-coated newspaperman asked as the couple sat together at a trestle table in the reception hangar.

Several menacing, gull-winged Goshawk scouts lined one end of the building, heavy equipment had been moved out of the way to accommodate the buffet breakfast counters where sausages, bacon and eggs sizzled on hotplates, and Navy stewards poured endless cups of tea and cocoa, buttering slice after slice of fresh bread. Plates and cutlery sang in constant collisions, and the throng built-up as every new bus disgorged its passengers.

"Germany?" Albert Stanton frowned, like Maud he had not really been paying much attention to the news the last few days.

"Parts of Berlin are supposed to be battlegrounds. The story is the Electors tried to *elect* some mad guy from Bavaria to replace the old Kaiser and the Crown Prince called in the Imperial Guard to acclaim him Emperor!"

Maud was blinking disbelief.

That sounded like the sort of thing that happened when the Roman Empire was going down the tubes!

Her intended was earnestly scratching his chin.

"Um, the last time I heard about a civil war I went charging off to see what I was missing," he recollected ruefully. He glanced conspiratorially at Maud. "That's a mistake I won't make again!"

He introduced Maud to the other man.

"This is Fred Barnett of the *Albany Express*," he explained, grinning broadly. "He taught me all I know. Fred, this is Maud Daventry-Jones, who has done me the honour of accepting my proposal to be my wife."

The other journalist heartily slapped Albert on the back and reached over to shake Maud's hand. He was a large, florid man with thinning hair and a physiognomy with a naturally sceptical look which had suddenly transformed into sunny satisfaction as he digested his younger friend's news.

"Some people are cut out to be war correspondents," he remarked wryly, "hopefully, somebody not a million miles from here has learned his lesson now!"

There was a lot of hanging around with nobody knowing what was going on that morning. Albert Stanton explained to9 Maud that this was pretty much 'par for the course' in most reporters' days.

Maud did not care.

She was constantly being introduced to Albert's friends, acquaintances, and detractors. It was a little disconcerting to discover how many people wanted to speak to her beau, and to be photographed with him and at Albert's insistence, her.

"Ah, the famous Mister Stanton, a broad, bluff, ruddy-faced naval officer with an unbelievable number of rings on the cuffs of his dress uniform and a chest bulging full of medal ribbons, declaimed from a distance, as he approached with his sword clanking, pursued by a retinue of other senior officers.

Maud had not realised that she had met Admiral Lord Collingwood, C-in-C Atlantic Fleet until some minutes later.

And then Kate Lincoln, her baby son in her arms, accompanied by a slender, attractive woman in her later thirties or early forties, waved to the couple.

The woman with Kate took her son.

"Go on," she mouthed, a little maternally.

And the next moment Kate had flown into Albert Stanton's arms.

"Abe's coming home! Ted's coming home!"

Maud did not know what to do with herself.

The other woman was about her own age, height, stature, her skin a lot less dark than she had anticipated, her long dark hair a flowing mane down her back.

Before Maud knew it, she was looking into Abe Lincoln's Mohawk-born wife's almond brown eyes.

Albert made the introductions. It was the hundredth or more that day yet the first one which Maud knew she would never, ever forget.

"In sorrow and longing we are sisters, Miss Daventry-Jones," the other woman said solemnly. "Let us be sisters in our happiness also."

Maud hesitated, stepped close.

The two women embraced briefly, and moved apart.

The older woman, whom Maud now realised was accompanied by three youngsters, her children, presumably, could only be Melanie Cowdrey-Singh, the wife of the former second-in-command of HMS Achilles. Her children, thirteen-year-old Indira, ten-year-old Peter junior, and eight-year-old Maryam, all politely greeted Maud. Indira, having held fourteen-month-old Tom Lincoln, while her mother stepped forward, now rather reluctantly, returned him to Kate with a shy smile.

Maud could tell that the strain was taking its toll on Melanie Cowdrey-Singh, the spokesperson for and acknowledged leader of the families of the Achilles's lost and missing men.

"Next time it will be Peter and the others coming home to us, Melanie," Kate murmured. If her arms had not been full, she would surely have hugged the older woman, and for the moment, oblivious to the churning crowd around them she leaned forward and kissed her friend's cheek.

Maud blushed, guilty that she was intuitively somewhat jealous of the quiet, supportive intimacy between the other two women. Her closeness with Leonora had just happened, come upon her, them both really, out of the blue. It had seemed, from the outset, something indefinably precious, unique and it often occurred to her that it was unusual to see such 'oneness' in others. She was glad that the redoubtable Melanie Cowdrey-Singh, so indomitable in front of the cameras knew she did not have to maintain her pretence in front of her friend...

Things got a little confused when the plane – one of the big new four-engined, high-wing Gloucester TR-4 Manitoba class transports allegedly capable, implausibly, of landing on a strip less than five hundred yards long in an emergency - carrying the returning heroes landed.

Today, there was to be no demonstration of the remarkable aircraft's short take-off and landing tricks; the Manitoba touched the tarmac a quarter of the way down the one-and-a-half mile main runway, braked in a leisurely fashion, slowed, and eventually joined the perimeter road a hundred yards from the end of the strip.

Albert Stanton tried not to smirk.

The Navy was stage-managing this whole thing as if it was a melodrama, which, of course, that was and why the Manitoba was in effect, taking the long way around to reach the welcoming committee and the now, hundreds, possibly thousands of media people, civilians and service personnel corralled into the relatively small secure area in front of the base's main hangars.

He thought about explaining the 'optics' of the way the Navy was orchestrating events to Maud; stopped himself because he could tell she was loving every minute and he did not want to spoil her fun, or her anticipation of the moment the two returning heroes would be revealed to the crowd, and indeed, the whole Empire.

To return from the dead was no mean feat...

Ted Forest appeared first in the door.

Dressed in a dark blue jump suit that was as near as dammit black with one leg torn to accommodate a bulky splint, he had had to be lifted down to the tarmac. And then the tall, spare figure of Abe Lincoln paused at the top step, waving diffidently before loping down to the ground and in a moment enveloping Kate in his arms as Melanie Cowdrey-Singh, holding young Tom again, with her three children standing protectively around her amidst the gaggle of senior officers and Virginia big wigs, watched on, blinking back her tears.

Remarkably, among the close-packed gang of VIPs, mostly Virginian politicians and planters, Roger E. Lee and his normally sour-faced wife, were today grinning incongruously, eagerly awaiting their turn to be photographed greeting the homecoming heroes.

The fact that in the aftermath of the Empire Day atrocities Roger Lee and other luminaries of his Planters' Party clique had labelled Abe as a quote 'half-breed traitor who deserves to be hung, drawn and quartered,' and repeatedly referred to Kate as a 'fellow conspirator and an untrustworthy harlot squaw,' seemed wholly forgotten in the excitement. All that was conveniently forgotten now that they were here to welcome home the Empire's latest favourite son.

Politics was ever thus in the South...

Ted Forest, perched on his crutches was smiling a laughing smile, just out of reach of the reunited couple; but only until Kate focused on him and then he was self-consciously swept into his friends' mutual embrace.

Presently, Melanie stepped forward so that Abe and baby Tom could be reunited, before she retreated out of frame as Kate, Tom, Abe and Ted posed for photographs in front of the aircraft – which until now had been something of an unacknowledged secret, the subject of 'S' notices which occasionally got unwary editors and TV producers hauled up in front of magistrates, or even High Court judges - which had whisked them north from Florida that morning.

At that moment there must have been hundreds of snappers, and at least three bulky outside broadcast cameras trained on the group.

Lord Collingwood watched it all with a broad, paternally indulgent smile on his face, waving away attempts by his staffers and impatient dignitaries to cut the initial scenes of the homecoming short. Then, when eventually, he stepped forward, he motioned Melanie Cowdrey-Singh and her children to join him, and a trim, wiry man in the uniform of a Commander in the Royal Naval Air Service, finally stepped out of the anonymity of the great crowd.

Alex Fielding stood, eyes twinkling with mischief and pleasure as he looked at the two prodigals returned. He had deliberately kept out of the way since he got back to Norfolk that morning. This was Abe's day; Abe and Kate and Melanie Cowdrey-Singh's day. A real day of hope for the families of the men still listed missing after the Battle of the Windward Passage.

A day to *Remember Brave Achilles*!

And he, for one, was not about to rain on his little brother's parade, whatever those clowns at the Fleet Public Relations Department thought about it.

He planned to catch up with Albert Stanton later, he had a few hours to kill before he had to report back aboard the Perseus.

There had been a great deal of misinformation circulated about the state of, and the current deployment of the Atlantic Fleet's big ships: rumours of operations deep into the Caribbean, and of ships and crews worn out by recent operations.

It was all a veil of lies to mislead the enemy's spies in New England. Security, such a little considered thing even in the run up to the war, had suddenly acquired a bear trap-like grip on everything that happened at Norfolk. Up until now it had been as if the Spaniards knew every move the fleet planned to take, the disposition and fighting efficiency of every ship, and even the now obvious flaws in the Royal Navy's hastily learned manner of large-scale air operations at sea.

Well, mistakes had certainly been made.

Plenty of them!

But that was then and this was now. Inevitably, the Navy would get a lot of things wrong in the future but it was not about to repeat the blunders and miscalculations of the first weeks of the war. Secrecy and misdirection were henceforth to be treated with the same obsessive attention to detail as war-fighting operations.

Word had been put around that the Perseus would not be fit for sea for another eight to ten days but in fact, the carrier was due to cast off a few minutes before midnight. The task force's screening destroyers would depart soon after dusk, then the cruisers, and the big ships would be the last to idle out to sea with the ebb tide, with the battleship Princess Royal and the old battlecruiser Indefatigable – the formerly partly de-activated fleet gunnery school ship – now fully crewed with all four of her main battery turrets restored to battle order, preceding the Perseus, her flight deck and hangar deck crammed with every available aircraft.

The Triple Alliance had had it all their own way thus far.

That was a situation which was about to be rectified.

Ten-year-old Peter Cowdrey-Singh junior stood to attention and saluted the two aviators, a moment recorded forever by the nearly deafening clatter of firing camera shutters.

Both Abe and Ted Forest returned the salute and shook the kid's hand.

Lord Collingwood oversaw the tableau like a proud uncle.

That was when Kate spied Alex stepping forward.

"They said you were still on Long Island!" She shrieked in happy complaint, flinging her arms around her brother-in-law. Abe, likewise embraced Alex. Only Ted Forest – who had never met Alex – like any true Englishman, contented himself with an uncomfortable handshake.

Alex was astonished at how well the two aviators looked.

"Getting yourself shot up was a bit careless?" He guffawed to the airmen.

"You should see what the other fellow looks like!" Ted Forest retorted, much to the mirth of all within earshot.

However, the circus was clearly beginning to tell on the injured man who slumped gratefully onto his chair on the small presenting stage erected in front of the big hangars, where a veritable hydra-like profusion of microphones awaited the welcoming speeches.

Presently, after much fanfare and hyperbole, which Abe and Ted – sat either side of Kate, cradling a surprisingly quiescent Tom - bore stoically, despite neither of them having slept for thirty-six hours and ached to luxuriate in the privacy of the circle of their friends, family and old comrades.

Abe rose, a little stiffly, to his feet and turned to offer his hand to his friend to help him stand up. Together they advanced slowly to the microphones, where they paused, their clasped hands raised high.

"This is all a bit overwhelming," Abe started. He had tried and failed to memorize the script handed to him on the flight from St Augustine to Virginia Beach.

It was all nonsense, anyway.

He glanced over his shoulder to where Kate rocked his now, for the first time, restive infant son in her arms. He exchanged a tight-lipped smile with Melanie Cowdrey-Singh, guilty to have been unable to bring her any news of her husband.

"There are so many things that I want to say," he shrugged, "and some I can't say because they are secret. As you can imagine, there are a lot of people I would like to thank for saving Ted and I, people without whom we would both have been goners. Again, for the moment secrecy means that I cannot thank them properly at this time. Ted and I are both aware, painfully aware, actually, that so many of our shipmates on the Achilles will never be, cannot be reunited with their families and friends; today, it is with them that our thoughts must be, and will always be. All I can say is that if Ted and I, our standing here in front of you proves anything, it is that one should never, ever give up hope."

Now that he was home a great weariness was falling upon Abe's soul; and all fear, dread, anger was draining away.

"After this afternoon Ted and I will be disappearing from sight for a while. My colleagues in the medical fraternity will be giving us a good going over, and I know that the Fleet Intelligence Staff will want to properly debrief us about our adventures. So, I apologise in advance; but for the next few days at least, neither of us will be making further public appearances or statements. I understand that an account of the last few weeks is to be issued shortly, covering the events around the Battle of the Windward Passage and our escape to Little Inagua Island," he grinned, momentarily baring his teeth as would a predator, "where we had further *dealings* with the King's enemies. However, for the time being I cannot speak of the circumstances of our rescue. You will understand that neither Ted, nor I, want to risk giving the enemy *any* information which might be of assistance to the Triple Alliance."

Belatedly, probably a sign of his mental exhaustion, he registered the breadth and depth of the sea of faces before him.

"I don't want to say much more. The important thing is that so far as Ted and I are concerned, this is a day to think of what Melanie and the wives of the men of the Achilles have gone through, and continue to go through. There is always a lot of attention on the chaps at sea and in the air; but just remember those we leave behind, without whom none of us would be any use to man nor beast, let alone our King and our country."

That was when the clapping started.

Abe put his arm about Ted Forest's shoulders, worried his friend was about to fall over.

They leaned into the microphones and chorused, hoarsely: "Remember Brave Achilles!"

Behind them Lord Collingwood motioned for Alex, Kate and the Cowdrey-Singhs to join the two flagging aviators, joining arms as the applause reached a tumultuous crescendo and the chant was picked up by the crowd.

REMEMBER BRAVE ACHILLES!
REMEMBER BRAVE ACHILLES!

The television pictures were beaming across New England, and via Empire Broadcasting Corporation relay stations, around the whole world.

There would be no other story on the front pages of newspapers throughout that quarter of the land surface of the planet that was painted imperial pink on maps of the globe.

How odd it was that two of the three sons of the traitor Isaac Putnam Fielding now stood before the whole Empire, rehabilitated and lionised, like prodigals returned heroes both.

Chapter 25

Friday 5th May
Imperial Concession, Guaynabo, San Juan, Santo Domingo

The survivors of the Achilles had been billeted in the makeshift, hurriedly thrown up barrack camp bordering the jungle about a mile south west of the nearest coastline, which now entertained the men of the SMS Emden. There were only thirty-three men left under Peter Cowdrey-Singh's command, existing rather than living in a hut surrounded by the five-hundred-and-thirty-seven men disembarked from the German cruiser.

Ironically, having initially been in such a screaming hurry to expel every 'heretic and unbeliever' off their new toy, the Dominicans had quickly realised that the one-hundred-and-eighty men of their own religion and navy already on board the Emden – supposedly 'in training' – were, when push came to shove, patently incapable of running the big, modern, complicated and in many ways, very delicate prize even when she was tied up alongside the quay.

"The idiots have already damaged number two boiler and short-circuited the aft fire control station!" Kapitan-zur-See Claude Wallendorf, the Emden's former commanding officer, an irascible man of Franco-German heritage, could barely contain his mounting outrage as he and Peter Cowdrey-Singh accompanied the German Minister and his wife on a tour of the new 'Naval Camp' situated about half-a-mile into the jungle. "My people say they can hardly bear to watch the fools monkeying around with the guns; they expect the idiots to inadvertently loose off a salvo at any moment. The Dominicans are like children, spoiled, ignorant children!"

Prior to handing over the ship Hans von Schaffhausen had asked Wallendorf to transmit a list of the names of the British 'guests' under the protection of the German Concession, and of those men who had died in the Weser's action against 'pirate elements of the Santo Domingo Navy', to the Admiralty in Berlin in 'the plain', so that the Royal Navy would, at least, be able to intercept the signal and therefore, be able to communicate what little good news there was, to the comrades and relatives of the men under his protection on the island.

The High Command had wanted to know why Wallendorf had transmitted in plain text; he had peremptorily wired back: "CODE BOOKS DESTROYED TO AVOID SAME FALLING INTO THE HANDS OF THE TRIPLE ALLIANCE."

Yesterday morning, Peter Cowdrey-Singh had been invited by the German Minister to sit with him awhile on his balcony, to drink tea and to enjoy the ongoing slapstick chaos on the quayside and on the upper decks of the Emden.

After touring the jungle camp, the Royal Navy man accompanied the German Minister, his wife, Claude Wallendorf and a protective escort of former crewmen of the Emden – each carrying side arms – on a walk through the Concession's small port.

"The Dominicans have had militiamen swarming all over the ship looking for things to steal," Wallendorf went on disgustedly. "The chap they've put on board to command the ship has a bloody Inquisitor standing behind his shoulder all the damned time!"

The previous day the Anglo-Indian former Executive Officer of the Achilles had watched the 'idiots' dismantling several heavy anti-aircraft guns and dumping crate upon crate of treasure ripped out of the bowels of the cruiser onto the dockside.

He grunted his barely concealed contempt: "I wouldn't be surprised if we wake up one morning and the bloody ship has capsized alongside the dock!"

Personally, Peter Cowdrey-Singh would not shed many tears if that happened. Although Claude Wallendorf seemed like a decent sort, and he and his officers were obviously unhappy about the part they had played in recent events, the Royal Navy man was not about to forget the death, destruction, and blood spilled that Wallendorf, and all the other 'good' Kaiserliche Marine men like him in the Caribbean, had caused while fighting for *his* King's enemies.

"And now," Wallendorf protested to the German Minister, his ire and the violence of his language only restrained by the presence of a lady, the German Minister's effervescent wife, Angela, "you are telling me that not only has the Empire broken off diplomatic relations with the British, but that normal, customary channels of communication with our brothers in the Royal Navy have also been outlawed!"

Hans von Schaffhausen nodded.

"Yes. Since then I have received further updates from Berlin and a communication from the Governor of New England in respect of the message, that you, Kapitan Wallendorf, kindly transmitted in respect of the survivors of HMS Achilles."

The Emden's ex-commanding officer listened, still scowling.

"My information is that although the Kaiserliche Marine supports the administration of the new Kaiser, it is taking no part in the fighting in Berlin or in quelling the ongoing disturbances in the other cities, other than providing peace-keeping detachments in the major ports, Hamburg, Bremen, Kiel, Cuxhaven, Stettin and Danzig."

The German Minister had learned that further 'disturbances' had flared-up, and were 'ongoing' in the Rhineland and the Palatinate, and in Bavaria, where the state government in Munich had declared, in unison with neighbouring Baden-Württemberg, a 'state of emergency' and summoned a 'joint representative council to consider the promulgation of a Declaration of Independence from the German Empire.'

Short-wave radio broadcasts from Europe also spoke of *Kriegsluftflotte III* – the Third War Air Fleet – of the *Deutsche Luftstreitkräfte* (German Air Force) which was based in Hesse, Bavaria and Württemberg, having sided with the civilian administration in Munich.

The whole situation was a nightmare.

Kriegsluftflotte III, in addition to its twenty or so operational *staffeln*

– squadrons – of modern fighters and medium bomber aircraft, also included several cutting-edge specialist units: the *Hochgeschwindigkeitsflug Entwicklungsgruppe* (the High-speed Flight Development Group) at Regensburg, the *Düsenturbinenantrieb Experimentalflügel* (the Jet Turbine Propulsion Experimental Wing) at Nuremburg, and the *Rakete und geführt Design-Mitarbeiter* (the Rocket and Guided Minitions Design Staff) at Augsburg.

The most organised, arguably the best-educated, certainly the most militarised continental European power had, practically overnight, begun to fracture.

Consequently, right now nobody in Germany gave a damn about a 'piss pot concession' like Guaynabo. Almost overnight, Von Schaffhausen and his fetid little fiefdom had turned from a sub-tropical paradise – of sorts – into an open-air prison at the mercy of the Dominicans.

The German Minister struggled to put aside his darker premonitions.

"My repeated requests that the Wilhelmstrasse be asked to arrange for the repatriation of Commander Cowdrey-Singh's men have thus far met with no response…"

"What of the message from Philadelphia, Herr Minister?" The Anglo-Indian asked pointedly. So far as he was concerned the Germans could carry on shooting at each other for as long as they wanted. In fact, the longer the better!

Von Schaffhausen hesitated.

"In the interests of clarity, I must re-iterate that the message in question was actually sent to the Dominican Government. Its form was that of an unconditional demand that you and you people should be placed on board a ship and sent home by noon tomorrow. The communication spoke, apparently, of the severest repercussions for the leadership in particular, and for the Dominican people in general, in the event that any of you are harmed in any way, or are not returned as demanded."

"Well, what are the fools going to do?" Wallendorf inquired.

"Nothing. They claim that our British guests are in fact *our* prisoners and that it is up to *us* to take them home."

The German officer shrugged.

"Why don't we, Herr Minister?"

"We don't have a ship," von Schaffhausen replied tartly, "and even if we did the Dominicans would never let it out of the harbour."

Peter Cowdrey-Singh was unimpressed; wondering how long it was going to take his 'hosts' to join up the pieces and realise that they were in as bad a position as he and his men!

"How many German nationals are there within the Concession?" The question was asked rhetorically. "A thousand, perhaps?"

The German Minister nodded.

"There were about three hundred and fifty adults and seventy or eighty children and young people below the age of eighteen years, before the men from the Weser and the Emden came ashore," Angela von

Schaffhausen said, helpfully. "So, that's around five hundred people."

"And what," Peter Cowdrey-Singh continued, "do you think is going to happen to you all when the Triple Alliance has got hold of all your ships and the Royal Navy starts to blockade the Greater Antilles and the Caribbean? Or when the first fifteen-inch shells start falling on their coastal cities in the middle of the night?"

The others were silent.

"I think it is high time we all put our cards on the table," he went on. "I think you know exactly what *those people* across the bay and their Inquisitors will do. Dammit, there's a bloody ironclad out there in the bay pointing its bloody guns at you!"

Still, the others said nothing.

"Up until now they've been waiting to get their hands on the Emden. In a day or two they'll have looted her from stem to stern, and then they'll warp her out into the bay and see if they can figure out which levers to pull and switches to flick, assuming they haven't completely wrecked her, to get her back to sea. Then, what use will they have for you?"

"I'm sure it won't come to that," von Schaffhausen objected, without real conviction.

"They tried to disarm your men when they disembarked from the Emden!" The Anglo-Indian snarled. "Open your bloody eyes, man!"

"But what can we do, Commander," Angela von Schaffhausen asked quietly.

"They sent out two destroyers to arrest the Weser because some religious nutcase over there," he jabbed his arm to the east where the capital lay across the other side of San Juan Bay, "wanted, and presumably, still wants, to get their hands on me and my men, presumably to do whatever the bloody Inquisition does to heretics!"

"But you are safe," the German Minister insisted. "We will not let them take you..."

"How would you stop them?"

Again, Peter Cowdrey-Singh gestured around them.

"I don't see any castle wall, or artillery. Dammit, you've got less than a hundred firearms and probably, damn all ammunition. What are Kapitan Wallendorf's people supposed to do if the Dominicans walk in one day and start arresting, or just killing, whoever they want? I'm sorry; but I don't think relying on stern words and sticks and stones is going to cut it against several thousand soldiers with automatic rifles!"

The four of them had halted, not quite out of earshot of several Kaiserliche Marine officers and men; others around them were halting, pausing to listen.

"But we still don't have a ship?" The German Minister's wife reminded him.

"Forgive me," Peter Cowdrey-Singh objected, genuinely apologetic to be gainsaying Angela von Schaffhausen. "We have two. The Weser and the Emden, neither in tip top condition, I grant you. But at least the Emden still has some shells in her magazines?"

He looked to Wallendorf, who nodded.

"Thirty or forty reloads per main battery barrel," the German officer muttered, almost under his breath. "But the Dominicans plan to move the ship in forty-eight hours."

The Royal Navy man was not telling them anything they had not thought about themselves. He had already decided that sooner or later he was going to have to get his men out of the Concession, with or without the help of the Germans. One option was to demand firearms from von Schaffhausen and to escape into the jungle, more attractive was the notion of stealing a boat, any boat, even one of the old sailing barques moored in neighbouring Catano Reach. Anything was better than meekly awaiting the pleasure of the religious maniacs who were prepared to arrest a friendly nation's ship – the Weser – to get its hands on him and his men. It was a racing certainty that the Dominican regime had been plotting its revenge ever since the Weser limped into port.

Hans von Schaffhausen sighed, sucked his teeth.

"The authorities have issued an edict forbidding the sale of foodstuffs to foreign nationals. I suspect that from the gratuitously bad behaviour of many of the alleged new crew members of the Emden, that they are thugs, not seamen, sent into the Concession to make trouble. It is no longer safe for a woman to walk alone. I suspect the Inquisition is looking for any excuse to enter our territory."

The German Minister's wife touched her husband's arm.

"There are still some of our people outside the Concession?"

It transpired word had gone out some weeks ago for all German nationals to report back to the German Minister. Many of these were individuals who had 'gone native', and chosen to live elsewhere. Among them were a small clique who had actually embraced the brutal Catholicism of the Church in Santo Domingo, and subsequently, been expelled from the Concession on account of their 'disruptive' conduct.

"For all you know, your people outside the Concession are already in the regime's jails," Peter Cowdrey-Singh said impatiently. "In any case, I have no intention of sitting on my hands waiting for those bastards to toast my feet over an open fire. Frankly, if it hadn't been for the cowardly actions of members of the Kaiserliche Marine in the Battle of the Windward Passage, I and my men would not be in this situation. If all you people can think of is twiddling your thumbs waiting to get stabbed in the back like Achilles was, then," he shook his head, "shame on you!"

Claude Wallendorf's nostrils flared with anger.

"Commander Cowdrey-Singh," he barked, "I had no part in that affair."

"How dare you, sir!" The Anglo-Indian rounded on the other officer. "How dare you! Answer me this: how many innocent civilians on Jamaica are dead because you forgot the honour of the Kaiserliche Marine? What did you do when those fucking Cubans sacked Kingston and started raping and murdering their way across the island?"

He turned to walk away.

"Commander," Angela von Schaffhausen snapped irritably. "None of us here need a lecture about imperial morality from a Royal Navy officer. But arguing among ourselves doesn't help anybody. You and Kapitan

Wallendorf can have this argument another time. Right now, what I am really, really worried about is the safety of *my* children."

The German Minister's wife was angry and she was not the sort of woman a wise man ignored when she was in this kind of mood. Her blue eyes flashed with exasperation as she looked back to her husband and the Emden's former captain.

"Commander Cowdrey-Singh is right. There is nothing we could do if the Dominicans violated the sanctity of the Concession, you only have to see how those toughs 'working' on the Emden have behaved to know that they know it as well as anybody. If they attempted to arrest our British guests all we could do is endanger the lives of the German civilians in the Concession. In effect, we too, are prisoners here. Either we accept our fate," she looked around defiantly, "or we rattle our chains."

"What have you in mind, meine Liebe," her husband inquired almost inaudibly.

"God sent us the Emden. I suggest we take advantage of *His* divine intervention!"

Chapter 26

Thursday 4th May
El Palacio de Los Pinos de Oro, México City

Professor Arturo Gutiérrez Ortiz Mena of the University of Cuernavaca's infant Department of Nuclear Physics, spoke with a quietly spontaneous, and after a few minutes, unselfconscious intensity which soon began to chill the souls of the other three men in the President of the Republic's office.

"You must understand that if we, or anybody else, were to set out from scratch, as it were, to produce sufficient fissile material for just a single, very rudimentary atomic device it would probably involve the expenditure of great treasure, the diversion of perhaps ten, or possibly fifteen or twenty percent, of our national scientific, technical and industrial capacity, assuming absolute priority was given to the project over its whole lifetime, and even once we had sufficient fissile material, it might still take us several years to resolve the technical design, and the implosive technologies required to initiate a chain reaction, and then, even assuming we had access to sufficient ongoing quantities of Uranium, which we do not have because most of the World's known deposits are in Australia and those parts of Southern Africa controlled by the British and German Empires, we would still not be capable of refining, or more correctly, enriching Uranium, chemical symbol 'U', from its most naturally occurring isotopic form of U238 to its fissile state, given a critical mass of around fifteen or sixteen pounds – incidentally, we have established that by theoretical means but what actually constitutes a critical mass for a given materials configuration would still need to be established by experimentation – to U235..."

The academic paused for breath.

President de Soto, and Chief of Staff of the Army, General Santa Anna, were viewing the dishevelled physicist with increasingly glazed expressions.

Arturo thought he had gone through the basic, what he regarded as schoolyard science with Rodrigo several times but clearly, the President and General Santa Anna were still completely baffled.

He hesitated.

I have been babbling like a fool...

He took a deep breath and started all over again.

"Uranium is a silvery grey metal with the symbol 'U' and an atomic number of 92, because it possesses the highest atomic weight of the ninety-two naturally occurring primordial elements. It is an actinide; all actinides release radioactivity over time as they decay and therefore, have a half-life, which, for isotopes of uranium vary between hundreds of thousands and billions of years. The isotopic form of over ninety-nine percent of all the Uranium naturally occurring in the environment is U238, so described because it has one-hundred-and-forty-six neutrons, and ninety-two protons, and theoretically – although in fact very unlikely to because it is unknown for it to occur in the concentrations necessary for it to happen – it is capable of spontaneous fission in nature, that is, a chain reaction splitting the nucleus of the atom and releasing exponentially large quanta of energy. However, as I say, since U238 is almost invariably found only as a trace element, that remains, to the best of my knowledge, a purely theoretical proposition. This is because at a sub-atomic level the ratio between neutrons and other particles reduces in relation to the number present in an atom. Therefore, to made U238 into fissile, or weapon-grade U235, it must be enriched so that the neutron count falls to one-hundred-and-forty-three, at which level the probability of the energetic random incidence of collisions with the constant ninety-two protons in the nucleus becomes, mathematically at least, unavoidable, and thence, given the presence of a critical mass of enriched Uranium – about fifteen or sixteen pounds, by my calculations - results in an immensely violent explosion."

Disappointingly, Arturo's interlocutors were still looking a little bewildered. However, a university lecturer soon got used to that; so, he decided to press on regardless.

"The important things you must take into consideration are that there are only a couple of viable methods of enriching U238 to U235," he frowned, momentarily distracted by arcane, positively existential possibilities, "although, several recent papers suggest the possibility of deriving U233 from Thorium, of course but forget about that for the moment. More realistically, you might employ some kind of gaseous diffusion process, or you might use cyclotrons to separate our matter," another stray thought intruded, "deuterium oxide," he muttered, as if making a mental note, "heavy water, perhaps... Anyway, the point is that it is impossible to enrich to the U235-state other than by creating an appropriate enrichment infrastructure, I suspect, on an industrial scale previously unknown in the whole of human history. The cost of this alone would be, as I alluded to earlier," he thought about it, "perhaps twenty percent of all the Republic's revenues tax revenues for as long as a decade, without even taking into account the weaponization costs of the end product, which itself, would be extremely cost, not to mention very hazardous to everybody involved in the processing, and consequently, very dangerous to store, other than in very small, well-shielded facilities. As to the specific problem of the weaponization project..."

Nobody interrupted, so the physicist continued.

"The geometry of bringing two smaller, non-critical masses together to form an instantaneous critical mass, thereby initiating the spontaneous chain reaction required to release a small part of the energy within the atoms of U235, would in itself, be a remarkable piece of science..."

"And yet," Santa Anna sighed, "the English have, it seems, solved all of these problems and produced, we think, judging by the test grounds in northern Sonora, a significant number of viable atomic weapons?"

"Yes, but they have the resources of an Empire that encompasses a quarter of the globe, General. Moreover, respectfully, they possess a centuries-old scientific tradition of free inquiry, that we do not. They also have access to Uranium, in small quantities in the British Isles and New England, and in significant deposits in Australia and Southern Africa, and the pre-existing, well-established advanced, large-scale, well-established academic, technical and industrial infrastructure in place to expeditiously implement such a huge project. True, the cost to them would be enormous; but in comparison to ourselves, that cost would only equate to a relatively small drain on their overall wealth." The physicist hesitated. "I would guess that the English have been able to keep their atomic research secret simply by hiding its costs in major military and civilian infrastructure and research and development projects. We have made great strides in the last few years but our universities and industry were constrained by the dogmas of the Mother Church even while I was studying for my first degree, and in the fields of the natural sciences and other realms of pure theoretical and experimental inquiry, we remain in many respects, like babes in arms, children taking their first steps into the future in comparison with our *friends* in New England and Northern Europe."

Santa Anna sat back and looked, thoughtfully to Hernando de Soto before again focusing on the scientist.

"You intimated to Don Rodrigo that you were afraid that the English might already have progressed beyond the testing of 'rudimentary' devices, Professor?"

Arturo Gutiérrez Ortiz Mena swallowed hard and nodded.

"Yes, in testing the samples brought back from the 'test' area, I detected traces of radioactive isotopes which my theoretical studies indicate ought not to be present in the environment after the testing of a U235 device. Specifically, I suspect that at least one device employing a product of Uranium enrichment called Plutonium may have been tested in Sonora."

"And why is this particularly worrying?" The President asked, his face a little ashen.

"Because using Plutonium it is conceivable to produce a fusion reaction, much like that in the heart of our Sun, Your Honour. It infers a technology which, if combined with that of a U235 *bomb*," he stumbled after the inadvertent use of *that* word, "might make possible the development of a weapon which could destroy the largest city on the planet and obliterate everything around it for ten, twenty, or possibly fifty miles in every direction."

The physicist's thoughts had already moved on.

He was thinking of the papers – a steady stream, a drip, drip, drip of them – on ionising radiation-related subjects published in the last decade in the British Isles, and several, fascinating ones which had been published under the auspices of the Kaiser Wilhelm Institute in Berlin. Until a week or so ago, he had complacently imagined the majority of these fascinating papers must have been based on the classified research carried out by the great powers back in the 1950s and early 1960s, and perhaps deliberately de-classified in the wake of the Submarine Treaty which, in effect, abolished the building of submarines and the development of under-water technologies in its title; but more importantly, had supposedly halted all bar theoretical atomic research either for civil usages, other than for medical applications such as x-ray or imaging, and banned outright all military applications of nuclear science.

He had wondered about the datasets many of those papers had been based on, and assumed that the Europeans must have had access to animal testing experiments prior to the signing of the Treaty in 1966. However, now two things struck him, both like unexpected blows to the guts.

One, either or both of the British or German atomic programs must have been far more advanced by 1966 than either of the parties had admitted; and two, that the English at least, must have continued to develop their program in secret in the intervening twelve years.

"When Don Rodrigo spoke to me," he said, picking up the threads of his racing, jostling fears, astonished that the first relatively short telephone conversation with his esteemed university colleague had only been seven days ago, "I explained the things that I would need to look for to confirm, or rule out, the provisional conclusions he had already drawn from visiting the Ojo del Diablo district, and the areas to which the local Indian population had taken him, where reported pathologies and fragmentary morphological evidence suggested possible contamination by non-naturally occurring ionising radiation. The literature I have read on the research available on the radioactive pathology of mammalians is, surprisingly, remarkably informative, if somewhat speculative. Nonetheless, the mechanisms in play are schoolboy stuff, basic high school physics, really..."

Don Rodrigo caught his colleague's eye and glanced at the nearest wall clock as if to say: "President de Soto and General Santa Anna are busy men and their time is very precious!"

"I apologise," the physicist stuttered, "as my beautiful wife keeps telling me, I am not a very practical man. I tend to digress at the drop of a hat..."

Hernando de Soto smiled patiently, paternally.

"What you have told us thus far is most thought-provoking professor. Pray continue."

"Yes, thank you, Your Honour. It was suggested that I stick to layman's language. That is hard, the subject is complex and there are many variables."

"We understand, Professor," Santa Anna confirmed, a little distantly as if his thoughts were suddenly hundreds of miles away with his troops in West Texas.

"Anyway, once I'd spoken to Don Rodrigo, I knew what to look for. If, that was, the Sonora site was indeed a testing range for atomic *bombs*..."

He had said that *word* again.

Employed the plural form of it...

And he was about to say *it* again, and he suspected, again and again in the next few minutes, days, weeks and years.

He took a deep breath.

"There are likely to be three relatively long-lived isotopic substances, isotopes, if you like from the detonation of an atomic bomb employing U235. There are other 'fallout' isotopes injurious to human health, and to the general ecology of local and distant sites from an atomic explosion, or more accurately, a significant fission event. In any event, there is nothing our present state of medical knowledge can do to mitigate, or to alleviate the effects of irradiation caused by the numerous exotic short-lived isotopic fission by-products, the majority of which would already be present only in unimaginably minute quanta by now, and therefore undetectable to the equipment available to us. So, I will disregard those. As I say, there are three particular isotopic markers, or contaminants, which are identifiable and tend to linger in the tissue of living mammals, and or, to collect in the fibre of the local flora and fauna."

A part of Arturo Gutiérrez Ortiz Mena wanted to believe that he was not having to explain this, any of it to the two most powerful men in México, especially not in the middle of a war with an enemy who might, at a whim, start wiping the cities of his homeland off the face of the Earth, much in the fashion of an angry god.

"Had atomic devices been tested in the desert of northern Sonora one would expect to find the presence of trace elements of isotopic Strontium-90, Iodine-131 and 133 in the surrounding landscape and in the tissue of living organisms. It is my understanding that of these, Strontium-90, or in scientific shorthand, Sr90, is the most dangerous. Sr 90 is a so-called *bone seeker* which biochemically mimics Calcium, coincidentally the next lightest of the *group 2 elements* in the Periodic Table. Like Calcium, after ingestion the body routinely excretes about seventy to eighty percent of the dose; unfortunately, all the rest, typically over twenty percent of the remaining Sr90 accumulates in bone and bone marrow. In all cases at least one percent of the total dose ingested lodges in blood and soft tissue. It is believed that minimal concentrations of Sr90 in the bones massively increases the risk of developing bone cancers, and cancers in adjacent soft tissue, or full-blown leukaemia. Sr90 attacks the bone marrow and consequently, destroys the body's ability to produce the white blood cells necessary to fight infection. In the immediate aftermath of an atomic explosion, anybody breathing in air, or consuming food or fluids heavily contaminated by Sr90 might easily die of something as innocent as the common cold, within say, a week."

The President and General Santa Anna were trying to tune out their mounting horror.

"Sr90, like I131 and I133 remain dangerous for a long time. The biological half-life of Sr90 inside bone and tissue is about eighteen years."

"Half-life?" Rodrigo queried softly, mainly for the benefit of the other men in the room.

"Yes, after eighteen years half of the original contaminant survives. Eighteen years later one-quarter of the original dosage, and so on. The mammalian risk factors remain, therefore, in statistically significant concentrations in the general environment for many tens, or in the case of Sr90, perhaps, fifty or sixty years and do not revert to the normal, background levels of contamination for hundreds of years."

"Is there nothing that can be done for the victims?" Santa Anna asked, his voice dull.

"The papers I have read speculate that calcium citrate, taken in large enough doses might help the body resist Sr90 take-up. The theory is that bone and bone marrow can only absorb isotopic contaminants at a given rate. By inducing biological competition, calcium citrate will therefore, at least reduce Sr90 assimilation and, possibly, reduce the total level of contamination. The dosages of calcium citrate suggested are a thousand milligrams daily – for both adults and children – immediately after contamination and, thereafter five-hundred milligrams per day for at least three weeks. Logically, in addition to calcium citrate prophylactic doses of vitamin C, that's ascorbic acid, may help to regulate the production of healthy bone protein and promote the formation of white blood cells. The recommended dosage of Vitamin C is three-hundred milligrams a day for a month and one hundred milligrams daily thereafter for several months."

"How effective are those measures likely to be?" Santa Anna inquired, dreading the answer.

"We have no way of knowing, General. It may be that people in the peak of health may benefit, and others not. Unfortunately, even if by some miracle one survives more or less uninjured in the proximity of an atomic explosion, one might easily already have suffered a fatal or disabling dose of X-ray or gamma-ray radiation."

President de Soto tried and failed to prevent a groan escaping his lips.

"Would such a death be immediate?"

"No, Your Honour. One would die within days. High doses of ionising radiation destroy all the internal biological mechanisms that support life. A victim dies from the inside out, with every organ disintegrating, causing heavy bleeding from every orifice. This pathology would be consistent with the symptoms described to Don Rodrigo by his Navajo scouts."

"Oh, God," the President breathed.

"You said that there were two other major contaminants indicative of atomic explosions, Professor?" Santa Anna reminded the physicist.

"Yes, after Sr90, the next most dangerous fallout isotopes are I131 and I133. Both collect in the thyroid gland in the neck. The literature suggests that mature mammalians exposed to these radioactive isotopes probably infer a massively elevated risk of a wide range of cancers in later life, and because the thyroid gland regulates growth, children exposed to these isotopes are likely to be stunted – or possibly afflicted with giantism, the literature is ambiguous about this – and excessively prone to infantile cancers. It is thought that potassium iodide, taken in daily doses of one-hundred-and-thirty milligrams for several months after first contamination, may inhibit the build-up of the two isotopes in the thyroid."

"So," Santa Anna prompted, leaning forward, "did you find these Hellish things in the samples Don Rodrigo recovered from Sonora?"

Arturo Gutiérrez Ortiz Mena nodded.

"Yes, in places, in concentrations many thousands of times higher than that which one would expect to find in the environment. Mapping the 'fallout', abnormal results were identified at seven sites father than twenty statute miles from the nearest identified test site."

None of the men spoke for some moments.

"Do we know how big the bombs they tested at the Eye of Diablo were?" Santa Anna posed, running a hand through his hair.

He had looked at Don Rodrigo, who, in turn had glanced, tight-lipped to the only physicist in the room.

The Professor of Nuclear Science at the University of Cuernavaca pondered this, his face a mask of concentration as his brain clicked methodically through the relevant algorithms and coefficients.

"I cannot be precise, even though Don Rodrigo was most particular in his surveying of the test sights. However, other scientists in England and Berlin, and I believe at the Academy in Paris, have published papers on the kind of explosive yields predicted by a minimum critical mass of very pure enriched U235. All their calculations are expressed in thousands of tons – or kilotons – of standard high explosive equivalence. From this, and the dimensions of the blast circles and craters, I estimate a range of explosions in the low tens, to the high thirties of kilotons..."

"Ten to thirty thousand tons of high explosive?" Santa Anna objected, as if he wished it was not so.

"Yes, General. Not of dynamite or gunpowder, but something like the most potent military grade substances, which would be between three and four times as potent as old-fashioned dynamite. Out of idle curiosity I parsed the numbers for the explosion, probably caused by a meteorite from outer space, as posited by my learned colleague, Don Rodrigo, which created the Eye of the Devil crater which, as I am sure you know is three-quarters of a mile wide and about five hundred feet deep even now after thousands of years of erosion and back-filling with wind-blown sand..."

A scowl was forming on the face of the Chief of Staff of the Mexican Army.

The physicist smiled apologetically.

"The number I came up with was, plus or minus a megaton – that is a million *short* English tons – that the ultra-high-speed impact caused an explosion equivalent to about ten million tons of the most powerful non-atomic high explosive known to science."

The others were staring at him.

Arturo Gutiérrez Ortiz Mena did not notice.

"Anybody looking at the fireball from thirty miles away would have been blinded for life. Everybody within twenty miles of the impact would probably have been killed or very seriously injured. Had the debris cloud thrown fifty to sixty miles into the atmosphere by the meteoritic impact been radioactive everybody for about a thousand miles downwind would have been heavily contaminated..."

"That's very interesting, Professor," the President of the Republic said quietly.

"Yes, isn't it," Arturo agreed, lost in his thesis. "Do you remember I mentioned about Plutonium earlier? Well, my preliminary work strongly supports the hypothesis that at least one of the tests in northern Sonora was of a bomb utilising isotopic material with the properties of P239."

Suddenly, the three other men in the room knew things were going to get worse and really did not want to hear about it, not then, not until they had had a stiff drink and an opportunity to get their mind around what they had already learned that afternoon.

The physicist ploughed on.

"If one built a Plutonium bomb inside a Uranium bomb the explosion of the outer, Uranium bomb might, theoretically you understand, implode the Plutonium core of such a weapon and lead to a fusion chain reaction like that which powers the Sun. In that event, it is conceivable that one might construct a bomb with an explosive potential equivalence of *much more than just ten megatons!*"

Chapter 27

Friday 5th May
Viano do Castelo, Portugal

Yesterday, when Melody had finally got back to the old hotel overlooking the Atlantic after a lonely, day-long journey by road and rail from Lisbon, she had been in a very odd mood.

Her 'interview' at the British Embassy in the Portuguese capital had been, as she had expected a job interview for the Imperial Intelligence Service. In itself, this was a little surreal: she had been working for the IIS all the time she was in Spain! Moving on past that little quirk she had discovered that back home in New England, the CSS – the Colonial Security Service – was to be wholly subsumed into the IIS, thus removing it from either the oversight, or the funding peccadillos of individual New England Crown Colonies. This change had not wholly recommended itself to her; she was at heart a proud daughter of the Crown Colony of Vermont first, and a New Englander second, and in any event, she had not decided if she even wanted to go *back home* quite yet, anyway.

Thinking about it, it was not until she had left New England that she had recognised that she did not like living in a Commonwealth where individual colonial administrations honestly believed, that they had the right to legislate for its citizen's sex lives.

She got it that if a woman slept with a man that she was not married to then she was, according to the prevailing sexual mores of the East Coast, de facto, a slut or a tart. That sucked but the notion that if she slept with another woman both parties could, theoretically be put in prison for it, and in practice sometimes dragged through the courts and the gutter press, had got really, really old since she had been in a relationship with Henrietta. Worse, back in New England, if she went anywhere near the woman that she loved she was placing Henrietta, and unthinkably, her family in huge peril of scandal; a thing she wished on nobody.

And then there was Alonso...

Which was where she started asking herself what she even meant by thinking she was 'in love' with somebody. It seemed to her that she was 'addicted' to Alonso, and 'responsible' for Henrietta. And that too, was a very peculiar way to look at things!

That first conversation with Queen Sophie had impossibly muddied...everything. She had thought she knew where she stood, known what she felt, and had understood her own motivations and then realised, she had been wrong all along.

In hindsight she had been *hot* about Alonso from the moment they met, and he, she guessed, for her. She had always been going to end up in bed with him and yet, she had had no real inkling that sleeping with him was going to have the effect it had had, if not entirely innocently then carelessly, on her part, on poor Henrietta. Melody had thought it was all about her; a mistake she made a lot but self-knowledge usually dawns far too late to stop one putting one's foot in it. It had never occurred to her that, in her way – albeit in a much less carnal and rather beautiful, in a girlish, naïve sort of way – Henrietta was as stupid about Alonso as she had, obviously, become since she arrived in Spain.

And...now she was hearing her mother's voice in her head reminding her what a selfish girl she was!

Things had never been this complicated when she was living a life as carnally blameless as any cloistered nun. She had loved being a detective, right up to the moment she had acknowledged that she was burying herself in her work to stop herself worrying about how she had screwed up the rest of her life.

No, that might just be her mother's voice again.

Anyway, the Imperial Intelligence Service wanted her to come on board 'for real', this time. That meant spending a while in England which probably was not going to work for Henrietta. Her mother was ill, of course, and although there was no family obligation or expectation for her to return to Philadelphia she wanted, needed to go back some time soon.

Yes, things were...messy.

And that was before she even tried to figure out how to cope with the Pedro situation...

The boy had come running down the first floor landing laughing and calling 'Mama Melody' to welcome her back, and clung to her like she was the edge of a cliff. And, well, she had loved it. She had known the boy less than a month – some of which she had been away being a complete slut with Alonso – and he had missed her.

'He asked where you were all the time,' Henrietta had confessed.

Hen was devoted to the little rascal who seemed to get more confident, more precocious with every passing day.

Melody had been happy just to be back with Henrietta and last night had been gently, marvellously blissful; and with the women waking up this morning to discover that Pedro had inserted himself between them had been...perfect.

None of which made Melody feel any more settled that morning.

She had meant to have *the big* conversation with Henrietta, instead, they had kissed their lips sore and in the darkness of the night they had been far, far too preoccupied with each other's bodies to worry about the future.

The two women had spoken daily on the telephone when Melody had been in Lisbon and Vila Viçosa with Alonso, they had gossiped away to each other, as usual. Henrietta had been fascinated to learn about Alonso's business interests and estates, including a large winery in the Algarve, in Portugal. Henrietta had talked a lot about Pedro, and been frankly flummoxed by what little Melody had felt free to confess regarding her meetings with the exiled Spanish Queen.

Melody was still teasing out a rough outline of how, exactly, Alonso and his 'allies' had safely extricated the Queen and the two Infantas from the chaos, a parallel adventure which probably made her and Henrietta's travails pale into insignificance.

It was a bright, warm day, so, Melody suggested they take Pedro for a ramble around the hilltop on which Viano do Castelo perched. Alonso was due that evening; and time was short.

"Things were a lot simpler when we were on the run in Spain," she decided.

They had been walking for some minutes, not talking.

"Yes," the younger woman agreed.

"We haven't really talked...about things."

"No."

"But we should, don't you think?"

Henrietta said nothing for several steps.

"I want to adopt Pedro," she said, in a voice suggesting she had been a little afraid to say it.

It was Melody's turn to lose her courage, she said nothing.

"How do you think Alonso will feel about that?" Henrietta asked anxiously.

Melody panicked, forgot everything she had meant to say and said the first thing that came into her head.

"Why wouldn't Alonso agree? He loves you, after all!"

The women stood, blinking incomprehension at each other.

Pedro broke the trance, tugging at Henrietta's skirt.

They each took one of his hands, and set off again.

The boy loved this game, the women gently lifting him off the ground so that he could swing, an inch or so off the cobbles, giggling and laughing, kicking his feet.

"No, he doesn't," Henrietta objected half-heartedly.

"He fell for you at first sight. Probably at one of those dreadful diplomatic receptions you used to host for your father in Philadelphia," Melody speculated. "You were always the most, well, only interesting woman in the room and the most beautiful..."

"That's silly!"

"Okay, who was the first person you went to talk to when all those middle-aged, awful planter types hit on you at official functions at Government House? Who was the man who always made you laugh? Who was the guy who always listened to everything you had to say to him like it was the most fascinating thing in the world?"

"No, that's impossible. How on earth could you know that stuff?"

"Because that was the sort of *stuff*, he confessed to the Queen of Spain in the letters he sent her practically every day from Philadelphia!"

Oh, shit, I really, really did not mean to tell Hen that!

Henrietta was momentarily dumbstruck.

"Alonso and the Queen were teenage sweethearts or something," Melody said in a rush, desperately trying to repair the damage she imagined, in her confusion, she had just caused. "Queen Sophie was telling me about all sorts of things because she's terrified that Alonso will waste his whole life trying to restore her to the throne. She doesn't want that; she just wants her daughters to grow up like normal kids. Preferably without anybody trying to murder them all the time."

"Alonso and Queen Sophie were..."

Henrietta just stopped herself in time, not wanting to go there.

Nevertheless, both women were suddenly looking down at Pedro,

"No," Melody blurted.

"No, of course not," Henrietta agreed, like her friend suddenly very aware of the boys wide, Hapsburg eyes. "But..."

Pedro tugged at their hands and they walked on, started playing the swinging game anew.

"I know we don't want to go there," Henrietta whispered, as if they were not alone on a remote hilltop but in the middle of a crowd, "but Alonso did say Pedro's mother was a high-born lady..."

"Oh, God," Melody groaned. "Look, you know Alonso was supposed to have had a fling with Roger Lee's sister? Shortly after he arrived in Philadelphia?"

"Yes, everybody was scandalised..."

"That was the point. Queen Sophie talked about Alonso being like a monk. Although, the way she said it made it sound more like his 'monk' incarnation was more like he was some kind of latter-day Templar. But anyway, that he was a reformed character after Pedro's birth."

"Until he met *you*," Henrietta said pointedly. "But we're getting off the point. What is *she*, the Queen, I mean? Is she Pedro's mother?"

This time Melody halted abruptly.

Pedro, thinking that this was all part of the game laughed and resumed pulling at the women's hands.

Melody looked into her lover's eyes.

"If she is," she said, her voice a hoarse whisper, "then it has to stay our secret, Hen. Forever."

Belatedly, Henrietta had already worked that out for herself.

"So..."

"If you adopt him it works perfectly," Melody concluded, relieved that at last they seemed to be getting somewhere.

Walking on, Henrietta tried to join up the pieces; although, not very successfully because she was still a little shaken by the notion that Pedro might actually, be the secret love child of the Queen of Spain...and its potentially terrible ramifications

"So, what happens if you marry Alonso?" She asked stupidly.

"Me!" Melody yelped in alarm.

Pedro looked up, possibly aware for the first time of the very, very strange mood his two 'Mamas' were in today.

"Of course, *you*," Henrietta insisted, mulishly stubborn now. "Don't tell me you aren't crazy about him."

"It would never work, Hen!"

"Why not?"

"Even Queen Sophie knows it wouldn't work," Melody insisted doggedly.

"How could she possibly know that?"

"She was the Queen of Spain; she knows a lot of stuff!"

Melody coloured in embarrassment.

Did I really say that?

She tried a second time.

"I don't know, Hen. I really don't. But think about it. I'm nearly forty, I'm pretty self-obsessed, selfish actually. I'm driven, never really satisfied with anything. And," she sighed, "even if I wanted to have babies it is too late and I can't anyway. I'm Alonso's mistress, that's all I ever was. Maybe, I'll always be his mistress but I certainly don't want to ruin his life by marrying the poor man!"

Henrietta's face was a picture of baffled hopefulness.

Melody leaned towards her and planted a kiss on her mouth, which was reciprocated, unhurriedly.

"So," the younger woman sighed, at a loss, "that means that we're back at square one, aren't we?"

"No," Melody said patiently, acknowledging that there was no tactful way of wrapping this up. She gathered her courage. "The sensible thing to do," she began, hesitated, "is for you to marry Alonso, make lots of beautiful brothers and sisters for Pedro, and to live happily ever after."

Melody suspected her lover was going to claim that she only liked 'girls' but neither of them actually believed that for a minute. She put a finger to Henrietta's lips.

Suddenly, she was giggling.

They were both giggling.

Pedro, somewhat mystified looked from one Mama to the other, beginning to get a little miffed that he was so obviously, not the primary centre of attention.

He stamped his small feet.

Both women dropped to their haunches and started tickling him, still giggling, tears running down their cheeks now, and a moment later each hugging him between them.

And Pedro knew he was in the safest place he had ever been...

Chapter 28

Saturday 6th May
HMS Perseus, 235 nautical miles NNE of Anguilla

In the knowledge that two fleet oilers had been pre-positioned out to the east, lost in the vastness of the Atlantic with their escorting destroyers, Task Force 5.1 had battered south at twenty-five knots almost from the moment it passed out of sight of land and turned to the east-south-east. Shortly after dawn it had rendezvoused with Perseus's sister ship, the Hermes, and her escorting cruisers and destroyers, and soon afterwards Perseus had started flying off the fifteen extra Goshawk IV scouts and fourteen Sea Eagle II dive bombers stowed on her flight deck.

Once those aircraft had successfully landed on the Hermes, the two carriers would boast a combined strike force of sixty-three scouts, thirty-five torpedo bombers and forty-nine dive bombers.

The Hermes had crept out of her home port, Pembroke Dock in South Wales the previous weekend, rendezvousing with her escorts in the approaches to the Bristol Channel, six nights ago, supposedly to exercise in the Western Approaches with the 3rd Battle Squadron of the Home Fleet. Instead, operating under conditions of complete radio silence she and her consorts had disappeared into the fastness of the North Atlantic, worked up to twenty-three knots and steered south west to meet up with Task Force 5.1.

By now the Spanish would know that Perseus had left Hampton Roads; and the enemy high command would be worrying about a single big carrier at sea, possibly about to launch an attack somewhere...

If all went well the Triple Alliance would have no idea what had hit it when the combined Air Wings of two of the new super carriers struck!

In addition to the two big gun capital ships, the Princess Royal and the valiant old Indefatigable, both with eight-gun 15-inch main batteries, there were four heavy cruisers with a total of thirty-two 8-inch guns, seven light cruisers armed with a total of fifty-eight 6-inch guns and nineteen fleet destroyers now in company. Thirty-four warships covering nearly thirty square miles of ocean on a mission to strike the Triple Alliance a series of blows designed to send shock waves all the way back to México City, and to halt, as bloodily as possible, the enemies' run of victories at sea.

'Forget all that nonsense about knocking the Triple Alliance out of the war with a single punch. That isn't going to happen. Whatever people say about the ships and the crews we have, and they do not, this is going to be a bloody long fight. Not a one round knock-out but a twelve to fifteen round slog. We weren't ready and they were; we thought they had second rate kit, they do, but they also have some good ships and men, too. Mostly, we could not legislate for the existence of submarines that, moreover, the enemy was actually prepared to use against us outside his own coastal waters. Or, for that matter, the large number of modern aircraft he seems able to whistle up at the drop of a hat. So, having tried to do this the elegant way, we're going to have to get our hands dirty!"

Those had been the words of Rear Admiral Sir Anthony Parkinson, Flag Officer, Task Force 5.1.

Parkinson was by repute, one of the Navy's finest minds, a man who had written a book back in the 1960s about the problems facing a Navy trying to come to terms with the quickening pace of technological progress, and the dilemmas inherent in attempting to reform traditional tactical doctrines given that it had not been involved in a major shooting war for over a hundred years.

Alex Fielding, the Commander of Perseus's Scout-Fighter Group, had wondered if Parkinson was going to be a straw man, obsessed with the minutiae of tactics and planning. In fact, thus far he had turned out to be a 'details' man; but not in a bad way.

'Courage and a carry-on spirit will only get us so far; the object of the exercise is not to be, per se, heroic, it is to defeat the enemy any way that we can without incurring unnecessary casualties and loss of materiel!'

Parkinson had been unrelentingly grim in his pre-sailing address to his senior officers.

'There's no point having a bloody great big sword if you are not prepared to twist it once you have stuck it into the other fellow. Forget about *playing up and playing the game.* We did not want, or start this war. We are losing this war precisely because we chose not to make warlike preparations for it lest we inadvertently provoke it. The time for that sort of circular argument is over. The gloves are off. It is going to take time to mobilise the industry and the manpower of New England and the Empire to defeat the Triple Alliance and its allies; until then all we can realistically hope to do is to staunch the flow of blood from the wounds we have already sustained, and to give the enemy something to think about. Something he won't forget in a hurry, if ever!'

The Spanish believed they had knocked one of the Atlantic fleet's much-vaunted big aircraft carriers out of the fight; well, there were plenty more of them in the rest of the fleet and the transatlantic transfer of the Hermes was just the start. A signal that the tide was about to turn as progressively, more and more of the military muscle of the Empire was brought to bear upon the Triple Alliance.

Operation East Wind had one minor, and one major objective and a single, over-riding purpose: to send a very specific message to the Spanish high command.

Be very, very afraid!

Under the auspices of Operation East Wind, Task Force 5.1 was to calve off two of its heavy cruisers, the Naiad and the Sussex and four destroyers – as Task Force 5.11 - to seek out, engage and to destroy the Spanish squadron cruising the northern Lesser Antilles, the so-called Leeward Islands, each of which including the former French colony of Guadalupe, were either crown dependencies or, like Antigua, newly and somewhat experimentally endowed with limited dominion status. The Spanish had twice bombarded English Harbour and the island's capital, St John's in the last week; hit and run raids which had as yet done little damage to the small naval base but nevertheless, caused over a hundred casualties, and understandably, no little panic. It seemed the 'raiders', which had switched their attention to Plymouth on the neighbouring volcanic island of Montserrat within the last twenty-four hours, were old-fashioned coal-burning ironclad cruisers in company with a gang of several three or four stack torpedo boat destroyers. In the breaks between attacks it was assumed this motley collection of antique warships rendezvoused with one, perhaps a couple of small 'coalers' to top off their bunkers, before deciding who to 'pester' next. The original scare stories about Spanish marines coming ashore on Antigua had now been discounted.

Both Naiad and Sussex carried long-range, fairly nimble two-man Southampton Seaplane Company Gimlets, single-engined amphibians, for over-the-horizon reconnaissance, gunnery spotting and if required, search and rescue missions.

Meanwhile, the primary mission of Task Force 5.1 was to attack the capital of Santo Domingo.

The *order of service* went something like this: one, sink everything that floats in San Juan Bay and its adjacent anchorages; two, destroy all port facilities including dry docks, maintenance sheds, oil and coal depots; three, bomb Santo Domingo Government House and its associated Legislative Council complex; four, attack targets of opportunity in and around the city, and; five, all scouts not required for top cover over the target would attack, at low-level the major air base – one of only two on the main island - some six miles east-south-east of San Juan Bay.

This latter attack would commence approximately five minutes before the first wave of Sea Eagle torpedo bombers swept in over San Juan Island from the north at dawn on Monday, less than thirty-six hours hence.

'We are not going to be squeamish about this,' the Task Force Commander had said, proceeding to make his intentions unambiguously, brutally transparent, 'if civilians, churches, or Germans loitering near the docks within the boundaries of their Concession get killed, that is just too bad. I'll say it again. We did not want this war. We did not start it. The Triple Alliance sowed the whirlwind, now its members are about to start reaping the wind. Let me be plain about this: the reason we are going for the Dominicans first is because they are the most ideologically inimical to our way of life. Granted, their Hispanic and Cuban allies claim the same sort of Hell-fire thing but we now know that it was the Dominicans who were behind the Empire Day atrocities two years ago. Now, as they say, the whirlwind will visit San Juan. So, as I say, let us not be squeamish about this!'

To emphasis the point, orders had been issued that no aircraft was to bring back bombs or torpedoes, or external 'drop' fuel tanks. If there was no ship worth torpedoing, or easily identifiable 'military objective' available – for example if the whole area was obscured by smoke - then pilots were to climb to five thousand feet and release their fish 'somewhere' over San Juan city; likewise, unused bombs and superfluous drop tanks were to be discarded over 'the target area'.

Of course, no drop 'tank' was ever truly empty and when it hit the ground the highly inflammable vapour within it, still, in most cases, under pressure, would probably explode like a fireball. Normal practice was to jettison drop tanks over the sea before landing back on board but this was not peace time any more.

Both the Princess Royal and the Indefatigable, with two light cruisers, the Penelope and the Galatea, and five destroyers in hand would part from the Perseus and make a high-speed dash to be in position to commence a thirty-minute bombardment of the coastal forts guarding San Juan Bay and suspected military targets up to eight miles inland in the vicinity of the Santo Dominican capital.

Operation East Wind was designed to be, and would indeed be, a terrifying demonstration of firepower.

Alex Fielding stepped onto the Flight Control Bridge, situated on the third level of the Perseus's island just in time to see the first two of his Goshawk IVs roar off the carrier's bow. They had been among the aircraft sitting down below in the hangar deck, while the aircraft loaded at Norfolk for delivery to the Hermes, fresh from her working up trials off the Scottish coast and in the Western Approaches to the English Channel, still occupied much of the deck topsides.

Notwithstanding the Hermes had commissioned within a month of the Perseus, with the main Goshawk production lines now established in New England, at the huge Gloucester-Camm Works outside Philadelphia, and the major Empire flight training programs now coming on stream in Virginia and north of the border in Alberta, Canada, given that the Ulysses was temporarily out of commission and time was of the essence, it had made excellent sense to deliver Hermes the balance of her air group – and over forty ready battle-seasoned surviving pilots and 'back seat' crewmen from the Ulysses - at sea rather than freight them and their brand new flying machines all the way back to England.

Perseus's aft elevator was hard at work bringing Goshawk's and Sea Eagles up from below. For the coming hours, only four of the scouts and a pair of the bombers, fuelled and bombed-up as the ship's QRA – quick reaction alert – flight would be sufficient.

However, ahead of the forthcoming 'big op', the hangar deck would become one of the most explosive places on the planet as the tanks of seventy or more aircraft would be topped off with high-octane aviation spirit, gun boxes and bomb racks would be filled full, and torpedoes and rocket packs winched and heaved onto hard points below fuselages and wings.

After what had happened to the Ulysses, extra non-flammable packing and fire-suppression systems were to be urgently installed in all the new carriers; as yet, there had been no opportunity for either Perseus or Hermes, to have their forward or stern aviation spirit mains modified. There had been no time for that. It had been nothing short of a miracle that both ships had rendezvoused as planned and that the aircraft transfer had been achieved with only minor incident, several relatively inexperienced pilots only getting down on the Hermes after two, or in one case, three attempts.

Alex watched his Goshawks climbing.

It was hard to believe that the men of his old squadron - No 7 (New York) Squadron of the Colonial Air Force – whom he had led out to sea that first day, only seven weeks ago, remarkable as that seemed, carrier landing virgins to a man, were now among the most experienced and battled tested 'flight deck jockeys' in the Navy.

Of course, of the original dozen or so men, five were no longer alive. A couple of others had not cared for the odds, stayed in the CAF, another had gone ashore to instruct at Virginia Beach; meaning that only Alex and three others of the old guard were still aboard the Perseus.

War, as the old-timers used to say, is Hell.

Fun, too in a macabre, exhilarating way but nonetheless, Hell...

Alex had already known that combat was the cruellest of taskmasters from his own hard-won, harum-scarum experiences down on the Border. And also, that if a man chanced to survive his first trials by fire he was changed, tempered forever by the heat of battle.

The second pair of Goshawks rumbled past, picking up speed, hurtling over the bow, dipping and then rising above the waves, turning to starboard to climb up to their assigned quadrant of the grey Atlantic heavens.

There had been questions about 'the submarine threat' at the final command briefing in Hampton Roads.

"That situation," the Task Force Commander had smiled, ruefully, "is under control, gentlemen."

That had raised a lot of eyebrows.

Rear Admiral Sir Anthony Parkinson had gone on to explain further, albeit a little vaguely which was not at all his style: "Special measures have been taken; we do not anticipate the submarine menace to be a major factor in the prosecution of Operation East Wind."

Alex Fielding was sceptical.

Nobody had shown him the magic wand!

Presently, the Hermes was driving through a squall some ten miles away to the south east. Both Princess Royal and Indefatigable had forged ahead of the carriers to conduct a full-bore offset shoot; just to blast the cobwebs out of their main battery turret crews. Both carriers were in relatively close company with their light cruiser guardships – the Ajax was twelve hundred yards off Perseus's starboard beam, the Cassandra, was staying close to the Hermes – while a 'chase' destroyer zigzagged in the wake of each carrier ready to react instantly if an aircraft went over the side, ditched or crashed.

In retrospect, even a couple of months ago, nobody had really worked out the half of the basics of operating the big new carriers; true to form, the Navy had worked it out in quick order. Even a month ago, not even standard cruising stations had been established, now everybody took the new practices for granted.

Perseus's Captain, Patrick O'Mara Bentinck, one of the men who had written what were now only the first chapters of 'how to do carrier operations' well over two decades ago, had had the inevitable talk with

Alex about whether or not, *in the circumstances*, he ought to 'sit this one out?'

Alex had already had that conversation with the ship's CAW, and fast-found firm friend, Commander Andrew Buchannan.

Both men had made their points, because that was their duty, and given in gracefully. They knew this was his last 'outing' aboard Perseus and that, understandably, he wanted to go out with a bang, leading from the front and in their hearts, Patrick Bentinck and Andrew Buchannan knew he was the man best qualified to be the master of ceremonies over the target.

That was another completely new innovation.

With so many aircraft in the air it was no longer good enough to allow individual squadron, flight and section commanders to call the shots; somebody, had to retain the big picture in his head and to keep the show on the road when, as was likely to happen, the confusion of battle intervened and the attack faltered, or became dispersed. One day, not long ahead, there was talk about ELDAR and scrambled telecommunications making it possible for a high-flying 'command and control' aircraft to safely hang back many miles from the battle and for a master of ceremonies to conduct operations from afar. However, for the moment nothing was going to supersede the Mark I human eyeball or the wily old scout pilot's brain it was attached to.

Alex's Goshawk was being modified to carry a one hundred gallon drop tank under each wing to enable him to loiter over San Juan for up to forty-five minutes – five to ten before, thirty minutes during the attack, and another five to permit him to assess the results afterwards – and still have a twenty percent margin of safety when he got back to the Perseus, which at no time during the operation would risk approaching nearer than eighty-five nautical miles from the Santo Domingo coast.

For Alex, to have spent a couple of days with Leonora again, to have held his new baby son in his arms, to have been there at Virginia Beach when his brother returned from the dead and now to be overseeing the preparations for the greatest carrier-borne aircraft strike in history, was...surreal.

Am I living in a dream; or am I living my dream?

It was hard to tell. Of one thing he was absolutely sure, he had never been more alive.

Chapter 29

Sunday 7th May
Trinity Crossing, Unincorporated District of Northern Texas

Flight Lieutenant Greg Torrance and his ground crew chief, Sergeant Fitter Bill Fielding wiped the sweat and grime out of their eyes as they stepped into the Headquarters Tent.

George Washington's sparsely furnished lair in the midst of the ever-expanding tented, shack camp, swollen daily by new arrivals, retreating stragglers from the south and west and new recruits from the surrounding hills, was a cool haven from the noon-day sun.

"Forget about trying to get one of the Fleabags ready for a search mission," the tall Texan said decisively as he rose to his feet to greet his visitors. "You guys look hot, take a pew," he said, waving at two collapsible canvas camp chairs. He stuck his head outside the open end-flap. "Bring us some coffee please."

Tea was a beverage they drank back on the East Coast, out here in the wide-open spaces of the West people preferred something with 'bite' and a real blast of caffeine.

The big man came back inside and perched on the edge of his desk, something a local carpenter had hammered together from old timber salvaged from around the derelict airfield.

"We ain't going to waste avgas looking for a damned fool who had the fuel to go on a pointless sightseeing tour but wouldn't send us a goddamned drop of the stuff!"

Headquarters back in the Delta had requested all units to search for the missing plane – maddeningly, the only remaining serviceable Manitoba 'heavy lift' transport aircraft in the South West - which had been commandeered to carry the C-in-C Lieutenant General Sir Roger 'Chinese' Forsyth on a 'grand tour' of his new command. The aircraft, which in the present dire circumstances, was irreplaceable and had previously been working twenty-four hours a day evacuating wounded men from just behind the fragmented front lines around San Antonio, had, apparently, broadcast a desperate, truncated MAYDAY signal reporting it was under attack from several Spanish scouts south east of the beleaguered city. That was twenty-four hours ago, and nothing had been heard of the aircraft since.

Washington had been out with his Navajo scouts that morning, and been mightily unimpressed upon returning to Trinity Crossing, to be informed of the order to mount an aerial search received GCHQ in New Orleans.

"I'm sending a message to GCHQ reporting that I have no fuel to mount air operations at this time," he told the two younger men. "I've been promoted major general, by the way," he went on, as if it was of no importance. "Which in time of war gives me the right to make field, brevet promotions of up to two ranks without prior reference to the high command."

The two CAF men exchanged looks, wondering where this was going.

Both men had already acquired no little respect for the 'old man', whom all his fellow Texans regarded as the font of all military knowledge and trusted implicitly in all things. Just the news that he was in command at Trinity Crossing was bringing men and boys, not to mention camp followers, women and children in from the surrounding prairie from up to twenty or thirty miles away.

"So, you're now a Squadron leader, Mister Torrance," he declared matter-of-factly, and you're," he said, nodding to Bill Fielding, "bumped up to Flight Technician, Warrant Officer First Class, Mister Fielding. I apologise if I'm out of date with my CAF terminology but that ought to make you my local Air Force Commander and Maintenance Chief respectively."

He paused to let that sink in.

"Right," he went on, "now we've got land lines re-established back to the Delta and Caddoport on the Big River to the east, get on the phones and beg, borrow or steal, I don't care which, some aircraft, spares and fuel. Some ammunition and bombs would be good, too. In the next day or two I hope a couple, maybe a few more, of my old Texas Ranger boys from the old days will be swinging into Trinity Crossing. They'll be forming patrolling and raiding parties, and hopefully, drilling a little military sense into the people we're collecting hereabouts."

Greg Torrance took this in.

"Actually, we've syphoned enough fuel from the bottom of tanks and such like to get one of the Fleabags in the air, sir," he reported.

"How far out can you go and be damned sure you can get back?"

"Fifty, sixty miles…"

At present the two CAF men were it. There were a handful of CAF electricians, artificers and fitters around; but no pilots.

George Washington thought about it.

"I don't reckon the Spaniards will head up this way. But I need to know if I'm wrong about that. Right now, I'm more interested in knowing if any of our people got out of San Antonio and if they're heading our way."

Again, as was his way, he gave his words a moment or two to register.

"Don't fly farther west or south than fifty miles. Like I say, I don't think General Santa Anna has any intention of coming this far north. He needs to take San Antonio; that gives him control of the railways and the roads connecting the rest of New England to the borderlands. Up here, he knows the country is bad news for any modern army. The same goes for the Colorado Country and Sonora, that's why the Army and the CAF went out there for their proving grounds all those years back. But I'd rather know for sure that there isn't a column coming up that road from San Antonio; far too many people who ought to know better haven't been making damned sure they know what they're talking about lately."

The older man made and held eye contact with the young pilot.

"But no risks. I need you more than I need peace of mind about what that wily little scoundrel Santa Anna is up to. Understood?"

Viciously bitter black coffee arrived in dented tin mess mugs.

"How we getting on with the extension to the strip?" Washington asked Bill Fielding. "I saw the dust from miles away," he guffawed.

"Not so bad, sir. The new runway is going to have a dip in it but that's better than having a hump, and anyway we're only talking about a four or five degree drop over about three hundred feet. We don't have the diggers to fill up a gap like that and it would take weeks, anyway. One of the new two-engine high-wing transports, like a Manchester Loadmaster could safely put down on what we've already completed. The real problem we've got is that because of the way the ground gradually falls away to the north, every time we get rains like last week, we're going to have to check and repair the strip..."

George Washington nodded sympathetically.

"Can't be helped. The CAF built the strip in the wrong damned place," he recollected ruefully. "There's way better ground a few miles north east; and a lot closer to the rail spur, too. Like I say, it can't be helped. We need to get this field operating. We don't have the time or the wherewithal to build a new aerodrome up on Indian Heights."

Bill Fielding thought about this.

"We'll be through with the heavy lifting extending the runway here in three or four days, sir. I could send the bulldozer, some of the tractors and a work squad north to flatten out a road between here and Indian Heights?"

George Washington raised an eyebrow.

Said nothing.

"I looked at the maps, sir," the younger man explained with a shrug. "Obviously, I've never walked the ground but what you said about this site, that's God's truth. They shouldn't have put an aerodrome here. One big flash flood and the runoff water will cut a new arroyo straight across the field."

The older man nodded, mildly amused.

"Do you ride, son?"

"No, sir. I'm a city boy, I guess..."

"I'll get Connie to put you on a good horse. Her and Julio can take you up to Indian Heights. You can take a look around and report back to me. I think the place will make a good airfield; you tell me if I'm wrong."

"Yes, sir," Bill Fielding muttered with no little trepidation. A year ago, he had been a dead man walking, waiting for the day they put the noose around his neck. Now he was...

What am I?

I am the guy the general wants to survey ground for a new air base. Life was full of surprises...

"Do you think Command will reinforce us, sir?" Greg Torrance asked, respectfully.

"Maybe. That rather depends on whether the high command keeps on sending us people like Chinese Forsyth, who'd rather fly off on 'fact-finding' jollies than actually sit down and make the hard decisions."

George Washington sighed wearily, rubbed his jaw with the back of his right hand.

"The fact of the matter is that we're an awful long way from the real fighting up here. I confess, this talk about scorched earth and trading territory for time would actually make sense if that had been the plan from day one; right now, it's irresponsible, negligent because we aren't actually using the time and space it might gain us. The only reason to waste the country as you retreat is to starve and diminish the enemy ahead of a counter attack. I don't see anybody preparing to counter attack; all we're doing is giving Santa Anna a free ride all the way to the Red River country when we ought to be bleeding him white. The longer we let the Mexicans call the tune the harder it will be to throw them out. Once there are Spanish troops and land cruisers on the west bank of the Red River, and their scouts and raiders are poking around in the bayous beyond it, we're in big trouble."

The younger men were dismissed.

At a few minutes after one that afternoon Greg Torrance coaxed his hastily repaired Fleabag off the ground and set course, very slowly – nothing happened fast in a Fleabag – to the south west.

He had been tempted to ask Washington who exactly, was actually in command down in the Delta; deciding against it because he suspected that he probably did not want to know the answer.

Chapter 30

Sunday 7th May
Imperial Concession, Guaynabo, San Juan, Santo Domingo

Commander Peter Cowdrey-Singh had talked with his men earlier that morning, establishing that he and his fellow survivors of the Achilles were of the same mind. There were still three of their number incapacitated in the Concession infirmary – they would have to be carried by their comrades – but every man was behind him. This, despite the fact he had told them he rated their chances of 'pulling it off', escaping, as one in ten.

If they were very lucky!

When it got dark, they would melt into the jungle and make their way down the banks of the Rio Hondo to the coast, seize a boat and probably...all get killed.

However, anything was better than waiting to be gutted by the Inquisition.

It was a counsel of despair; of the last glint of hope.

Then, a little before mid-day, Angela von Schaffhausen had walked into the camp and asked to speak to the Achilles's former Executive Officer. The German Minister's wife was well-liked by the Royal Navy contingent who knew that she worked tirelessly in the hospital and had been extremely solicitous about their wounded friends' wellbeing and their own living conditions. She was also chatty, maternal, with a wicked laugh no matelot could resist.

'Might I speak with you, Commander?' She had inquired.

Outside the barracks she had got straight to the point.

'Claude Wallendorf is being a perfect idiot. He refuses to discuss re-claiming the Emden. He says his honour has been impugned.'

'I speak as I find, Frau von Schaffhausen.'

'That's all very well, Commander. You are right, and Claude is wrong. I know that, you know that and secretly, so does my dear husband. The problem is that unless we do something to save ourselves, we'll all get roasted over an open fire or crucified sometime in the next few days because of two otherwise highly intelligent and able officers' stupid pride!'

Put that way Peter Cowdrey-Singh had blown hot and cold for some seconds; and asked the obvious question.

'Okay... So, you honestly think that's all that's standing in our way?'

'I don't know. My husband suspects that Claude is still deeply affected by the death of Kapitan Weitzman, who was his commanding officer some years ago, I believe. And of course, he has just had to hand his ship – the love of his life - over to those...barbarians!'

Peter Cowdrey-Singh had experienced a moment of burning, irreconcilable loss as he thought of Captain Jackson, the finest man he had ever served with, who had gone down with *his* ship in the Windward Passage.

'I'll speak with Kapitan-sur-Zee Wallendorf.'

He had not beaten about the bush.

'Forgive me, sir,' he had begun, without ado. 'Earlier, my language to you was intemperate. I confess I am still not myself; one cannot be after losing so many of one's shipmates and friends so recently. I apologise unreservedly to you and hope that you will do me the honour of shaking my hand.'

To his own surprise the Royal Navy man had meant it, and after a short delay, the former commanding officer of the Emden had nodded curtly, and taken his hand.

Now, as the tropical dusk closed in over the bay with a rush, the two naval officers studied the activity on the dock and the cruiser's deck from the German Minister's balcony.

In truth, they and their spies on the dockside had observed very little 'activity' that could reasonably be described as 'purposeful', that afternoon.

The Dominicans had succeeded in getting at least one boiler lit, a plume of grey smoke – sometimes clear, and at others far too dark for any self-respecting engineer in either the Royal Navy or the Kaiserliche Marine, or his commanding officer, to tolerate – spewed from the cruiser's funnel.

Much of the time the two gangways, at bow and stern, were unattended and there was still a large amount of equipment, and boxes of all sizes, haphazardly strewn along the quay. Ahead of the cruiser, the Weser seemed to be listing slightly to port, away from the dock; but nobody on board seemed to care. Meanwhile, out in San Juan Bay the ironclad cruiser San Miguel had dragged her forward anchor and nobody had bothered to do anything about it. This meant that presently, the ancient ship's bow was at an angle of about forty degrees to the Weser and because of the movement, at the nearest point, only some fifty yards distant from her stern.

It was all very sloppy, more than a little offensive to both men's professional pride. As darkness fell a large number of men streamed off the Emden and began to wander, in gangs to the south and the nearest exit from the Concession, possibly, decamping to return to their barracks or homes ashore for the night.

"There can't be more than a hundred or so men left on board her?" Peter Cowdrey-Singh suggested to Claude Wallendorf.

"Maybe less," the German agreed thoughtfully. "Although, my people tell me that several dozen civilians crept onto the ship last night…"

Nobody seemed to be in command on deck although there were lights on in the bridge and shining through several of the bow and stern portholes.

Pumps still thumped below decks on the Weser but apart from a man coming topside for a smoke from time to time, otherwise, she might have been an abandoned hulk.

Leutnant Kemper who had been watching yesterday, and throughout the day joined the older men and speculated that there might still be as many as one-hundred-and-thirty men still on the Emden. If yesterday was anything to go by, the rest of the crew would not start to come back to the ship until after eight o'clock tomorrow morning.

The first prostitutes began to slink aboard once it was fully dark; whores, pimps, drug dealers and the normal scum of the earth who had been excluded from the Concession until recent weeks, driving decent people indoors at night.

"Well," the German Minister asked, lighting a cigarette as he joined the officers on the balcony of his office to gaze at the lights of the ships in the bay, "what do you think, gentlemen?"

"That bloody cruiser in the bay still has her guns trained on us," Claude Wallendorf sniffed, irritably.

"At the Weser," Peter Cowdrey-Singh offered.

"At the dock, whatever," the German muttered, very nearly lost in thought.

"When the tide ebbs I noticed it pulled a lot harder than I expected on the Weser's moorings," the Royal Navy man said, similarly distracted. "I wouldn't be surprised if, were she to be cut loose, she'd drift straight into the San Miguel the way she's dragged her anchors."

"That wouldn't help," Wallendorf apologised. "If that happened the Weser and the San Miguel would block the Emden in…"

"Ah, yes, but only if the San Miguel remains moored fore and aft," the Anglo-Indian suggested, unhurriedly eyeing the movement of flotsam in the muddy waters of the bay.

Hans von Schaffhausen was studying the near-deserted quayside; until a couple of days ago, there had been several armed men guarding the gangways, stationed onshore and on the decks of the ships.

"Still no communication from your normal contacts in the government, sir?" Peter Cowdrey-Singh inquired of the German Minister, gesturing across to the other side of San Juan Bay.

"No, this is the third day running I've been fobbed off by a particularly supercilious underling. Ever since I refused point blank to discuss the future of you and your men other than to raise the repatriation issue, in fact." Von Schaffhausen sighed, and made an admission. "My last conversation with the authorities ended badly when it was put to me that the surviving Kaiserliche Marine officers of the Weser should be put on trial as war criminals."

"Cheeky beggars!"

"Yes, just so. Anyway, there are more soldiers posted on both of the roads leading into the Concession this evening. For all I know, the jungle around us may be crawling with Dominican troopers. If we act, we must act tonight, gentlemen."

The two Navy men looked at each other.

"Is that possible?" Von Schaffhausen pressed.

"This would be a thing fraught with great risk, Herr Minister," Claude Wallendorf cautioned. "Also, I must remind you that I have no idea what damage those idiots have done to my ship!"

Von Schaffhausen did not reflect overlong.

"How would we proceed?"

Wallendorf looked to Peter Cowdrey-Singh.

"We keep things simple," the Royal Navy man declared. "We send your Marines in to seize the Emden and the Weser. No mucking about. We shoot anybody who makes trouble. Thereafter, everybody just piles onto the Emden pronto, and all non-operational personnel are sent down below decks behind some armour plating. Obviously, even those dozy beggars on the San Miguel out there in the bay will eventually notice something is going on; however, personally, I doubt her captain will do anything without first *consulting* higher authority because that's the way joke navies like the Armada del Santo Domingo work. In the meantime, once we've got the Emden in our hands, we send your Marines back onshore to guard the port area while the civilians are chased onto the ship..."

Claude Wallendorf opened his mouth to speak.

Peter Cowdrey-Singh had not finished: "The tide begins to ebb at two-fifteen tomorrow morning. That's when we set fire to the Weser and cut her moorings. In the confusion the Emden puts a couple of broadsides into the San Miguel and we do our level best to get out to sea!"

Nobody said anything for several seconds.

"Then what, Commander?" Angela von Schaffhausen asked in a whisper.

The former Executive officer of HMS Achilles laughed a little unkindly.

"I have no idea, dear lady. That was a thing I planned to worry about it if I am still alive at the time!"

Chapter 31

Sunday 7th May
Government House, Philadelphia

The Governor of the Crown Colonies of the Commonwealth of New England, Edward Philip Cornwallis Sidney, 7th Viscount De L'Isle, The Lord De L'Isle, Dudley and Northampton, bent and kissed his wife's cheek before her chair was wheeled into the adjacent morning room. That Elizabeth had been well enough to accompany him to church the last two sabbaths, and to stand for short periods – granted, with a stick and his arm for support – was the one thing which had given him any real solace in the last few days.

Well, that and the news – the best part of three weeks ago now – that Henrietta was safe and sound in Portugal. Her disappearance and the coming of the war had stilled, for the moment at least, all those mendacious rumours about his youngest daughter and her companion, Melody Danson; as if he and Elizabeth cared a fig so long as their remarkable little girl was safe, well and happy!

God in Heaven!

Did people not have better things to worry about?

A sheaf of new telegrams had arrived in the two hours he had been away; presumably, further endless tidings of bad news. It seemed that if things had been going badly in New England then his woes might soon be trumped by developments in Germany. All talk of sending as many as six divisions of the Indian Army to New England had been comprehensively quashed overnight; with chaos threatened along parts of the Franco-German border most of those men would probably be needed to beef up the Army of Occupation in France...

Sir Henry Rawlinson, De L'Isle's Chief of Staff knocked and walked in through the open door to join the Governor in his office.

"Elizabeth seems most chipper," the other man observed, cheerfully. He was one of those irrepressible old soldiers whose mood often brightened the darker things looked

"Yes, getting out and about helps a great deal."

The Governor of New England had poured himself a stiff drink, now he poured a second whisky for his friend and indefatigably loyal comrade in arms in Philadelphia.

Both men glanced at the pile of telegrams. A few more minutes unread would do them no lasting harm, the Governor decided.

"That the King and Queen and our ministers successfully got out of Germany in one piece sounds ever-more like a minor miracle, Henry. It is a damned disgrace! As for the notion that the new, self-appointed dictator is threatening to confiscate all the Empire's property and investments in Germany, well, that's..."

"Not very hopeful," the other man, the elder by a handful of years murmured, joining the Governor in comfortable chairs below the large portrait of a long dead predecessor, Lord John Murray, 4th Earl of Dunmore. Not for nothing had all subsequent Governors kept a portrait of John Murray, who as Governor of Virginia, having been forced to flee from Williamsburg after the burning of Norfolk by the rebels in January 1776, returned only after the destruction of the Revolutionary Continental Army on Long Island in the autumn of that year. Lord Dunmore's experience in 1776 had served as a salutary lesson to all successor governors over the last two centuries.

The lesson that must never be forgotten was that: adversity came and went; but the Empire prevailed through thick and thin.

"It's a bloody disgrace, that's what it is!" Philip De L'Isle shook his head, forcing himself to get a grip of his ire.

"Lady Henrietta managed to get a call through to Government House while you were out," Henry Rawlinson reported.

"Oh, damn," his friend groaned, horribly guilty to have missed his daughter's transatlantic call. "How did she sound?"

"As bright as bell. I think she plans to stay in Portugal a little while longer. Apparently, it is likely Miss Danson will be travelling to England soon."

"Of course," De L'Isle nodded. "Matthew," he recollected, feeling a new pang of loss for an old friend no longer in this world, "always maintained *that* woman might have been made for intelligence work." If anybody had been qualified to make that judgement it must, assuredly have been Matthew Harrison, the long-time Head of the soon to be defunct Colonial Security Service.

"Hen spoke of plans to adopt that young orphan boy that she and Miss Danson rescued in Spain."

"Oh, surely an unmarried woman can't do that?" Philip de L'Isle queried. Such a thing would certainly not be entertained in any of the East Coast Colonies.

"I didn't like to delve into that. However, she seemed confident that she had everything under control."

The proud father relaxed, chuckling under his breath.

Reluctantly, he turned his thoughts back to business.

"Henry, what am I supposed to make of what I'm being told about this Washington fellow down in," he forgot where the damned man was from, scowled and tried very hard to remember.

"Trinity Crossing, Unincorporated North Texas," his friend helped out.

"Yes, that must be the chap."

"He was captured by the Spanish in the last unpleasantness down there. He met General Santa Anna while a prisoner of war. The two of them got on quite well, by all accounts. Anyway, had it not been for Washington, and his men's heroics, some historians think we might have lost that war too. Or rather, certainly taken a lot longer to win it!"

"We haven't lost this one yet, Henry!"

"No, of course not. Not yet."

The Governor grinned ruefully.

"I gather he's a man of around our own vintage?"

"Yes…"

Philip De L'Isle recollected how hidebound certain sections of the

British Army had been in his time in uniform, and doubted an awful lot had changed in the intervening decades.

"Why on earth isn't he in charge down there?" He couldn't possibly have made a bigger mess of it than dear old Chinese Forsyth; I can't think where London found him?" He had another thought. "Does anybody know what happened to Forsyth, by the way?"

Sir Henry Rawlinson recognised that this was an entirely rhetorical interrogative and held his peace other than to ruminatively shake his head.

"Washington?" The Governor of New England thought aloud. "Why does that name have such a familiar ring to it?"

His Chief of Staff looked up, meaningfully, at the portrait on the way.

Philip De L'Isle groaned anew.

"Oh... Yes, he was that rascal the Howe brothers finally cornered on Long Island, wasn't he? What was it that bounder Isaac Fielding wrote about him? *With the death of George Washington, the Revolution's last best hope of survival died!* Or something like that, what!"

His old friend chortled.

"Oh dear," he rumbled, "we've been over here too long, Philip!"

"I'll drink to that," the Governor of New England smiled.

Not everything was lost; nobody was exhorting him to pack up his chattels and flee from Philadelphia. Unlike poor old John Murray, he still had a passable hand to play in this game. So, all things considered, he was not about to be run out of Government House like a whipped dog. Not quite yet, anyway.

The first time Philip De L'Isle had been briefed about the existence of Project Poseidon – by Cuthbert Collingwood on his appointment to Government House some three years ago – he had known that when news of the scandalous disregard for the Submarine Treaty finally broke that there would be repercussions for whoever had the misfortune to be in residence in Downing Street at the time.

Back in London, the Prime Minister, Sir Hector Hamilton had submitted his immediate resignation to the King on their return from Germany. Poor old Hector had been the man in possession; axiomatically, he had had to fall on his sword. De L'Isle hoped, without much cause for optimism, that the cull would end there but doubted it. The Government would almost certainly fall; there would be a General Election and probably, sometime in the next few weeks, he would be reporting to a new Foreign and Colonial Secretary.

Given that he was one of only half-a-dozen men, the others were nearly all senior naval officers, 'in on the great secret', it seemed more likely that his days in Philadelphia were numbered.

I ought to feel a little more upset about that than I actually do...

However, the fact was that all things considered, right now, the idea of spending his declining years pottering around the De L'Isle family seat, Penshurst Place in Kent, bouncing his grandchildren on his knee, was positively seductive!

He shook his head.

"Washington," he breathed wryly, "George Washington, indeed." He snapped out of his reverie, coming to an abrupt and by any rational criteria, very nearly reckless decision of the type he had studiously avoided taking during his military and diplomatic career. "Right, if that nincompoop Forsyth doesn't turn up again in the next forty-eight hours, we'll tell London we want Washington put in charge down in Texas."

Something like alarm flickered in Sir Henry Rawlinson's rheumy eyes. His whiskey glass might easily have fallen out of the numb fingers of his hand at that particular juncture.

"Is that wise, Philip?"

"I'm not sure *wise* comes into it. Dammit, Henry," the Governor of the Commonwealth of New England sighed, "this isn't India. We don't have a ready-made British Officer corps in situ who have lived among and understand the people. It is high time we trusted a New Englander. I sometimes despair of London. Don't they know their history? It was New Englanders like that fellow Sherman, you know the one, the chap with the funny Indian name, and Roger Lee's great-great-great grandfather – I can never work out whether he was three or four times removed, not that it matters – who finally made the difference in France in the Great War. If we had learned the lessons of the last couple of wars with the Mexicans, which our military people have singularly failed to do, we wouldn't be in this position now!"

The Governor's friend had recovered his sangfroid, and nodded sagely but elected not to offer any comment.

The Governor of New England drained his glass.

"You and I know that this war has been coming for a long time, Henry. We both tried to warn the Prime Minister and the Foreign and Colonial Office, and we've talked ourselves blue in the face with the people at the War Office, and the bally Army Department," Philip De L'Isle went on, his exasperation simmering just below the surface. "I know the King has always been on our side but time and again the needs of the Commonwealth of New England have been subordinated to those of the broader Empire. So, we are where we are, and now this trouble has blown up in Germany we aren't going to get anywhere near everything we want or need. At sea, we know that Lord Collingwood will do what he can do. Operation East Wind is hopefully the start of the fight back, notwithstanding, I suspect that if the FCO didn't have its hands full with the Berlin imbroglio they'd probably be trying their best to tie Cuthbert's hands behind his back. That's the trouble with Whitehall, they're obsessed with organising the peace without a thought for fighting and winning the damned war first! Honestly, it's ridiculous, here we are in a major war in the Americas and might soon be in another in Europe, and those fools in London are still behaving as if there's nothing a little bit of gunboat diplomacy can't solve!"

The Governor's Chief of Staff remembered his whisky, drank deep.

"I think Cuthbert Collingwood is more your man if your taste is for 'battlefleet diplomacy', Philip," he smiled grimly.

"Well, hopefully, this chap in Texas will turn out to be a man with real mettle, Henry!"

"The King!" Henry Rawlinson proposed, finishing his drink.

Chapter 32

Sunday 7th May
Viano do Castelo, Portugal

Alonso Pérez de Guzmán felt like a complete cad, that most contemptible of double-dealing excuses for manhood. In fact, he was beginning to view himself as no better than the despicable breed of men he had always despised. To arrive at Viano do Castelo and to be welcomed like a prince by his mistress and the woman he adored; but to whom he had never dared to confess as much, and to be reunited, anew with the son he had thought he had lost forever a little over four years ago, in a funny sort of way, actually contrived to make him feel even worse.

And then he had artlessly compounded his misdeeds.

He had been morose, absurdly sorry for himself as Melody and Henrietta had sat him down to enjoy afternoon tea with them, and his son had gambolled around their feet without a care in the world, safe from all evil with his two beautiful 'Mamas'.

He had not actually been rude, not gratuitously; simply a little distant, reserved, untalkative, overly polite and correct, almost formal in his introspection and brooding, hoping above hope that the two incomparable ladies in his life would assume he was just weary from his travels.

Coincidentally, those travels also, were a thing coming to an end now he had got a fresh grip upon his estates and holdings in Portugal – now his country of exile – and his Queen had summarily, almost but not quite cruelly, for he perfectly understood the reasons why and that her motivation was not, and had never been, ignoble, dismissed him from her service. He had, and he had not, expected that; just not believed it was going to happen until it did. That Sophie, whom he had known, seemingly forever, had reluctantly balked at the cost of fighting on, to her and more so to her many loyal supporters, had come as no real surprise. But to be exiled from her circle, well, that had been...a shock.

It ought not to have been, of course. He had known the woman who was to become his Queen from earliest childhood; possibly, no man in Spain knew, or even began to understand the bewitching enigma which was the once, and possibly, future Queen Consort of the Spanish Emperor, as intimately as he.

As any true, devoted courtier must, he had accepted his fate, knowing that to do otherwise would be to cause *his* Queen even greater distress.

So, here he was, the disinherited – in the lands of Spain at least – 18th Duke of Medina Sidonia, feeling sorry for himself, having made his excuses and retired to his rooms where he had dismissed his footman, and ordered that he not be disturbed.

He had lain these last forty minutes or so in a slowly cooling bath, alone in the steam with his thoughts.

At some stage he had opened up the hot water faucet to warm the water, almost to overflowing and sunk back into the warmth up to his chin. Later, he must have dozed off because whoever was at the bathroom door had had to knock twice, and then thrice.

"I don't want to be disturbed!" He protested irritably, albeit without genuine angst. No man with any self-respect raised his voice or belittled a subordinate, an arms man or anybody else in his service. That was a lesson his father had, when he was young, beaten into him; probably the best thing the old monster had ever done for him...

There was another knock.

"Yes, what is it?"

The door opened a crack.

"May I come in?"

Henrietta?

What was she doing here?

The door opened and closed quickly and in a moment Henrietta De L'Isle was standing with her back pressed against it. She was still dressed in the cream blouse and pleated peach-coloured skirt she had worn earlier.

Alonso, naked and desperately covering up his submerged manhood with both hands, inadvertently splashed and caused a minor flood around the overlarge bath tub.

"Henrietta," he muttered, like an idiot, obviously.

"Yes," the woman agreed, shifting uncomfortably on her feet and trying very hard – and failing – to stare at the man in the bath. In the steamy humidity of the room short strands of her boyishly cropped auburn hair stood on end. The fog rising off the waters could not begin to hide her flushing embarrassment.

"I acted like a fool before," Alonso said, not knowing what else to say.

"No, you didn't," the newcomer objected. "This is all very awkward, and it must be horribly, well, strange for you... But Melody is right, we can't go on like this and besides, we, Melody and I, had a long chat about things yesterday."

"You did?"

"Yes," Henrietta agreed. "And there's Pedro to be considered..."

Talking had enabled her to slough off a little of her initial discomfort; now, she looked around for the stool that was always somewhere in the mansion's bathrooms, and finding it, drew it close to the tub and sat down. Primly, she clamped her knees together and folded her hands in her lap before again, attempting to focus on Alonso's face, rather than his leanly muscled torso and manhood, presently concealed beneath the water and his hands.

"Melody has decided to carry on being a spook," Henrietta continued. "Only, this time, officially. She loved being a detective. But she knows she can't go back to that, any more than you or I can go back to our old lives. And, as I said, now there's Pedro to think about. I'd want to adopt him even if he wasn't your son. As he is, your son, I mean, that makes it even better. Perfect, in fact. As if it was meant to be..."

Alonso was speechless.

Henrietta frowned.

"I suppose if I was Melody, we'd be having this conversation *in* the bath," she added, clearly on the cusp of losing her courage.

Suddenly, she was looking to the man for a sign, a moral prop, something that told her she was not making a complete fool of herself, or that she was not about to be utterly humiliated.

Alonso vented a bewildered laugh.

Henrietta began to rise from the stool, near to flight.

He touched her arm with the tips of the fingers of his left hand.

"Don't go. Please stay."

Henrietta shivered.

Betwixt and between she was momentarily at a loss.

She squeezed her eyes shut, berated herself for her uncharacteristic timidity.

Forcing a smile, she suggested, hoarse: "I think You will need to let a little water out of the bath..."

Alonso half-smiled in askance.

"If I get in with you, I mean, we'll flood the whole bathroom," Henrietta explained, looking at her feet.

This had all seemed so simple when Melody had suggested a way to 'break the ice' with Alonso. She was suddenly afraid what she planned might come across as sluttish, as if she was throwing herself at him and that was no basis for a lasting relationship.

"This was Melody's idea?" The man asked rhetorically.

Henrietta nodded.

"She says one of us should marry you but," she shrugged, "she thinks she'd make you unhappy. She says she's not the wife a man like you needs or deserves...but I know you are crazy about her and that she loves you."

Alonso gritted his teeth and tried to step past the unreality of the conversation.

"Melody and I have never discussed such things."

"No," Henrietta giggled, venting a little pent up nervous energy, "you were too busy..."

Her voice trailed away.

"Having sex and generally endeavouring to exchange bodily fluids?" The man in the bath suggested, dryly.

"Yes... I've been a little jealous about that, actually," Henrietta confessed. "I cried my eyes out when you slept with Melody back at your house in Chinchón, by the way. I was angry with Melody, but I blamed you for seducing her. How stupid is that? Mostly, I was hurt because I thought I'd lost you forever. Sorry, all this must sound completely weird..."

That was the moment Henrietta realised she needed to stop talking: rising to her feet she began, jerkily horribly uncomfortably, to peel off her blouse, over her shoulders and head, revealing her arms, shoulders, and – she had always thought – slightly overlarge breasts, presently, teasingly contained in a lacy, white bra. She knew better than to risk meeting Alonso's eye as she stepped out of her skirt, and turned away and with oddly numb fingers, unhooked the clasps of her bra, letting her breasts sag a little, free. She kicked away her knickers.

Still not daring to renew eye contact she stepped, feeling very bovine and clumsy, right foot, then left into the tub. The water was cool and she shuddered involuntarily. The man had drawn up his knees to give her space as if he too, was wary of actually making physical contact. She lowered herself, dropping the final few inches into the water, thinking how impossibly hard it was to keep one's legs together when getting into a bath with a handsome man with whom one had been unrequitedly besotted for the last two years...

Presently, her arms crossed over her breasts, Henrietta raised her eyes.

"This is," she grimaced, "more uncomfortable than I thought it would be. I seem to be getting a lot of things wrong lately," she murmured.

"And the water is cold," Alonso observed, apologetically. It was hard to resist the urge to pinch himself.

Was this, any of it...real?

He began to cautiously re-arrange his legs.

Henrietta shivered as if tingling with electricity at his touch as his ankles brushed her hips.

"Move forward, perhaps," Alonso suggested, as if he was standing before her about to lead off into a slow step on the dance floor rather than sitting with her, stark naked, in a bath tub.

She too began to open herself up.

In a dream she wriggled closer until legs akimbo, shamelessly but by no means unpleasantly, she decided, she looked in Alonso's eyes.

Their faces were barely inches apart.

"I'm sorry, I need to reach past you to turn on the hot water tap," he said hoarsely.

"Yes," Henrietta gasped. "You should..."

His chest touched her breasts; her nipples Henrietta became aware, were suddenly as hard as nails as warm water roared behind her, spreading around her ribs and hips.

It was dreamlike.

Still, naked together they were playing the game; pretending they were not, yet, lovers.

The bath filled; the tap was turned off.

Alonso smiled, raised an eyebrow, teasingly.

"You were saying, My Lady?"

Now, for the first time it was Henrietta's turn to laugh, and with it all her pent-up terrors seemed to flee away.

"Melody says if she married you, she'd ruin your life," she confided. "And she loves you far too much to do that to you."

The man was hardly listening.

"You," he whispered, "were the most beautiful woman in that room in Philadelphia the first time we met. The most beautiful and by far and away the cleverest," his gaze was roving over her bare shoulders and torso and coming back to hold her face, mesmerically in its focus. "I loved you from afar from the start even though in those days, I knew it was hopeless."

Henrietta just wanted to melt into his arms.

"So," she gasped, knowing that her words were about to fall, one over the other, "*we've* decided, that you have to marry me instead!"

The man was laughing again.

"You've decided that, have you?" He chortled. "You and Melody?"

"Yes. We have! Oh, and just so you know," Henrietta was crying and laughing now, "I want a whole brood of babies!"

Chapter 33

Sunday 7th May
HMS Perseus, 133 nautical miles NW of San Juan

One of the three experimental London Aircraft Corporation R-1 Albatrosses based at the St John's River Naval Air Station at St Augustine had flown, unseen, undetected – and in the absence of ELDAR virtually undetectably - at an altitude of thirty-eight thousand feet, over eastern Santo Domingo and onward to the east and south east, quartering the Leeward Islands shortly after dawn that morning.

Commander Alex Fielding was probably one of less than twenty men among the sixteen thousand at sea with Task Force 5.1, who even knew of the existence of the remarkable reconnaissance-bombers. The Albatross, of which only two test prototypes and ten pre-production variants had been built to date, was so secret that any reference to a 'super plane' being test flown in New England had been rigorously embargoed, and such fragmentary reports of a 'new warplane that flew like the wind at extraordinary altitudes' which had leaked into the public domain had instantly been quashed as 'imaginary sightings', or contemptuously written off as 'unidentified flying objects', with witnesses who claimed to have seen one of the aeronautical marvels of the age in the flesh, cavalierly dismissed as 'sad' and 'delusional'.

Alex was in the Captain's day room digesting the texts of the terse intelligence digests literally hot – some of them honestly and truly warm out of the print box – from one of the ship's two (also ultra-secret) digital decoding computers, in the company of the carrier's Captain, Executive Officer, the ship's CAW, Commander Andrew Buchannan and his newly installed deputy, Lieutenant-Commander Francois de Montfort Percival. The six men were briefly locked in such intense concentration that they might have been antiquarian treasure hunters studying freshly discovered maps revealing exactly where several previously unknown stashes of ancient pirate gold were buried.

The London Aircraft Company already had a long – although admittedly, in the early days of flight now and then chequered - history of designing lightweight, high-performance aircraft, and for 'thinking outside the box', innovating in proudly open defiance of Air Ministry or Royal Air Force requirements or operational specifications, that *its* legendary design bureau considered to be out of date, or just plain wrong. The R1-Albatross had the potential to be the LAC's most revolutionary product yet, seemingly so far ahead of its rivals that it had very nearly created a new genus of aircraft.

Although still powered by twin turboprops – supercharged Derby-Royce Wyverns rated at over 2,500 horse power – by constructing eighty percent of the airframe from wood rather than metal to minimise weight, the Albatross was capable of flying at nearly four hundred miles per hour in level flight at altitudes of up to forty-two thousand feet. It was as fast or faster than any other propeller driven aircraft in service in any air force anywhere, and higher-flying than practically any other aircraft other than the first generation 'turbojet' powered test beds, the majority of which were still just twinkles in their designers' eyes.

Several pre-production prototype bomber variants of the Albatross (type B-1), capable of carrying a two-thousand-ton payload to a target over a thousand miles away had been delivered to the RAF late last year for operational testing in Scotland and Nova Scotia.

"Where the Devil did that Mainz class cruiser come from?" Alex inquired, whistling softly.

"It has to be one of von Reuter's ships," the CAW, Commander Andrew Buchannan grunted.

"Probably one of the cruisers that took part in the bombardment of Kingston…"

"Well, we've got her bloody number now!" Buchannan decided, grim determination in his voice. "This just gets better and better. There must be three or four other warships in the bay, including that ironclad anchored out in the bay opposite the German port."

"The lazy beggars haven't even put out anti-torpedo nets!"

There were at least two large vessels, possibly old-fashioned ironclads, in dry docks, and other smaller, more modern frigate-type vessels moored within the main tidal basin of the Santo Domingo Naval Dockyards to the north east, across San Juan Bay from the German Concession.

And if that was not good enough news, the Albatross had made a possible sighting of one of the Dominican coal-burners plaguing the Lesser Antilles which had killed so many people on Antigua, coaling some twenty miles east of St Kitts and Nevis. Task Force 5.11 was already working up to its best speed, about twenty-nine knots in the relatively benign Atlantic swells east of the Leeward Islands, dashing to 'pin' the enemy squadron between its gunline and the rising sun at daybreak tomorrow morning.

On board the Perseus, the CAW and his henchmen, were very nearly salivating over the prospect of catching one of the ships of the despised Vera Cruz Squadron tied up alongside a quay, helpless in their sights!

"That bloody ironclad out in the bay is going to make life difficult for our Sea Eagles to mount torpedo runs on the German cruiser. The waters of that part of the inner bay are too shallow for a normal 'drop'," Percival, a solid, pragmatic man belying his aristocratic lineage – he was the third son of a Viscount – who had transferred over from the Ulysses only last week, remarked thoughtfully.

Air-launched torpedoes, no matter what fancy fins one fitted them with, or how low or slow a 'dropping aircraft' flew, tended to dive several tens of feet deep before 'finding' their 'set' running depths. In a harbour with a relatively shallow, sandy bottom, they could easily 'plug' or hit the bottom and 'porpoise' wildly off course.

The carrier's Captain, Patrick Bentinck stroked his beard.

"Let's not get over-excited about this, gentlemen," he guffawed. "We've got the Dominicans on a decidedly tricky wicket here. Let's not get carried away and start bowling too many full tosses, what!"

The other men in the day room listened respectfully.

"We can't have all our torpedo-carriers concentrating on that damned ship to the exclusion of all the other juicy targets moored alongside or anchored elsewhere in the harbour. And I certainly don't want our bombers drawn away from their targets in the docks and the government complex in the heart of the city. By all means detail off a couple of Sea Eagles to attempt torpedo runs at that cruiser but otherwise, I plan to recommend that we leave *that* ship to the tender mercies of Princess Royal and the Indefatigable."

Two eight-gun 15-inch broadsides dropping one-ton shells in and around the quayside of the German Concession were likely to cause almost total devastation for hundreds of yards, perhaps a mile or so, all around the target. But that was not their problem; it was the Germans' problem.

"With your leave, I'd like to assign two or three dive bombers to have a go at that cruiser before the big ships open up, sir," Andrew Buchanan responded, simply registering his point of view.

Patrick Bentinck thought about it.

"Two aircraft only."

The final decision would be adjudicated by the Task Force Commander, Rear Admiral Parkinson. That said, thus far Parkinson had not demonstrated the least propensity to countermand or in any way disregard the expert advice of men under his command who were self-evidently, well-qualified in their fields.

The Princess Royal and the Indefatigable would jump at the opportunity to rain Hell on one of the ships of the Vera Cruz squadron, the harbingers of this evil war, already covered in the blood of the men of the Achilles and the rape of Jamaica.

Presently, the ships of Task Force 5.1 were running without lights with the gun line still in company. The big ships would break away a little after midnight for their high-speed run to within as close as six or seven miles of the Santo Domingo coast. At one stage two escorting destroyers were to be detached to lay mines at the mouth of San Juan Bay; a scheme abandoned shortly before sailing because to be effective the mines would have to be laid inordinately close in shore – perhaps as near as two hundred yards from known shore battery locations – and whatever else Operation East Wind was about, it was not about presenting thin-skinned targets to Dominican gunners shooting over open sights at point blank range!

A month ago, nobody would have blinked an eyelid at taking a chance of the Dominican's being caught napping; but a lot of things had changed in the last few weeks and no more unnecessary hostages to fortune were to be offered until further notice.

The command group meeting broke up a few minutes later.

Alex knew he ought to try to grab a couple of hours sleep; but also knew it was not going to happen. Every single aircraft under his command was going to be in the air tomorrow morning, and nobody was getting much shut-eye tonight!

The Dominicans and their foul Triple Alliance friends must be thinking that they had their God on their side. To date the war could hardly have gone much better for them, at sea, in the air and on land, not to mention beneath the waves if the Indomitable's fate was anything to go by. Well, around dawn tomorrow morning the enemy was going to get a very, very rude shock!

One-thousand-pound semi-armour piercing bombs were being slung under the bellies of Sea Eagles, and an additional pair of two-hundred-and-fifty-pound high-explosive 'eggs' under each bomber's wings. Eighteen-inch air-launched torpedoes, each with a warhead of over four hundred pounds of high-explosives, and capable of racing through the water at upwards of forty knots, were lined up on dollies to be maneuvered under the fuselages of the 'fish carriers' parked menacingly in the midships section of the hangar deck, while most of Alex's Goshawks were already topside, their gun boxes stuffed tight with bullets, with lightweight fuel 'drop' tanks topped off and hanging beneath cockpits or in the case of Alex's aircraft, also on two underwing hardpoints in lieu of the rocket pods mounted by twenty-three of his other scouts.

Those pods packed a fierce, short-range punch, fourteen 2-inch missiles armed with a three-pound high-explosive or anti-personnel fragmentation warhead, with a range of up to fifteen hundred yards. In practice, the unguided munitions were only accurate up to about two to three hundred yards and best unleashed only when one could literally see the whites of ones' enemies' eyes.

Before leaving Norfolk there had been some discussion about the notion of several of the carrier's aircraft dropping 'Greek Fire' cannisters over the target. Nobody was entirely clear if employing such weapons – basically, when they hit the ground they dispersed a sticky, burning jelly-like form of Hades on earth across a broad swath of ground and anybody unfortunate enough to get in the way was likely to be burned to death of to suffer dreadful bone-deep wounds – was either legal, or in any sense moral. However, given the horror stories one was hearing about the way the junior parties to the Triple Alliance, the Cuban, Hispanics and particularly the way the Dominicans treated their prisoners of war, and at times, their own people, the debate was one of splitting hairs. Discarded drop tanks, virtually empty, apparently went off like mini 'Greek Fire' bombs, anyway.

Philosophically, Alex knew that he ought to retain at least a modicum of unction about the rights and wrongs of the subject; but actually, he was already well beyond that point.

Even had he not already known it, war was a nasty, brutish, kill or be killed business, and anybody who tried to pretend otherwise was an imbecile, or a charlatan, or both, in his book.

In the air over the target he would have no problem whatsoever jettisoning his near empty drop tanks over enemy territory. If there was a 'military' target underneath him at the time, all well and good. If not, well, that was too bad. Either way, he was not about to start crying crocodile tears over it.

Chapter 34

Monday 8th May
Imperial Concession, Guaynabo, San Juan, Santo Domingo

The SMS Weser's mooring lines parted with a series of very loud 'clunking' noises as sledge hammers demolished the winding gear at the ship's bow and stern. By then most of the aviation spirit in the cans the looters of the Armada del Santo Domingo had left lined up on the quayside, presumably for collection in the morning by the criminals and war profiteers they had sold them to, had been carried on board the half-wrecked merchant raider, tipped on the decks and set alight.

On the bridge of the Emden, Commander Peter Cowdrey-Singh could honestly not believe how smoothly things had gone, or how unobservant the lookouts – assuming there were any – on the ironclad San Miguel had been thus far.

Hans von Schaffhausen's troops had walked aboard the cruiser virtually unchallenged. Those Dominicans on the quayside, or not yet roaring drunk or pleasuring themselves with the chorus line of tarts they had invited onto the ship, had just watched the Germans walk back onto the cruiser and take control. Not even a few muffled gunshots deep in the bowels of the warship had attracted anybody's attention.

Yesterday, the German Minister had belatedly confessed that he had always had an emergency evacuation plan for 'his people', in the event 'something untoward' came to pass. The man loved everything about Santo Domingo except the Inquisition – which had not always been 'this pernicious' – and the members of the ruling cabal, for whom he had unrelenting contempt. All it took was the word 'CAVILIERI' to be spread and everybody, men, women, children, the sick and the infirm dropped, on pain of being left behind, everything, and headed for the port. The first civilians were being ushered up the cruiser's gangway as the last crew member re-boarded her.

It had immediately been apparent that the Dominicans had indeed, regarded the ship, as a treasure trove to be looted. Parts of the vessel were effectively electronically dead, the ELDAR fire control and air search installations had been ripped out, and most of the store rooms emptied. The aviation spirit on the dockside had been siphoned out of the tanks for the Emden's SWF Model 157 seaplane. The only surviving working radio on the whole ship was that in the cockpit of the aircraft which was positioned half-in, half-out of its hangar. It seemed that the Dominicans had, no one could tell how, managed to burn out the motor that turned the crane which loaded and unloaded the SWF 157 and the ship's boats.

"Unglaublich!" Kapitan-zur-See Claus Wallendorf muttered repeatedly as he stalked the bridge of his almost bloodlessly re-claimed command.

Unbelievable!

"What did they think they were doing?"

Answer came there none because the mind of their enemies was utterly unfathomable to any self-respecting Royal Navy or Kaiserliche

Marine man.

As they came aboard the civilians were swiftly ushered below and ordered, in no uncertain terms 'not to get in the way'.

Most of Peter Cowdrey-Singh's men had been assigned to the cruiser's Deck Division, where their general training and familiarity with weapons systems – most of which differed from their British equivalents only by the variation in the calibre of their barrels – enabled them to easily dovetail into the ship's hastily thrown together restored order of battle.

A runner hurried onto the bridge.

"I respectfully report that number four boiler is lit, Herr Kapitan," the man reported breathlessly. "The Chief Engineer reports that his department will answer engine room telegraphs on both shafts."

None of the status boards on the bridge were working and the Gunnery Officer had reported that the main battery fire control circuit was dead, meaning that the ship's main armament could now only be fought in local control.

By Angela and Hans von Schaffhausen's count there were still some thirty or forty civilians yet to arrive at the port as the fires on the Weser took hold and the raider began to drift, imperceptibly at first, clear of the dock.

The missing citizens had only minutes to make an appearance.

Problematically, since there was no daily or weekly, or any meaningful or trustworthy roll call of any kind within the Concession – it was a civilian trading entity, not an armed camp or prison, after all – there had been no way of knowing precisely how many people there were to be evacuated and by now, surely, some of the Dominican domestic staff, many of whom would have been regime spies, within the Concession, must have reported that something funny was going on...

The missing people might already be in the hands of the Inquisition or the authorities, and might have been for several days.

Men were standing by to cut the Emden's lines.

Peter Cowdrey-Singh was convinced the Weser's stern was going to foul the cruiser's bow right up until the moment it did not. All the while Claude Wallendorf had watched the other ship's drift, apparently unconcerned.

"There is movement on the deck of the San Miguel!"

"About time!"

The cruiser's Captain's voice was suddenly abrupt.

"Reset engine room telegraphs!"

Bells chimed, seemingly deafeningly in the gloom.

In a moment the Weser would begin to obscure the forward part of the cruiser from the bridge of the San Miguel.

"Main battery turrets Anton and Bruno may traverse and operate under local control! Turret Caesar will remain trained fore and aft!"

Both forward turrets began to track slowly to port.

The rear triple 5.9-inch turret was unmoving; if the idiots on the San Miguel shone a searchlight on the Emden they might, conceivably, still believe the ship was dormant.

The lookouts were reporting regularly, their voices pitched low.

"There is activity on the deck of the San Miguel..."

Activity but precious little action.

The old ironclad might by now have attempted to warp sidelong against the hold of her anchor chains but obviously, nobody had thought about letting out a few fathoms of those chains, or of dumping a new anchor over the side so she continued to wallow in the path of the Weser, now burning from end to end and inexorably bearing down on her.

There was a small explosion near the bow of the Weser.

And a few seconds later, another on the stern well deck; thereafter, the twenty-millimetre ready use lockers containing ammunition for the raider's anti-aircraft cannons began to cook off at regular intervals.

Finally, the clamour of ringing alarm bells drifted across the water as the Weser ran into the bow of the San Miguel. Instantly, there was the rattle of chains running out as the ironclad belatedly abandoned her forward anchor. Yet still, the old ship made no attempt to turn her shafts and back away from the burning merchantman, now fiercely burning, looming above her decks.

"She's still anchored at her stern!" Peter Cowdrey-Singh muttered, not quite believing his eyes.

Finally, the San Miguel's crew cut her stern chains.

By then it was too late, the ebb tide was pushing the bigger, much heavier Weser broadside on against the warship, and they were grinding rails, locked together.

HMS Achilles's former Executive officer swore under his breath.

He would not have believed it, any of it unless he had just seen it. Not only could the San Miguel's guns no longer bear on the Emden, it was odds on that the tide, and the fluky wind coming off the land would push both the Weser and the ironclad onto the sandbanks on the opposite shore of the bay.

By now the Weser's fires were casting crimson shadows around the whole bay.

Claude Wallendorf turned and called: "RELEASE ALL LINES FORE AND AFT!"

He waited to hear acknowledgements.

"SLOW ASTERN STARBOARD! SLOW AHEAD PORT! FULL LEFT RUDDER!"

The ship began to gently reverberate as her turbines began to turn her shafts and her propellers stirred the mud and sand under her transom.

And, astonishingly, still nobody had fired a shot in anger.

Chapter 35

Monday 8th May
SMS Emden, San Juan Bay, Santo Domingo

With no specific duties to perform Peter Cowdrey-Singh had watched, to all intents, transfixed, by the Weser and the San Miguel's slow-motion dance of death. It was not until some minutes later, as Claude Wallendorf fought to back the Emden out into the deep-water channel, that the Royal Navy man realised that very gradually, the ironclad's guns were coming to bear on the cruiser as she swung around, locked together with the burning, slowly sinking commerce raider.

"Herr Kapitan!" He called lowly from the port bridge wing, where he had migrated to watch the ongoing drama. "I believe that the San Miguel's forward guns will bear on us within the next sixty seconds or so!"

"Very good," the German acknowledged bloodlessly. Who simply commanded: "Gunnery Officer! If we are fired upon return fire immediately, if you please!"

That was when the cruiser's bow had grounded for the first time, some distance inside the marked channel where there should have been at least five and possibly as many as ten feet of water under her keel.

Oh, well, the former Executive Officer of the Achilles thought, that explains why the San Miguel moored so close to the *other* side of the inner channel!

There was no substitute for a little local knowledge!

The cruiser's screws went half astern, her bow slid free, continued to swing, slowly to the east, across the tide. This of course, was where it would have been damnably handy to have had a couple of tugs pulling and pushing, and an experienced harbour pilot standing on the bridge beside Claude Wallendorf.

Notwithstanding, Peter Cowdrey-Singh was mightily impressed with the way the Kaiserliche Marine man was going about his business, unflappably, phlegmatically, with only the memory of how the small boats which had greeted his ship outside the port, had slowly led the Emden to her berth, to guide him. Having to retrace that tortuous passage through the shifting sand bars of what was a rarely dredged anchorage in the middle of the night, with the tide running fast, ebbing and the bottom reaching up for the Emden's keel, all the while knowing that shore batteries and other ships could open fire on his vulnerable command at point blank range, was perhaps, the greatest challenge of Claude Wallendorf's long career.

There was a flash of light and huge explosion, or so it seemed for a moment. One of the 3- or 4-inch casemate-mounted guns of the San Miguel had put a shell into the side of the Emden somewhere below where the Anglo-Indian had been standing.

Somebody grabbed him and hauled him back inside the conning tower; not that its seventy-centimetre-thick armoured carapace was going to keep out even a small calibre shell at a range of only a few hundred yards.

The 'big explosion' had actually been Turret Anton opening up with two of its three 5.9-inch rifles. As the hatch banged shut behind him the ship rocked as all three of Turret Bruno's guns discharged.

Staggering to his feet, he squinted through one of the observation slits on the port side of the bridge just in time to see Turret Anton's second salvo slam into the Weser and the San Miguel.

At a range of probably significantly less than four hundred yards the one hundred-and-twelve-pound armour-piercing rounds carved straight through the Weser's thin-plated side and probably, the four or five inches of cemented steel protecting the San Miguel's vitals. Had that armour been inclined to deflect shell impacts, or manufactured to the specifications of that fitted to the ships of the great powers at any time in the last forty years, it might have offered some small protection to the dozen or so heavy shells which hit her in the next minute.

As it was, it was safe to assume that practically every 5.9-inch round which struck home penetrated her outer carapace and exploded in her vitals.

There was a blindingly white flash from a gun near the old ironclad's stern as the Emden's fourth salvo, and first full broadside, with the guns of her aft Caesar Turret joining in, in the instant before the old ironclad's whole starboard side lit up like a Roman Candle.

It was impossible to say where the massive detonation which ensued began; it was as if the whole ship, from the bridge to the taffrail just disintegrated in a giant, crimson-yellow fireball, and when the spots in front of Peter Cowdrey-Singh's eyes began to clear there was nothing, literally nothing recognisable, left of the five thousand ton cruiser while nearby, the wreck of the still burning Weser – her whole port side now stove in - was slowly capsizing, practically already on her beam ends.

Chunks of wood and metal began to rain down across the inner bay, thudding into Emden's upper works and driving the men manning her anti-aircraft guns scurrying, diving for cover.

On the other side of the bay searchlights began to play across the sky. It was as if the people over there thought there was an air raid in progress!

It was surreal.

Tracers looped lazily across the water, kicking up spray, pitter-pattering on steel somewhere far aft. Something whooshed through the air, a column of water rose between the ship and the abandoned port of the Imperial Concession.

"MAKE SMOKE!"

"All secondaries may return fire at will in local control!"

Rifle and machine gun bullets were clunking harmlessly off the armour of the conning tower.

Peter Cowdrey-Singh spared a thought for the men manning the Emden's anti-aircraft gun pits; many of those positions amidships were protected only by relatively thin splinter guards which were liable to spalling if struck by even a rifle-calibre round.

Finally, the cruiser's bow was swinging across the channel, clearing the wrecks of the San Miguel and the Weser. The water all around was fouled by floating debris, and dull with coal dust from the ironclad's shattered bunkers.

Idly, Peter Cowdrey-Singh wondered if one of the Emden's shells had ignited a magazine or perhaps, a gun room full of cordite might, or conceivably, simply triggered a chain reaction of coal-dust explosions along the flank of the old ship.

Astonishingly, it was as if the people on shore still could not make up their minds if the cruiser was a friend or a foe!

Nonetheless, that the harbour master should still be sitting back, presumably in a fog of indecision, and carrying on watching as a vessel which had just sunk two of the Armada del Santo Domingo's ships, not even challenging her defied credulity.

But then when the Emden had arrived at San Juan she had pretty much, sailed into the bay without a by your leave to anybody in particular. Claude Wallendorf had had to order a pair of small tugs to assist him to navigate the main channel; with the harbour authorities never at any stage really catching up with events as the cruiser edged towards its berth alongside the main quay of the Port of the Imperial Concession.

Hans von Schaffhausen had been as surprised as anyone!

Although, on reflection, the German Minister had confided that it was not at all uncommon for one hand of the Dominican government not to have the remotest idea what *any* of the other agencies were up to. Add into the mix the machinations of the autonomous organs of the Inquisition and obviously, the potential for chaos was unlimited. Likewise, as implausible as it sounded, it might well have been that the only reason the badly damaged Weser had been allowed to enter the port unmolested was that *nobody* had forewarned the harbour authorities at San Juan that the Inquisition had ordered two Dominican Navy torpedo boat-destroyers to intercept the commerce raider.

Peter Cowdrey-Singh flinched as a heavier shell erupted in the water near the bow sending a jolt through the deck at his feet. Briefly, he spared a thought for the hundreds of German non-combatants below decks, huddling in claustrophobic, humid compartments dogged shut to guarantee the maximum possible watertight integrity in the event of a hit below the waterline.

Anecdotally, his understanding was that the Emden's design incorporated approximately three the times the weight of armour as Achilles – a ship a little less than two-thirds of her tonnage – had, and that below the level of the main deck, itself protected in places by up to two-and-a-half inches of modern Krupp cemented plate, there was up to five inches around her magazines and engineering spaces at the waterline, tapering to about two at the joint with the main deck.

As a rule, all German cruisers tended to be more heavily protected than their Royal Navy counterparts, a thing the Kaiserliche Marine could get away with because range was not the priority for it – historically a North Sea and Baltic Fleet – as it was for a Navy with global responsibilities. In essence, Emden's weight of armour and general protections system was roughly comparable with that of the latest class of British heavy cruisers.

In other words, Emden was built to be tough for her size, and ought to be capable of taking a fair bit of punishment. Which was just as well because if the gunners manning the batteries guarding the main entrance to the port got their act together, things were going to get somewhat more than middlingly unpleasant if and when, assuming she did not go aground, the cruiser rounded Point La Puntilla, turning her bow to the west following the deep water channel before she made the long, slow, very predictable turn to the north and if she was still under control at that time, ran for the open sea.

The bridge chronometer reported it was 04:07; although dawn was around six o'clock that did not mean they had another two hours of darkness in which to fight their way out to sea. Twilight, the pre-dawn brightening would be with them in about an hour. After that, if there had ever been anywhere that a ten-thousand-ton cruiser with a fighting top seventy to eighty feet above its waterline could hide, it would not be inside this port no matter how much smoke she was making.

Presently, a long, choking pall of steamy, half-burned oil was drifting ahead of and a point east of north of the cruiser as she crawled, barely at walking pace away past the graveyards of the San Miguel and the Weser.

Whatever awaited the Emden around the headland of Pont La Puntilla, there would be no dodging it. If she deviated from the channel she would ground and thereafter the Dominicans would surely shoot her to pieces at their leisure.

Chapter 36

Monday 8th May
San Juan, Santo Domingo

No plan survives first contact with the enemy, and one simply had to be philosophical about these things. But when the enemy started the battle before one had even arrived, when the nearest of the Perseus's and Hermes's aircraft were still over thirty miles away, that was ridiculous!

Approaching the enemy coast at three-hundred-and-forty-knots, Alex Fielding flicked across UHF frequencies, picking up the excitable, panicky, oddly angry babble of Spanish on both of the frequencies the Armada del Santo Domingo was known to employ before re-selecting today's designated command channel.

Up at twenty thousand feet the pre-dawn twilight began to turn the blackness of the night into subtle greys, with the diamond twinkle of the stars above fast winking out while down below, on the deck, the darkness clung on another few minutes. Or rather, it ought to have lingered a while longer.

In the distance the flash of big guns sparkled, many, many fires were burning and a plume of grey-black smoke was drifting across the San Juan Bay and the city around it.

Racing south, giving a wide detour to the Princess Royal, Indefatigable and their escorts – they were bound to be trigger happy on a morning like this – Alex's Goshawk was closing the range with the northern coast of Santo Domingo at nearly six miles a minute.

Down lower there was tracer fire reaching up into the sky.

Anti-aircraft fire?

How the Devil do they know we are out here?

The Princess Royal and the Indefatigable would have launched her Gimlet amphibians by now. They were supposed to stay well to the west of the line of the Rio Hondo, which marked the western border of the German Concession and report the big ships' fall of fire as best they could from a safe distance away.

Oh, well, there was nothing for it but to go and have a closer look!

Alex put the nose of his Goshawk down, he was not going to see an awful lot of ground detail from four miles high!

He rocketed over the long isthmus protecting San Juan Bay where the original conquerors had established their city in that long-ago post-Columbian epoch, where, nowadays, the Armada del Santo Domingo had its only large, relatively modern base.

At least, for a few more minutes...

There was a near impenetrable smoky haze across much of the anchorage; so much for the meteorologists promise of a lovely clear morning!

And then he saw it.

The same Mainz class cruiser that was supposed to be tidily moored alongside the German wharf in the inner bay, meekly, unknowingly awaiting her fate.

Instead, she was in the main channel, heading for the open sea. And...

She was shooting at the Dominicans!

Alex realised instantly that the haze was the cruiser making smoke.

He kicked the rudder pedals, and without consciously thinking about it began to climb into a wide circle over where, hidden in the murk, the German Concession lay.

The cruiser's forward turret spat fire to the right; moments later her aft guns blazed away at targets to the left as the ship began to turn to the north for the final run for the open sea. There was a fire somewhere near the ship's bow, another amidships, belching black smoke and even as he snapped his eyes away for a lightning check of his cockpit instrumentation, he saw at least two shells smash into the ship as countless near misses threw up a sudden forest of water spouts around her stern.

There was oil streaking the water in her wake and she was steaming very, very slowly...before the haze hid her from view.

All this he saw, parsed using a fraction of his mental capacities as he flew the Goshawk, weighing odds, intuitively joining-up the pieces of the jigsaw. In the heat of battle a thing was usually what it seemed to be. When the bullets were flying all around one, the time for artifice, clever stratagems and slights of hand were over.

He opened the command channel.

"BAD BOY ONE TO NAUGHTY CHILDREN!"

He paused.

"BAD BOY ONE TO NAUGHTY CHILDREN!"

Another pause.

This needed to be succinct; unambiguous.

"HERE THIS! HERE THIS! ONE MAINZ CLASS CRUISER ATTEMPTING TO ESCAPE, REPEAT, ESCAPE FROM THE PORT. THIS SHIP IS CURRENTLY ENGAGING SHORE TARGETS. DO NOT ATTACK THIS SHIP. UNDER NO CIRCUMSTANCES ENGAGE THIS SHIP. ALL OTHER OPERATIONS WILL PROCEED AS PLANNED. TALLY HO! TALLY HO! BAD BOY ONE OUT!"

He waited for his Squadron Commanders to tersely confirm receipt of his orders, each snapping back an affirmative, their call sign and calling a terse 'OUT' in the designated sequence so they did not jam each other's transmits.

Alex switched to the Princess Royal's circuit.

He guessed that if the German cruiser did not sink in the main channel first, she would reach the sea within the next twenty minutes. In which event he would leave her to the 'big boys' out at sea.

"Roger to that, Bad Boy One," a laconic voice confirmed, "we'll deal with her when we've got a moment. Out."

Somewhere in the back of his mind Alex recollected that the Task Force Commander had mentioned the need for a secondary 'gunfire support plan' just in case the gun line's objectives had to be modified during Operation East Wind.

There were plenty of targets around San Juan Bay...

Alex had climbed back up to about eight thousand feet when the first Sea Eagles began to swoop onto the dockyards on San Juan Island. Other Sea Eagles, torpedoes slung under their bellies raced in from the east, squashing down low over the inner bay, their fish splashing into the water heading for the merchantmen and small warships moored to the north and alongside the naval and civilian piers.

High overhead a flock of Goshawks patrolled; others would already be strafing the aerodrome to the east.

Alex banked his Goshawk, and tried to establish if the German cruiser was still under its own steam. To his surprise it was almost at the neck of the bay and nobody seemed to be shooting at it now.

He forgot about the ship.

The dockyards were rapidly disappearing under billowing clouds of smoke and dust, there were new, very big fires burning along the shore of the bay. To the east great eruptions pocked the crowded city streets and plaza to the south east.

Time was telescoping.

Huge explosions walked across the western edge of the inner bay where, presumably, the port and headquarters of the German Concession lay.

Although here and there tracer climbed aimlessly through the clouds of destruction, to all intents the defenders had stopped fighting back.

There were no Dominican scouts struggling for altitude to distract the carrier-borne air fleet.

The enemy had been caught with his pants proverbially, around his ankles!

It was pure murder even before Alex summoned the bulk of his thus far, unengaged Goshawks of the high cover squadron, to fall upon the now defenceless airfield to the east of the burning city.

Far out at sea the livid flash of either the Princess Royal's or the Indefatigable's broadsides lit the now fast-brightening northern horizon.

Pure bloody murder...

Chapter 37

Monday 8th May
Viano do Castelo, Portugal

"Alonso has to make some phone calls," Henrietta De L'Isle murmured, blushing deeply as she entered the small, private dining room where Melody, with Pedro on her lap happily spreading butter, egg and breadcrumbs over himself and his other 'Mama', were breakfasting.

On mornings such as this Melody could not stop herself feeling just a little bit...maternal. That was nice, every now and again but she knew it would soon get old if she had to do it every day. It had been fun despatching Henrietta to her fate yesterday evening, and when neither her friend or Alonso had appeared for dinner last night, she had known that 'the big gamble' had paid off.

That was fine.

Better than 'fine', in fact; and she had had Pedro to herself. Granted, it had seemed a little odd bathing him without Hen in the bath, too. Later, reading to him in patient, indulgent Castilian from one of the books of nursery rhymes Hen had acquired in her absence had been blissful. The boy had listened with rapt fascination, and slept like a little angel in her arms all night.

Henrietta had reported that his nightmares were going away.

That too, was good.

And as for the flush of guilty embarrassment on her friend's face when she finally made an appearance that morning, well, that had been exquisite.

There was nothing like knowing a plan had come together like a dream!

That was not to say that Melody had not experienced a brief pang of selfish, somewhat adolescent angst in acknowledging the new reality of their lives. In the future, she and Henrietta would be friends first, not lovers, or at least, that was what she had reconciled herself to; that being the worst-case scenario, etcetera.

Henrietta was wearing a cotton frock which reflected her sunny mood, *and* that revealed her shoulders and arms and a discreet suggestion of cleavage.

She kissed the top of Pedro's head, and then Melody's cheek, her lips touching the side of her mouth, and lingering a moment.

"Did you sleep well, dear?" Melody asked mischievously.

"Eventually," Henrietta giggled.

Melody waited expectantly.

"It was completely lovely, actually," the younger woman confessed, avoiding Melody's gaze.

"And?"

Henrietta's expression was, momentarily, confused.

"Oh," she sighed, recognition dawning. "Er, that's what one of the telephone calls is about. Alonso's mother's engagement ring is in a deposit box in a vault in a bank in Lisbon. He's getting one of his arms men to bring it here."

All the while, Pedro was earnestly wrestling with the concept of boiled eggs and 'soldiers', thin strips of toasted bread which one dipped in the warm, runny yellow yoke, ideally without spreading bits of both liberally about one's local environment.

He was still a long way from mastering this latter trick.

Henrietta looked at the boy, a dob of yellow yoke on the tip of his nose, and smiled proudly. She picked up a napkin and tenderly removed the spillage.

Melody arched an eyebrow.

"Did you?" She asked, pointedly, wanting to know if her friend had obeyed her 'plan of action' to the letter.

"Yes, I got into the bath with him."

Melody waited patiently.

"And I took off my clothes first," her friend confirmed.

"Good girl," Melody said, smiling.

She knew how hard Henrietta would have found that, making herself weak, vulnerable. Although, on the other hand, she assumed Alonso must have been similarly...deliciously naked at the time.

Henrietta giggled like a schoolgirl.

A maid came in with fresh hot water for the teapot.

Shortly afterwards, Alonso entered the room.

He bowed and kissed Henrietta's hand; Melody thought that was sweet and it allayed her guilt, a little, when the man gave her an apologetic grimace.

Poor man, this was all rather odd for them all.

Alonso poured himself a cup of black coffee and sat down to Henrietta's right and Melody's left at the small round table. In their discomfort the adults focused on Pedro, who, like any small child thrived on being the centre of attention.

"Well, here we all are," Melody declared, gently restraining the boy on her lap, knowing it would not help the ambience of the moment if he tipped her cup of tea down her front.

"Yes," Alonso agreed, pausing to sip his drink. "Melody," he began, halted, and looked to Henrietta for help.

If Melody had learned anything in her – certainly by New England standards – eventful, sometimes fraught, unconventional and lately, overly dangerous life as she rapidly approached her forties, it was that for her at least, nothing stayed the same forever. She had been Alonso's mistress for a few short weeks, with a civil war in between; and Henrietta's friend and lover for less than a year. Those were ecstatic interludes and she had known as much. Real life was more complicated and she was not so good at that. Given that fate had decreed that there should be a sweet-natured, adorable four year old boy who called her 'Mama Melody' presently sitting contentedly on her lap – that was a thing she had never expected – and that both her lovers were only know embracing the change already turning their lives upside down, it was proof positive that one never really knew what life was going to throw up next.

She was also wise enough to know that notwithstanding her two lovers *probably* did not want to risk losing her, that it would be profoundly foolish to attempt to carry on as before. So, putting aside she was going to cry her eyes out later, and possibly in the days to come, the time had come to recognise that things were what they were.

"I expect to be this little rascal's godmother," she said, brushing her lips across Pedro's mop of tousled still fair hair. "And for us all to stay friends. We can work out how that actually works in practice another time."

Nobody broke the silence except Pedro, happily chuntering to himself as a youngster will, as Melody gently wiped his face. Having exhausted the possibilities of his boiled egg and soldiers, he was seeking new challenges. He began to squirm, soon he was standing on Melody's lap, his hands transferring crumbs and tiny gobbets of congealing egg, to her hair.

Never mind, now my hair is so short it washes out easily...

She looked to Alonso.

"I won't deny I completely loved being your mistress, Alonso. I wouldn't have missed that for the world but," she shrugged, "if I'd known the way Hen felt about you that would never have happened. I'll go on feeling a little guilty about that for a while, most likely. So, staying as friends is good for me. And to be your kids' favourite Aunt, obviously."

Chapter 38

Monday 8th May
SMS Emden, 8 nautical miles NNE of San Juan

As the noon-day sun beat down on her scorched and torn up decks the cruiser was sinking. Slowly but surely the water was filling her battered, cruelly abused hull and the few remaining pumps were fighting a losing battle.

Peter Cowdrey-Singh and Kapitan-zur-See Claude Wallendorf stood together in the shadow of Caesar, the aft main batter turret jammed at an angle of forty degrees to port, its right-hand gun warped out of alignment by a direct hit.

The two men watched the last of the wounded being transferred to HMS Venom, which with the other two destroyers, the Electra and the Express, had taken off the last of the civilians and three-quarters of the Emden's survivors. The only men on board now were volunteers manning the pumps, and acting as runners enabling Wallendorf and his officers to fight to keep the ship afloat as long as possible.

Had the waters not been very nearly a millpond, almost glassily calm the destroyers would have had no opportunity to come alongside, and many of the women and children, the sick and the injured, would have surely drowned in the oil-fouled sea.

Peter Cowdrey-Singh was ever-more grateful for mercies large and small.

During that last, slow-motion turn to the north the cruiser had been systematically dismantled by those shore batteries, perhaps a dozen 6-, 5-, and 4-inch guns smashing away at her over open sights, albeit poorly handled by guns crews who had probably not drilled in months, soon after the bombing and the shelling had begun. The cannonade had ceased within a minute of that torpedo exploding somewhere near the stern, possibly when it encountered a sand bank. That had seemed like the end of the world at the time. The detonation had opened up the packing around the starboard shaft, probably bent it out of true and within minutes flooded one of the machinery compartments.

Suddenly, the ship had been crawling, slewing sideways, drawn helplessly on the ebbing tide into the mouth of the anchorage. Once, twice she had touched bottom and then, capable of only making two or three knots under her own steam, she had been carried out to sea...

Anything and everything pale or white had been waved at the Gimlet amphibian, which they now knew was from the Indefatigable, which had come to investigate the sinking hulk, flying wide, slow concentric circuits of the dying ship.

And then the destroyers had come racing out of the haze with streaming white crescent bones in their teeth.

And miraculously, the rescue had begun.

The Emden sagged under the two men's feet.

"Not long now," Claus Wallendorf sighed. He turned to face Peter Cowdrey-Singh. "I hope my old friend Weitzman has been looking down on us these last few hours. Honour in the Kaiserliche Marine is not dead."

"Indeed, it lives, Her Kapitan," the Royal Navy man agreed.

The two men shook hands.

"We shall meet again on the other side, sir," the Anglo-Indian promised, straightening to his best impression of attention, and crisply saluting the older man.

It was time to go.

For Peter Cowdrey-Singh life continued; Claude Wallendorf was travelling another road.

They would never meet again in this world.

EPILOGUE

Chapter 39

Saturday 13th May
Vera Cruz, México

Forty-year-old Vice Admiral Count Carlos Federico Gravina y Vera Cruz, the Chief Minister and Commander-in-Chief of the Armada de Nuevo Granada, and High Admiral of the Fleets of the Triple Alliance, welcomed his guests with impeccable respect and charm. This was hardly surprising because if there was one man in New Spain, or for that matter, the whole of Catholic Christendom he feared and respected in equal measure, it was General of the Army of New Spain Felipe de Padua María Severino López de Santa Anna y Pérez de Lebrón, the Chief of Staff of the Armed Forces of the Mexican Republic.

As to the other, tall, distinguished man in the uniform of a Colonel of the Chapultepec Horse Guards, the elite Presidential Cavalry Regiment, he assumed that if the man was with Santa Anna, then he too, was to be taken very, very seriously.

Behind his haughty public façade, Gravina was not the arrogant, seedy aristocrat that many of his enemies in the House of Representatives or in the Army took him for. In the Navy, tradition and what the British might term 'keeping up appearances' were the twin pillars upon which high command rested. Besides, if his underlings regarded him as a puffed-up buffoon – an image his family's tendency to florid corpulency in middle age inflicted upon him – who knew no better than to charge headlong into any battle, that was fine so long as they remained afraid of him. In the meantime, he was in the business of playing what was a relatively weak hand, with every ounce of panache he could beg, borrow or steal.

Moreover, Santa Anna understood as much.

The Chief of Staff of the Armed Forces of the Republic introduced his companion.

Gravina's eyes widened in curiosity.

Colonel Rodrigo de Monroy y Pizarro Altamirano of the Geological Department of the National Academy for the Natural Sciences, of Cuernavaca University.

Gravina had spared nothing in his report of the week-old disasters which had befallen the Dominicans at San Juan, or the sinking of the Hispanic squadron charged with 'harrying' the King of England's beard in the Eastern Caribbean.

The violence of the sudden attack on San Juan had initially, left Gravina stunned. In an air attack and an naval bombardment which together, had probably not lasted more than ten to fifteen minutes from start to finish, San Juan Island had been wrecked from end to end, the port and dockyards severely damaged – perhaps, put out of actions for at least six months - and the Dominicans were reporting several thousand naval and dockyard personnel, and civilians dead or missing under the rubble of the towns around the bay.

Moreover, the English had mercilessly shelled the German Concession!

Fire-bombed the city!

Destroyed over forty aircraft on the ground!

And torpedoed or dive bombed nine ships moored in the bay, or tied up alongside the docks or under repair in two completely flooded and wrecked dry docks!

Worse, at some stage in the hours before the attack the cruiser Emden, only surrendered to the Dominicans days before, had been spirited out of San Juan Bay, and a Kaiserliche Marine commerce raider, the Weser used as a fire ship to prevent the ironclad San Miguel intervening.

Needless to say, both the Weser and the San Miguel were among the wrecks now littering the anchorage!

Nobody knew what had become of the former SMS Emden, which had not been in Dominican hands long enough to be re-christened, 'Santissima Trinidad'.

As for the Hispanic squadron Gravina had sent to the Eastern Caribbean to draw the Royal Navy back into the periscope sights of his patrolling submarines, those idiots had allowed themselves to be trapped between the rising sun and a massively superior English cruiser force and consequently, shot to pieces without ever being able to see, let alone hit back at its attackers.

In retrospect, baiting a *new* trap for the Royal Navy's big ships had proved wholly fruitless. After the Indomitable had been hit and the Ulysses set on fire, there had been no similar successes and ominously, one by one the submarines operating west of Havana – four to date - had ceased to radio in their daily position reports.

The English, with no little fanfare, had announced they planned to land the first of four hundred-and-twelve men they had pulled from the sea after the battle in the waters west of Montserrat, in New England in the next few days.

"I am honoured to receive you on board my flagship, Your Excellency," Gravina bowed, before leading his visitors off the quarterdeck of the Nuevo Leon, the former SMS Breitenfeld, down one deck to his day cabin. A battery of fans, and the air filtering in through the open port holes was a cool relief after the blistering heat of the open deck.

The heavy cruiser was moored alongside the south pier, dwarfed by the great Hamburg-Atlantic liner Friedrich der Grosse, currently preparing to get under way, transporting the Kaiserliche Marine crews of the Nuevo Leon and the Sonora (formerly the SMS Lutzen) back to Europe.

Gravina had turned out well over half the crew of the flagship to greet Santa Anna even though the visit had been announced at less than twelve hours' notice.

The High Admiral of the Fleets of the Triple Alliance threw a thoughtful look at Rodrigo Altamirano.

"Rodrigo is my personal scientific advisor, Don Carlos," Santa Anna said, his tone implying that his companion was *their* advisor. "All three of us in this room," he smiled apologetically, "cabin, know from hard-won experience that war always throws up surprises and that things often go wrong. The Navy has distinguished itself with great credit against a formidable foe. I am not here to rake over what happened in Santo Domingo, or in the Leeward Islands, or why the performance of our submersibles has been so disappointing after such an encouraging start. Setbacks, such as the one our Cuban and Hispanic allies suffered on that stupid little island, Little Inagua, shortly after the outbreak of hostilities are to be expected. Let us be thankful for all the things which have gone well. We have much to discuss today."

Gravina nodded, saying nothing.

"In fact, if any of us in this cabin," Santa Anna observed wryly, "were truly the God-fearing men our confessors would have us be, I would be tempted to conclude that *He* has a perverse sense of humour."

Gravina frowned: "I don't understand, Your Excellency?"

"Don Rodrigo has recently returned from a survey mission to the Sonoran Desert north of the old demilitarised zone. We now believe that up until as recently as two to three years ago," Santa Anna explained, suddenly deadly serious, "the English were testing atomic bombs. The test range Don Rodrigo discovered covered many tens of square miles of territory; we can conclude that as it was abandoned long before the current war, that the English had no further use for it. From which it follows that they have mastered the technology necessary to build atomic bombs, and to harness the power of the atom for both civil and military applications."

Visibly, the colour drained out of Gravina's face.

"They ignored the Submarine Treaty," he murmured, his psyche pummelled from all sides by the literally earth-shaking implications of the revelation.

"Yes," Santa Anna agreed urbanely. "It may well be that quite soon, the English will be fighting the Germans and that," he shrugged, "they will need to settle with us or face a World War. A war on several fronts which they cannot possibly win, or survive with their precious Empire intact."

[The End]

Author's Endnote

'George Washington's Ghost' is the fifth book in the **New England Series** set in an alternative America, two hundred years after the rebellion of the American colonies was crushed in 1776 when the Continental Army was destroyed at the battle of Long Island and its commander, George Washington was killed.

I hope you enjoyed it - or if you did not, sorry - but either way, thank you for reading and helping to keep the printed word alive. Remember, civilization depends on people like you.

Oh, please bear in mind that:

Inevitably, in writing an alternative history this book has referenced, attributed motives, actions and put words in the mouths of real, historical characters.

No motive, action or word attributed to a real person after 28th August 1776 actually happened or was said.

Whereas, to the best of my knowledge everything in this book which occurred before 28th August 1776 actually happened!

The sixth book in the series **Imperial Crisis** will be published later in 2020!

Other Books by James Philip

The Timeline 10/27/62 Series

Main Series
Book 1: Operation Anadyr
Book 2: Love is Strange
Book 3: The Pillars of Hercules
Book 4: Red Dawn
Book 5: The Burning Time
Book 6: Tales of Brave Ulysses
Book 7: A Line in the Sand
Book 8: The Mountains of the Moon
Book 9: All Along the Watchtower
Book 10: Crow on the Cradle
Book 11: 1966 & All That
Book 12: Only in America
Book 13: Warsaw Concerto
Book 14: Eight Miles High

A Timeline 10/27/62 Novel
Football in The Ruins – The World Cup of 1966

A Timeline 10/27/62 Story
The House on Haight Street
La Argentina
Puerto Argentino
A Kelper's Tale

Coming in 2020-21
Book 15: Won't Get Fooled Again
Book 16: Armadas
Book 17: Smoke on the Water

USA Series
Book 1: Aftermath
Book 2: California Dreaming
Book 3: The Great Society
Book 4: Ask Not of Your Country
Book 5: The American Dream

Australia Series

Book 1: Cricket on the Beach
Book 2: Operation Manna

For the latest news and author blogs about the Timeline 10/27/62 Series check out thetimelinesaga.com

Other Series and Novels

The Guy Winter Mysteries
Prologue: Winter's Pearl
Book 1: Winter's War
Book 2: Winter's Revenge
Book 3: Winter's Exile
Book 4: Winter's Return
Book 5: Winter's Spy
Book 6: Winter's Nemesis

The Bomber War Series
Book 1: Until the Night
Book 2: The Painter
Book 3: The Cloud Walkers

Until the Night Series
Part 1: Main Force Country – September 1943
Part 2: The Road to Berlin – October 1943
Part 3: The Big City – November 1943
Part 4: When Winter Comes – December 1943
Part 5: After Midnight – January 1944

The Harry Waters Series
Book 1: Islands of No Return
Book 2: Heroes
Book 3: Brothers in Arms

The Frankie Ransom Series
Book 1: A Ransom for Two Roses
Book 2: The Plains of Waterloo
Book 3: The Nantucket Sleighride

The Strangers Bureau Series
Book 1: Interlopers
Book 2: Pictures of Lily

The River House Chronicles Series
Book 1: Things Can Only Get better
Book 2: Consenting Adults
Book 3: All Swing Together
Book 4: The Honourable Member

NON-FICTION CRICKET BOOKS
FS Jackson
Lord Hawke

Audio Books of the following Titles are available (or are in production) now

Aftermath
After Midnight
A Ransom for Two Roses
Brothers in Arms
California Dreaming
Empire Day
Heroes
Islands of No Return
Love is Strange
Main Force Country
Operation Anadyr
Red Dawn
The Big City
The Cloud Walkers
The Nantucket Sleighride
The Painter
The Pillars of Hercules
The Plains of Waterloo
The Road to Berlin
Travels Through the Wind
Two Hundred Lost Years
Until the Night
When Winter Comes
Winter's Exile
Winter's Pearl
Winter's Return
Winter's Revenge
Winter's Spy
Winter's War

Cricket Books edited by James Philip

The James D. Coldham Series
[Edited by James Philip]

Books
Northamptonshire Cricket: A History [1741-1958]
Lord Harris

Anthologies
Volume 1: Notes & Articles
Volume 2: Monographs No. 1 to 8

Monographs
No. 1 - William Brockwell
No. 2 - German Cricket
No. 3 - Devon Cricket
No. 4 - R.S. Holmes
No. 5 - Collectors & Collecting
No. 6 - Early Cricket Reporters
No. 7 – Northamptonshire
No. 8 - Cricket & Authors

———

Details of all James Philip's published books and forthcoming publications can be found on his website
www.jamesphilip.co.uk

———

Cover artwork concepts by James Philip
Graphic Design by Beastleigh Web Design

Printed by Amazon Italia Logistica S.r.l.
Torrazza Piemonte (TO), Italy